D1396525

Everything Happens For A Reason

By: Raven Soars

To: James.
Thanks For All The Talks over the years &
your inspiration. I truly appreciate you.
you're up Next....

Raven ♡

ISBN: 9781089350644

DEDICATION

This book is dedicated to everyone whose ever been told to give up on their dreams, and didn't. To anyone who has ever tried to break the path of a destructive lifestyle, by changing their lives to better themselves. This book is for the people who are always trying to help others just because they know it cost nothing to do the simplest act of kindness. This book is to Love, and the hearts that have been broken by love. Without you, I wouldn't have gained the strength to move forward. May God continue to help us all do our part during this journey called, life.

Dear Reader,

"If you always remain **HUMBLE,** and **DON'T EVER GIVE UP**

when **SURVIVING** is your only option. You will become **WISE**

when making decisions, and your full potential will no longer

be over looked. The knowledge you have obtained through

experience will be at its **BEST** *which will allow you to spread*

wisdom to others. Be **TRUE** to yourself always, and know that

there is nothing in this world that is greater than you but, God.

It will help you be **UNBREAKABLE** even at your weakest

moment. Your legacy will then go on to **LIVE**

UNCONDITIONALLY through the hearts you've touched

positively during **YOUR** life's journey. Helping others just

because, or even the simplest act of kindness is worth more

than any amount of money. Simply, because the cost is

nothing to spread **LOVE.**

Raven Soars

P. S. Only **"YOU"** can soar high enough to **Never L.A.N.D**.

Never (Leave, Abandon, Neglect, Dreams)

Prologue
Dear Diary,
8/23/2014

I can honestly say that I am lucky to be alive. I once read somewhere

that in order to change and move forward you have to forgive your past as

well as yourself. This is the first step of changing your life with

"acceptance and forgiveness". Once you conquer those two you are free to

move forward towards "repair and restoration". It took me a long time to

understand this, but I am thankful I can finally see the truth. It was so hard

walking around life wearing rose-colored glasses that blinded me for so

many years. One day my soul just opened up, and I finally understood the

lesson's behind all I had been through. I had finally found that peace of

mind that I was always searching for. It was by the grace of God that I was

still breathing and able to start a new life. That is when I realized that

"everything happens for a reason". The tipping point of my life brought

me closer to my turning point so I decided to change the rules. Truthfully

speaking, after surviving the dangerous game that I was playing with my

life, itself, I knew it was time for a change. That is when I began to face

the music even when I did not like the tune. Life had a hard way of

teaching me that "there are no shortcuts to any place worth going; and no one listens until you make a mistake". I realized that I was just like a quote I once read by Raven Soars: "Why speak to death ears, when there's always someone else ready to tune in." I had been foolish for far too many years, and my stupidity was holding me back from living my full potential. As, righteous as I wanted to be, I knew in my heart I would never be a saint when sinning was what got me where I was today. I had to learn to take the good with the bad, and treat them equally in order to get what I wanted out of life. Being bad, got me to places that being good would have taken me years to get, too. That's also the main reason that I believe, there's some truth to the saying: "Pussy rules the world". I say this simply because the way I can mentally seduce any man, and send him straight to fantasyland has to be the reason Usher recorded his single "Good Kisser". With lips like mine, I can easily give you the "Kiss of Life or The Kiss of Death" depending on how you play yourself. It is amazing to have so much power over such a vulnerable creature with just words, yet men have the nerve to call us weak.

"Please…"

The only thing weak about me is my whimper when I'm in ecstasy from the deep strokes that unleashes the beast in me. My motto on sex is simple. Take me to your boudoir and a lovesick, mentally seduced, sex addicted nympho, is bound to leave out behind me. I call it the "**CUMBACK**," because you're guaranteed a round trip on this flight. I am porn, hardcore to the bone and triple X-rated. Leaving my victims hypnotized off my juices during lovemaking, and my name imprinted on his brain. Moments later, his body's yearning for an instant replay of my session of straight mind fucking. Call me a Succubus, the way I can seduce any man with my powerful potion of pure pussy. I always knew I was a natural born sex goddess without the film or magazine. You've heard Apollonia 6's classic hit from the 80's right? I'm every man's perfect little modern day "Sex Shooter!" It's still very hard to believe that as of today, I'm the most craved, spell-binding, heart throb vixen to ever dance in the strip game. I honestly feel as if I went off and joined Zane's "Alpha Phi Fuck' Em," sorority chapter during my years of college, then graduated with a Masters in "Sexology" instead of Business Management. The irony of it all; is that I always fantasized my life to turn out differently once I was adopted by my foster parents. I guess, the hard truth is not even a knight in shining armor could rescue me from the evil villain called "life". In the end, nothing in life is ever what you dream of and reality can be harsh with only moments of happiness. Sometimes, in order to survive you have to learn from yesterday, live positive today and hope for a better tomorrow. Even when your faith seems like it's nothing more than a fragment of your imagination.

Hypnotized
Dear Diary,
March 10, 2015
(Present Day)

"Where the fuck are you, Ize?"

I whined into the phone as the answering machine picked up for the tenth time today almost causing me to throw my phone against the wall. I was just about to head out to the stage to do my last show of the night at club "Dirty Secrets". Instead of breaking my phone, I picked up my wrist bag and reluctantly handed it over to Sazhay, my house mom, and headed out the dressing room irritated as hell. I had been calling Izes' phone since 6 pm, which happens to be the last time we talked before I decided to come in. This also happens to be the time Ize claimed he had to call me back. It was now 1:30, in the morning, and I hadn't heard a word from Ize's trifling ass. It's really starting to piss me off that every time I've tried to call I got the "VOICEMAIL". I could hear the DJ calling me to the stage and people shouting Teaz, but I took my time walking through the crowded club. I knew exactly what Ize was doing. The feeling, I was having were all too familiar, because Ize, and I, have been down this road a thousand times before.

"Don't I suck his dick well, enough?"

"Don't I keep this pussy tight and wet just for him when I could be selling it to every trick ass Mark or John that comes through here

claiming that he'll take care of me?" My mind was raging with kinds

of questions as I walked towards the stage.

"What the fuck, Ize?" I thought again as I began to wipe down the pole

before I started my performance.

Handing my towel to Sazhay, I could hear Akon over the loud

speakers saying, "You got me so hypnotized," then Sazhay slapped me

on the ass and told me to "Kill 'em all," liked she always did. I could

feel the words deep in my heart as they played but not for these

tricks in here throwing their money and shouting, because I was all

into my performance. The men I was dancing for didn't even know,

nor do I think they would've cared that the show I was putting on

for them was more for the man in my head. Ize had me GONE, and I

was making love to this pole letting him know I was his. By the time,

I snapped back to reality, this new chick name Mona was tapping me

on my shoulder to let me know her turn was up. I figured because they

never would have sent me out to "Come Here Bitch," by Weebie,

anyway. I quickly left the stage, ignoring my usual fellas that I'd kick

it with every night before leaving. I wasn't really feeling any

meaningless conversations tonight. I had to get dressed fast! I needed

to know where Ize was and what he was doing. My heart wasn't

going to rest until I knew why he was avoiding my calls after endless promises he made to "never" do this again. Ize knew **this type of behavior** caused me pain, because he would just disappear for weeks without a word. I stormed into the dressing room and got dressed as quickly as I could. I paid Sazhay for the night, and told her to give Duty, the owner of the club, the tip out money I'd made. It was around 2:30 in the morning, when I hopped into my Aqua colored Lexus. I tried to call Ize one more time before I decided to just ride pass his house. Believe me when I say there were a million other things I could have been doing right now. I could have been hooking up with any person who would truly appreciate me being their girl, but Lord knows, I love, Ize! I would do anything for that man, which is part of the reason I started dancing in the first place. I would give him my very soul if he needed it, so I really didn't understand why he won't commit to me. When will Ize realize I'm his soul mate? If Ize really wanted to marry me, I would leave this whole strip game behind me for good. My mind, told my heart in comfort.

I even went as far as to ask Ize to marry me before, but, he just sold me some lame excuse about it's not time bullshit. Ize even had me convinced that I wasn't ready to take on the responsibilities of being a wife. No matter how I sat there trying to analyze the whole "Us" thing, I knew in my heart that I loved Ize more then he would ever love me. Love is so crazy to me! When it's just us two he really makes me feel like he could be the one. I was disgusted as I sat in my car pondering over our relationship. The one thing Ize always said to me from the beginning to be clear now:

"The one, who loved less, was the one who always controlled the relationship."

I was pissed as I sat with my thoughts that kept going from zero to a hundred really, quick. He was right, and I hated it deep down inside. I was the one sitting in my car with all the crazy thoughts while Ize was out somewhere in La La Land, literally. I stuck my key in the ignition and drove off with a purpose. I was "Dangerously In Love," with Ize! I put in the song at the thought of it and bumped Beyoncé on repeat as I drove all the way to his house.

"No the fuck he doesn't have the nerve to be home!" I yelled to myself more a loud than in as I pulled in front of his house.

"I can't believe this shit," I chanted over, and over like a mad woman to myself when I noticed a silver Mustang parked in my usual spot right next to Izes' Challenger.

"Oh Hell No," I screamed as rage began to fuel my now flaming mind...

"Who the fuck car is that?"

"And, has the nerves to be in my spot?" was all I could muster up before I cut off my car, and parked.

"This nigga, Ize must've lost his damn mind," I screamed out loud to the wind as I snatched opened the glove compartment, and removed the set of keys Ize had left a t my house the other night. I stepped out the car, and slammed my door so hard I had to check and make sure I didn't break my own window. I marched up to the gate like a drill sergeant ready to command his troops and entered the security code, then crept around to the back of the house. Opening the back door to the kitchen, I could hear music playing.

"Damn, Ize, you couldn't even make it to the bedroom," I mumbled, then started instantly get madder than I originally was walking into the house.

 I stood there in a state of shock with all kinds of wild thoughts in my head as "Secret Garden," by Quincy Jones played. I could hear the woman Ize was with moaning and begging him to fuck her. I shook my head in disgust as I continued to tip toe closer to where the sound of the voices was coming from. The whole thing was so surreal to me. Of course, I knew Ize had been with other women before today, but he always told me they didn't compare to what we had built together. I was mad as fuck on the inside as I walked down the dark hallway. It's just something about catching a guy you have feelings for in the act that makes you question yourself. What happened to the loyalty Ize swore he had, and is always stressing me about? Where is the bond, I thought we once shared? Right now, I swear if this is the link I gotta be chained to forever, you can best believe I'm about to break it. This shit right here just shows me that no matter how much a guy lays under you, tells you sweet nothings, and you provide, there is always going to be somebody who can fuck him other than you! I stood at the entrance of his entertainment room listening until my heart couldn't take the pain it was starting to feel, and then I walked in.

"You piece of shit!" I shouted as I entered the room throwing his keys at him.

Ize couldn't believe what he was hearing as the keys came crashing into the back of his head right before he could manage to pull his face from between the bitch legs.

"Teaz?" Ize responded in shock as he began to rise to his feet.

"What the hell are you doing here?" Ize managed to ask me with a bit of attitude in his voice.

I just cut him off with my "**WATCHING YOU EAT THIS BITCH PUSSY**," reply, like I hadn't just snuck up in this mans' house while he was clearly making another one of his homemade dirty movies he loved to watch so much.

"Teaz are you, crazy?" Was all I heard before I charged him like some raging bull. We tussled for a few minutes while Ize tried to gain control of the situation. I was so mad the only thing I heard were the screams from the "other lady" to be released from the pole he had built into the ceiling months ago. I was furious listening to this bitch. All I could think about at the time was the fact that this hoe was cuffed to the pole I asked him to install so that I could give him private shows. I was enraged by the sight of it all, so I wasn't backing down. He finally grabbed me up in a bear hug and then carried me kicking and screaming all kinds of profanity to the couch and slammed me into it. As soon as my bottom hit the couch, he smacked the shit out of me, causing me to calm down.

"Teaz, how dare you sneak up in my shit and attack me because you see me with another Bitch!" Ize finally spoke.

All I could do was concentrate on was the stinging feeling I was having in my face.

"Are you fucking crazy or something?" He asked with a sinister laugh as he looked at his arm where scratches were now starting to form.

"You know what, Teaz, don't even answer that." Ize snapped.

"It's obvious that you are crazy the way you up in here trying to kill a brother like we're married and you came home to find me, cheating." He yelled.

"What the fuck is up with this shit, my baby?" He inquired, but I was at my wits end with Ize, and all his cheating.

"I guess you just straight disrespecting me now, huh, Teaz?" He grunted, raising his hand to slap me again, and I screamed.

"Wait Ize please, baby," I begged, knowing that I probably wouldn't be able to stop the obvious.

"I'm so sorry for acting like this," I whined, putting on a little waterworks to make it look believable.

"I was calling you to return your keys, baby," I thought quickly.

I can't tell you where I was going with my story, but I hoped to God it worked. I paused, and took a deep breath before I went into my next line.

"I was trying to surprise you by coming in, and giving you some head, and this good pussy while you were sleep,"

"But," …

I stumbled over my words as I lied, watching his penis go from soft to erect as my words began to sink in.

"Baby," I sighed, now dropping to my knees and taking his manhood deep into my mouth.

" I got kind of jealous when I saw you with her," I confessed.

I then started licking all over his shaft that was now at full attention begging for more.

"You know I would never act like this on a normal basis," I added, while letting spit roll out of my mouth as I sucked vigorously at his penis playing on the vulnerability of the moment.

"You mad at me, Daddy?" I cooed.

It's just something about good oral sex that makes men weak even in their strongest moments.

"I can make this up to you," I promised pulling his penis out of my mouth, and walking over to where ole girl was still hand cuffed.

I gave her a look that said, "I was doing this more for him, then you."

Before, either of them could say a word, I went down on that hoe. I sucked that bitch's pussy until she begged for us both to fuck her. I couldn't believe I'd just ate out some hoe I didn't know from a back alley, but when it comes to my man there was absolutely no limits to what I'd do. Once, I felt like Ize was satisfied with my behavior. I, told Ize to come fuck us both, and little did I know this was just the icing on the cake. In my mind, this was the beginning of a war; because I will be damn if another bitch was gone ever have, what I felt was rightfully mine.

Trick No Good...

Dear Diary,
August 25, 2014

I bet you're wondering how I even got into the whole stripping game or even how I ended up with Ize. To be perfectly honest, they both go hand in hand like our tainted relationship. I started dancing when Ize got locked up a few years back. It was a fast way to make some money, and I just so happen to be born with the exotic look. The job came easy, too! I got my girl, Rozilan to put in a good word for me with the club owner of this new hot spot that her, and a couple other chicks I knew from around the way were dancing at called "Dirty Secrets". Once the owner Duty, set his glassy slanted little eyes on me, I was hired. I strolled in the club liked I owned it on amateur night. The girls who worked there were all right looking, but none of them compared to me. Rozi had already informed me that Duty would want to meet privately in his office. She also told me he was quite the perverted type so I wore the skimpiest outfit I could find. I had recently brought this sheer zebra print one piece from a boutique I stumbled across a few weeks ago. I love what I was wearing simply because the outfit happened to compliment all my curves. I decided to dress the outfit up with a pair of red Louis Vuitton pumps, the matching clutch bag, a pair of red feather earrings that hung past my shoulders, and a single red feather that sank perfectly between my two perky average B-cup breasts. Duty took one look at me from head to toe, while admiring my naturally long wavy black hair thanks to my Mama's side of the family. Once he looked into my dark-brown, almond shaped, dreamy eyes, he damn near melted. I could not refrain from laughing just looking at the bulge Duty was starting to get in his pants. I was use to this type of reaction I was getting. I could not blame him either, because I was flawless. Standing at 5'4" ft tall, about 5'7" in heels, a light honey golden complexion with a hint of caramel, and an ass so round and firm you would've thought I paid for it. I looked like I could have easily stepped out of one of Playboy's Bunny chocolate edition magazine. I always took pride in my appearance, and I loved that my unique style often made me out to be a "trending topic". Dirty Secrets was an all-nude club. At first, I almost turned the job opportunity down, being that I had never stripped before, today. I always had a resentment towards being a stripper until I needed a job to pay off my probation officer, and fast. Once my home girl from school, Roziland, informed me of an easy way to make some money every night; I reluctantly had a change of heart once I found out how easy it would be to get the job. Although, I was confident that I would be hired, I was also very skeptical about becoming a stripper. My Mama, use to tell stories about her younger sister who was a stripper. Zion, was always known as the black sheep of the family. She wasn't talked about much because she died when she was in her early twenties'

from HIV. My mother always told me her whorish ways was what caused

her death, but I secretly believed Mama envied Zion, too. Zion, could have

been anything she wanted be in the future, being that her IQ level was

higher than any other child her age. She was also very gifted when it came

to dancing, and any form of arts. Once she met her high school crush,

Deniro, and fell in love with him, it was over for all her dreams. They

moved in together after graduation, and life was never the same for Zion.

The fact that Zion was throwing her life away with some no good man

drove my grandmother to an early grave. Before, Zion was nineteen years

old; Deniro had introduced her to the street life. Deniro's abuse began

shortly after they moved together. He began with pressuring my aunt into

threesome's with other woman, and that soon progressed into prostitution.

Zion, wasn't too fond of his ideas especially when her heart belonged to

him, but she did everything she could to keep him happy. She hated the

fact that he was willing to sell her body to random men she would meet

off the street when they were supposed to be a couple. Deniro didn't care

much about love when money was what he needed. Zion often ended up in

the hospital brutally beaten for refusing to do what was expected to make

ends meet. Several beatings later, and Zion's constant threats to report

Deniro to authorities, Zion decided to become a stripper as a way to defuse

the constant drama between them two. After a year of dancing at random clubs in Michigan, Zion met the trick of a lifetime, or so she thought.

Jarvis, was a smooth talker who promised to save her from the lifestyle

she was currently living, and she fell for it. Therefore, I guess it is safe to

say, "Beauty doesn't always come with a brain attached." It wasn't even a

full month after meeting, Jarvis and having an affair that she began to feel

ill. Zion would soon find out that her illness would be death of her. Not

only did Jarvis disappear long before she found out he had given her HIV,

he was also an undercover homosexual who preyed on woman as a sick

way to deal with his denial of being gay. Her vulnerability and the desire

to be in love with a man made her the perfect conquest to manipulate. I

always wondered what Zion would do if she had a second chance at life,

and Mama punishing me for having any type of compassion for Zions

situation. The night, I went to audition at Dirty Secret's I thought about

my aunt Zion, and prayed that God protected me from any people like,

Deniro. I knew was flawless from head to toe as I sat across from Duty. I

just prayed this new found lifestyle wouldn't leave me with regrets.

 "So what do I have to do?" I finally say, breaking the silence.

It was clear this fool forgot I was here to talk business. The entire time I

was sitting in my chair, I watched Duty stare at my outfit as if he were

doing a trick that would magically remove my clothes.

"What do you do?" Duty, replied sarcastically while running his hand across his penis.

I knew I had him exactly where I wanted him, then. I just licked the tip of my upper lip. I loved this new "Lady at Play," Mac lip stick that I'd been wearing lately, and tonight the way I'm feeling I might just act out the part too.

"Well, baby," I paused.

"You know what they say," I, continued seductively, and methodically.

On the inside, I was memorizing myself by the spell I was putting on, Duty with only mere conversation. I was mind fucking him with every word that left my mouth. I could actually envision the pre-cum beginning to ooze out the tip of his penis just at the thought of him ever getting this pussy. I smirked, and then took a seat at one of the two chairs that were closest to his desk and opened my legs.

"I'm known for being a teaser," I smiled, and then looked him straight in the eye, and licked my lips one last time.

"If you pay me right," I paused.

"I can be you, Pleaser." I smirked.

The line came so natural being that I have always had the gift of gab. Besides, I'm a finesse, Queen when it comes to charming men out of something I want.

"Is that right?" Duty spoke in his sexy Italian accent, meeting my stare with a straight face and a wicked little snicker.

I had to admit; Duty was a very attractive man. I knew if this were any other circumstance, I would probably be throwing this pussy at him.

"Just tell me when you can start baby girl," Duty stated standing up from his seat, and walking over to where I was.

"To be honest umm,"

"Umm, what is your name again?" he asked then laughed, realizing he never asked me my name.

"La'Teazya, and yours?" I asked.

"My name is Gianluca Fortunato, but around here, everyone calls me Duty," he smiled as he confidently straightened his tie.

"Well, you can call me: "The Teaser" then," I replied, and we both laughed.

It was obvious that, that was exactly what I was doing to his ass at that very moment: Teasing him.

"Well, La'Teazya," he smirked with this naughty look in his eyes while placing his hands on my shoulder.

"The job was yours from the minute you walked through the door".

"I was thinking I need to start as soon as possible," I replied, standing up and sashaying over towards the door.

I needed a drink, or maybe I just needed something cool in my system because of all the flirting I had done. Just looking at Duty was beginning to turn me on.

"Well how about tomorrow night if it's alright with you?" he proceeded to say then walked over to open the door for me.

He escorted me out into the now crowded club, and I could see why it was the hottest topic of everyone's discussion. I watched Duty's every move as we walked towards the bar. He was about 6'2" ft tall, his perfectly tanned complexion complimented his thick black curly hair, and his eyes were even dreamier than mine were. His cocky yet muscular build could have easily been mistaken for one of the bouncers at the club, yet everything about Duty's overall appearance down to the tailor made Italian suit he had on screamed business.

"Would you like a drink, Ms. Teaser?" he asked in his thick Italian accent.

"Because, I'd like to make a toast to the loveliest lady I've seen all week," Duty announced, and then snapped his finger to get the attention of one of the young girls working behind the bar.

"Pepper, darling," the girl approached us with a big smile on her face.

"Sup, Duty," she answered all bubbly, and then placed two shot glasses in front of us as if she already knew what he wanted. She poured two glasses of Patron, and was about to walk away until Duty said, "I'd like you to meet our newest addition to the family Ms. Teaser."

Then he turned to me and gave me a little wink.

"I'm sure she's going to be a nice asset to my investment."

"Let's toast to the finer things in life," he chuckled, and then raised his glass."

I just smiled, admiring myself in the mirror as "Tell Me," by Bobby Valentino played.

"I've always had an eye for quality Ms. Teaser," he smiled showing off his pearly white teeth and right now business couldn't get any better".

I had to agree with Mr. Fortunato. I was definitely one of the finer things from the looks I was getting, and quality just so happened to be my middle name. I threw back my shot of Patron, and quickly ordered two more shots. The way I was feeling at that m o m e n t a l l I could see was dollar signs.

"Pass go, please collect $200.00." I giggled inside.

My goal was to make triple that every night. I sat there chatting for another twenty minutes with Duty, then he excused himself. I could finally feel the five shots I had earlier slowly taking effect on me as "Rock Yo Hips," by Crime Mob started to play. I couldn't control myself as I began to do exactly what the words were saying. I was feeling myself tonight, and I damn sure had every reason, too. Rozi finally came to join me by the bar to play catch up on my little meeting with Duty.

I gave her the "You know I got the job, Bitch," look, and it was on.

Rozi ordered me six more shots, and before I knew it she was throwing all that ass of hers on me. Dancing with Rozi caught the eye of some of the ballers who was up in the club that night. It wasn't long before a couple of them approached us. Of course, some were trying to get us to leave with them right, then, and there, others wanted their own private show later on, but my eyes were glued to this one guy who didn't seem to pay us any attention. I loved m e n who played the "High and

Mighty" role. That type of guy seem to open up rather easily once you got to know him. I whispered in Rozi's ear " I'll be back," because I spotted something I liked, and then I made my way over to his table. Everything about the man read "Money," because he damn sure looked like the part.

"Please tell me why the finest brother up in the club is sitting over here all alone?" I inquired as I approached the table.

"You must be married," I paused.

"No, wait, let me think," I say with a chuckle, taking in the man's overall appearance, while making sure to glance over at his bare ring finger.

At first glance, you would have thought Nasir Jones himself was in the building, but I knew I wasn't that lucky. The jewelry he wore was flawless! I watched the diamonds in his jewelry reflect everywhere in the club each time the light caught a glimpse of his chain, pinky ring, and Rolex. I started to feel like I was one of the girls from Belly's beginning club scene when Nas first walks in with DMX. At that moment, it was only us two, and the only thing I wanted to do was rob him of his heart.

"Or what," he questioned, and I knew at that moment I wanted the man inside me.

"Or just maybe," I proceeded to say while snapping out of the fantasy I was having.

"You're a pimp, and you're back here making sure your girl gets all your money made for tonight," I joked taking a seat.

"Woman or No Woman," I wasn't leaving without mystery dude's number.

"Actually, I'm neither," he laughed, and then took out the bottle of Ace of Spades he had on ice and poured himself a glass.

"Would you like a drink?" he offered, and then raised his hand to get the young waitress attention before I could even answer.

"That's right, baby," I thought as "Swimming Pools" by Kendrick Lamar played.

"Take charge of your woman," the naughty voice inside my head screamed.

Just the thought of being his woman sent chills through my entire body.

"I'd love one," I lied.

All the shots I'd taken before walking over here were starting to make me feel a little queasy. After the waitress brought me a glass, he poured me a drink, and I continued with my line of questioning. This man definitely intrigued my interest, and the chemistry he was letting off was strong. It was something about him that stood out from the other men in the club.

"If I can't have the real Nas, I guess I'll take the doppelganger," I mused before I began my next question.

"So, are you single?" I asked admiring his overall appearance.

"I damn sure wouldn't want to let you out of my sight if you were my man," I flirted.

"Really," he replied, and I didn't even say a word.

I was ready to decode this mystery, and I could tell he was enjoying the question game.

"Are you single?" he asked me, and I was almost at a loss for words.

Technically, I was single. Ize was the furthest thing on my mind, and I was free to do as I pleased. "Helluva Life," by Gorilla Zoe started to play, and all I could think of was I wanted this "Dope Boy" sitting in front of me.

"I might be," I replied, trying not to come off to easy, and then he laughed.

"What's so funny?" I asked, because I had to have missed the joke.

"It's nothing too, major," he smiled.

"I just figured you would say that, " he replied sincerely as I watched him take a couple more sips of his drink.

"So what do you think about us two single people possibly getting out of here, and going somewhere that we can get better acquainted?" he suggested.

I noticed he made sure to put emphasis on the word single. All I could do was laugh, because not only did I "not" get the man's name. He obviously had to think I was as dumb as they came for even thinking I would leave the club with a total stranger.

"Now why would I do that?" I asked sarcastically when "R.N.S." by a Detroit artist named Icewear Vezzo came on, and changed my mood.

I laughed just thinking back on the meeting I had with Duty earlier.

"Introductions were definitely lacking on everyone's part tonight," I concluded, sipping my drink.

I watched the way "Mr. Nas," look-alike was staring at the opening in my jumpsuit, and I knew my name was the furthest thing on his mind.

"Guys are a mess," I giggled, as I sat thinking to myself while we chatted for a few more minutes about sweet nothings.

"He's only been talking to me for twenty minutes, and he already trying to get me to leave with him," I laughed sipping some more of my drink.

"That's some real Nigga shit alright," I laughed along to Vezzo's song.

"You were saying?" he asked with a look in his eyes that read, "You know you want me," and I just shook my head.

Those Patron shots were doing a number on my system, and all I could think about was getting out of that hot spot.

"I was saying," I repeated, and then stood up so he could get a better look at what I was wearing. I watched his eyes trace my curves then land right where I wanted them. I walked over to his chair and leaned in real close. I was so tipsy I could have sworn he leaned towards me too. We were so close to one another that I almost kissed his lips before I whispered in his ear.

"Maybe we should step outside and continue this conversation," I stated, pulling myself away from the table and heading towards the exit.

I made sure to put a little twist in my hips as I headed to get some much-needed air.

"Two fine men in one night," I thought, fanning my face with my hands.

"Somebody was liable to get fucked," I giggled to myself as the air hit my skin.

I stood there admiring myself in the windows of the club. I was the true definition of a "Bad Bitch," and the outfit was damn sure bringing out the animal in me. Five minutes later, he stepped out the door, and my pussy almost got moist on sight. He was even finer outside under the moonlight than he looked in the club. I swear I could have, had sex with him right there outside the club with everybody watching. The fantasy was quickly, interrupted by the sound of him asking me: "Did you make your mind up yet?"

"How do I know I can trust you?" I asked as he handed the valet woman his ticket to bring his car around to the parking lot.

"Don't tell me you're shy," he replied with a slight smile on his face as his candy red 2014 Camaro finally pulled up.

"I didn't expect you to be the "scary type," he joked, walking over to the driver's door, and letting down the top.

"You look like the type of girl I'm into," he added, hoping in the seat and closing the door.

I wanted to faint, thinking I was blowing a chance of a lifetime.

"So are you a daredevil, or what?" he inquired so seriously that I felt like a naughty schoolgirl being scolded by the teacher.

"Or are you just a tease?" he implied, and I rolled my eyes to the heavens.

"Was he taunting me?" I asked myself, and then grinned at the thought of being called a tease.

"If I wasn't already e l e v e n shots of Patron, and a glass of Ace of Spades into my drinking," I continued.

I'd show this guy how much of a dare deviling tease I could really be.

"Fuck it, like fuck it though," I thought.

"What did I have to lose?"

"If tonight's my last night,"

"Then its three sheets to the winds, BITCHES," I giggled, walking over to the passenger door, and opening it.

'I'm gone off this Patron, and I'm out with this fine curly head, Motherfucka."

As soon as we pulled out the parking lot my song came on. I couldn't help but sing-along to "Tonight," by John Legend as my long black, naturally wavy hair blew in the wind. Everything about this night seemed magical, and it was damn sure turning out to be one of the best I ever had. I was relaxed as I sang along to the song while the wind whipped wildly through my hair. I just stared into the night sky as we drove through the city. I was in shock at what happened once we pulled up at the light just before the freeway's entrance. I was singing along to John Legend in my own little world when he just leaned over, and kissed me. Before I could say a word the light changed, and I just sat back and enjoyed the ride. Puff Daddy's "Roll Wit Me," poured out the system as we drove on the half empty freeway. We exited downtown on Jefferson, and pulled up at this little secluded spot by the water. At first, I was nervous, but I shook the feeling off quickly as the song changed to R Kelly's "Half On A Baby," and sex began to fill my mind.

"So are you ever going to tell me your name?" I finally asked while running my fingers through my hair to straighten out the parts that were out of place.

"It's Haji," he replied then leaned over to grab something out of his glove compartment and my heart began to beat fast.

This dude could be a mass murderer for all I know, and I have the nerves to think about that now. I shook my head then let out a deep breath, but I couldn't shake the panicky feeling that was starting to come over me.

"All my friends call me Ace," he continued, pulling out a blunt.

"Do you smoke?" he asked, passing the perfectly rolled blunt.

I hit it to try and balance out the liquor that was starting to make me feel like I was spinning. I passed him back the blunt after taking a couple puffs and tried my best to keep my composure. I sure as hell didn't want to start throwing up in front of Haji. I knew first impressions were everything, and I wasn't about to be the known as the "drunk bitch," that threw up all over his ride. I asked him if he would like to continue our little escapade at my house. Of course, he did not mind. This would give me enough time to sober down on the ride and then freshen up once we got to my place. The drive to my house seemed like it was taking forever because of all the alcohol floating around in my system. All I could do was secretly pray that I got home before it decided to show the way I was truly feeling. The weed only seemed to intensify my drunken state of mind. I was beginning to wish the night would end the minute I reached my doorstep. The sound of sirens coming from behind us got my attention as I tried to make sense of what Haji was saying to me. Somewhere between me giving him my address, fantasizing, hitting the weed, and us driving, I must have dozed off, because I never even notice the police until I heard then announce that they wanted us to **"PULL THE VECHICLE OVER"**. **I just** looked at Haji liked he had lost his mind. This was starting to feel like a scene out of a movie as I tried to gather every ounce of soberness I could muster up in my body.

"Why don't you just pull over?" I asked.

The thoughts from earlier about him being some type of killer of some sort played tricks on my mind. It was clear to me that he was even considering pulling the car over. I watched Haji push the pedal to the metal while staring through his rearview with a sinister smirk on his face. Something about that very moment just watching his reaction to everything that was happening told me that he was no good. I was trying my best to talk some sense into Haji, but everything he said sounded like a bunch of mumble-jumble as I zoned in and out of consciousness while we talked. I was so pissed at myself now for drinking all those shot earlier, because Haji wasn't taking me serious.

"Look, La'Teazya!"

"I know we just met, and this may seem like a fucked up way to end a good night," he paused staring through his rearview.

"I need you to do a big favor for me right now, boo," he asked, and I instantly sobered up.

"What the hell did I get myself into?" I w o n d e r e d.

Haji was fine, but he going to jail wasn't worth the dick I was trying to get. Besides, the dick might not even be good and here I go just throwing myself at him because he looks good on the outside.

"What is that?" I asked flabbergasted.

This fool, Haji was really starting to press his luck with me. He already got me to leave the club with him without me even knowing his name.

"What else could he possibly need from me?"

I swear if it wasn't for the fact that my car was in the shop getting a new paint job, and the liquor didn't take over my better judgment, I wouldn't even be here right now.

"Lord, please let me get home safe," I prayed to myself as my conscious started to kick it.

"I need you to hide this for me," he asked, placing a sandwich bag filled with tiny packs of cocaine on my lap, and, I just looked at him like the fool that he sounded.

"I can't get caught with this, or I'll go back to jail," was all I heard.

He was rambling on about something else, but it all started to sound like a blur. I moved the dope off my lap back to his as "Never Been," by Wiz Khalifa began to play.

"How do you expect me to do that?" I inquired, looking at my clutch bag.

"You're a girl," he tried to explain, as if I didn't know the game already. I was fresh out of prison my damn self, and I wasn't about to take a chance on going back for a fool I hardly knew anything about.

"Even if I stop they won't search you," he tried his best to negotiate.

All I could think was where the hell did he expect me to put the shit?

"So what exactly do you want me to do?" I asked again, confused.

I knew if I heard the officer say: "**PULL THE VECHICLE OVER**", one more time, and we didn't; we were going to be in for a hell-of-a night once we did.

"I need you to put this in your pussy for me until we get to your house," he stated, and all I could do was laugh like the drunk I felt.

"Are you fucking kidding me right now Haji?" I asked, looking at the drugs he wanted me to shove inside of my pussy as if it was a personal storage. Before I knew it, I was asking that fool where his pussy was. I laughed again, but this time I told Haji that he had better do what he had to, to get us out of this mess. I also informed him that if it came down to me, or him, he could best believe it was only one of us going home, tonight. We argued the entire time the police were chasing us. I couldn't believe the nerves of this nigga, Haji. I'm sure the police knew something was wrong between us, because at one point I reached out, and slapped, Haji. He just shook his head, and stepped on the gas as we headed out of the police's eyesight. A couple blocks, a freeway, and an alley later we had lost them. I had never been so happy to see my place in my life once we pulled in front of my building, and never so disappointed to have to turn down a fine guy.

"This clown better be lucky I made it home safe," was all I could think as I let out a sigh of relief once we reached my apartment building.

I didn't even want to say "goodbye" to Haji as I opened his car door but, a part of me knew I had to be respectful despite how things turned out, just in case I ever ran into him again.

"Wait, La'Teazya, I," Haji pleaded, while trying his best to apologize to me, but I wasn't even trying to hear it. I was pissed, and there was no talking to me once I was mad. I was so disappointed in Haji, as I took one final look at his fine ass before I shut car door.

"TRICK NO GOOD," I giggled throwing my ass as I walked towards the door.

I couldn't believe this was one good night gone to waste all because this fool wanted me to shove some dope up my pussy while getting chased by the police.

"What the Fuck!" I laughed, opening up the front door to my building.

P.S. **It was definitely a good thing I went to my girl Molly's toy party the other day. I was damn sure going to put one of my new gadgets I brought to work before I went to bed.**

Do You Really Love Me???

Dear Diary,

August 27, 2104

I remember my best friend, Stazy telling me that her mom and dad would have bible studies and random talks about God, and his son Jesus at their house. My Mama never taught me anything about God, or Jesus. To be perfectly honest, my Mama sold my soul straight to the devil the day I was born. I was six years old when I lost my virginity. My Mama got into this bad situation with my sister's dad, Bono during one of their little gambling parties she was having one night; and she basically let some man rape me just so her, and Bono didn't have to pay him back. Bono and my Mama were the scum of the earth, literally. I hated my Mama, and the feeling was mutual. Mama only cared about herself, money, and drugs. Mama always prided herself for dating Bono, but he was nothing like the real men I knew. He was more like a Bozo, which is what I always called him behind his back. My Mama was always drinking, on drugs and having gambling parties so, she never really had time to watch over us. To her, we were just a way to keep up with her lifestyle. As long as Mama got her monthly income, she kept us, I once heard her tell someone. I remember asking my Mama, "Did she really love me"? She gave me one simple drunken response: "Maybe, you did at least get my hair, you little Heffa".

Mama then laughed at me as tears rolled down my face. Secretly, I believed my mom envied me. I was a reminder of the one man my Mama could never have. I never knew my biological father. Once, I overheard that he was the love of my Mama's life. Mama did everything she could do to impress my dad but he already had a family. After years of chasing him, and making a fool of herself, she started drinking. She never could accept the fact that the only thing my father ever gave her was a nut, and a baby. It drove my Mama crazy to see my dad strutting around town with his wife and kids while she struggled with me. Eventually, he moved out of town with his family when Mama showed up at his doorstep drunk demanding him to take me. Shortly, after Mama would drink for days and curse the day that she ever had me. I hated the constant reminders day in and out that I was only born because she thought it would make him leave his "other" family. Shortly after that, she met Bono. Bono was a real asshole whenever he was drinking, or on drugs. He also had a gambling addiction. I guess that is why I always called him Bozo. He was a real clown ass nigga if you asked me. Mama and Bono started their own after hour spot once Bono was kicked out of all the casinos, and that became his way to support his drinking and drug habit whenever he hit big. T'Aira was born a year after they met when I was four, and Mama actually started to like the fact that she had two kids. The increase in her monthly income and food stamps was a "blessing," she had called us but she treated us more like shit. Well me, really, because T'Aira seemed to be her pride and joy. Things got a little better once Mama was approved for her Section 8 housing voucher, and we moved into our townhouse. That also happened to be when I met my best friend Stazy. Stazy was more like a sister to me, because I could tell her all of my deep, dark secrets about my crazy life living with Mama, and she never judged me. Stazy never treated me like the other kids from my neighborhood that would pick on me for not having the latest toys or clothing. One day while Stazy and I sat playing Barbie dolls, she kept going on, and on about God and Jesus. I tried my best to refrain myself from asking her if God, and Jesus were such good people why didn't they love kids? Stazy told me that God loved everyone, and that he loved us all so much that he sent his only son Jesus here to die for our sins. Stazy also explained that God knew some people were just plain old wicked. That explained it all, because my Mama had to be one of those bad people she always talked about. Every time, I would play with Stazy she would teach me more about God. I was actually starting to like him until Stazy died from cancer. I never did understand why God would take away the only person who ever told me anything right in my whole life. It was downhill from there. I cursed God, and before I knew it, I was headed down a path of destruction. I went from playing hide-and-seek, to hide-go-getty-ooh with my best friends' brother, my first kiss was with an ugly eighth grader, and by the time I could count well my virginity was gone. I was six years old when I was, raped. My Mama, and Bono were having another one of their little gambling parties and I guess Bono owed out more than him, and Mama could afford. That's when I became part of the deal. I will never forget the big, strong, drunk man coming into my room, or Bozo telling me to do what he said. Nor would I ever forget the fact that Mama acted as if she didn't know what happened, or even care to know what happened to me when I tried repeatedly to tell her about the man. She never could look me in my eyes while she cursed me out for making up such a story. I hated the fact that she had the nerve to tell me I better not tell anyone else what I'd just told her or she was gone beat the hell out of me. The liquor and drugs always took over Mama's better judgment. I also knew the only reason they picked me instead of T'Aira was because, I was the child Mama hated, and T'Aira was her sick twisted love child in her mind. Favoritism was a part of my everyday life and at times, I really resented having a sister. T'Aira would lie about any and everything, and Mama would blame me for it. She always told me I could lie my way out of anything because I was the spawn of the "devil" himself. T'Aira even got better clothes and toys than I did, and all I wanted to do was rid myself from them all. Bono and Mama started to use and excessive amount of drugs as a way to escape the harshness of their reality. He had just lost his job at the post office, because he was caught on camera stealing credits cards out of people's mail. Plus, he owed so many people out in the streets due to his gambling debits that Mama damn near sold everything we had that wasn't nailed down to keep folks from killing him. She eventually got a part time job at the market up the street from us as a cashier to support their habit, but with Mama bringing in all the money, and Bono smoking it all up things began to clash between the two lovebirds. They would get drunk, high and then argue and fight all night long. I was eight years old when I, eventually started sneaking out of the house. That is when I met, Zarbreah. Zarbreah, became my best friend instantly because we clicked during our first conversation. We both had mothers who drank all the time, other siblings who irritated us, subjected to rape at an early age, and absent fathers. Her mother's brother had raped Zarbreah, and months later, the police found pieces of his body at the City's dump. Zar always swore that was the real reason why her dad was locked up in prison. Her mother also drank to cover up her past, but she was more functional able than I ever knew my mother to be. Whenever things went wrong at my house, I would find myself over Mrs. Emerson's house for days, sometimes weeks after introducing our mothers' to one another. Mama never really cared what I did as long as I catered to her. I hated listening to my Mama when I was in her care so I would convince Mrs. Emerson to let me stay over even when Mama wasn't tripping. Eventually, Mrs. Emerson starting letting me come over without having to ask. I guess that is when you can say I started to like Izir, who was Zar's older brother. Sometimes when I would spend the night I would sneak out of Zarbreah's room while she was asleep, and stay up playing truth or dare with her older brother Ize. Ize would literally stay up all night sometimes talking to me, about their father and things they would do before he was locked up. This was cool to me because Zarbreah never talked about their father. Izir was the total opposite. He seemed to idolize their dad, and he swore he was going to grow up to be just like him one day. He promised his dad that he would be the man of the house once he left, so all Ize ever talked about was ways to make money, and I admired that. All, I needed was my own money to be free from all the bullshit my Mama was always putting me through. At home, I was my Mama's personal slave. I always compared myself to Cinderella because one day, I was going to get away from her, Bono, and my evil little sister. Mrs. Emerson was like my fairy Godmother, because everything Mama lacked on teaching me, she made sure I knew. I was grateful to have Zarbreah, and her family because without them who knows what would have happened to me. One day, while Zarbreah and I were playing Monopoly I told her about my secret crush I had on Ize. She explained to me that she already knew, because some nights she would wake up, and I would be gone. When she would come to look for me, I would be talking to Ize with the biggest smile on my face. She also said that she didn't mind the fact that I liked her brother, because that would make us sisters if we were to ever get married in the future."

"Married…" I laughed, thinking Zar had to be crazy. The only person I ever knew of that was married was my father, and I damn sure didn't want a husband like him so marriage was the furthest thing on my mind for my future.

Four years had come and gone, yet my Mama hadn't changed one bit. My Mama was pure evil in my eyes, and I couldn't wait to be grown. Izir was having his 14th birthday party and all the kids from the neighborhood came. We ended up dancing together to Aaliyah's "Are You That Somebody", and Ize was the only thing on my mind the entire time. The marriage idea Zarbreah mentioned before wasn't sounding that bad as I watched Ize from across the floor dancing with another girl wishing it was me. Once "Hey Lover" by LL Cool J came on, I knew I liked Ize! There was only one problem: I knew he didn't feel the same about me. Ize had told me plenty of times before that he enjoyed having a second sister he could talk to because Zar had a big mouth. Secretly, I always wished he were mine, because LL was right. This was definitely more than a crush, and the feeling was something I never experienced before. The party was going great until I'eyzha came. I'yezha happened to be the most popular girl in our school. She was fully developed, for her young age, and all the boys liked her but she liked Ize. I envied her for being able to get the boy I only dreamed of having. I'eyzha, and her little "Stuck Up Crew" as I called them, suggested we all play a game called "Seven Minutes in Heaven" which is a popular party game amongst teenagers where two people are selected to go into a closet or other dark enclosed space, and do whatever they like for seven minutes. When it was my turn, I got paired up with Ize's best friend, Roj. I hated it too because Roj was a big lipped, bubbled eyed boy who always reminded me of a frog. When we went in the closet together, I wanted to faint as he slobbered all over my mouth, and I just stood there. This was the worst first kiss I ever had and it pissed me off even more that I'yezha had to kiss, Ize. For the rest of the entire evening, I wouldn't talk to anyone but, Zarbreah. I even declined to play any of the games at the sleep over. The next day, I went home earlier than all the other, kids did. I also didn't spend the night over Zar's house again until Mama and Bozo started fighting. She had put him out one weekend for stealing money out of her purse but, of course, he came back, and it was the same old routine with them. One afternoon while I was standing at my locker getting out my books for class, Ize approached me. He asked me why I didn't come kick it with him anymore while I was at his house. I had to laugh, because I could have sworn he was spending most of his time with I'eyzha lately.

"I'm sure you and I'eyzha have plenty to talk about" I snap slamming my locker while heading towards my classroom before the bell rang.

"You sound jealous" Ize teased, and I wanted to slap the smirk he had off his face.

"Me, Jealous?" I lied, because his arrogance got the best of me sometimes.

I knew that if I were two years older or had a body like I'eyzha's, he would be my boyfriend. Instead, all I could be is a second sister who listened to all his dreams, knew all his secrets, while somebody else wore the title I, wanted. Sometimes, I hated that we met, because I was his sister's best friend.

"You must think I don't know," he blurted out, now walking in front of me so that he could look me in my face when I responded to his comment.

I stopped dead in my tracks and rolled my eyes to the heavens while clutching my book tight to my chest.

"Know what?" I demanded, rolling my head with a bit of attitude.

"That you like me, Duh," he laughed while moving out of the way, so I could continue walking.

All I could do was say: "I don't like you," while putting some pep in my step.

He had caught me off guard with that statement, and I was about to let him know I was secretly crushing on him when he already had a girlfriend.

"If you say so," he replied, and I just turned around and shocked the shit out of him.

"See… I know you like me now, La'Teazya," he taunted, while rambling on as the bell rang, and I just kept walking.

"Zarbreah been told me you had a crush on me weeks ago," he laughed again, while following close behind me as I reached my classroom door.

"I also know that you stopped talking to me, because you had to kiss Roj at my party, but you wished it was me," he teased, and I just walked in the class without answering.

I was going to kick Zar's ass the next time I saw her. She never could control that motor mouth of hers and it was time somebody taught her ass a lesson. After school, I decided to walk home by myself, but Ize insisted that he would walk with me. He suggested that we go chill at the park for a few before we went home, and I agreed. Once we got there, he pulled out half of a joint he stolen from his mom's personal stash and made me try it with him. He told me that he had been thinking about smoking weed but never actually tried it. He knew Zar would snitch, Roj was too scared, I'eyzha was indecisive, and the only person he knew would keep his secret was, me. He even confessed that he never really liked, I'eyzha. I'eyzha s was a freak, and she would let him do anything he wanted to her down to taking golden showers as long as she could keep her virginity. She didn't want her parents finding out that she was fast due to her father being a Preacher. Passing me the joint, Ize stood up and looked off into space. For a minute, I thought the boy had lost it. I knew if I was zoning out from the puffs of marijuana I inhaled, he was, too.

"Do you love me, La'Teazya?"

I damn near choked hearing the words come out of his mouth. After catching my breath, I looked at Ize as if he had lost his mind.

"This weed shit was a serious drug," I announced, then threw out the rest of the joint we were smoking. Ize had to be tripping, I rationalized but the look on his face said it all. He was dead serious! Just like, I was the time I asked my Mama did she love me.

"Seriously, Teaz," He stated.

"I need you to tell me do you really love me," he repeated, and I wanted to disappear.

I was so confused…

"Why did it even matter if I loved him?" I wondered, because love never did anything but let me down.

"Besides, wasn't he I'eyzha's boyfriend?" I concluded.

"Shouldn't you be asking I'eyzha these types of questions?" I asked him before answering.

I was only twelve years old. What the hell, did I really know about love anyway? Yes, I liked, Ize, but maybe it was all because of our circumstances. Ize's house was my safe haven from my reality at home. Life had bonded us together as far as I was concerned. Who knew what the future held?

"I guess I love you, Ize!" I finally managed to say.

I really didn't know what love was. I knew in my heart I felt a way for his family that I didn't even feel for my own family. I guess that was love, because when I was at home, I liked to pretend to be invisible. This often led to me packing up my things to go over to Zabreah, and Ize's house.

"I guess I can accept that answer," he replied, and all I could do was wonder why he even asked that in the first place.

"Why do you want to know," I asked, as he began to gather up his book bag so that we could go home, and all I got was a simple, "because".

"Because what?" I drilled him, as I picked up my belongings to catch up to where he was.

Ize wasn't about to get off the hook that easy.

"I just needed to know if you loved me, La'Teazya," he answered sincerely.

"I'eyzha said she didn't when I asked her," he explained to me, and I just shook my head.

"If I ever get a girlfriend in the future, Teaz," he paused.

"I'd like her to love me like my mom did my dad."

"I don't ever want to be with someone just because we look cute together," He finished.

I just listened to him as he talked about love, relationships, and him dumping I'eyzha soon. Those were the best words I had heard him say since we started talking about this love mess. I actually wanted to hear more about Ize dumping her, than the whole love crap he was selling me. I sat there taking in his every word as I always did, and that's when he said the words I'll never forget.

"I love you, La'Teazya."

"You're really one of the best friends I ever had," he stated, and I just smiled.

It was getting late once we approached our block. The streetlights were coming on, and I was wondering where all the time had gone. Once we arrived at my house, I told Ize I had fun walking home with him. I even promised to start talking back to him more whenever I spent nights at their place. He just laughed, and I ignored him while I looked for my keys. I figured he was still high off the weed we smoked earlier. The next thing I knew he called my name, and when I looked up to answer him, he kissed me. I was so shocked, that I didn't even try to move as he stuck his tongue in and out my mouth while caressing my hair. Finally, I gave in and kissed him back then pushed him away, realizing we were standing right outside my Mama's bedroom window. I didn't need her to catch me kissing Ize, because I knew she'd take away the one thing that I truly might have loved.

"I knew you loved me," Ize said, smiling ear to ear as he skipped off towards his house.

"One day you gone be mines, Teaz," he shouted, and all I could do was stand there and smile.

I was looking forward to that one day. That night, I dreamed about Izir and for the first time, I knew what love was. He had to love me to share all his secrets with me, to kiss me, tell me he loved me, and to ask me if I loved him, too, I convinced myself. I was just hoping that the he would keep his promise and dump I'yezha soon.

"Love or no love," she was definitely "Getting In The Way Of What I'm Feeling," I thought as Jill Scott sang her heart out.

In my eyes, the end was near for I'yezha's trifling ass, and all I could do was laugh.

"Now who's the shit, Bitch," I thought as I listened to "If," by Janet Jackson.

"You're looking more, and more like yesterday's trash, slut!" I smirked, then let out the evilest laugh I could.

Just thinking about I'yezha getting pissed on by Ize and other boys she had dated before Ize made me shake my head in "total disgust". I secretly could not wait to become her replacement. Alicia Keys was right. I used to be jealous of your girlfriend, but I guess she never shared that special part of you that "I Do".

What Is Love; Because It Hurt So Damn Much

Dear Diary,
September 9, 2104

It was the end of summertime in the year 2000, when Mama finally left Bono. I will never forget it because, it was the cruelest summers I ever had. I hated living with my Mama, and her stupid boyfriend, because they weren't good role models. Everyone knew they didn't need to be parents, and I wished I was grown. My Mama was a junkie, who liked to keep up with the Jones's. She would do anything she could to keep living the lifestyle she loved so much. I truly believed that my Mama would sell her soul to the Devil, himself if the price was right. I assumed Mama's little gambling parties and job was finally starting to pay off, but that was far from the truth. Mama had talked the manager at Quick Mart into paying her under the table at the market so she could keep receiving her cash benefits from the government. Mama wasn't about to take a cut back in her monthly income, so she persuaded the manager of the market to have sex with her one night after work, and he was like play-dough in her hands. Bono, on the other hand, happened to be on a lucky winning spree with him hitting the lotto a couple evenings. It literally felt like Christmas in July. It seemed like everything they wanted they got. Mama even bought us some new things to keep us occupied while they lived their lives. T'Aira loved every minute of it, too, but I didn't. A couple of Barbie dolls, and a new game system wasn't enough to make-up for all the bad things my Mama did to me on a daily, basis. Sometimes when Mama was sober, she would try to apologize for her actions, but I knew she didn't mean it. Time and time again, I tried to believe in my Mama, but she always let me down. Yes, she kept a roof over my head, clothes on my back, and food in our fridge, but she never could love me. When it came to love in my household, Keith Sweat is absolutely, right: There really is a "Right and Wrong way to love somebody," and I was on the wrong side. The only real love I ever got during my childhood came from the Emerson's. They were the ones who had my back without a shadow of doubt. They understood, and empathized with all my life's trials and tribulations. I had to learn the hard way that not all family is blood, but loyalty is what makes you family. Ize had also kept his promise. He dumped I'eyzha the next day, and every time I would walk home, he would walk with me. Sometimes, we would just sit at the park and talk, but others times we smoked and practice on my kissing skills. Ize was starting to become more of a best friend to me than Zarbreah. We started to do everything together. I even had to start lying to Zar about seeing Ize, because I could tell she was getting jealous of our relationship. She told me that she felt Ize was taking me away from her. She even went as far as to tease me about letting him take my 2nd, virginity.

"I know you're fucking, Ize," I remember her saying to me one day, as we got ready to go roller-skating. I admit, I had been sneaking around hanging with Ize a lot lately; but he and I both knew I was too scared to go all the way. I often told myself that I was still technically a virgin, because that situation with the drunken man was something a six-year old child could not control. I wasn't physically strong enough to fight off the man as he ripped off my panties, holding me down on the bed with his one hand while wrestling to restrain me, and unzip his pants with the other, as his liquor stench breath filled the air.

"Please don't hurt me," I pleaded and begged, hoping my Mama would come to my rescue. The cold words of Bozo's, "***YOU BETTER DO WHAT HE TELLS YOU***," kept playing over, and over in my head like a broken record. I watched the man pull out his penis and shoved it into my vagina. I can't even tell you what happened next, because I blacked out. When I woke up, all my Mama did was tell me I was a liar as I stood there holding my bloody, swollen vagina. I hated her and Bozo, and I truly believed I would still be a virgin if it wasn't for them.

"I'm not fucking Ize," I snapped, putting on my clothes. Lately, since Mama and Bono had been traveling in and out of town, I had been staying at their house a lot, while T'Aira stayed over one of her little random friends of the week house.

"Sure you're not," Zar laughed!

"I guess that's why I caught ya'll kissing with his hands down your pants," she teased, and I slapped her with a pillow. Zar's sneaky ass was always lurking around for gossip, and I damn sure didn't need that being told to anyone. The following week, Mama was having a going away party right before Bono took her to Vegas. She was blasting her jam, "Summertime," by Fresh Prince while talking shit as usual with her friends, as they all had the time of their lives. I, on the other hand, felt more like Bananarama, because it was starting to be a "Cruel Summer" all over again. I guess they hit big while they were in Vegas, because once they returned home from their trip all they did was party. Some nights, I hated it, too. I would literally stay up all night listening to them and their drunken friends fuss, fight, then fuck. Mama's house had only one rule: "Pay to get in and pay to get out."

I'll never forget this one particular evening; I had begged Mama to do my hair in a bunch of spiral curls. Even though she acted as if it were going to kill her, she went on ahead and did it for me. Being that my hair was naturally wavy, Mama had to wash and straighten it before she could actually curl it. While we were sitting in the kitchen waiting on the pressing comb to get hot, we heard a loud noise coming from the living room. I looked at my Mama, terrified, as we both stared in the direction the noise was coming from. We heard the front door fly open and then three men in masks stormed into the kitchen where we were. The first man ran over to my Mama, demanding to know where Bono was. Before she could even speak, he grabbed Mama up by her hair, and smacked her with the back of the gun, causing blood to drip down her smooth chocolate face. He then grabbed her by the arms and dragged her out the kitchen kicking, and screaming. She tried her best to fight him off while he repeatedly asked for the location of the drugs and money. The third man put a gun to my head. Mama just screamed and yelled some more until the second man starting kicking her. The second man finally started tearing up the house looking for the drugs, and money. T'Aira came screaming from her bedroom, and was thrown to the floor with a gun put to the back of her head. That's when my Mama finally attempted to beg for our lives. I was in total disbelief as I sat in my chair watching the guys' every move. Even in a time of life or death, it was clear to me who Mama chose. I hated my Mama as I sat there with the gun pressed to my head. I really couldn't see a point worth living anymore. The person that was holding Mama smacked her again with the gun and cocked the trigger, and I thought they were about to do us all a favor.

"Bitch, you better tell me where the money is!" he screamed at Mama, kicking her limp body into the floor. He then pointed the gun at Mama, who was playing the best role I had ever seen in my life of not knowing what the men were talking about, or wanted. Secretly, I knew she did. I just closed my eyes and tried my best to concentrate on the lyrics to the song that was playing. The reality of the situation was more like a dream I wish I could wake up from, but knew would never happen.

"I'll kill you if I don't get what I want, Bitch!" he yelled, and then placed the gun to her head one last time. I just knew it was over for us all as I hummed the words to "November Rain" by Guns-n-Roses. I guess that was when the dumb bitch finally came to her senses, because she just pointed towards her room and said, "Mattress". Once the three masked men got what they came for which was seven keys of cocaine and eight thousand dollars, they left. I, on the other hand, secretly wished they had put us all out of our misery. Hours later, Bono strolled in the door and Mama damn near lost it. I couldn't believe it either! I could have sworn her main reason for chasing him out the door with a butcher's knife was that somebody could have killed "her kids," all because he starting robbing people. His last hit almost had him sitting carefree, but Bozo wasn't as smart as he thought he'd been. He robbed the spot he'd been copping his drugs from one night, and he would've pulled it off had he not got high and pillow talked to one of his little tricks he saw behind Mama's back. This was the first time I ever heard my Mama stand up for me in my whole life. I never would have thought my Mama would ever leave Bozo's triflin' ass! It wasn't until another one of Mama's little gambling parties did the truth really come about the robbery. Mama only begged for our lives because if they had killed us, she knew her livelihood would have been over. We were Mama's bread and butter! Without us, the money she received from the government that she loved so much would not exist. All I could do was shake my head in disgust as I sat in my bed with a face full of tears. If there was one person in this world I knew didn't "*LOVE ME*" for sure it was "*MY MAMA*". I promised myself that day that if I ever got a family, I would never treat them like my Mama did me. I also prayed to that person, Stazy called "God She always told me once before that he helps those who pray, and believed in him. I begged him to get me out of my situation. I knew in my heart there had to be somewhere better for me than living here in this misery. The new school year was going to be starting in the next couple of weeks, and I was pissed, being that Izir was starting high school. I just hoped that the next couple, years of my life would fly by so we could run away together liked we always talked about. The first part of the school year was actually going better than I had expected. Until this one day during lunch, Zarbreah announced to our friends that she had caught Ize, and his new "girlfriend" named Angel doing it. I was fuming sitting there listening to her ramble on and on about the details. All this time here, I am sneaking around and freaking with Ize, and he repays me by having sex with some "Devil," and caught by his big mouth sister.

"Love ain't shit," I thought as I zoned out on Zar's story. Sometimes, I

wondered did Zar even think before she spoke. She would just blab out the

latest gossip without evening caring if it was fact or not. As long as it got

to her ears, her big mouth told it. Zar was terrible at keeping secrets, and

for the first time in our friendship, I was glad she snitched. I was just

happy she never told any of my dirty little secrets out in the streets. This

is the main reason I always considered Zar a best friend. That night as I

lay in my bed, I could hear Mama and her friends at it again at their usual

weekly gambling party. Boys II Men's "Please Don't Go", and Jon B's "R

U Still Down" came on, and all I could do was cry. Ize was the first boy to

ever break my heart, and he wasn't even mine. How could he make me

feel like he cared about me when he knew my circumstances, then do

something like have sex with another girl other than me? I knew we only

went to second base when we messed around, but he always told me that

was enough for him. So why would he go off and go all the way with

some Angel chick? He always promised that we would be together once

he got a new girlfriend. I was confused as to why he would betray me, and

hook up with Angel in the first damn place, and I hated love! I began to

pray again to God that he would just make my heart cold like everyone

else that I knew. I wasn't built for all the hurt people kept doing to my

feelings. This world was cold and callous, so, I took heed at twelve years

old. When I was the age of six, I had to learn the hard way that all I will ever have in this cold world is I. Right now, I was having a Déjà vu

moment. I constantly prayed that eighteen came fast! You can't tell me

that God doesn't answer prayers, because I will never forget being woke

up out of my sleep by the sound of fire trucks and police sirens. The next

thing I knew, my bedroom door was being broken down, and men rushing

me out of the burning house with T'Aira close behind. I could hear the

neighbors whispering something about "those poor children," and I just

knew my Mama was dead. Somebody had set my Mama's body on fire

while she was sleeping. Just like that, my life's burden was gone, forever.

I didn't even cry as the police officer explained to me, and T'Aira what

happened. I felt Mama deserved to die, because she never truly gave a

fuck about us anyway. T'Aira and I were taken by social service, and

temporarily placed in a girl's home. I hated it there at first, because some

of the girls tried to test me daily. After beating down a couple of them and

earning my respect, I finally found some peace in writing poems and raps.

The fights only seemed to make me a stronger person. There was no way

in hell I was ever going to let anyone in this world punk me now that my

Mama, was dead and gone. Once the girls had gotten over their little beefs

with me, I ended up with a couple new friends. My grades drastically

began to get better after my Mama died. As much as Mrs. Emerson tried to

help me, I was only managing to maintain a "C" average when it came to

my overall G.P.A. It was hard to learn properly in my household being that Mama always had company, so I always did just enough to keep me passing each semester. By the time I was a junior in high school, I made the honor roll a few times. That also happens to be when I began to take my education seriously. I remember using all my free time at the girl's home to research different colleges, and learn about scholarships. Miss Grace, the woman who ran of the girl's home, was always assuring me that I would do "great things" in life, some day. All I could do was hope that day came soon, because my whole life up until this point was a day-to-day struggle. I felt that I deserved a second chance in life, but I, did not when that day would come. My only goal was to stay focused on the books. I knew my education was my ticket out the ghetto. By the time, I had graduated from high school I was accepted to five out of seven of the colleges that I applied for in Michigan. I would soon find out that God had different plans for my future. Little by little, life was changing for me, yet it wasn't a day that went by that I didn't miss Ize, and Zar. I even tried to write them letters, but no one ever wrote me back. I used to wish Ms. Emerson would walk through the door and adopt me, but I knew in my heart it would never happen. I started to pray often and read the bible when I wasn't writing in my journal. I begged God to send me a family that would love me, and treat me kind. Months had passed, and I was starting to give up on the idea of a new family. I knew that surviving the rest of this life would depend solely on me. There wasn't anyone I could turn to when the world turned its back on me. I was learning to be unbreakable as a loner, because even my own sister had turned against me. I expected nothing less from her being that Mama always raised her as if she was better than I was. I guess praying to God works in mysterious ways. Not only did he take me away from my Mama, he took me away from my bratty little sister too. As fate would have it, I was placed in a foster home before, T'Aira. Since we didn't really have a bond as siblings, I didn't mind the fact that the couple wanted me over all the other children. It was a long process, but the Franklyn's eventually adopted me, and I moved to Ohio. I stayed in Ohio until after my first year of college. I was an honor roll student with a 4.O G.P. A, and I was only a month away from receiving my Associates degree in Business Management. A few months after my nineteenth birthday had passed; I transferred to Michigan State University with my roommate and best friend Barbara Hernandez. Barbie had it made being that she came from a wealthy background. Barbie's father, who is a Mexican immigrant to the United States, would marry into a wealthy family in his teenage years. After, seven years of being married to Roseatta Barbara Garcia, she died from complications of Sickle Cell, and left Roberto a nice fortune. Three years later, he married Maria, and Barbra was born. Barbra's, mother had no problem naming her daughter the middle name of the first woman her husband, married. After, seeing pictures, and hearing so many great stories about the kind-hearted, dainty, humanitarian, who was known for her demurely appearance. She obliged Roberto's request to name his first daughter, Barbra. It was also ironic, that once Barbie grew older, she started to look more, and more like her father's first wife than her biological, mother. People all over town mentioned the resemblance to her father once they saw Barbara. She was pure beauty without even trying, with a Cola bottle shape that could put any woman's figure to shame. She was also dating a rich white boy who had a plug in damn near every drug you could think of. Cazhmere Dongotti also happened to be a part-time owner of a nightclub with his dad in Atlanta. Barbie and Cazh hooked up after she helped him get his license back while he was finishing his Masters year at our last college. She used to make a couple of runs for him here, and there her first year of college after he got a D.U.I., and it was love ever since. Both businesses were going good for Cazh, and his reputation definitely exceeded itself. He was a legend to all the people he grew up with, and he took pride in his work. He had managed to come out on top of both worlds. He was the head of the family business, and a well-known drug lord. Barbie and I moved to Michigan so that Cazh could be closer to his connection who was bringing in a lot of revenue. She wasn't even considering the whole "moving" idea unless I agreed to go with her. She even promised to let me in on half of the money she made if I went with her. I agreed, and in less than a week, we were applying to Michigan State. Once we both were accepted, we found a little house close to campus, and Cazh paid the rent up for a year. It was supposed to be a quick way to make a couple extra dollars outside of school, but everything that glitters isn't gold. When I first got back to Michigan, all I could do was think about Zar, and Ize. I often wondered how they had turned out seeing that my life since my Mama had went in a different direction. I smiled thinking about how much the Franklyn's did for me to show me that they genuinely cared, despite my fucked up attitude at times. In my spare time, I would go back to my old neighborhood. One day, while I was cruising the block bumping "No Love" by Eminen, I ran into I'eyzha pushing a baby stroller. I found out that Ms. Emerson had moved out of her townhouse right after my Mama's death. Looking for Zar and Ize was like looking for ghosts, because no one that lived in our project knew what happened to them. That never stopped me from wondering where they were, though. One day, while I was in the library studying for an exam, I ran into, and old friend of mine name, Tye. Tye had the biggest crush on me when we were coming up, but I liked, Ize. We sat conversing about our lives, the past, and the future for a couple hours and I wished I had given Tye a chance, now. Tye had his life all mapped out, and was achieving every goal he set out for himself. I admired that he set obtainable goals each year. I always believed that people fell short of achieving greatness when they tried to have unrealistic expectations for themselves as well as others. The conversation that I had with Tye that day made me want to do better just in case I ever ran into another great man like him. Fast forward, three years later, and I never would have expected my life to turn out the way that it did.

Dear Dairy,
September 15, 2014

It was the end of my summer vacation, and I, planned on enjoying every minute of it before school started. I knew it would be crunch time once the fall semester started, being that I was working on getting my Bachelor's degree in Business management. I didn't have a care in the world as far as my life went. Barbie had kept her word on her end of the bargain, and I loved the fact that I moved back to Michigan with her. I couldn't wait to go to Cazh's yacht party that was coming up in a few days. All week long, Barbie told me stories about previous parties she had been too. She bragged about the fact that all the ballers around the globe always attended them. I had never been much of a gold digger being the Franklyn's spoiled me rotten, but, I had to admit the stories were turning me on. For some odd reason, I couldn't wait to meet me a guy like Cazh. It was a couple days before the big event, and I was getting ready to go shopping with my new friend, Roziland. We both were studying the same major, but she already had a Bachelor's degree in Business Management. I was singing along with Amber Rose's part of Wiz Khalifa's song "Never Been Pt2," and I felt her. I knew I could pull any man that I wanted. I honestly, wasn't that pressed about having a boyfriend because I loved my independence, plus, I wasn't sure if I was fully ready to commit to anyone.

"So much peer pressure," I laughed looking in the mirror once I got

dressed for this party Rozi had invited me too. If my Mama wasn't good

for shit else, she sure did bless me with that cold ass figure of hers that

guys loved so much. That is how she claimed she snagged my father; I

remembered her drunk rambling on one night about their affair.

"He loved this pussy," she blatantly stated, rubbing her hands all over her

vaginal area.

"I used to make him go home to that raggedy, Bitch," she slurred,

grabbing her cup of Martel.

"At first, I use to make him pay for the sex, I gave him on a regular,

because I was pissed that he married that hoe over me. Then I fell deeper

in love with the son-of-a-bitch, and told him he didn't have to pay me

anymore. One night, Taz made love to me so good I actually thought the

bastard loved me. That happens to be the night I got pregnant with you.

We used to mess around all the time, too. Folks knew about us, but no

one would ever tell, or dream of crossing Tazmund. Taz had real power in

these streets as far as his reputation went. I actually loved being his

sidepiece, because I got to do things with him that his wife didn't even

know about. I was his wife in his other life! I guess that's why I'll never

understand how he could just stop seeing me, just because, she found about us. As hardcore as Taz was in these streets, he was soft as butter when it came to that bitch, and her children."

Mama would always get pissed after saying those words, and never finish the story. Secretly, I knew it was more to the story then she was willing to tell me. I could see it in her drunk, teary eyes that tried to hold back all the pain it held as best it could. I knew Mama was hurting deep down inside by the way my father would treat her. It wasn't anything she could do to hide those feelings. Not even all the alcohol and drugs she consumed on a daily basis could bury the wounds he left on her broken heart.

"What is love any old ways?" She would finally say after staring off in a daze.

Then she would consume the rest of the contents in her cup while looking at me, shaking her head. She would always finish by saying, "Love hurts so damn much," and I would just laugh inside.

I truly felt that my Mama deserved everything my father ever did to her. I hated that I had to suffer because of his negative feelings towards her. I always wished one of them loved me like a parent was supposed to love their child, but the idea was only a dream. I never could sympathize with my Mama's pain, because I honestly felt like she didn't deserve love from anyone. She had been a total bitch my whole life, because of her past. Why should she get the one thing she never could give her own child? As much as I hate to admit it, my crazy ass Mama was right all those years. Love really did hurt.

"Sometimes you win, sometimes you learn." The choice is all yours.

It's Always Choices Too Be Made
Dear Diary
September 26, 2014

It was the 9th day of September in 2007, and Cazhmere was having a yacht club party for his clients. This was a formal way to meet up, and talk about when the latest shipments would be in. It was also a way for everyone to celebrate their yearly earnings, and award the person with the most earnings "Hustler of the year". Barbie was use to these yearly meet and greets Cazh would have. Being that this was all new to me, I was excited.

Barbie, and I had been up all morning getting prepared for the evening. I had to look my best being that my potential "Boo Thang," could possibly be at the party tonight. My Dad had just brought me a new Lexus for my 20th birthday in March, so I was feeling myself. "Bossy," by Kelis was pounding from my radio as we cruised through the city streets. It felt good riding through the city with one of the finest girls in Detroit in my passenger seat. Kelis song lyrics were right on point for the way I was feeling. I was definitely one of the chicks that hoes loved to hate. My grades in school were good, my life was great, and I didn't have a worry in the world. It wasn't anything a chick could tell me. My life was great, and I damn sure was living right! The only reason, I never work a real job is because I didn't have too. As long as I kept up my good grades, and stayed out of trouble, Mommy and Daddy took care of me! I was actually

spoiled rotten being the Franklyn's only child, and the fact that I was,

adopted. I was truly, blessed to have a loving family for once in my life. I

will never forget the feeling I had once the adoption papers were finalized

the end of the summer in 2001, when I was thirteen years old. I was really

starting to hate the summer time until we took our first family trip that

would put the glue on our bond we have now. During a campfire, I shared

with the Franklyn's some of the horrible stories of my broken childhood. I

could see the sincerity in both of their eyes as they sat listening to my

horrific tales about Mama, and Bozo while trying hard not to judge me. I

knew that the Franklyn's sincerely loved me after our talk, and I was

grateful, because I needed all the love they could give. I knew it was going

to take a miracle to repair the damaged spirit that was living within me. I

guess the Franklyn's somehow felt they owed me for what Mama had

done to me, so they spent a lot of time trying to make up for all of her past

mistakes. It never did sit too well with Mrs. Franklyn's "good side" as

she'd called it, that I had been raped at such a young age, so she tried to

protect me from everything my whole teenage life, and she promised me

that nothing like that would ever happen to me again as long as I lived

under her roof. I often wondered what her "bad side" even looked like,

because I never even heard Mrs. Franklyn yell. She always said, "The

God" in her kept her sane even when chaos arose. She even cried the first time I drove a car, and went to a dance that I practically had to beg Mr. Franklyn to make her let me go, too. He was the cooler, yet down-to-earth parent out of the two, and I was proud to have him as a father figure. I was definitely a "Daddy's girl" as people often called me, and I loved it. Being in their care growing up made me grateful for my friend, Stazy from when I was a little girl. The fact that Stazy introduced me to God at an early age played a major part in living with the Franklyn's. I had to get use to regular Bible studies and church every Sunday but the whole experience only brought me a little closer to God, and his son. Church was literally Mrs. Franklyn's second home. I cannot lie, at first I wanted to connect with God right away because of all I had been through before my new life. Little did I know that it would take me some much needed self-realization time, and a lot of growing up to really understand him. I was too real to be perfect, and sin seemed to keep following me wherever I went.

It had been a year since Barbie, and I had moved back to my hometown. It was a beautiful September day, but my mood was bittersweet because it was also my Mama's birthday. I tried my best to put the mixed feelings I was having about the day aside as we drove through Detroit. I even thought about going to pay my Mama's grave site a visit just to rub the fact that I had made it in her dead face.

"What good would that do me now?" I wondered as I drove feeling emotional. I was torn on the inside just thinking about her but, I wasn't going to let the past get me down. All kinds of old school jams were pouring out of the system, sending us into a zone as we blew out the strongest weed in Detroit. "Cash Rules Everything Around Me" by C.O.I. was blasting that famous Detroit style music while we were on our way to do one of our weekly drop offs of either pills, drugs, or weed to one of Cazh's trap houses. With the money we had collected on this run; we were told to do whatever we liked with it. I popped in T.I. switching up the mood at the thought of being catered too all the time by another man other than my Daddy. I could finally feel where Barbie was coming from dating a drug dealer. The lifestyle she was living wasn't so bad looking from the outside in. It was crazy that so many years ago all I wanted to do was be far away from people like Barbie's boyfriend when I lived with my Mama. It seemed like everyone Mama ever knew was the worst of the worst! Straight gutter if you ask me, which is why I had more Respect for the type of drug dealers Cazh, and his entourage was. Cazh, the chameleon, was as gangster as they came on the inside, because he grew up in one of the roughest areas in Detroit. Although, Cazh came from money, he always admired the hustlers from his neighborhood, which is how he got started in the drug game. Cazh became interested in selling drugs when he started transporting small amounts of drugs to other dealers when he was little. The fact that he was an innocent, yet nerdy looking white boy always kept him off the police's radar. Cazh's parents never expected him to be hanging around with the scum of the neighborhood so they continued to shower him with expensive gifts as long as he did right in school. Once he established a name for himself with the popular dope dealers in his area, Cazh became everyone's "ticket out the hood". Money was never the issue for him because his father spoiled him rotten. Cazh had it made simply because nobody ever thought to look into the well-educated white boy's past; and Cazhmere seemed to use to his advantage. Cazh always admired the power, and extravagant lifestyle drug dealers lived because his best friend Don's father ran with a notorious drug cartel. Mr. Lucky Gonzelli's was the first person Cazh ever knew that was able to maintain a real job, household, and good reputation while reaping the benefits of the underworld. Cazh admired Mr. Gonzelli's ability to hide his bad side from the people closest to him about as much as he looked up to Superman when he wasn't Clark Kent. With Cazhmere being the only child to a very well-known and respected family in the Motor city, he got away with anything he pulled off. Cazh, relished in the fact that he was "Untouchable" as he would always say. Cazh, had it made, but greed would soon become his downfall.

"Stacks on deck, Patron on ice, you can pop bottle all night, baby."

"You can have whatever you like," We sang, as I pushed the pedal to the medal down I-75 towards our exit.

"You gone absolutely love tonight, Teaz," Barbie beamed, as she puffed the blunt then passed it back to me.

All I could think about was how good I was going to be looking tonight at the party, tonight! Earlier that day, Barbie, and I, decided to hit the mall, and Starters Downtown for some of my favorite steak bites, and key lime pie. After our lunch date, we got our nails, and feet done, and then headed home to get ready. Excited was an understatement of how I was feeling as I drove back to the house to get dressed. A party like the one Cazh had planned was something I have only seen in movies. Tonight it was nice to know that I was part of the main entourage, and it felt even better knowing that my best friend was the "Head Niggas In Charge's" main chick. I had never been to a black tie affair before, so I was a bit nervous.

"Pretty Girls," by Wale had me feeling some type of way as I stepped into the shower. I sang along as I washed my thick and luxurious body thinking about all the fun, I had planned on having, tonight.

"Ugly girls be quiet,"

"Pretty girls clap, clap like this." I slapped my hands together causing soap to splash in my face as I sang. I had to laugh at myself, because I was definitely on my level, and I was going all in. The night air was just right for my outfit of choice. I wore a long black Iggy style dress by Affliction with slits on both sides. It also had a slight opening in the front, and my back was completely, exposed. I decided to wear my diamond cluster stud earrings with the matching bracelet, and necklace. The shoes I wore had a crystal heel that made me feel like Cinderella on her way to the ball. I was glowing as I did a once over of myself in the full-length mirror right before I shut my bedroom window that was blowing in a nice breeze.

"Hopefully, I'll meet my Prince Charming tonight," I giggled, as I walked out the door.

Barbie was looking exquisite herself in her hot pink one piece. I swear my girl was a pink wearing, Diva! Nobody in this world wore the color pink like Barbie, could wear it. Barbie could have been a Victoria secret "I love pink, model," because the color pink was her favorite. We headed out the house on a mission as we stepped into her pink, and black custom painted Cadillac truck.

"One big room, full of bad bitches," The music sang once Barbie put the key into the ignition, and I was ready for "whatever".

"We be stunting like, Gucci, Gucci, Louis, Louis, Fendi, Fendi, Prada,"

"The basic bitches wear that shit so I don't ever bother". We sang in unison to Kreayshawn, as we drove through the city with the night air whipping through my long wavy hair. I was actually feeling like Tupac, tonight, because when we pulled up all eyes were on us.

"We don't rock the same clothes,"

"Fuck the same hoes,"

"Cause its levels to this shit." I sang as Meek Millz rapped, and I had to agree with him.

There really are levels to this crazy life, and I was living out my dreams for once. It felt good to have great friends with benefits, and I was extremely appreciative of everyone, I had in my life. I was extremely, captivated by the arrangement of vehicles parked outside the clubhouse. You could tell that the party was jumping inside just by looking at the number of cars. I had a good feeling that I was going to meet my future man, tonight. I can even bet that Barbie tries to play "match maker" before the night is over. I could tell by the facial expressions she kept giving me whenever, I mentioned a person to her. Barbie always thought she had the best taste when it came to men, and I could not wait to see what she had lined up from me. She also kept talking to me about her "special guy of interest". I was going to see how the entire evening played itself out before I let her talk me into her pick of the night. I, on the other hand, already had my heart set on meeting Cazh's secret business partner. The man was Harry Houdini in my eyes, but tonight, I was sure I was going to get to meet him. Barbie always acted as if Cazh wanted to keep him top secret whenever I inquired about him. Not only that, whenever we would have to make any drops to him in particular, we would always go through his right hand man, Pzyco. He definitely wasn't my type. His demeanor told it all, and the name damn sure fit. In my world, he was the underdog, and I was not a "Little niggas, little nigga," type of chick. My motto was always point me to the "Boss," and tonight, I was feeling like Gucci Mane's "Bosses" lyrics. The moment we stepped onto the bridge leading to the clubhouse, and boat dock we were greeted by two handsome, young men with a white rose, and two glasses of champagne.

 "Cazh really does know how to treat his guests," I thought as we strolled, sipping our drinks.

"This is definitely my kind of party." I announced to Barbie, taking in the scenery. I couldn't help myself from flirting with one of the guys as we made our way to the entrance. Everything about this evening was beautiful as we walked toward the golden trimmed glass doors. I loved that pictures were being taken of each guest as soon as you stepped on the red carpet, and I every moment. I, honestly felt like a star going to one of the award shows as we stood there getting our picture taken. I wondered who was here in the private jet that I spotted as the man snapped the last picture of us. I made a quick mental note to find out just whom it belonged too as we walked into the clubhouse. Barbie didn't seem impressed at all. This was the usual for her, and Cazh. All I could do was take in the beautiful atmosphere, and smile. Everything about this night was perfect! The clubhouse was packed with all kinds of people, and it was hard to believe that everyone there had their hands in the dope game of some type. I started to wonder about my own father after a few conversations with some of the guests. I knew he was a successful, Engineer but I always wondered what else he did outside of work. The more I stood talking to people; I began to realize that everyone I knew was far from those goodie-to-shoes type that Stazy always talked about to me as a kid. Don't get me wrong, I didn't run with killers, but the fast life was all I ever knew; and bad boys seemed to be all I ever attracted. Barbie tapped me on the shoulder to get my attention. I was in awe just taking in the scenery. I followed Barbie's lead through the crowded rooms thinking it was nothing but endless opportunity. It was so many single men in the building that it literally looked like it had rained them. I followed Barbie to a little room with a group of guys seated at a round table. At the head of the table sat Cazhmere. Cazh motioned for us to come take a seat next to him. As I walked to my seat, I could feel the men's eyes glued to my every move. I did my best at acting as if I hadn't noticed. Once we were both seated,

Cazh introduced me to the gentlemen, and Barbie began to talk about future shipments and plans for the organization. As she talked, I couldn't help but notice that one of the finest brothers in the room kept staring at me from across the table like he'd seen a ghost. I was we never met, because if we did, "I'd be married to him", I marveled to myself as Cazh wrapped up the meeting. Once the meeting was over, everyone except the one guy left the room. Cazh just grabbed Barbie's hand, and headed out the door. I was instantly attracted to his smooth chocolate skin when walked closer to me. I actually wanted to take a bite out of him when he asked me my name again.

"Perfect smile too." I admired, and then thought back to the only boy I ever knew with a perfect set of teeth like those. I stood there taking in the man's over appearance. Savvy, yet debonair. He was so handsome that I was honestly intrigued with his natural charm.

"I'm La'Teazya, and you are?" I asked in a flirtatious way.

"Your future," he replied, and I just laughed.

I loved his confidence, and I knew he was every bit of the prince Charming that I was looking for. He had to be one of the big guy's in this league, because he was sitting at the table with Cazh in his private meeting. Too bad "Sexual Chocolate," would have to wait in line. A couple of smooth lines by "Mr. Smooth Operator" weren't going to win me over that easy. May the "best man" win, I mused, breaking out of my daydream.

"We should be heading to the party," I announced, walking to the door, and opening it to leave the room. I didn't even wait for him to respond. I just left mystery guy standing there. I was on a mission, and the brother was definitely right. "My future," was about to be found. I walked through each crowded room, meeting and greeting all kinds of people from all over. The women there were extremely friendly unlike some of the females I would usually meet. I guess when you have as much money as they did; there is no need to be jealous of anyone else. As impressed as I was by all the activity going on around me: I was shocked that not one man in the entire party that I had conversed with after Mr. Chocolate caught my attention.

"Teaz." I heard Barbie call out to me, and then I made my way over to where she was. She wanted me to accompany her to the ladies' room before we took our seats for the ceremony, which I figured she wanted to use the time for some girl talk.

"So are you enjoying yourself, Teaz"? She inquired from her stall as I fixed my makeup.

"Did you like ole, boy," she added with a laugh.

I was having the time of my life, but I still hadn't found Mr. Right, yet. The only person that kept standing out in my mind from the entire night was the chocolate brother from earlier with the perfect teeth. Once she did her final touches of make-up, we headed to our table to take our seats and the ceremony began. I swear everything about this night was like being at the BET awards. The only difference was people were given an award for being drug dealers. Cazh stood up to announce the last award of the night. Ironically, it was presented to none other than the handsome chocolate brother from the meeting earlier. Barbie gave me a look that said it all. This was the guy I'd been dreaming of meeting since we got here to Michigan. I just shook my head, and gave her the "I'mma Fuck You Up Later," look. Before I could even get my thoughts together, Cazh was telling "Brother Wize," how honored he was to have him as a comrade and business partner. Barbie was one "slick bitch." I laughed as I gave her the middle finger. I was blown away when Brother Wize walked over to our table, and whispered in my ear for me to come accept his award with him. I hesitated at first, but I obliged his request. We looked perfect together walking up to the stage, and I honestly felt like I had known the man for years. Once the award ceremony was over, we all headed out to the dance floor. "Forever My Lady" by Jodeci filled the air with a soulful tune as I danced with, Wize. Everything about him seemed so familiar. It was starting to feel like we had danced like this before in our past life; and

I loved every moment of his body pressed to mine. The scent of his cologne was starting to lubricate my vagina as I tried to think of the name of the fragrance.

"Are you ever going to tell me your real name?" I asked as we danced.

He just smiled, and pulled me in closer to him. I wanted to kiss him so bad, but I fought the urge off with every ounce of power within me.

"I've been waiting on you my whole life, La'Teazya," he responded, looking me deep in my eyes. For a moment, the way he said my name took me back to my first love, Ize.

"Is that right?" I inquired sarcastically, looking him back in the eyes.

Wize didn't know a thing about me other than my name, and here he was running the best game I'd heard in years. His pompous reputation was definitely getting the best of him, tonight. I could just about put any amount of money on it that he was this way with all the women he encountered. He had to be reading my mind as we danced, because before I could say another word he dipped me, and landed a kiss on me that I will never forget.

"I'm going to be leaving here soon," he stated, and I wanted him to get straight to the point.

"My jet is outside." he mentioned, and then went on to explain that he had just flown in from Mexico to collect his award, as a way to show respect to Cazh.

"Once I laid eyes on you, La'Teazya, I knew I couldn't leave. I decided to stick around so I could convince you to leave with me," he explained, but I was shocked.

I had already moved here to help Barbie transport drugs for him, and Cazh. Now he wants me to just up, and fly to Mexico with him on the first night we meet without me even knowing him. How crazy was that? Everything about him was exactly what I was hoping for when I first came tonight, but Prince Charming was moving a little too fast for me.

"So what's your answer, La'Teazya"?

"You don't have to worry about anything," He claimed; before he went on to promise to have me back to Michigan in a couple days unharmed, just liked I left it. I was impressed by the offer, but I wouldn't dare run off into the sunset with a complete stranger no matter how much of a connection I thought we were having.

"I'm sorry, but I have to decline." I said, making sure to watch his facial expression.

"I'm sure we'll have another chance to spend time together once we exchange phone numbers, and I get to know you better," I explained, releasing his grip.

"There're always choices to be made," he stated, looking me in the eyes.

"Right now you're passing up a chance of a lifetime," he continued, and I just shook my head.

His arrogance was really starting to get to me because, "Money or No Money," I wasn't leaving with a guy I didn't know. I just turned around and began to walk away. He was absolutely, right: There are always choices to be made, but flying to Mexico wasn't one of them.

"La'Teazya," he called out to me just before I hit the exit. What he said next could've made me pass out, and die right there as long as he could've kiss me, and brought me back to life like Sleeping Beauty.

"It's me, crazy girl," he laughed as I just stood there in total shock.

"I'm really surprised you could forget my face after all these years."

"I guess the promises to be together "**FOREVER**," meant nothing." He sighed, and I was confused.

"OH MY GOD... Izir is that you?" I responded, so clueless all he could do was laugh. I couldn't believe my prince Charming of the night turned out to be my childhood sweetheart all grown up. That was all I needed to

know before I ran, and jumped in his arms and told him, "LETS GO"!

Wicked Games

"Bang, Bang…"

"Order in the courtroom," I watched the gavel hit the beautiful cherry wood colored podium that I had been staring at the whole time in a panicky state of mind. The judge then instructed the juror to read the verdict.

"We, the jury, find the defendant guilty on all charges," the old woman read aloud to the courtroom.

 It was so surreal being found guilty on drug charges right along with everyone I had grew to love. Subsequently, my mind flashed back to my childhood best friend, Zarbreah, and tears began to roll down my eyes. She had lost her life because of the wicked games we were all playing with life. I was shocked when I found out Barbie would be an older woman once she got out of prison. Barbie's parents were so disgusted with her actions that her father literally disowned her before she even went to trial. There was no one in the courtroom for her when the jury read her the cold verdict that would change her life, as she knew it. Barbie knew she was facing more than twenty years in prison because she never snitched on Cazhmere, and took full responsibility for her actions. She had made a conscious decision to move to Michigan to help Cazh with his drug organization in the first place. Barbie was given up to thirty-five years in prison. The reign was over faster than it began. Everything, Cazh had built over the years had just crumbled to pieces in a matter of seconds.

Barbie was loyal to Cazh, so snitching on her man to get a lighter sentence never crossed her mind. Cazhmere had provided a life style for them that not even her own parents could have done. It was sad to see their entire empire that had taken years to build crumble before our very eyes. I also respected Barbie for her decision to take most of the charges filed against me. I hated that Barbie even suggested that we move back to Michigan to help Cazh, now. We were all guilty in the eyes of the law, and I damn sure was not about to start pointing the finger because a Judge was standing before me. Where we came from, snitches were murdered, and you damn sure didn't want to be known as the snitch behind bars. My only option was to take whatever was about to be given to me, and mover forward whenever I got out of prison. My fate was slightly different from my friends, Barbie. I was sentenced to five years in prison, but I only served three years behind bars. I still thank God each day for the lawyers the Franklyn's hired. If it wasn't for them, Barbie's testimony, and the fact that some of the evidence against me wasn't creditable; I'd probably be an old lady before I got out of prison, too. It was a shame we had all literally threw our young lives away chasing money. I could not believe that I was going to be twenty-seven years old before I came home. It was two weeks past my 22nd birthday, and this was by far the worst year of my life.

Prison life was so different from the life I knew. I couldn't believe I had traded in my freedom for a cell block, a number and a jumpsuit. I had to adjust to the fact that I was now living under someone else's rules. I couldn't have any contact with the man I loved or the outside world except letters, visits, and timed phoned calls. Prison was like living in the hell of my childhood all over again. My reality was far worse than my experience at the girls' home. My first week in prison, I found myself in solitary lock up for a brawl I was involved in with a group of girls. I had to defend myself because they had been riding my back since I got there. As fate would have it, I, was switched to another cell after another fight I had. This time, I ended up being bunkmates with the leader of the first group. I wanted to rip the bitches' throat out the minute I entered the cell. I could tell the feeling was mutual, but I played it cool. I couldn't sleep that night. I patiently waited until we were both in the shower the next day, and I made a move on that hoe. I knew I had to get her before she tried to get me. I waited until everyone was done showering, then I ran up on her, while the guard was being distracted. I strangled her with my towel, pushing her body into the wall as she swung her arms uncontrollably. She wasn't so tough now that her little crew wasn't around. I pulled out my shank knife I had made with a toothbrush, and placed it near her ribs.

"Be calm, Bitch!" I whispered.

"I said be calm, Bitch!" I repeated tightening the towel up on her neck.

"Move one more time!" I grunted through clinched teeth.

"I swear I'm going to fuck you, like you've never been fucked before" I continued.

She finally surrendered, hearing the seriousness in my voice. I was not playing with this crazy bitch. Today it was either her or me.

"Look bitch, I suggest you be cool," I whispered in her ear.

I then pushed the shank I held into her side just enough to draw blood and make my point clear.

"Since we have to be Bunkie's' from now on," I hissed, pushing her closer into the wall.

"Let's just say you're my new, bitch." I stated.

It never did sit well with me that I was moved into a cell with, Mizz. It was as if someone was playing a sick game with my life, or she had people on the inside.

"You're also gonna call off your little pussy licking crew so the rest of this time we both have here can go pleasant for the both of us," I paused, and thought real hard about killing the bitch right then, and there without anyone around to see anything. One of us was going to die, today, and I wasn't backing down. I stabbed her again in another spot in her side, and she didn't even scream. She just laughed, and it made me wish I had killed her. It was crystal, clear to me that this bitch wanted to die, or that she wanted me dead.

"Let's just say I'mma let you walk out of here with your life, baby girl," Mizz laughed right before the officer walked back in.

"You're probably one of the luckiest bitches who's ever gonna walk this cell block after this conversation," she boldly stated, still laughing while leaning in real close to me.

"Let's go, Mizz." The officer interrupted before I could respond.

I couldn't believe the nerve of this hoe. Even when death was on her, she had a heart of steel, and an imaginary pair of steel balls to match it.

"I have to admit, I like your style, baby girl," Mizz laughed sarcastically before walking out of the shower, and grabbing her towel.

I was in pure shock. I had literally seen the face of crazy that day, but, I wasn't about to let this heathen punk me. Anyone who could laugh in the face of death had to be crazy in my opinion.

Later on that night, before it was lights out. Mizz didn't forget to remind me that she wasn't the push over that I'd taken her for in the shower incident, earlier.

"You remind me of someone I once knew, La'Teazya." Mizz told me as we laid on our bunks.

"For that reason alone, I'm going to spare your life," she continued to say, and I rolled my eyes towards the ceiling.

"Lets' just call this a life for a life," she replied.

When I didn't respond, she hopped out of her bunk, and looked me deep in the eyes. Everything about this girl's demeanor read psychotic as I stared back at her. Her actions were so appalling that I couldn't even move, or say a word. All I could do was lay there in pure disbelief because I knew I was sharing a cell with the Anti-Christ. I hated that this was my life, and I hated it even more that it wasn't much that I could do to stop her.

"I'll call off my crew," she smirked sarcastically.

"There's only one catch, baby girl," she added while my inner voice screamed, "kill her, Teaz"!

"From this point on, little mama, you're my bitch," she stated, getting back in her bed.

"Good night, sweet cakes," she giggled, and I was furious on the inside.

Mizz was the only bully, I had ever dealt with in my life next to my Mama, and a part of me knew exactly what the outcome would be. I wasn't scared of Mizz, but I knew I wasn't going to make it in prison being somebodies', "Bitch". I also knew this whole prison experience was going to change the person I once was. The question I needed answered was; was it going to be for better, or worse?

The Turning Point:
"The Choice's You Make In Life Is All Yours... Remember That!!!"
Dear Diary,
September 27, 2014

   Before I knew it, I had spent two weeks with Ize in Mexico. I almost hated the fact that he had kept his word, and brought me back home safe in one piece. The moment I saw the "Welcome to Michigan" sign, I shed a tear because it felt like my honeymoon was over. I had spent so much of my life wondering where Ize and Zar were once we moved out our townhouse after Mama's unexpected death. Now that I had them back in my life, I never wanted to let them go again! It's funny how life plays itself out. Whoever would have thought the man of my dreams would come back to me after all these years apart, and would turn out to be one of the wealthiest drug dealers I knew in Detroit. Maybe Anita Baker was wrong all these years as I thought back to my old school jam, "Fairytales". This moment was a dream come true, I never in a million years would have expected to end up back with the boy I loved as a child. Ize had his hands in a few businesses here and there, but he was mostly the outside resource who provided money to each company. Ize did not seem to mind that fact, either. As, long as the companies kept him financially compensated, and his account with thousands, he didn't need to actually work from them. Ize never wanted to work for anybody other than himself, so he became an Entrepreneur when he was a teenager. Ize actually enjoyed being out of the spotlight while everyone else handled his dirty work. Ize made a name for himself, a long time ago in the streets but, it was his strategic approach to eliminating all his competition and never being caught up that earned him the name "Brother Wize". The moment we arrived in Detroit, I made Ize take me to see Zarbreah.

Zar also looked exactly like I knew she would when she grew up. I always use to tell Zar she was Tisha Campbells doppelganger, and looking at her now that we were adults, I was right. Everything about Zarbreah's personality, style, and body shape reminded me of the younger version of Tisha Campbell. She was outgoing, dynamite, and stylish like Tisha when she played in "House Party," and as charming, fierce, yet strikingly beautiful, Diva as she was in her "School Days" appearance. Of course, we were crying when we reunited but, after a three-hour conversation of some much needed catch up talk, we had put all the missing pieces together about each other lives, and we were back hanging together like the old days. Zar, was also one of Ize's business partners, and the person who ran his organization while he was away on business. Zarbreah, already had a degree in Business Management, and Accounting. Zar, was working on getting her Master's degree when we reunited. She had also recently opened up a boutique as a way to clean all the dirty money, Ize was bringing in a regular basis. Pzyco was his personal bodyguard, and the person who eliminated all Ize's beefs or potential enemies. They had

been best friends since Ize went to juvenile his second year of high school,

right after T'Aira, and I were taken to the girl's home.

Two years later, Mrs. Emerson had moved out the hood to Grand Rapids,

Michigan, which explains why nobody knew where Ize, and Zar where

when I came home. During my conversation with Zar, she told me that the

move to Grand Rapids was a surprise, and they didn't get to say goodbye

to anyone once their mom got her new job. Later that evening, I

introduced Zar to my new best friend Barbie, and we were inseparable. I

used to joke all the time that we were the female version of the "Three

Musketeers," because we were three of the strongest women behind the

city's well-known drug dealers. Cazh, the kingpin name ringed bells all

over the streets of Detroit, along with Brother Wize, whose name was

feared in certain parts of the Michigan. I hated that sometimes, we

couldn't even go out to eat without being stopped as if we were celebrities.

Ize and Cazh were definitely legends in every hood. Barbie, Zar, and I,

were just lucky to know them, personally. Weeks had gone by, Ize, and I

were starting to do everything together when he wasn't out of town and I

wasn't doing runs for Cazh. I absolutely loved the fact that he would fly

me in and out of town on random occasions just because he called me to

hear my voice and began to miss me during our conversations. I was so in

love with the fact that Ize was in my life again that I didn't even want to look at another man. I never would have imagined in a million years after moving here and looking all over the city for him that he'd fall right in my lap and we'd end up living just like we always planned when I was twelve years old. Everything seemed to be going "perfect" with our rekindled love affair. I felt as if I were living a fairytale until our trip to California. We had been out in Cali a month living the good life at our new beach house I'd talked him into buying. We've all heard the song by Lil' Wayne, that warns us not to ever get too "comfortable," right? It seems to me that no matter how you play your cards just when you think everything is good, Murphy's Law strikes you. I was sitting in our room picking out my outfit for dinner while Ize took a shower, when Ize's phone rang. On a normal day, I'd never pick up Ize's phone but after seeing the number call back repeatedly, I decided to just answer the caller figuring it was one of his clients. To my surprise it was this angry female on the other end claiming to be the mother of Ize's son and demanding to know his where-a-bouts!

"Did you just say you were the mother of Izir's, son'?" I inquired like I hadn't heard her right.

I began to wonder what part of the game was this, because Ize clearly never mentioned a son to me. All Ize ever talked about is me having his daughter in the near future and how we're going to be a real "family". So please tell me why this bitch is screaming in my damn ear about ruining her relationship and destroying "her family?" I could've died standing there listening to the bitch repeat the words "where the fuck is my baby daddy, Bitch?" I wanted to snap. I felt betrayed as I listen to this bitch ramble on, and on. I started to think back on my Mama and Daddy. Mama always said it was all downhill once he married his wife and had kids by her. I didn't understand how Ize could keep something like having a son a secret from me with me knowing he grew up a "Daddy's Boy". I knew his own son had to be his pride and joy as I sat on our bed staring at the water with tears rolling down my eyes. "Wicked Games," by Chris Isaak crossed my mind as I reminisced about how I was at a point in my life when I wasn't even trying to fall in love then Ize came along. You're absolutely right, Chris," I thought to myself

"This world is only gonna break my heart," I sobbed, and then hung up.

"How could you make me fall in love with you Ize after all these years, just to hurt me this bad?" my heart asked my mind.

"You a fucking cold hearted bastard just like the rest of these no good men!"

I screamed at the air like it was Ize as "Situationship," by Fabolous began to play. I contemplated storming into the bathroom and acting the fool that was growing deep inside of me. I wanted to tear Ize a new asshole literally for the way I was feeling inside. This wasn't the first time Ize had broken

my heart, either. I reminisced back to him having sex with the girl Angel

behind my back when I was twelve. Even though, I was the one sneaking

around and freaking with his ass. I wanted to hurt Ize the way I was

hurting on the inside at that moment, but I started praying instead.

"Why do you constantly make me feel like my life is finally going perfect

God, and then snatch away that little piece of happiness right from up

underneath me?" I cried out through tears.

"Haven't I suffered enough this lifetime?" I continued to ask God all kinds

of questions that I desperately needed answers too while thinking back on

all I'd been through and overcame growing up. I stood up from my bed,

wiped away my tears and walked out the patio door in our room leading to

the beach. I took a seat by the water and let the tide brush up against my

feet and cried some more. I didn't ever want Ize to see me cry. Men saw

crying as a sign of weakness. I just sat there pondering over everything

that I been through up until this point with Ize, and I really didn't know

how I was going to deal with this situation. My Mama always drank to

cover up her love for my dad, and right now, I was feeling her pain.

Maybe a drink could help me escape the harshness of this cold realization

I'm having because the fact of the matter is that I'm no better than my

Mama herself. Ize was turning out to be the modern day version of my biological father, and we've all heard of the ancient folklore that says: History repeats itself. The cruel but true reality of my situation was starting to hit home hard like a ton of bricks.

"That still didn't give my Mama the right to treat me like shit all those years that I was in her care." I reasoned.

 I knew I had a lot to learn about him, because we had missed so much of each other's past. I was clueless when it came to decoding the mystery behind, Ize's behavior, lately. I didn't just want to give up on the bond we were starting to rebuild just because he hadn't mentioned that he had a son to me yet. It's only been three months since we'd been dating after reuniting at Cazh's party. Maybe with him being gone in and out of town all the time on business and just wanting to spend all his free time with me. I reminisced over our past months together searching for a moment that Ize could've told me about his child before today. It must've slipped his mind, I reasoned, but I knew I was just trying to comfort my own feelings to better cope with the current situation I was facing. Everything about this very moment reminded me of the lyrics to "Opposites Attract," by Kendrick Lamar. We always "hurt the people who love us, and love the ones who hurt us". Love was backwards as hell to me sometimes, but I made up my mind right then and there that I was with Ize, right or wrong! I'd been down with Ize since our very first conversation and "loyalty" was something we expected out of one another from as far back as I can remember.

"There had to be a reason for it all," I concluded, and I damn sure was going to get too the bottom of things. I remembered the missed calls and me finally picking up Ize's phone the last time his "Baby Mama" called. I ran back into our bedroom, snatched the phone off the dresser and deleted the calls from his log. It was obvious that Ize had been avoiding the bitch for whatever reasons by the way she was blowing his phone up in the first place, I convinced myself. Ize would just have to deal with our little talk I had with her whenever we crossed that path. I smirked just thinking about how I was gone let his ass have it the day the subject ever came back up. I sat his phone back down on the dresser just in time because he came walking out the bathroom with a smile from ear to ear. Ize was so handsome, I had to force a smile through my madness. He always did have this effect on me that even I couldn't begin to explain. I played it cool our next couple of weeks we spent together. Ize took me on shopping sprees, spa trips, dinners and dancing at the local hot spots. You name it, we did it and the whole time, I acted as if I didn't know anything about his son. We were in the jewelry store my last week in Cali getting matching watches when we decided to look at rings. I was almost impressed by everything Ize had been doing for me, but I knew in the back of my mind it was all just a part of the role he was playing. It felt so real the love we shared, but

I wasn't even thinking about marriage until I found out the truth about Ize's, son.

 I flew back to Michigan solo the following week and that's when all the bullshit began. A month had gone by, and I hadn't heard a single word from Ize. I instantly knew that he'd talk to his "Baby mama", and found out about our little conversation we had. I couldn't believe that he'd gone this far just to stress the fact that he didn't like me answering his phone. I was flabbergasted that I still hadn't heard as much as an "I'm alive but, Fuck you," from Ize. He had become the ghost he'd been to me before he magically walked back into my life. Avril Lavigne crossed my mind as I lay in bed writing while listening to the "Blame Game" by Kanye West. Guys love to make things more complicated than they have to be and females are so gullible, we fall right into their traps. No matter how fucked up men can be at times, they will be quick to put all the blame on you. These fools really need to stop listening to some of this music they play on the radio now-a-days because it seriously has their minds all messed up. I laughed as K Camps "Cut Her Off," began to play.

"It ain't shit to cut you off, bitch," I mocked in my K Camp voice. E 40 was absolutely right because some niggas really do act like bitches once you do something to them they feel is wrong. The next day, Barbie and I were having one of our usual weekend ladies' night. I was so depressed about not talking to Ize for a month that it was hard for me to really enjoy myself like I'd usually do. I was missing the hell out of Ize. The fact that he didn't even care enough to pick up his phone and call me once was really starting to get to me as Ashanti's "Scared of You," followed by "Rescue Me" played in our stereo system. She was right: I was scared to love him anymore, and yet he was the only man who could rescue me from my own fears about him. I even went as far as to ask Zar about Ize's where- a-bouts one night while we were at the bar with my girl, Rozi and she just acted as if she didn't know where Ize was, or what he'd been up too. I could tell she was lying by the way she answered me stuttering through each lie she tried to sell me. I was finally getting over the whole "Ize and Me" being together theory when a "restricted" caller came in on the other line of my phone while I was conversing with this new guy I'd met. Something inside of me knew it was Ize before I even answered my other line and just like I thought it was him once I clicked over. I wanted to curse him out and just hang up in his face, but to my surprise he was telling me that he didn't appreciate the bullshit I'd done in Cali and he'd be to see me as soon as he got back to the city.

"The nerve of this Nigga," I thought before clicking back over and telling ole boy I'd call him back. I don't know who Ize thought he was but he wasn't about to keep running in and out of my life like this. I bet he's going to have all kinds of excuses for his actions and try to blame me for him being so inconsiderate, but you heard Zhane: "You're sorry now, but sorry won't relieve the pain of my broken heart." I was pissed just thinking about how Ize was trying to play the blame game, and then Angie Stone came on saying everything I felt in "I Wish I Didn't Miss You Anymore". This fool was playing with my heart, and I didn't like it one bit. I sat there for a brief moment feeling sorry for myself, and then thought back to this one night when my Daddy showed up at our house unannounced. He was actually trying to buy my Mama's secrecy about me being his child. It was all starting to make sense now as to why she just showed up at his house demanding that he helped her raise me. My Daddy wasn't shit, and I guess that's part of the reason why the first man I ever really loved treats me like shit. Mama used to always say: "Karma was a bitch scorned," and I guess I'm paying for the bad decisions he made in life. How could he do his only daughter, and first born the way he did is beyond me. After listening to them argue that night, I made it up in my mind that I'd never need my Dad for anything.

"I'm good enough to fuck, hold your dope, and suck your funky dick, huh, Taz?" Mama asked him while calling him every bad name she could think of.

I just stood in my bedroom with my door cracked so Mama wouldn't see me as they went back and forth with the blame game, but the fact was neither one of them loved me.

"All I need to know is why did you chose to marry her over me, Taz?" Mama went on to question him about his love for his wife instead of her.

My dad clearly didn't care about my mom, because he just threw some money at her, and then walked out her house calling her the "Stupidest Bitch" he'd ever stuck his dick in.

"Fuck you, Taz!"

"You're a real son of a Bitch!" she'd scream after shouting at him from her front door.

I finally understood how betrayed she felt. That bastard of a sperm donor didn't give two shits about her, or me, and right now I felt her pain. Maybe, my Mama did try to love me at some point, but decided to grow bitter inside instead. I could see how people's hearts just turned cold due to other people's lack of love. It's a hard pill to swallow knowing the one person you love, and desire to be with will never love you back.

"Paybacks a coldhearted bitch scorned named Karma," she chanted over and over, searching for her liquor bottle that always helped her escape her pain, and secretly I hoped that Karma came back on the both of them for treating me, the innocent child, like shit because of their past issues. Next thing I knew the music would be blasting, and Mama would be drunk again in one of her rages. I was just happy I wasn't the primary target for the night. I hated being the person who got blamed for all my Mama's life fuck ups.

The following weekend, I wasn't really up to driving out to this cabin in Lexington, Michigan the day Ize called me and told me he wanted to see me. I popped in my SWV classic cd, hit random, and it was ironic that the first song to play was "Use Your Heart". As of this point, I couldn't even trust my heart when it came to making wise decisions about me and Ize's relationship. My mind was telling me "NO" but my body and heart was yearning for Ize. I missed his touch, his scent, the tone of his voice, and his smile even when I knew he was up to no good. We were destined to be together in my eyes. Without Ize, I really thought "I'd die," like P M Dawn said. It wasn't a man that compared to him as a far as I was concerned.

"Ize was quite a charmer," I blushed as I walked through the front door with "Just In Case," by Jahiem playing in the background as I stared captivated by the scenery, letting my eyes drift off then land on the fire place. I fantasized about Ize fucking me right in front of it later that evening while the tiger rug that laid in front of it watched us take its place on the floor. Ize wasn't anywhere in sight, so I took the opportunity to look around the beautiful log cabin when I noticed a trail of white, red and hot pink roses. I followed the beautiful arrangement of all my favorite colors to a small hallway leading to a door with candles lit out front, as Jagged Edges' "Walked Outta Heaven," began to play. I was secretly hoping to catch Ize in the tub once I opened the door, but to my surprise it was an envelope with my name on it next to a Victoria Secrets' bag. I opened the envelope that was sealed with two doves kissing in a heart. I smiled as I read the note: "Enjoy and Don't Forget to Wear Me", and I couldn't help myself from screaming once I peeked inside the bag and saw the set I was telling Ize I wanted. He was so romantic when he wasn't on the bullshit that he's been on lately. I just followed the instructions ignoring the fact that I'd been mad about not seeing Ize for a month. I stepped into the rose filled Jacuzzi with a bottle of wine waiting for me. I started to think 'breaking up to make up," wasn't so bad after all but it didn't take away the fact that Ize had been lying to me and had the nerve to ignore me for a month. "Love Jones," by Melky Day started to play, and I couldn't help but cry. I had a love jones for Ize and it was crazy how I just let him constantly get away with things. I knew he had to know hurt me. Even when we were little, I let Ize betray me without even saying a word, so maybe he felt it was okay to just walk all over my feelings behind my back and shower me with false love in my face. I threw the glass I was drinking out of against the wall out of anger then picked up the bottle. My mood went from happy to sad as Faith Evans "Used to Love Me," took the place of the love/hate relationship I was starting to feel in my heart. I was standing in the mirror, staring at my reflection of the bitter woman I was secretly starting to become, and I couldn't hold back the tears that started to flow.

"Fuck you, love!" I screamed, throwing the entire bottle of wine against the wall now.

"T-Rone was right, and Ize gone get somebody killed the way he be fucking with people's emotions," I yelled then went on to conclude that love wasn't shit but a word that people used to their advantage. Somehow, someway, I was going to start using it to mine. All I could think about after listening to all those sad love songs and drinking the entire second bottle of wine to myself was letting it rip once I saw Ize. I wrapped the towel over my body, looked at the Victoria Secrets' bag again, and opened the bathroom door instead.

"This nigga must really think he is "King Ding-a-ling," or "The Don Juan," himself the way he's always trying to play me, and buy my love with material items!"

I screamed as I paced back and forth angrily in front of the mirror leading to the steps.

"Money can buy a lot of things, but my love wasn't one of them," I yelled into the mirror as if it were Ize.

"If Ize would just open his eyes, he'd see that I'm his soulmate," I yelled, as tears rolled down my face.

It was this very moment that I began to realize that some men are just plain dumb when it comes to being in a healthy relationship. I stood there screaming at the mirror for about five more minutes, and then I decided to just let go and let God handle it all. I couldn't understand why this fool has my love for free, and still doesn't know what to do with it.

"I guess it doesn't matter how good of a woman you are, or have been in the past once a man finally thinks he's over you." I reasoned as I stood there deep in my thoughts.

I'm sure he knows that all he has to do is be honest with me, and I'd always be his "Ride or Die" chick. When it came to Ize, I was loyal to a fault, and I definitely had his back without a shadow of doubt. I walked down the stairs as "Don't Let Go," by En Vogue started to play, and all I could think about is the fact that I never wanted to lose Ize. I strolled into the kitchen, and opened up another bottle of wine and an hour later, I was passed out on the couch with the music still blasting. A few hours later, I heard the front door open as I watched Ize walk in and hang up his coat. Just the sight of him turned me on. I fantasized about Ize playing in my moist vagina while "Already Wet" by Lil Scrappy played as I walked towards the door. Before he could say a word, I took off my towel and watched his eyes follow it as it fell to the floor. Ize just stood there admiring my naked body, but, I wanted to feel him inside of me. I desperately needed to feel his hands on my body like he had the quantum touch that I needed to survive. Ize gave me a feeling that I couldn't find in anyone else. I was addicted to the man, and even he knew I was strung out on his love. We were like any other couple in a relationship. Sure we'd probably fuck, fight, argue, then we'd make up, to break up, and do it all over again; but, at the beginning and ending of each day I knew I loved him, and in his own crazy way, Ize loved me, too. Life was full of lessons for fools in love and if loving him was wrong, I was damned, because I didn't ever want to be right. I removed the bags he held in his hands, placing them on the floor then pushed Ize up against the wall with my naked body. I began to slowly caress his upper and bottom lip with my tongue while I unbuckled his belt to unzip his pants. The moment was so perfect, I clearly forgot we were standing directly in front of the glass doors, as Ize slide his tongue inside my mouth, causing me to moan, because I was enjoying the moment so much. I was feeling like Jace Everett at the moment, because, I definitely wanted to do "Bad Things," to Ize right here and now.

"That's right, baby," I thought as we kissed then began massaging his erect penis.

"Show me I'm the best you ever had," my mind demanded but my mouth didn't say a word.

I just let the moment speak for itself. I had him right where I wanted him. Before, I knew it he was pressing me up against the wall, pushing every inch of his manhood into my throbbing wet walls as Sons of Funk's "Pushing Inside of You," played. The perfect song for a perfect moment, I beamed inside, and encourage him to fuck me harder. Ize had been giving me the business for a while up against the wall until I turned around, and started throwing my ass back at him. I knew he liked it when I matched his strokes, and it was also a quick way to get us to both climax at the same time, which I loved. After we finished our little session of love making, I headed back to the bathroom to take a quick shower. Before I could even open the door, I remembered the glass and bottle I broke, earlier. I was on cloud nine right now, and standing here looking at all this broken glass I had to clean up made me think I needed to learn how to control my emotions a lot better. Ize crept up from behind me, placing small kisses on the back of my neck while humming "Now That We're Done," by 112, and once he noticed the glass, he just shook his head and looked at me puzzled. I quickly tried to make up a lie, but I could tell he wasn't buying the story I was trying to sell him. After cleaning up all the glass, we hopped in the shower, and continued to make love. After out nap, we went to this bar in town called the Blue Grass, and had a really good evening. I felt ecstatic as we drove to our cabin while Sade's "Cherish The Day," played. On the way back to our cabin, we decided to go for a night swim. The night air was perfect that evening, and everything about that day was turning out to be a dream come true. I thought about saying something to Ize about his disappearing acts he pulled on me before we got out the car but I couldn't. I didn't want to ruin the moment with my personal issues, but, I couldn't let him get away with doing that, and the fact that he'd been hiding a son from me for months now. The stars reflected so beautifully off the water at night as we swam nude. I had never done this before tonight, and I loved how peaceful and relaxing it felt as I floated on my back watching the stars in the sky. I felt like Halle Berry in my favorite movie, "Their Eyes Were Watching God," and, I knew that tonight would be the perfect opportunity to get clarity.

"So why did it take a month to hear from you, Ize?"

"And why haven't you told me about your son?" I asked when we finally took our seats in the sand to dry off, because I couldn't hold it in any longer. Everything about whatever Ize, and I thought we were trying to build together was starting to feel like the lyrics from "Wicked Games" by The Weeknd.

"It's complicated, Teaz," he answered, looking up in the sky like it could somehow save him from this very moment.

I guess we both were watching God, because he was the only person except, Ize who knew the "truth" about this entire situation at hand. I was sure Ize knew this conversation was going to happen one day soon. No matter how he tried to justify his action, we both knew Ize was dead wrong. I had every right to feel the way that I did right now, but, I played it cool. I always knew that you get more bees with honey, and all I wanted was the truth. I deserved that, because I had been loyal to Ize in the past. The more he prolonged his answers, I tried my best not to lose my temper, or let his puckish ways get the best of me. I knew anything I didn't feel was the truth could irritate me immediately, and change up the entire vibe. I just wanted to be as understanding as possible once he explained his situation to me.

"It's not like you think, La'Teazya, I promise," he replied, drying himself off.

"I wasn't trying to avoid you for this long, but, some things happened, and I had a lot to take care of before I could just spend time with you again."

"As far as my son goes, Teaz", he added

"Yes, I have a son, but I'm no longer with his mother, despite whatever you all talked about."

"Trust me," he continued, and I noticed that he frowned a bit at the thought of us talking about him behind his back, but, I just shrugged it off.

"The truth is, we haven't been together since Izir junior was born, and the only thing we have in common is our son".

He then went on to tell me everything about his son's mother, how they met, and then separated right after the baby shower. He also admitted that he wanted to marry her. He never wanted to have kids with random women, and he even explained that he always wanted to be a family man. It wasn't until the betrayal she did to him before the wedding that he changed his mind. After finding his ex-fiancé in bed with his favorite cousin who was raised like his brother, Ize called off the engagement before his son was even born. "Billie Jean," on the other hand, as Michael Jackson would have called her, never did forgive herself for losing out on the chance of a lifetime, and the one man that was willing to help her fulfill her lifelong dreams. That's mainly the reason why she always tried to cause drama with any woman she thought Ize was going to potentially be with in the near future. He was so sincere about everything we talked about that it reminded me of the times when we would talk as children. All

I could do was give him a winsome smile as I listened to him tell me about a part of his life that I'd missed out on. I didn't know much about his past life before, today but, I knew Ize wasn't the type of guy who'd just tell me lies to keep me in some twisted love triangle. That one conversation seemed to bring us closer the next two days we stayed in Lexington. It was back to my normal routine with Barbie the following week, doing our usual pick up, and drops for Cazh. Some weekends just like before, I'd fly out to see Ize whenever he wasn't in the city. I had forgiven him for everything, and we were starting over with a clean slate. I truly believed he wasn't seeing his baby mama anymore, or any other girl for that matter. After, Ize confessed to me that I was the "only woman," he would ever need in this lifetime, I put it all behind me. Everything was back to normal until one day out of the blue, he pulled one of his famous disappearing acts without even as much as a phone call for yet another month. I just wanted to fall out of love with, Ize. One night, while I was laying in my bed listening to "Can't Let Go" by Mariah Carey I cried my heart out. I knew that I needed to let go of the love I had for Ize, but I knew I couldn't. I felted enthralled when it came to my love for Ize, because he made me feel like his personal love slave. He was my only weakness, and I was sure he knew he had me hanging on strings like Loose Ends said. Ize had a way of making me feel lost, and turned out whenever he wasn't around. Even, Zar had started to act like she didn't have much time to hang out anymore.

At first, I swore she knew something about Ize and I, until I found out that it was all on account of this new guy she recently started dating who just moved to Detroit. Legend was a small time hustler from Ohio, who moved here to start his own empire in the drug game. Legend, was actually a very down-to-earth, savvy, yet, humble man, but, Cazh saw him as an arrogant young prick who wanted what he felt was his. Cazh was jealous that Legend, also sold everything for a cheaper price, which got him well-known in some parts of the city his first weeks in Detroit. Cazh envied anyone he couldn't benefit from. It was even worse, that whenever women took a break from gossiping, and fantasizing over the mid-thirties, well-dressed, stocky but, muscular, smooth cappuccino skin-toned, heart-throb with the perfectly trimmed goatee, and thick wavy hair; they boasted about how they would love to be with the guy who was up next. Little did we all know, Legend was about to be the downfall of us all. With Cazh, and Barbie being in and out of town on business, lately, Zar handling Izes' personal affairs while he was missing in action, and me being depressed I didn't have time to keep up with the latest street gossip. All I did was sit around moping over that fact that I was starting to feel lonely. Ize was still missing in action along with the only friends I had, so the streets were my last concern. Lately, I had found some comfort in drinking. It seemed like liquor and wine had literally become my new best friend whenever I wasn't shaking my ass at the club. It helped me deal with the pain I was always feeling in my heart. I was cruising through Belle Isle one evening, smoking and drinking while trying to rid my mind of any thoughts of Ize, while Faith Evans "Catching Feelings" played, when my phone rang. I almost didn't answer it when I read "My Future" on my caller Id. I had programmed that as Ize's name in my phone the day we went to Mexico and didn't see why I should ever change it, but lately I'd been feeling some type of way, so I just picked up the phone and let him have it. I couldn't continue to ignore my feelings any longer. I was hurt and quickly falling out of love with Ize, and it was time he knew it. I snatched up the phone, taking another sip of my drink.

"What do you want, Ize?" I asked so sarcastic that if the words had been a knife, I knew he was cut.

I wasn't just some random hoe he could call upon every other month when he felt like being bothered. Just the thought of him trying to play me like one filled my heart with disgust as I waited for him to come up with his lie. Before he could even say a word, "I Get So Lonely" by Janet Jackson began to play, and I snapped. I was fuming on the inside, so I started to curse his ass out until I heard silence on the other end. I threw my phone back in the compartment that it was sitting in before I picked it up and replaced it with my bottle of peach Ciroc, and I didn't even bother to pour me a new glass. I took a swig straight form the bottle instead, and I felt just like my Mama as I reminisced about her always walking around with her personal bottle she would carry in her purse that she called her "savior". I pulled over and began to cry, because Ize was playing with fire, and only God knew what my next move was going to be.

"You gone get what's coming to you, Ize!" My mind whispered to me as I drank some more.

"I swear to goodness that one of these days you, gone get more than you ever bargained!" I chanted as if I were putting a personal hex on Ize myself. This was the first time in my life since I'd fallen in love with Ize that I wanted to just completely walk away without any regret but something inside of me just couldn't. It was like he had a spell on me because every time I tried to leave there was something that kept "Pulling Me Back". I wanted to cry as Chingy started to play. Even the songs on the radio were trying to tell me something, but I ignored all the signs that clearly stated that Ize was out of my league in every aspect of the game. We just weren't the same two people we were as children no matter how much I wanted us to be, and this life we were living wasn't turning out to be that bright future we always talked about. It was all "Just a Dream," I thought as Nelly replaced the thoughts in my head because this relationship with Ize was turning out to be everything I never wanted.

Meanwhile, Cazh had finally heard the rumors about Legend moving in from out of town and trying to take over the drug game here in Detroit. At first, he blew off the rumors about Legend trying to take over, because he wasn't losing out on much money. Cazh was the man of the City let him tell it and there was no way in hell some low life "nobody" was taking over his turfs. All that mucho man talk went out the window the moment a couple of his favorite clients stopped copping their usual shipments. Legend became a part of Cazhs' personal interest once he lost three more of his favorite clientele in Michigan. It was quite evident that the rumors were true about Legend trying to make a fast come up, and Cazh became pissed at that fact that just maybe this "nobody" would take over the entire city in less than a couple months.

It wasn't until Ize showed up unexpectedly at my place did I over hear him talking to Cazh about Legend. I didn't pay the conversation Ize was having much attention being that Legend was dating Zar. I automatically assumed they knew each other until a phone conversation Zar, and I had when she mentioned that Ize and Legend hadn't officially met yet being that they were both in and out of town all the time. I started to tell Zar right then and there that I overheard Ize talking to Cazh about Legend, but before I could get out a word she ended the conversation saying: "she had to call me back later because she was in the middle of packing for a trip they were about to take to Ohio". I just hung up and went on about my day, making a mental note to talk to her more about the rumors I heard once she got back. I didn't want to ruin her weekend get-away with all the negative he said/she said.

A month, had gone by, and I hadn't heard anything else about, Legend. Of course, Ize was still running in and out my life as usual, and it was back to the normal routine for me and Barbie. Zar had finally came back from Ohio with Legend, but, he stayed behind on family business. The first semester was coming to an end, and I was happy to still be maintaining my same grade point average. I didn't care how much my personal life crumbled as long as I made the Franklyn's proud each school year. School was my way to escape my everyday lifestyle. I knew as long as I finished my degree in Business management I'd make it out this hood shit one day. I was having lunch with Zar one day at this new place downtown called, Macabee's, and she literally spent most of the time talking about how good Legend treated her. I was so jealous on the inside just listening to how much Legend loved Zar after only knowing her for a short period of time. I hated that I couldn't get the same love from her brother who I knew since we were children. Ize and his disappearing acts didn't even seem to faze me anymore. As long as we got to spend time together when he just popped up, I played it cool. I knew my role now, so I played it well. There was no way in hell that I was ever going to let Ize see me sweat over him anymore than he already had. There wasn't anything Ize could really do that affected me when it came to my feelings, or so I thought. It was like an icebox had literally started to form where my heart used to be. I had also found some new friends to occupy my time whenever Ize wasn't in town and whenever he was, I'd play like I was just as happy to see him as he pretended to be to see me. I had promised myself that I'd never get lonely again so I had a different friend for each day of the week. Secretly I knew some of them envied Ize, because he had so much control over me. I couldn't imagine the idea of sleeping with another man, so I'd wait weeks at a time, even months just so Ize could be the only man fucking this pussy, even though I knew I wasn't the only pussy Ize was fucking.

One night while I was lying in my bed, cuddled up with Ize, his phone rang. I could tell the person on the other end of the phone was mad about something by the way his mood changed the minute he answered the phone.

"I'll take care of it," I heard him tell the angry caller before he hung up and called his boy, Pzyco.

I didn't get to hear the conversation between them two, but I knew in my heart something was terribly wrong if Ize was calling Pzyco's crazy ass at 4:00 am, in the morning. It wasn't until the next morning; did I find out the extinct of their conversation when Mrs. Emerson called Ize hysterical. Zarbreah, had been murdered the night before at a gas station with her new boyfriend after they were last seen leaving an after hour. She informed Ize that she needed him to accompany her to the morgue to identify Zar's body, then Ize hung up, and began to cry.

"What's wrong Bae?" I asked rushing into the living room where I heard the sobs.

I had been in the kitchen making him breakfast when he left out to take the call from his mother. I had never seen Ize cry before today so I knew whatever Mrs. Emerson told him had to be bad news.

"Zarbreah's dead!" Was all he could manage to say once he finally opened his mouth, and I was in total disbelief...

All I could do was fall to my knees, and cry right where I stood.

"Why is Zar dead, Ize?" I, sobbed uncontrollably while hitting him in the chest as he repeated it was an accident.

"What do you mean, Ize?" I screamed.

I was so mad that I was actually yelling at him, like Zar was my sister instead of his. I needed answers that I was sure he wasn't really up to answering as he put on his coat and headed out my front door leaving me in tears, and I was sure that all of this was because of the call he made last night to Pzyco.

"This is all my fault." Ize repeated, again.

The harsh reality was that Ize introduced Zarbreah to this dirty game of drug dealing, and drug dealers. If it wasn't for him always wanting to follow in his father's footsteps, becoming a king-pin, flaunting his money and power around like he was a Demigod, the high rollers he would show her off too, and the so called "Ballers" he dealt with frequently, maybe Zar would have chosen a better man. Instead, he showered her with lavish gifts, and made her believe that the lifestyle they lived was much more than he could ever really provide. Ize wasn't as untouchable as he thought; Now, Ize had to do the unthinkable, and go identify his sisters' lifeless body on a cold slab in a morgue. It was sad just knowing that in the back of his mind the truth was, he was the one who had a hand in putting her there.

I on the other hand, couldn't believe Zar was dead all because she started dating a guy that just so happened to be her brothers' drug suppliers rival.

"Damn, Damn, Damn!" I screamed into the air thinking back on the conversation I had with Zar, a couple weeks ago. She told me that Ize, and Legend never met due to them both being in and out of town all the time. I couldn't believe I had failed to mention that I'd heard Ize discussing Legend to Cazh the last time I saw her. I was so busy in my own feeling about my failed relationship with Ize that it totally slipped my mind when we were out the other day. I had let my jealously of her relationship cloud my better judgment instead of warning my friend about the potential beef brewing, and in a way, I felt Zar's death was as much of my fault as Ize did.

"IF I HAD JUST TRIED TO WARN HER... MAYBE SHE WOULD STILL BE ALIVE!"

My mind chanted over and over but the reality of the situation was clear. Zar was dead, and there wasn't anything anyone could do to bring her back. All I could do was cry the entire day after Ize left. I kept thinking back on all the times I had prayed for Ize to get payback for the way he always treated me but this was far worse than anything I could have ever wanted to happen to Ize. It also didn't make it any better that every news station had a breaking story on the "double homicide," that left a couple dead, while the woman was pregnant. I was in shock, because I never even knew Zar was expecting a child. I really cried after hearing that news and decided against watching television for the rest of the entire evening. I felt so bad for my best friend and her unborn child. Murder was always a hard pill to swallow especially when it's a person you're close to and was so young and full of life. All I could do is lay in bed and pray for Ize and Mrs. Emerson all day. I could tell Ize was hurting deep in his soul once he returned to my house that night by the way he was acting. I also knew there was nothing I could do to stop the bitterness that was secretly growing in Ize's heart. The next morning, I woke up to Ize and Pzyco having a heated conversation about Zar's death.

"How did you not know that was Zabreah, Sco?" Ize asked repeatedly but what was done was done. It wasn't anything we could do to bring Zar back to life! The bullet that struck her in the head killed her instantly. I just sat in my bed listening to Ize go on and on, then threaten Pzyco until they started fighting. Hearing the guys squabble in my living room with one another really began to piss me off. I stormed out of my bedroom like a bat out of hell and demanded that they both leave my house immediately once I got to where they were at. Just looking at the mess they made brought me to a rage of my own. Before I knew it, I had grabbed the bat from my closet, and started swinging it at both of them.

"Get the fuck out my house!" I shouted to no one in particular as they tried to apologize

"I don't want to hear it!" I yelled as they exited the door with me slamming it behind them.

The fact of the matter was Zarbreah was dead. No matter who blamed who, she wasn't ever coming back. The funeral was the following Saturday morning. Mrs. Emerson nearly lost it, while Ize and I did our best to console her. Once they closed the casket it was nothing but uncontrollable crying coming from everyone in the church until the pastor stood up at the podium and spoke.

"Let this be the day that we dry our tears and remember what our lord Jesus promised."

"As long as you believe in me, and are baptized you will be saved,"

"But he who does not believe will be condemned."

The entire church was completely silent after that statement, and I assumed everyone was thinking about their own lives until he continued.

"Mark 16:16 reminds us what Jesus wants from us, and of his forgiveness of our sins, and trust me when I say that sister, Zarbreah no longer has to worry, because she paid her dues to life and resides in the heavens above now".

I could see the blankness in Ize's eyes as he tried his best to be strong for his mother throughout the funeral service. Once we reached the cemetery, I felt the coldness starting to take over the warm spot that was left in my heart. I knew this was the end of the road for my best friend. The weather even agreed with how everyone must have felt because it was freezing once we all gathered around her final resting place.

"Ashes to ashes, dust to dust," The preacher said as this lady began to sing "Coming Home" by Dirty Money.

I just held Mrs. Emerson's hand as the tears flowed wildly. I looked up at Ize, and I could've sworn I felt Ize bury his soul with Zar's.

It wasn't even a week after the funeral before the changes began to arouse. Ize was set on having a personal vendetta against everyone who was involved with Zar's death and it wasn't anything I could say to change his mind.

"Anyone Can Get It," Ize yelled drunk one night while he was sitting at my dining room table, loading his .40 caliber with bullets.

I just watched him load, aim, take a sip of his drink and fire imaginary shots at the wall. I shook my head because he was seriously turning into a mad man. He hadn't shaved in weeks and he was starting to look as bad on the outside as I knew he was feeling on the inside. He was so serious about getting everybody back for Zar being dead that he even called, and threaten to kill Pzyco a few times.

"This Ain't What They Want Thou, Bae," He snapped when I entered the room trying to convince him to come to bed. He just stood up, put on his coat and left.

I started to pray for Ize every night after that night. I knew he had gained a reputation long ago for "cleaning up" his messes as he would call them. My biggest fear was losing him to this war he was starting. Only the Lord knew what would happen this time around. On many occasions, I tried to talk some sense into Ize. It would only lead to us arguing, and Ize leaving me alone to wonder was he alive for weeks at a time, even months. I was really starting to hate the way Ize always treated me like I was the root of all his problems. It had been damn near a year, and six months since I ran back into Ize, and I wasn't a person he could continue to lash out on, and then run back too when he felt like it. I felt like his puppet at times because no matter how Ize did me, I always gave him the extra string to jerk me around with whenever he showed up at my doorstep with an excuse. I had already spent a whole year, and a half chasing him around trying to prove my loyalty. I really felt it was time for Ize to start proving his. I was in the shower one day with Mariah Carey's "We Belong Together" blasting as I sang along feeling really good after spending a week with Ize. The sex we'd just had before I got in the shower had me in a zone as I thought on how "Too good to be true" this week had been going. Ize was actually calmer than the last times I'd seen him. He was even back to looking and dressing like his old self. He also confided in me that he'd been branching out a lot more to meet new clientele being that he didn't mess with Cazh anymore. I knew right then and there that it would be trouble ahead. I also knew Ize could handle himself. I was all into Mariah's song when Ize walked into the bathroom. I knew it was about to be some bullshit in the game, but I was secretly hoping my intuition wasn't right for once. All of a sudden, he had a business meeting to go to when he'd just told me he didn't have anything to do before I got in the shower.

"Do I look stupid or something?"

My mind asked itself as I thought back to my jam, "B.A.N." by Sevyn Streeter, that I heard earlier today.

"What a Bitch Ass Nigga!" I thought, thinking about the title of the song.

I just gave him a smile then mumbled "Okay," under my breath. The so-called business meeting turned into another one of his little famous disappearing acts without a single word from Ize and I was fed up with his shit. I was such a fool in love, I thought as I sat having drinks with Barbie one evening. Toni Braxton's "Seven Whole Days" was on, and Barbie was really starting to get on my last nerve with all the questions about Ize that I knew were more for Cazh's ear than her own.

"Lately, I haven't been seeing, Ize," I said, playing into her little game.

I don't know what would make her think I would tell her anything about Ize when I knew the deal between him and Cazh. Even with me being mad at Ize all the time, she had to know I'd never betray him. Since, I could see where things were going, I had to show her where my loyalty laid. I knew Barbie's loyalty was with Cazh. After everything that was said, and done,

I couldn't blame her for trying to see where I stood in all of this chaos. It was sad to see our friendship being tested after so many years of being solid. I never thought our bond would be broken, but I also knew Barbie would do anything to setting people up when it came to her or Cazh's well-being. I was in total disbelief as I sat there, and listened to her every insult about my tainted relationship. I was so tired of her always trying to be my love counselor like her relationship was so much better. I just rolled my eyes to the heavens, and sipped my glass the entire time she ran her mouth. I didn't even respond to any of her foolish accusations, but, she definitely knew how to push my buttons. I let Barbie throw the shade of a lifetime at me, as I sat calmly under my imaginary palm tree with my shades on. I, literally had to refrain myself from punching the bitch in the throat a couple times during her visit.

"So where is Ize, now, Teaz?" she asked, passing me the blunt and my look must've said it all

"That's the typical Ize routine when it comes to you two," She chuckled, and I just got up and changed the music. This bitch was killing my vibe, and I see now that some friends ain't really friends; they just cool for the moment.

"I'd be tired of the disappearing acts by now," Barbie had the audacity to say as I passed her back the blunt, and I snapped.

"Well, I'm not," I lied while cutting her off before she could get out another word.

"It's actually better this way," I continued, trying to be my own personal comforter for my heart. I had realized a long time ago that Ize might not be the one.

"I get to do me more now that my feelings aren't all wrapped up into having a title," I explained, but I knew I was only saying that to shut her up. I always dreamed of being Izes' wife, and I planned on being just that one day.

"No matter what," I continued while hitting the blunt, and putting on "I Still Love You" by 702.

"I'm gone always have his back," I assured her then gave her, a look that could've killed her, and she just shook her head.

"Why so serious, boo?" she laughed.

"I'm actually happy that you finally got your mind right," she joked, then sipped her drink

"Ize reminds me of that song by Donell Jones," she replied as she hit the blunt one last time before putting it in the ashtray.

"You give him all your love,"

"And, he gives you his half the time," she scolded, sarcastically, and I was ready to put her ass out on that note.

By the time "Love Is Still Enough" by Savory came on it was time for Barbie to go. I was done with all her rambling in my personal affairs and trying to get information about Ize for Cazh from me. I made up a story about having something to do and an hour later I was alone in peace. I was glad I'd taken Ize's advice months ago and got my own place. Barbie was starting to seem real fishy in my eyes so I knew I had to keep my distance from her.

A couple weeks later, Ize showed up at my house and we flew out to Vegas. We had a ball that entire weekend and it made me think back to the summer that Bono took Mama to Vegas, and they came back living life on the edge. They were the modern day version of "Bonnie and Clyde" in my eyes and we were "Part 2 (On The Run) like Jay Z and Beyonce' said. Pandora was jammin' with all my favorite old school songs on the plane ride home as I zoned out to Aaliyah's "We Need A Resolution", Kem's "When Love Calls", Mary J's "Only Woman", Floetry's "Say Yes", Xscape's "Who Can I Run Too", 112's "Pleasure and Pain", and I felt like Alicia Keys. I just kept falling in and out of love with Ize, and I felt like it wasn't anything I could do about it. As long as my heart beats, I believed we were bonded for life. Somehow, I knew I would always be with Ize through the good or bad, like I always said. I was almost done with this new book I'd recently picked up a couple days ago in a bookstore called "How to Kill a Guy in 10 Days" by Kayla Perrin and Brenda Mott, before we landed. Just the title of the book made Ize keep asking me was I "okay" periodically throughout the entire plan ride. I would just laugh, and assure him that book wasn't anything like the title. It did turn out to have a great plot, twist and turn out. Ironically, it also got me the reaction I was looking for in Ize. Even before Zar's death, I wasn't sure if the boy had any real feelings left inside because of how he always treated me whenever he got mad. The things he did to me weren't right, but I knew Ize loved me in his own crazy little way even if life wasn't turning out to be the way we always dreamed.

"Maybe we just need a little more time to grow into our love," I thought to myself as I watched Ize sleep. Besides, it had been almost two years since the day we reunited, and I was still hopeful that one day we'd get it right.

"What is love anyways?"

I thought back to my Mama, and how she always said this when it came to her relationship with my dad. I realized she was right all these years because it really does hurt so much at times! The following weekend, I found myself at Club Ice with my girl Rozi, and a couple of her friends. We were all having a good time on the dance floor when a group of girls that Rozi had been beefin' with walked in. I knew it would be on and poppin' if they even blinked at us wrong. To our surprise, the hoes played it cool, but it was something about the way this one chick out the group. She'd been staring at me from across the room all night that confirmed my thoughts that she had a serious problem with me. I decided to excuse myself to the ladies' room, and just like I expected, she followed me.

"So you're, La'Teazya?" The chick asked me, when I came out the stall.

"Who wants to know?" I asked the female who was almost unbearable to look at.

 The only thing mystery lady had going on for her was a fat ass and a half decent shape. She was definitely the definition of a "Tip Drill".

"I'm Tazha," she announced, like I was supposed to know who she was or care to know her, as "Fuck You" by Yo Gotti began to play.

"Okay," I mumbled sarcastically, and then turned on the faucet to wash my hands

"I'm Izir's Baby mama" She stressed through a grin, and I just wanted to slap the smirk that was forming on the ugly bitches face.

"We talked on the phone once before," she continued, and I was waiting impatiently to hear what else she had to say.

"What the fuck, Ize?" I thought looking at the Shrek look-alike ass bitch.

I just laughed then continued to wash and dry my hands. I wasn't about to stand there and belittle myself with a bitch that was clearly jealous of me. Whatever this bitch thought she had to say to me could wait, as far as I was concerned. Honestly, after just looking at that ugly bitch I could care less what she had to say. Ms. Tazha, was a non-factor, and it was beginning to be a plus that Rozi didn't like her girls.

"Anybody can get it," I thought back to Ize saying this awhile back, then laughed, straightened my hair in the mirror, and walked past her like she was nothing.

"Take your issues up with your Baby Daddy." I snapped.

"This right here, Tazha," I snarled making sure my lipstick was just right, and then opened the door.

"Ain't what you want, baby girl." I laughed some more while sashaying my sexy ass back to our table.

 I quickly ordered myself a bottle to calm my nerves. Tazha's ass was lucky as hell I didn't open up a can of whoop ass on her in the ladies' room. I just laughed as I danced to "Blah Blah Blah" by Richie Homie Quan. I could see why Ize no longer wanted anything to do with Tazha's ass. She was nothing more than a used up Thot in my eyes.

"That Tazha bitch is too, comical." I giggled, while sipping my drink.

It was even funnier, that the bitch was so mad she kept trying to stare me down the entire time we were in the club. I knew in my heart she didn't want it with me, though. I just gave her a look that said it all and enjoyed the rest of my evening.

"You can get it if you with it," I sang along with the song.

"You're absolutely right, Trey Songs," I thought as "Uh Huh" played. Then, I promised myself that my next encounter with Tazha wouldn't be as nice.

The Outcome:
"Your Reputation Should Never Exceed Your Legacy."
Everything Happens For A Reason
Dear Diary,
October 3, 2014

There's certain secrets that I've hidden deep inside my soul about my life. I've also promised myself that I'd never tell anyone about my past who didn't know anything about the hurt that I went through, and survived. I guess that's why I chose to write down all my darkest moments in my diary. Writing is my form of self-help, and a way to reflect on what I've done. Writing also frees me from all the pain that I overcame in my past. Life itself has taught me all kinds of lessons. There's also different types of people who hang around you on a daily basis. Some good, but, the majority of the people we meet are wolves dressed in sheep's clothing. They prey on the weak, and, devour the souls of the innocent. Then there's the critic's. The judge without jury, convict without reason, and persecute without a sense of remorse, or credentials to do, so. I remember the day, I realized I needed each one of them in my life to survive. My favorite has to be the critics who will be judgmental no matter what you achieve in life. Then you have the go-getters who take charge of their lives and actions while constantly push you towards achieving your goals even when the back-stabbers betray you, and switch sides. My second favorite group of people, the motivators and inspirations. These people will always be known as the few who never doubted you, or lost faith. It's up to you to know which person you're being faced with on a day to day basis. No matter who you are or what you stand for: "You reputation should never exceed your legacy."

It had been four long, and stressful years since I moved back to Michigan, and as usual, Ize was missing in action. I stopped excepting, his phone calls whenever he decided to pick up and dial my number, and I even started to play like I wasn't home sometimes whenever he'd do his usual pop up visits. I needed a break from all the games he constantly played with my heart. I literally couldn't take the bullshit he was putting me through any longer. I had cut everyone out of my life, and it was starting to seem like my only real friend was my girl, Rozi. The year, 2010, was going to be my year to take back my life. I was now twenty-two years old, and I was more focused than ever on my life without Ize in it. One night, while I was lounging around the house, Rozi called me while she was working at another bar, and told me that she had just saw Ize in the club all hugged up with some Mexican chick. That was the night that I began to see things for what they really were between us. I was nothing more than a pawn in his sick little game he liked to play with females. Ize was nothing more than a player to me and I wasn't about to keep settling for being second best. Maya Angelou's poem, "Phenomenal Woman," was being recited by Janet Jackson from Poetic Justice, and something inside of me felt good about the decision I had made to finally leave Ize alone. I had also read these two new books I'd recently picked up from my favorite local book store called "When Love Calls You Better Answer", and "Redemption Song" by Betrice Berry, and I was starting to have a new outlook on the whole love concept. I even started to realize that there was a greater purpose for my life, and all I had been through after reading them and having a self-realization. I wanted to change, so I embraced that fact that God had to be working on me like Stazy always told me he would.

"We are all just a work in progress". Stazy would often say, and I was truly beginning to feel that in my heart.

Even though, I didn't know much about God growing up, I knew he would never forsake me when I needed him the most. He did after all bless me with the Franklyn's when I needed a loving and caring family, and I knew if I was patient in due time, he'd bless me with the love I truly needed and deserved. I admit that when I crossed paths with Ize, I wanted love for all the wrong reasons. I was so caught up in the life Barbie was living and listening to all her stories about her and Cazh, that I lost track of what I really wanted out of a man. I had settled for Ize when he came along because he was a love I always wanted as a child but was forced to give up due to my Mama's untimely death. As, I watched Poetic Justice, I thought back over the new couple of years that Ize and I shared. Everything was beginning to seem more clearly to me as if God was trying to give me clarity on the whole situation. We were on two different paths of life, and I could only give him the respect that he had earned which was becoming close to none each day that passed. I had also found out that Barbie was only looking out for my best interest as far as the beef between Ize, and Cazh went, but I knew things would never be the same between us because of it. I was also happy that I'd managed to graduate on time. My last semester was very stressful with all the bullshit I was dealing with on a day-to-day basis, but I pulled it off. Life wasn't perfect, but it was great, minus all bullshit. I knew a blessing was ahead of me, if I just stayed focused on the right things. I turned on my radio after the movie was over and decided to make my favorite meal for lunch. Red skin potatoes and onions, with a juicy steak and a cold glass of blueberry lemonade had my mouth watering just inhaling the aroma while "Brain" by Banks poured out the stereo system. I was feeling the lyrics deep in my heart as I prepared my food while singing along. Steve Harvey's strawberry letter came on with a caller during the break, who was talking about love and how women are starting to take the whole "Act Like A Lady, Think Like A Man," book to the extreme. He went on to say that: Women really didn't want love, and in some ways, I had to agree to disagree. Men have a tendency to put women through all kinds of bullshit then expect you to be the same loyal, faithful and dedicated women you were before the sent you to hell and back. Maybe the book was helping some woman obtain better morals while dating, I thought before the caller hung up and "Knights Over Egypt," by The Jones Girls came on. I sure as hell needed a copy of the book, so I could start setting better goals and standards when it comes to dating the next go round. I had my mind made up as far as the relationship I was having with Ize went, thinking back on this one night my Mama was having a party, and my Daddy decided to show up. Bono opened the door for him, and he just walked in the house liked he owned it and criticized my Mama about everything she was doing.

"You got some nerves, Taz," I heard her yell before I decided to peek out of my bedroom door.

"Get the hell out of my house, you, son-of-a-bitch!" she screamed while walking back to the door and opening it. He just put on his hat, gave Bono a little wink and smile then strolled out the door, looking my Mama up and down with disgust in his eyes. I was done with Ize for good, because he was never going to get the satisfaction of belittling me in public. It was already bad enough he was the ruler over my heart. The doorbell rang, breaking me out of my thoughts, and I almost decided against answering it because I figured it was Ize doing another one of his famous pop visits. "My Life" by Mary J. Blige began to play as I walked to the door. A strange feeling was starting to come over me, but I shook it off as I listened to Mary sing, because my life was a fucking trip at times and I damn sure needed a vacation from it all. I flung the door open, annoyed as hell that the person was now pounding on my front door like they had lost their mind. I was about to give the person on the other end a good tongue lashing once I opened it, but to my surprise they were police officers.

"La' Teazya Scorns-Franklyn?" The officer asked before I could get out a word.

 I just stood there staring at her, clueless.

"You're under arrest," she continued, and I went numb.

"You have the right to remain silent"

"Anything you say can, and will be used against you," I heard her say but the rest was a blur.

"What do you mean, I'm under arrest?"

I managed to ask right before the other officer cuffed me. I was fuming on the inside as I watched the officers walk inside my home while being escorted to the squad car.

"This must be my lucky fucking day," I said aloud as I laughed. I was feeling like the crazy bitch Zaria from this book I read called "One Night

Stand" by Kendall Banks, because all I could do was chant her favorite saying over, and over again.

"Smiley face, smiley face,"

"Can everyone see my Smiley face!" I laughed again.

"These fuckers have got to be kidding me," I whispered as the vehicle pulled away from my building.

"Game, over!"

Cold Blooded
Dear Diary,
October 13, 2014

"There's a big difference between being from the hood and being the hood". The only problem is if you don't know which side you were meant to be on it could lead to your downfall. I guess that's why they made sidewalks, because the streets damn sure ain't for everybody. I remember thinking about my life on my ride to the county jail, being locked up had to be some sick joke someone was playing on me, and I didn't want to understand what I had done to deserve this. Even with me knowing all the evidence the prosecutors were trying to use against me, I remained unfazed. Once I got to the county jail, I found out they were holding everyone in custody including my dumb ass ex-lover, Izir, and was still looking for a well-known hit man name Santwan Tyson, aka Pzyco. It still amazes me that sometimes we have to swallow a big dose of harsh reality to realize our own self-worth. Little did Ize know, the latest piece of eye candy that he had been flaunting around town with was a federal agent for the, FBI. According to the Mexican police offer that showed up at my doorstep to arrest me, she had been building a case against Cazhmere for a five years, and it became rather easy to get close to him and his entire organization once she started socializing with the pissed off, set on revenge ex-boyfriend of mine, Izir Emerson. The whole "boyfriend," concept she was rambling on about was so funny to me. As of three months ago, Ize meant nothing to me. Now here this woman is telling me about different rendezvous Ize, and I had shared together during her stakeouts. Just hearing Ize's name made me cringe on the inside. I had built so much dislike in my heart for Ize over the past years that I had to separate myself from him, just so I could have a peace of mind. I could have snapped just hearing her continuously mention his name. She also had pictures of us on our first trip to Mexico, and random pictures of us living in a fairytale that I really wanted to forget about. I always knew Ize's ego would be his downfall. Ize, was set on getting revenge on Cazh for Zar's death by any means necessary, that he was willing to sell Cazh out to Gabriella who claimed to be the sister of a well-known Mexican cartel leader. All he had to do was give up the information she wanted on Cazh, and he would get all the drugs and clientele he needed to put him back on his feet. Gabriella knew all she had to do was sweet talk Ize, sell him a dream, and he was like play dough in her hands. She had watched him in many stakeouts before she finally decided to go undercover. She knew he was most vulnerable after Zar's murder, so she used that to her advantage. Had he just faced up to his own actions in Zar's murder none of this would be going on, and Zar might still be alive despite what Cazh wanted done to Legend. The fact of the matter was Ize had made the call that resulted in her death so he was as much at fault for his sister's death as anyone else he tried to blame. For that reason alone, I knew the guilt was eating away at Ize, which made him make tons of irrational decisions lately. "Moments," by Nas crossed my mind as I prepared myself for my first arraignment. I was locked up immediately without bail, because I was considered a flight risk. The first visit I had with the Franklyn's they promised to get me a good lawyer for my case. They even swore to me on Jesus that I'd somehow get out of this mess I'd gotten myself into, but it was clear to me that Jesus didn't want anything to do with either one of us sitting behind bars. Our fate was now in the hands of the judge, and you heard Pac. We were considered "America's Most Wanted" and you can get life for selling drugs in this "White Man's World". Spending a lot of time alone behind bars made me start to reflect over my life once more. I began to write down the thoughts of my days instead of writing my parents whom I knew were waiting on a letter from me they never got. Ize would cross my mind periodically here and there, and in those moments I'd find myself asking why I even bothered. I don't know why I kept associating myself with him or anyone else for that matter to get myself into this situation but there was no turning back the hands of time. Maya Angelou said it best, "when a person shows you who they really are, believe them the first time". There is no excuse for the stupidity that I displayed dating, Ize, but I must say my feelings always got the best of me, and my logic. I couldn't blame anyone but myself as "Thugs Cry," by Rick Ross crossed my mind, and the lyrics hit me deep. I just wanted to be the one that Ize loved, and ran too when he was down so I could always be there to lift him up like I always promised. We were supposed to fly together landing "Nevermore," like the Raven quotes in my favorite Edgar Allen Poe poem. I guess now I see that I'm just like that bird in many ways, and I'll be soaring alone. I always knew Ize's infidelities would catch up to him one day, because he loved to play games with women's heart. What I didn't expect was for it to also involve me once Karma came back around. I was truly broken by love, and I had to bang my head up against a brick wall this time to learn that. For the first time in my life, I realized that "You owe life; it doesn't owe you". Everything that was happening to me were all the effects of me moving up here to help Barbie transport drugs for Cazh knowing what the outcome could be. I knew the consequences, yet I moved here anyway being greedy and chasing a lifestyle I knew very little about. I was so smart, yet naive in every way possible. Blinded by the hood's perception of what is right. We've all heard the saying: "a hard head, makes a soft behind". I guess, I needed to burst mine wide open to see clearly, again. The look of disappointment in the Franklyn's eyes their second visit didn't shock me one bite, and it made me feel sad deep down inside. I had let them down tremendously after all they had done for me. No matter how fucked up I was, they remained in high spirits and good faith about everything that was going on. The Franklyn's had been there for me since the day they took me away from the girl's home, and I admired that even in my darkest hours they tried to shed light on the situation. I honestly knew in my heart the Franklyn's had my back without a shadow of doubt; even if nobody else did.

"Never let your sun go down, La'Teazya," Mrs. Franklyn said to me right before they left.

"You will always be my sunshine." she finished in her loving voice with a smile, and my heart cried the tears my eyes wouldn't allow me too.

I had to be strong. I knew tears couldn't rescue me from my reality, so I didn't see a point in shedding them. It was a blessing that the county wasn't as bad as I expected it to be. Some days, I hated being in jail and going through trial. I hated the fact that my fate laid in the hands of people who knew nothing about me. Being that I was still in school most of the time when Barbie would do most of the drops, some of the evidence against me was dropped. I was still looking at ten years in prison, which I was trying to be reduced to five. I was laying in my bunk one evening thinking back on my last day I was free. I was sitting in my car listening to Tupac's "Staring At The World Thru My Rearview," and Memphis Bleek "I Get High," just reflecting on my life right before I decided to go in and watch movies. I realized that I had been surrounding myself with material things and people who didn't really bring me true happiness lately. My eyes were filled with tears when I pulled into the grocery store parking lot to pick me up a couple steaks that I couldn't even park right. I had been dealing with a man whose love was questionable, a dead best friend, and my home girl was slowly but surely turning into a potential enemy. I had so much negativity weighing on my shoulders that I felt I couldn't trust anyone anymore. Rozi, was the only real friend that I had at the moment. She was the only person that I felt I could trust with certain things about my life, and she never skipped a beat when it came to court dates and putting money in my commissary. I had been going through months of trail and they finally came up with a verdict. I was escorted out to the courtroom with a little white judge who'd been giving everyone before me the maximum sentence time for their crimes and I just knew I was in for the same treatment as I stood nervously staring at the podium. Once she instructed the juror to read my verdict, I felt a sight relief even though I was found guilty. Based on the guidelines, and the fact that I'd never had a prior record I was given five years which was still a long time to me being that I was only Twenty- one years old. I couldn't complain because after the speech she gave me I knew I was lucky! If it was up to her instead of the jury I'd be doing every bit of the ten years, the prosecutor was pushing for. The lyrics of "Silly of Me," by Denise Williams played in my head and I was feeling like a kid in one of the Trix commercials. It was silly of me to move here to help Barbie sell drugs, but I was even dumber for thinking I could just magically stumble into Ize's life and make him fall in love with me all over again. Fact was we'd hardly gotten to know each other after spending all those years apart. Tina Turner was right; sometimes you have to ask yourself "What does love really have to do with it?"

I spent another week in the county jail before I was moved to a prison called, Hard Knocks Correctional Facility. I wasn't even there a week before a group of girls started riding my back. This was just the type of attention I didn't need during my time in jail. I also knew it could only result in one or two things. They'd either beat the hell out of me or kill me, or worst I'd do the same to one of them and find myself doing more time than I wanted too. Either way, it wasn't any hoe in my blood so I was "Down For Whatever," like Nuttin' Nyce said. During recess one afternoon, I had to open up a straight can of whoop ass on one of the biggest chicks in the crew. This was my way of letting the hoes know I wasn't to be fucked with but it also got me on solitary lock up for damn near a month. Once I got out of lock up, I got into a fight with a new girl that was transferred to our facility. She was supposed to be my new Bunkie, but the bitch tried to stab me the first day we met and I damn near put the bitch out of her misery. I still can't tell you what possessed her to try me but I ended up back in lock up for damn near another month after that incident.

"I knew I should've just joined that fire fighters rescue squad," I thought back on a girl named, Maria asking me to join their group my first day there to keep me out of trouble. I refused because I was so mad at the world for even being in prison in the first place that I let anger take over my better judgment. Now, I wished that I had just accepted her offer instead of being so stubborn when I was first locked up. The minute that I stepped out of lock up, and back into my cell, I wanted to kill the warden. He had to be the Joker himself for moving me into a cell with this bitch named, Mizz whom everyone called "Mister". She was the leader of the toughest girl group in this prison, and, the main reason I got solitary lock up the first time. Mizz had also tried to recruit me into her crew the first day that I got here. When, I refused her offer she sent her crew after me thinking intimidation would make me run with them. After fighting one of the toughest girls in the crew, getting on solitary lock up twice, and shanking Mizz in the shower; I would soon find out that getting rid of Mizz, and her crew wasn't going to be as easy as I thought. She did manage to keep her word, and told her crew I was her "new property," which meant I was off limits to everyone. At first, I hated the fact that I had let her punk me out of my decision to kill her, because she tried to make me do everything for her on a daily basis. If I wasn't washing her laundry, I was providing her with things she needed whenever my commissary money was put in my account. I never stopped thinking about that one day we had in the shower when I should have put an end to it all. I swear to God I couldn't stand the ground that Mizz walked on but, I knew to always choose my battles wisely. I was just waiting on the perfect moment, and it was a wrap for Mizz's ass. One night while I was in bed sleep, I woke up to the sound of Mizz crying. At first, I thought I was dreaming because it was no way in hell big bad, ass had any feelings. I stood up, and went over to the toilet trying my best to act as if I didn't notice.

"I guess you heard me huh?" Mizz asked and I just played it off.

"Heard you what?" I asked her sarcastically because if she wasn't going to tell me the reason behind the tears I sure as hell wasn't up for any conversation.

"I'm sure you heard me crying," she stated, and then sat up on the edge of her bed to face me.

I just wiped myself, and was about to get back in my bunk without even addressing the statement she had just made. To my surprise, she asked me to have a seat next to her before I could make my next move. I didn't want to sit with her at first because I was so tired of Mizz's shit on an everyday basis. It was something different about the look in her eyes this time though that told me she needed me. I saw a touch of sadness behind her stare that I had never seen before so I took a seat.

"Do you ever wonder why I even spared your life that day you tried to threaten me in the shower La'Teazya?" Mizz asked me with sincerity in her voice and I was curious to know the answer to that myself. I knew why I had spared her life that day thinking I had met crazy itself that morning but it was always three versions to each story and it was time I knew hers.

"Before I got locked up, I use to run with this gang and we were as ruthless as the came! We had beef with different hoods, and even the name of our group "Da Hoodlums," was one people knew not to even mention unless you wanted a problem. We terrorized the streets for years without anyone ever thinking of crossing one of us. I was one of only two girls in the entire gang, and I had one of the best-looking girls in the city, on my team. Men were often jealous of me because I had the girl they could only dream of having. I had a hell-of-a reputation when it came to the streets, but the fact that I was a beautiful girl myself didn't seem to help the situation when it came to my sexual preference. Most men saw us as two sexy women who were experimenting with each other, being that Jazmine wasn't always gay. I happen to be the first and only girl she'd ever been with. After seeing each other around town here and there, we clicked after I saved her life this one night. Jazmine's parents didn't want anything to do with her once they found out she was dating a female so I moved her into my place. We were actually happy in love despite what people felt or thought about us. Two years had passed, and we were living a good life together while planning to run away together to a state that allowed gay marriage. Everything seemed to be going just fine; but it was all about to come to an end. One night while Jazz was at a club with her girls partying a group of men followed them out to their car trying to get their numbers. When the girls rejected the men advances, they decided to take matters into their own hands. After raping, and beating Jazz along with her friends; Jazmine ended up in a coma for six months. When she finally woke up, she had no recollection of what happen to her, or who I even was anymore. She didn't even remember the three years we had spent together prior to her being beaten. She did however remember her parents, and decided that she would move in with them when she was released from the hospital. They banned me from ever seeing Jazz again and they even got a restraining order against me claiming that I was a threat to Jazmine's life. The next time I saw Jazz again she was pregnant and married. A part of me almost died inside just seeing her look at a man the way she used to look at me. She promised herself that she would never be with another man after I saved her from being raped in an alley. She made me promise to keep her secret, and that bonded us for life because who knew what would have happened had I not turned that corner that night and had the reputation I did. Just seeing her that happy in love with the family I couldn't ever give her made me want to kill Jazz for leaving me broken hearted after I was the one who sat by her bedside day in and out. She had no idea that her being in a coma sent me into a rampage of my own. Once I found out who the men were that put her there, I made it a point to pay each one of them a personal visit. Men are right; "pussy is the root of all evil." All I had to do was dress up like a lady for a day, and I had each one of them right where I wanted them. "Checkmate," was all they found by each body except the leaders. I had others plans for him. Once, I found Oscar there was nothing to calm the bitterness that was growing inside of me. It killed me to know that the love of my life, Jazmine had woken up, and moved on with her life. I started taking all kinds of pills, drugs, and drinking, uncontrollably. I would get so drunk at times, that I would find myself playing Russian roulette with my own life. I would have rather went blind as Etta James said, then to see Jazmine living happily ever after with someone else. One night I had stayed up all night on a drinking binge. I decided to go see Jazz the next morning so I could convince her that she was once a part of my life. I wasn't just the enemy her parents made me out to be and it was time she knew that. I could tell she knew who I was once she opened the door for me and saw my face. I was so happy at first thinking that I could at least have my old friend back but the fact that she kept acting like she didn't know me and asking me to leave her house was really starting to piss me off and before I knew it I had

snapped. I pulled out my pistol and shot her in broad day light right there

at the front door where we had been standing causing a scene. I was in

such a drunken state of mind I didn't even leave the scene of the crime. I

just sat there holding her lifeless pregnant body until the police came.

That's how I ended up with Life, in prison".

I watched a tear roll down her face, and all I could do was say "damn,"

after wiping away my own tears. I felt sad for Mizz, because she was just

like me in so many ways. Love was a powerful thing and I could honestly

see how she just threw her life away because of it. It was plenty of

occasions where I wanted to kill Ize for the way he treated me. I wanted

him to feel as bad on the inside as he always made me feel. I couldn't even

judge Mizz for what she had done in the past, because a part of me felt

her. She had been through it all to get her love back, just to lose to her in

the end. I couldn't ever see myself actually going through with a murder,

but I knew everything happen for a reason. It was bad enough Zarbreah

had lost her life due to our foolishness, and I damn sure didn't ever want

to lose, Ize.

"You remind me of Jazmine," she expressed to me as tears rolled down

her eyes.

"It's just something about the way you look at me that reminds me of her," she sighed.

I knew the pain she was hiding deep down inside was the real reason behind her tough façade she always put on. I couldn't believe Mizz was sharing her life's story with me. I actually felt bad for her after listening to what she had been through, so I reached in to give her a hug.

"It'll be okay, Mizz," I said wrapping my arms around her and giving her a little pat on the back. She didn't say a word. Instead, she leaned in, and kissed me. I wanted to pull away, but the touch of someone else's lips against mine was a feeling I hadn't had in months, so I let her continue. Once she began sucking on my breast, I didn't even bother with trying to stop her. I just relaxed as I let her caress my body in ways that Ize never did. In only a matter of minutes, she had taken me to ecstasy and back to earth. After that night, I was hooked on Mizz and her "Bitch" was exactly what I became.

A year had come, and gone. I finally joined that fire fighters squad, and was actually in love for the first time in my life. I felt like Mary J. Blige's old song "Real Love," because everything about what we had was real. Mizz gave me a feeling inside that I only dreamed of feeling with Ize. I hated the fact that she would have to do life in prison, because I didn't know how I would feel once I left here. I knew this was probably all just a phase that I was going through being that I was an inmate, isolated from the world. I never let that stop me from loving her, and showing her how much I appreciated her for having my back while I was in jail. Sex with Mizz was better than it had ever been with Ize, and she didn't even have a penis. It was the emotional attachment that we shared that made us have an unbreakable bond after sharing our life stories with one another. Our past was somewhat the same, except Mizz wasn't blessed with a loving family to keep her off a destructive path like I did. The Franklyn's were my only redemption as teen. As I look back, neither of them lacked on giving me the love I needed. I was the one who kept making mistakes. Now, I was just grateful that I didn't do enough to keep me behind these bars. It had been three long months into the New Year when a new group of inmates were transferred to our prison. Amongst the group of girls was a prisoner who everyone called, "Ladibug". She was, as innocent looking as they came, but everyone knew the truth that lay behind that pretty baby face. When it came to eliminating her enemies, Ladibug didn't play any games. She was swift with a blade, and as ruthless as they came. This also happens to be what landed her in juvenile plenty of times before she was even, eighteen. She had quite the reputation for poisoning some of her victims, but she prided herself on always getting up close and personal with her victims. Ladibug also happened to be the sister of the leader of the gang that Mizz killed for raping, and beating Jazmine. She swore that one day she would get revenge on Mizz for what she had done to her only brother. As destiny would have it, jail would be the place they crossed paths again. Mizz once confided in me that she had tortured Ladibug's brother, right before she decided to kill him. The details of his murder were so gruesome; I could honestly see why Ladibug hated her so much. Mizz had cut off Ladibug's brother penis, fed it to him, and then beat him with a bat until his face was no longer recognizable. After she was satisfied, she set his body on fire along with his drug spot. Mizz was definitely stressing about Ladibug. She knew she had to kill Ladibug, before she tried to kill her. This wasn't the shower incident that we had when I first got here. This was far worst, and nothing in the world could stop this feud except, death. At first, Mizz ordered random hits on Ladibug. Mizz soon found out that Ladibug wasn't someone she could just bully into getting their act right. This was a fight for Mizz, and only Mizz.

"A life for a life," I whispered to Mizz one night right before we went to bed. I didn't want to see her hurt, or possibly killed over some past non-sense, but it wasn't anything I could do. Karma didn't come with deadline, and it was clear time was up. Sure, Mizz had killed Ladibugs' brother out of revenge; but he had also taken something away from Mizz that couldn't be replaced. I felt he got what he deserved for the cruelty that him, and his crew did to Jazmine, and her friends. Who knew how many other women had fallen victim to these psychopaths before Mizz put an end to them all.

"I love you, Teaz." Mizz stated with a blank face, and I felt depressed.

"I'll always love you,"

"No matter the outcome," she continued, and I began to cry.

"God has a plan for you, but you have to pull yourself out the fire first. He wants to see how strong you are without his help, as he continues to watch you first help yourself. He wants you to show him you want to live. Don't just talk about letting go, actually let go. Let go of all negativity, let go of all foolishness, and let go of the people who are holding you back from progressing. From this day forward, let go of anything that are not pushing you forward. Promise me, that you'll let it all go into that same fire once you finally pull yourself out of it." Mizz said through tears, and I did.

We sat talking for another thirty minutes, and "Payback was a real bitch at times," was all I could think about while I listened to Mizz. I was just lucky, that bitch happened to be a woman scorned named, Mizz. One afternoon during a pool game with my girl Azhley from Mizz's crew, Ladibug walked into the room. I wanted to squash their beef right then, and there. I could tell Azhley was thinking the same thing by the way she watched Ladibug's every move with a mean mug on her face. I gripped the handle of my pool stick, and was seriously contemplating cracking Ladibug right upside her head. Before I could even get to make my move, an officer announced that our time was up. Just as we began to make our way to the door I noticed Ladibug putting something in her pocket, but I didn't get a good look at the object. When I looked to see if she noticed me watching her, she gave me a wave, and a smile. I just flipped Ladibug the middle finger, and walked out the door.

"You gone get dealt with real soon, Bitch," I mumbled under my breath with a smile.

Later on that evening during dinner, I was pissed as we walked through the food line. Ladibug was standing directly behind me, and she was really annoying the hell out of me. I was trying my best not to pay her any attention, but she just kept rambling on and on about "sloppy joe," being served for dinner tonight.

"This bitch has to be off her meds," I thought to myself, because sloppy joe wasn't anywhere on the menu.

Usually, I would sit in the back with Mizz, but today I was going to sit with Azhley so we could discuss further details about the hit we were planning on Ladibug. I, swear every move I made towards where Azhley was siting, Ladibug followed me. I started to get a feeling of paranoia inside thinking maybe this bitch was up to something, but I held my composure. I purposely made a left towards the table that Mizz was sitting at. Mizz was looking right at me, and I was trying my best to give her the heads up that something was wrong. Before, I could motion to Mizz to look behind me; she was distracted by a chick that she had been on for weeks about money that was owed to her. I was just about to slap the taste out of Ladibug's mouth with my tray of food I was holding, when she switched directions. The next time I looked up to get Mizz's attention Ladibug was standing at Mizz's table. I saw Ladibug pull something from her waist, but I was in shock. Once the guards pulled her off Mizz, I knew it was over for my lover. Ladibug had beaten the hell out of Mizz with a pool ball she had stolen earlier, and then stabbed Mizz in the neck. Mizz died instantly, and I was devastated standing there looking at Mizz lifeless body. A part of me died with Mizz as I stood there letting the reality sink in.

The words "sloppy joe for dinner," kept repeating itself in my head. I finally understood what the crazy, bitch meant as I watched blood ooze out of Mizz's forehead. I couldn't believe her beautiful face was ruined by the ball that was repeatedly smashed into it. I felt paralyzed as I watched them finally carry out her lifeless body.

"Love sure does hurt," I wailed through tears then thought back to my favorite song "Never Want To Live Without You," by Eric Benet.

I was feeling just like Mizz, now. I understood exactly how she felt after her one true love was taken away from her. I also promised myself that I would get revenge for her death if it were the last thing I did. I was in the shower on day thinking back on the song "Set A Drift On Memory Bliss," by P.M. Dawn and all the pain in my life flashed before my eyes. I felt like the girl off the song "Memories," by T.I. because life makes you make some bad decisions at time in order to survive. I realized everything that had happen to me was either a lesson, blessing or curse depending on the situation, and the people involved. I had also had so many people die on me that I began to feel like I wasn't meant to love anymore. Everything, I loved seemed to be taken away from me. I let the tears roll wildly and free as the water washed them away. I feel you P.M Dawn, maybe it is my time to wish I could have them all back, but not be able to do a damn thing about it. All I could do was cry while the voice inside my head peer pressured my wounded ego.

"Ladibug thinks you're weak," my mind yelled at me.

"She's gonna kill you next," the evil voice laughed as tears rolled down my face.

"You ain't gone do shit about it either, but cry like a baby every night," it continued to taunt me, and before I knew it I was yelling at the wall.

"I'm gone kill that Bitch," I chanted over, and over and I meant every word. In fact, I was already ten steps ahead of whatever Ladibug thought she had planned for me. All I had to do now was put my plan in motion, and it was "OVER WITH" for her ass.

"Your time on earth is limited, boo," I laughed, and then grabbed my towel.

You know what they say: "keep your friends close, enemies closer." I couldn't trust a soul, and I couldn't be any closer to cutting that bitch Ladibug's life span short. The first thing I did was get Ladibug's flunky to turn on her. It didn't even take much to convince her, either. Being that I had recently taken over Mizz position in her crew I had a couple connects here and there. I had a point to prove, and Ladibug was my primary target.

It had been two long weeks, since Mizz was murdered. I arranged a special lunch in Mizz's honor just for Ladibug. I also purposely got in line directly behind Ladibug, just so I could play out the role she did on the day she took Mizz's life.

"How ironic," I let out a sinister laugh as I marveled in the moment.

I watched Ladibug put her food on her tray before she turned, and shot me a nasty look.

"Frown all you want, Bitch," the sinister voice yelled.

"Nothing can help you, now," my mind theorized.

I had been planning Ladibug's death for weeks, and I was glad my plan was finally falling into place. It was time for lunch, and I could wait.

"Looks like we're having sloppy joes, today," I acknowledged, and then gave the girl serving the food a little wink.

I followed Ladibug's every step once I got my tray. Right before she got to her table, I took a seat at a table facing directly in front hers. I didn't even eat as I sat staring at Ladibug from across the room watching her every move. When she noticed me looking at her I politely gave her a "smile and wave". Ladibug just roll her eyes to the heavens. A few minutes later, I watched her eat her entire meal then I got up and walked over in her direction. I could see the fear in her eyes but I played it cool as I walked past her table. Right before I walked past her seat, I stopped so she could be the only one to hear me.

"How does it feel to know that you're going to die before I reach the garbage can," I whispered.

"Heart attack," I laughed, and then told her I hoped she enjoyed her last meal.

I laughed some more as I walked away and she tried to get up and reply something. I turned around just in time to see her clutch her chest and fall to the floor.

"Are you okay?" I screamed, and then ran to her aid.

I leaned in real close to her shaking body, looked her straight in the eyes and whispered.

"It's a coldblooded world we live in," I giggled.

"I'm the bitch called, Payback," I finished right before she took her last breath, and the guards arrived.

Ladibug was so set on killing me, that she never even noticed the bottle of poison she kept hidden missing after the wild time she had with the girl I had serve her, her last meal.

"I bet she's still hearing my voice in hell," I laughed, but even her death wasn't enough to comfort my broken heart.

Dear Diary,
October 25, 2014

Three years later, I was counting down the days until my freedom. I had been showing improvement in my behavior, and was one of the top ranked girls in the fire fighters rescue squad. It had been a long, and draining three and half years in prison, but my day of freedom was soon to come. I was so happy when June 14, 2012, came because I was released from prison. I had to do two years of probation, and three hundred hours of community service, but that was the least of my worries. Prison was another lesson I had to learn the hard way, and I was just lucky I came home stronger than I went in. My girl, Rozi, decided to throw me a coming home party. Rozi even offered me a place to live until I got back on my feet. I was glad we connected during my first semester of college, because I really needed someone other than the Franklyn's in my corner. She also put me on with a job at a new club she was part owner at called "Dirty Secretz". Nobody, except me knew that about Rozi secret business venture with Duty. I was just grateful that I made good money there every night. Being a stripper can have its benefits, but some days I still can't believe this is how things turned out for me. I was extremely, blessed to be home nonetheless, and I knew soon enough I would be back to the old me. Even though, everything in my life seemed to be going perfect. It wasn't a day that went by that Mizz didn't cross my mind. I even made up my mind that I would never fall in love again. It was certain types of hurts in this lifetime that I could avoid, and love happened to be one of them. One day, while I was at Somerset mall with my friend Rozi, I met this guy named, Omega. We were walking into the Victoria Secret outlet when Omega followed us into the store. At first glance, I was impressed with Omega's overall appearance. I was unsure if I wanted to talk to Omega when he approached. We stood there conversing for a few, and then he asked me for my phone number. Even though I felt unsure, I was intrigued by his persistence, and confidence even after I turned him down a few times.

"How charming." I thought as I stood in Victoria Secret trying to figure out what new panties I wanted to buy.

"You're just not going take no for an answer," I asked him while laughing, and shaking my head.

"Take my number down," he insisted, grabbing my cell and entering his number in it before I could say, "NO".

I just laughed. Anyone who had the balls to take something out of my hands had to be a boss, so I let him give me his number, and promised to call him.

"If you need anything," he continued.

"Call me," he told me right before I approached the counter to pay for my items.

"Whatever!" I said, and then he walked away.

Later on that evening, while I was at home watching reruns of "The Wire," on demand, I was in need of some weed, but was too lazy to get up and go get it. I wanted someone to deliver some to my house, but everyone I called was busy. I thought back to my encounter with Mega earlier, and him telling me: "to call him if I needed anything," and decided to hit him up. To my surprise, he answered on the second ring, and I wasn't shocked when he told me he was the weed man. He also happened to stay in my area, so I ended the conversation by telling him I would text the address. A few minutes later, he was at my doorstep Johnny on the spot. I didn't even have to pay him, either. From that point on, Mega, became my new weed man. One day, while he was dropping off my weed for the week, he asked if he could take me out, and I agreed. We had a great first date at this Mexican restaurant in southwest, Detroit, and the next day he brought me a dozen white roses. He was such a great listener, I thought admiring my flowers. I never would have expected him to remember that white roses were my favorite because I only mentioned it once during a brief conversation. I was impressed that Mega was quite the gentle man every time we went out together, despite being a product of the hood. A few great dates later, I was happy that I had given Omega a chance to date me. He was nothing that I had expected him to be, and he even gave me a better outlook on life. I thought he would be like every other hood nigga with money who is constantly flossing everything they get, but he was the total opposite. Omega was humble, kind, a very respectful. I could tell that Mega, didn't really like the lifestyle choice he had chosen for himself, but I also knew it was what made him the man he was, today. Mega had a hard life growing up, so he was never going back to being broke, and I felt him on that aspect. On our first date, he brought me a Christian Dior outfit with a matching pair of Louis Vuitton gym shoes, just because. I had to admit, every date I went on with Mega after that impressed the hell out of me. Before, I knew it weeks had turned into a month, and I was falling for him.

"Mega was really turning out to be an amazing guy," I thought as we sat enjoying dinner.

"Could it be, love?" I wondered as Trick Daddy, and Twista, played while we drove on the freeway back to his apartment. I was so tipsy off the shots of Tequila I had during our date that it was really starting to feel like I could have been falling in love all over again! I quickly shook the feeling I was having off because I was scared to fall in love again. The only thing that was on my mind was the $850.00 dollars, Mega, said he would give me later that evening if I let him take me home, and have his way with me, tonight. Mega loved pleasing me, and seeing me smile on a daily basis, but he also loved giving me money more. I was nervous as we drove just thinking about us having sex for the first time, and I sure as hell wasn't about to turn him down, now. I knew that doing nice things for me was his way of showing me that he truly cared, but I didn't ever want him to think he could buy my love. Little did he know, I would have given it up if he hadn't given me that much money. He had earned this pussy, and tonight I was going to show him a thing or two.

"Are you serious?" I giggled taking another sip of my drink, and his look said it all as he passed me $800.00 crispy dollars.

"You know you didn't have to do this right?" I asked, and I could tell he wanted every inch of my body on his, and the way I was feeling after taking all those shots, I wanted him too.

"That's nothing." He replied, and I laughed even harder thinking about the night ahead of me.

"Tonight just might be your lucky night, Mega." The naughty girl in my head screamed, as "Bed Peace" by Jhene' Aiko played.

Now I Understand
Dear Diary,
November 5, 2014

"Baby," I whined, rolling onto my stomach.

I had been patiently laying on Omega's bed, gazing out the window at the water while waiting for him to put his dick inside of me. I was on fire after the unexplainably great head job he had given me a couple minutes ago.

"Ugh!" I sighed into the pillow, because the feeling of the orgasm I just had was wearing off and I was yearning for more.

"I'm sorry, babe," he muttered while going to work on his penis with his right hand trying to get it back erect.

"It's, Okay!" I whined, and then stood up off the bed and gave him a kiss.

 It was really starting to seem like it was hard for Mega to stay hard ever since the first time we had sex. The foreplay was always incredible, I must admit. I absolutely loved the way Mega worked his tongue in and out of my vagina as if he was their personal decorator. His touch alone sent chills through my entire body, causing me to explode all in his mouth, which he loves. Passion was something we always shared but our sex was horrible. I guess it was a good thing he has a big bank roll, because he sure knows how to make up for what he lacks. I also love that he doesn't mind the fact that I'm a stripper. This made me start to appreciate having Omega in my life, simply because he stayed true to his word just as he promised me. When I first met Omega, I had my doubts about him. He proved me wrong by being nothing but loyal to me. It hasn't been an easy process getting me to show my true feelings, but I honestly loved the way Mega handled my bitchy attitude. Other than my new boo, lifestyle, and school, I had recently finished with all my hours of community service, and I was real close to being off probation. I felt as if I could just reach like Goapele says in "Closer," and my dream will be reality. I can honestly say that I have been doing much better now that all the negativity is out of my life, too. I had also just gotten my Lexus painted, thanks to Mega. I wasn't sure what color to get at first, but I ended up painting my car Aqua, since I was born in March, and it was my favorite color. My car also happens to be the only Lexus I have ever seen that color. Mega was always on me about being original and standing out, so I felt it was only right to pick a color everyone would notice. I loved Mega's reasoning for many of the things he often did in life, and I adored the fact that he is also teaching me how to save my money, which is something I never really thought much about before. Sure, I stashed a couple dollars away here and there for a rainy day, but I never thought about opening my own bank account. Omega saw things differently. He was always giving me good advice and it all was helping me grow as a woman. Everything Mega ever got in life he had to work hard for in the streets. He always told me "to pave a better way for my future while I was doing well in my present". He was right because life as you know it can change in the blink of an eye.

""You have to be prepared for the unexpected bumps that show up in every road."

"You either learn how to drive in your own lane, or you're going to be broke down somewhere on the side of the road." He would always tell me.

"Nothing in life is just handed to you." Omega would always say, ending his sentence, and I knew it all too well that nothing in life was free. Everything in life came with a price. The real question was how much you were you willing to pay to get where you really wanted to go.

Mega, and I, both had learned early on in life that handouts were not something you could always depend on. Omega was the middle child of three. His older brother was born with Autism, so Omega took on the role as older brother. Although, Mega, always wished his older brother functioned like everyone that he knew, He also knew that he had to be his protector, forever. Mega became a force to reckon with at the age of thirteen. Being that his household lacked a father figure at times: Mega became just that after he learned of his father's unexpected death. His mother started drinking, and doing drugs after that. She would often leave the children home alone for days at a time. During those times, when the boys were out of food, Mega and his best friend Frankie would run errands for some of the dope boys in the hood to make money. Now, whenever his mother would decide to go on her weekly crack binges, which often led to them being abandoned for months, he was prepared. Omega was able to feed his two siblings, and buy them the things they needed around the house. To Mega, the streets were now his parents because the streets became his provider. One day, their mom disappeared for good, claiming that she was going to the grocery store. After a month went by without so much as a word from his mother, Mega, knew what he had to do. He made sure his brother and sister went to school on time every day, which kept the neighbors from becoming suspicious. He also was fronted a couple of sacks of marijuana by his boy Chico, to get him started in the game, and money in his pockets. After a year of hustling, it was over for the child he once was. At the age of fourteen, Mega, knew right then, and there that it wasn't any going back to the boy he once was. He was now the man in all their lives.

"The Three Stooges," he once called them, and their mischievous behavior was also, what landed each one of them behind bars at an early age. After a few lock ups in the juvenile corrections facilities, it was clear that Omega was going to grow up to be a menace. He never had a real family being that his mother was an only child and her parents were deceased. He didn't really know his father until a year before he died, so in his eyes it was him and his siblings against the world. He got into some trouble when he was seventeen, during a break in gone terribly wrong with a friend. After both boys were caught red handed in the act by the owners of the house, they ended up behind bars for two years. Once he came home when he was nineteen, the streets became Omega's new best friend. A couple years later, he earned the reputation of being a well-known dope man in his area, but he was also someone everyone easily loved. Mega was such a wonderful person inside, and many people respected him. He was very loyal, and someone most people trusted. He was a very outspoken person but if you ever needed him, he would be there Johnny on the spot. He was the kindest person I ever knew that was raised by the streets, but he didn't play when it came to his money. He was actually the one that gave me the "Pass Go Please Collect $200," saying I often liked to use. If it was less than $200.00, you didn't need to call Mega's phone. To Omega life was like Monopoly.

"It's all easy money once you have a name made for yourself in this game," he would often say, and I admired that. I was trying to build a brand that would continue to bring in revenue, even when I was long gone. When it came to current events, Mega, knew about any, and everything that was going on in the world. I can honestly say that in the little time that we've known one another; I have learned so much about life from

Mega, and how to really live my life to the fullest. Mega offered my soul so much in so little time. Mega, always kept a positive attitude, and I loved that he was always honest, loyal, and truthful with me. I loved being with Mega, because he was the total opposite of Ize, who was full of mystery. Mega never tried to make me feel insecure, or jealous during our time together. In fact, he would do anything for me, and he genuinely cared about my best interest. Mega was also very big on verbal affirmation. He was constantly reassuring me that I held a place in his heart that no woman would ever have once I was gone. I, on the other hand, was withdrawn, and confused when it came to being in love with any man other than, Ize. I figured the best thing I could do was be patient with love if I wanted things to work out. After dating Mizz, I wasn't sure if I could love, again even though, Mega, seemed like he could be the chosen one. It was a slow night, in Dirty Secrets the first time I invited Mega to see me dance. I gave him his own little private show after I worked the pole to "Fuckin' Problem," by A$ap Rocky. I had him gone off the Patron, and before I knew it, we were fucking in the V.I.P. section. It all happened so fast, and I loved every minute of it. I was giving him a lap dance, and it turned me on to know that he hadn't heard the song before I danced to it. I was even more excited to know that he loved the way I danced with grace, unlike the other girls he'd seen perform before me.

"You don't even need to dance, La'Teazya," he whispered in my ears as "She Gettin' It" by Cali Swag District began to play.

"I know," I answered.

"I do it simply because, it's easy money, baby," I giggled, twerkin' my ass cheeks.

I was always about my money before he came along, but Mega pushed me to be better when it came to saving it. He was pleased hearing that I never got involved with any of the people that I met here daily.

 "I'm bout that money, baby," I whispered, while leaning in to give him a kiss. During work hours, I fulfilled all fantasies. I was every man's dream woman turned professional stripper. Every show I performed spoke for itself. I was a natural born sex goddess without the film or magazine. The bonus for each of my tricks was the fact that I got nude each night. We both laughed in unison as I explained my logic behind my decision to become a stripper. Mega just smiled, and continued to listen. He knew I was dead, serious. I didn't plan on being a stripper my whole life, but for now I was going to use what I got to get what I wanted. Right now, all I needed was enough money to rebuild my life, and I was going to get that by any means necessary.

"The work I do joyfully is the only possible work for me," I giggled to myself as I danced, thinking about this Pisces affirmation of the year quote I read earlier in my horoscope.

I was so good at what I did that I only danced two, maybe three times a night, and I would leave the top paid stripper of each night. Mrs. Franklyn always told me "to be the best at whatever I did in life," so I shook this money, maker for all it was worth every time I hit the stage. Then I would go home and lay in my money like Scrooge McDuck. It felt good to be independent for once in my life. Sure Mega tried to spoil me, but at the end of the day, what was mine was mine. Nothing I had in my new life was something that Ize, Cazh, or the Franklyn's gave me. For the first time I was living the statement: "God bless the child who has their own". I even paid the Franklyn's back for all my lawyer fees they paid for me. I had to make them take the money by just leaving it on the dining room table after dinner one evening. I felt it was the least I could do, because they had done so much for me my whole life. I was only twenty-three years old, and I was finally living my life liked it was golden.

"You should just move in with me and let me take care of you forever," Mega suggested so sincere.

"I would marry you if you were ready, Teaz," he stated.

I just walked away after hitting him with the "I have to use the ladies room," line. It was the fastest lie I could come up with so I could avoid responding. I knew in a way I loved Mega, and ever since we met the man has done nothing but live up to his word. Mega, showed me nothing but unconditional love and has proven to be above my expectations.

"I just don't seem to know why I'm so scared to fully commit to him," I thought to myself through tears.

I stood there trying hard to make sense of it all. I finally have the perfect man in my life that accepts me for me, and yet I cannot fully give him my heart. I let the tears flow wildly down my cheeks as "Sanctuary" by French Montana played. Actions always spoke louder than words, and my actions right now weren't matching the way Mega was feeling. I felt bad, because I wasn't able to give him the same love he was giving me.

"Wow!" Mega's favorite song would be on while I'm in here crying over dumb shit.

"Why can't you just love him, Teaz?" my mind asked itself.

"The man is clearly in love with you and you're going to pass up the opportunity to have real love for what?" I questioned myself.

I stood there starring deep in the mirror, and Mizz popped in my head. I had tried not to even think about Mizz after her death. In a way, I felt like

Mizz now, except I was Jazmine. I just wanted to forget it all. I felt the love we once shared, and then I felt the sadness all over again.

"Maybe, that's it," I assured my weary heart, and then wiped my face.

"I'm scared that if I love Omega to much that he'll get taken away from me, just like everyone else I loved in my life," I concluded.

"I will not let my fears stand in the way of me getting what I deserve," I thought, and then checked my face so I could head out the bathroom.

As soon as I opened the door, Young Jeezy's song, "Tear That Pussy Up" began to fill the room. The club had picked up a bit with a few crowds here and there, but I could see Mega patiently waiting for me to return.

"Teaz!" he shouted with a big smile on his face before I could reach his table.

"I thought you got lost, babe."

"Are you okay?" he asked with a bit of concern in his voice

"I'm great, baby," I answered, and then walked up to him and gave him a big kiss before I put it down on his ass to Jeezy's song.

I could tell that he was feeling my performance by the hardiness growing in his pants. I told him I was ready to end my night and to meet me in his car once the song ended. I got dressed quickly and headed out the club to find Mega. I knew my Boo would be waiting to see what else I had up my sleeves. I only had one agenda, little did he know, and that was to give Mega the fuck of his life tonight. That little five minutes we shared in the V.I.P. section of the club had me open, and I was in need of some dick. "Dopeman," by a local Detroit artist name Jesse James was playing when I hoped in the passenger seat of Mega's new Benz SL class. A couple weeks after being pulled over by the cops in his black on black, BMW, Mega, got a new car. He swore his new vehicle was going to make his profile more low-key. I literally listened to Mega talk about staying under the radar for weeks after he brought his new ride. Once he got a new paint job, and matching Forgiato chrome rims, I knew that being "low key," idea was history.

"Here, baby," Mega said, passing me the blunt and turning up the volume as "Wicked Ways" by Raven Soars began to play.

"I swear the author Raven Soars, is multi-talented," I stated, as I rapped along with her verse. Once it was over Mega turned the volume down so he could continue to listen to me talk.

"She reminds me so much of myself," I acknowledged, thinking back on an interview I watched of hers. She was talking about her life, and the obstacles she had to overcome just to become a great author.

"I've read everything she's ever written, and I love her poems!" I told him, then starting reciting my favorite poem by her.

"Sometimes, I sit alone a lot, and stare right into space. Thinking about all the things, I have done in life; and will the bad things, be erased. I know I might be wasting time on this fascinating daydream. Far from a nightmare, because I awake without a scream. In fact, I think I like my past as crazy as it may be. It makes me who I am today, part of my "HISTORY". The shoes I wear are running miles, and slightly worn down. From carrying heavy loads and smiles turned upside down. A broken past of much regret, and secrets I will never tell. My life although it looks perfect, I know I have rose above my hell. I look back on things that have come to past, and call them "WAKE UP CALLS". Who cares about the things I have done, I am splendid "AFTER ALL".

"I See Me, The Turning Point, and Too Late," are all classics, but "I See Me" is my favorite. I smiled and so did Mega, as I thought back to when I read a couple of her poems from her poetry book. Raven was my daily escape from the whole prison life. She was also the one who inspired me to change after Mizz's death, so I joined the Firefighter Rescue Squad. Mega just sat there listening to me ramble on and on about Raven Soars, and I loved that he always let me be me. I felt free around Mega, because he never judged me. He always knew how to lift my spirit, and that was exactly the type of man I needed. Omega and I sat talking for a while, and then he changed the cd.

"So what do you want for dinner tonight?" he asked as my jam "Never Getting Back Together," by Taylor Swift came on.

"Since I already know what you'll be eating," I joked, patting my pussy.

"I guess, I'll have that new 24-hour soul food joint that delivers," I teased.

He just laughed, and then picked up his phone and placed our orders. Once he was finished, he told me to meet him back at his place for dinner. I agreed, then gave him a kiss and headed to my car. As soon as I put my key in the ignition, my jam "High Road," by Broken Bells came on. I instantly began to zone out to the song on my drive to Mega's, house. The group was absolutely, right. The high road is a hard place to find considering the fact that we live in a world full of corruption. By the time "Beautiful Ones," by Prince went off, my mind was all over the place. I knew Mega loved me, but I knew that my heart was elsewhere at times. I had to be a fool for loving, Ize after everything he had put me through in the past. I went to jail because I kept on associating with the man, yet here I was driving to see a man that loves me thinking about a man whose love is questionable. I pulled up at the gate to Mega's apartment building, gave the man a little smile, and then parked my car. I stepped on the elevator, and I could not help but think about how I was going to put it down on Mega once I saw him. It had been a month since we had sex and my body was yearning for some "Sexual Healing," like Marvin Gaye sang about. Food was the furthest thing on my mind once Mega answered the door. I showered him with kisses leading him towards his bedroom but decided to get it on right, then, and there in the living room. I unbuckled Mega's pants, pulling out his penis, and then I dropped to my knees and gave him some head. I had never done this to any man other than Ize before today, but I knew I had to try something new to get what I wanted. Mega was enjoying every minute of it too. Once I got him where I wanted him, I pushed him on the coach and slid down on his dick. I took my time riding Mega, looking him deep in the eyes as he matched my strokes.

"I love you, La'Teazya," he moaned, and I just rode him until we both climaxed. I was feeling ecstatic afterwards as I headed to the shower.

"That month without sex was definitely worth the wait." I thought to myself as my song "No Hands" by Waka Flacka played in the background.

"Girl, drop it to the floor I love the way your booty goes,"

"All I wanna do is sit back, and watch you move while I proceed to throw this cash." I sang along, thinking, that is right, Waka Flaka.

"I know, Daddy bout to break Mommy off something real nice after that session of love making I just put down." I laughed just thinking about Mega sleeping like a baby afterwards. Trust me when I say, "Ain't nothing like the powerful potion of pure pussy."

The club was packed the following Friday, night. For some odd reason, I wasn't feeling like my usual self that night. I decided to go home early after I did a few shows. I ended the night dancing to my new jam "Playhouse," by Raven Soars featuring Rayo Wolfgang. Once I made a quick $800.00 dollars, I was ready to go. On my way home, I decided to stop at the closest Buffalo Wild Wings before I went in for the evening and that is when I met Oz. First impressions were everything, and I could tell Oz was nothing like his brother Legend. I stood listening to the conversation Oz was having. He was very arrogant when he spoke, young, flashy, and hotheaded. Every other word he used was a curse word, and the word "Bitch" seemed to be one of his favorites. Although, Oz wasn't as attractive as his older brother, I knew his money is what made him so debonair. Oz was covered in tattoos, had three teardrops under his right eye, and I could tell he wasn't the charmer that Legend was from the few stories Zar had told me. Just listening to Oz talk made me feel sad.

"The good ones always die young, while the fools are left to walk the Earth." I thought as I shook my head in disgust. It was ironic that I would run into Oz, when I knew that Oz moved here set on revenge for his brother Legends' death. I tried to avoid him, but he was attracted to me from the moment I entered the door. He reminded me of the snake that came to visit Eve in the Garden of Eden as he approached me. Once he introduced himself, I turned him down without a second thought. I was happy to have a real man in my life, so I used that as my excuse to avoid exchanging phone numbers with him. I even went as far as to lie, and say my fiancé was outside in the car waiting for me to come back out.

Oz just looked at me, and laughed.

"I'mma see you around, Lil' Mama," I heard him say as I grabbed my carry out bag, and headed out of the door.

It was exactly a week later, when I ran back into Oz. The club was crowded with people the following Saturday night for my girl Champion's birthday party. This group of ballers sitting at one of the back booths kept asking for me, personally to dance for them. After turning the group down a couple times, I decided to just do one lap dance for the first person I ran into once I reached the table. I laughed inside once I walked over to the table and discovered why they were so persistent about having me dance. I watched Oz admire my figure, and then he asked me to come over to where he was.

"I told you I was gone see you around, Lil' Mama," he smirked, and then pulled out a stack of hundreds.

 He then slid three crispy $100.00 dollar bills in my panties, and I went to work. "We Up" by 50 Cent began to play, and I did the fool as Oz continued to tip me hundreds. Once "Real Nigga," by a Detroit group named The Lodge Boyz started to play, I felt like 50 Cent, as I now danced for the entire table. Oz was everything the lyrics rapped about, and I was showing out considering the fact that I was the only girl dancing at their table. I had literally made one night's pay in less than thirty minutes, I thought as "Money Trees" by Kendrick Lamar played. By the time "Whatever U Want" by Consequence came on, I was racking in the dollars from all directions. This time around, Oz, had my full attention because he kept spending money on me. I decided to invite him to one of our private rooms to dance for him, alone. My real plan was to get him alone to find out more information about him. Being that it was rumored that Oz wanted Ize, and Cazh dead, it was only right to try to find out how much he knew about them. Of course, he agreed, and then we made our way through the crowded club towards the steps leading to, Heaven. "Heaven" was the name of the room I was taking Oz to, and for a moment, I felt like Vanity in the movie, "The Last Dragon". I was definitely about to take Oz to "7th Heaven." I couldn't help but to watch Oz as we walked. I loved the fact that he was already on cloud nine. I watched him stare at my ass, and lick his lips repeatedly while I made my way to the room. The moment we stepped into the room, Gorilla Zoe's song "I Got It" came on.

"Perfect song, DJ," I chuckled, and then walked over to the stage.

I worked that pole as Oz sat enjoying the show. I threw my naked ass all kinds of ways as he continued to throw hundreds at me. I had to admit, I loved every minute with this fool Oz. This stupid nigga was paying me a week worth of tips in one night. I crawled to him so seductively once the song was over while "Lick," by Joi played. As soon as I reached his lap, I dropped my face into it, and he just sat back and relaxed. The illusion I was putting on of me giving him a blowjob had Oz, spellbound as I danced while watching him start to get an erection.

"You like this huh, Oz?" I teased him, while rubbing my breasts in his face.

"I'm diggin' the total package my, baby," he responded, and then took a sip of his drink he ordered during the last song I danced too.

"Really?" I replied, watching him caress his penis.

I had Oz right where I wanted him. I also knew what he wanted from me after all the seducing I was doing to his body. It was so amazing to have so much power over such a vulnerable creature, and men have the nerves to call us weak.

"Please," I giggled inside while watching the spell I was putting on Oz, take over.

"This was a piece of cake," I giggled inside some more.

Getting a man was like taking candy from a baby. The mere fantasy of being with me sexually made men weak in the knees, like SWV once sang.

"You must be quite the businessman?" I stated as the song ended.

I already knew what Oz did for a living. I just wanted to hear the words from his, own mouth.

"What makes you say that, Lil' Mama?" he asked as I continued to dance.

"Generally speaking," I replied.

"I get a lot of those guys in here," I added.

"I was really just wondering if you were always this generous with the ladies," I quizzed, but I wasn't really interested in the answer.

"I guess you can call me a businessman," he stated.

"I am the head nigga in charge in my organization," he boasted, and I took a seat before the song changed.

"What type of business do you run, if you don't mind me asking?" I asked, taking a sip of my drink I poured myself.

"I run the city right now, my baby," he boldly told me, and I smiled.

"You arrogant, Muthafucker," I thought, but I continued to smile and sip my glass.

"Do you?" I asked, acting clueless.

I had to admit, I was playing the best role of Ize's favorite saying: "Play dumb, but don't ever be a fool".

"Yea, really boo," Oz explained, taking a couple sips of his drink

"I came down here to take over once my brother got killed and that's exactly what I've been doing," he grinned, then finished his glass and poured another.

"I can see that, Daddy!" I assured him, leaning into him so he could look me in the eyes.

"You sure look like the Man to me," I lied, hitting him with the line Vanity used in the "Last Dragon" movie on Bruce Leeroy.

"Where is the, wife?" I asked, as if I really cared.

As far as I was concerned, I had to keep Oz close and his money closer. He was the best enemy a girl like me could have. He was literally a walking ATM machine that would eventually put out more than he could afford to pay.

"U.O.E.N.O." by Mega came on, and it amused the hell out of me that this fool had the nerve to be cocky. Oz didn't even know that I was the ex-girlfriend of the guy who was the cause of his brothers' death. I stood up, walked over to the pole, and showed out to the song that was playing. I was pulling out all the tricks I had in my bag while I danced for him. He was hypnotized by the performance I was putting on for him, but I was feeling like Elmer Fudd with a masterplan. Checkmate, I smiled then blew Oz a kiss. I had found myself, one silly rabbit, to prey on. We exchanged numbers, and he made me promise to let him take me out sometimes. I did, and that was one promise I was definitely planning on keeping. After closing, I jumped in my car and "You Won't See Me Tonight," by Nas started to play. I just laughed as I counted my money, thinking Oz was the biggest dummy I had ever met.

A couple weeks later, Mega and I had decided to take a trip to Mackinaw Island for the weekend. This also happened to be when I first started getting calls from Oz. One night while Mega was asleep, I answered the phone from Oz. I told him I was out of town with my girls and that I would hit him up whenever I got back to the city. To my surprise, he told me "that he'd be waiting on me, and I'd better call him as soon as I got back". I had to laugh because the only thing Oz could ever offer me was his money.

"Silly Rabbit," I mused.

"Trix are for kids!" I laughed as I mocked the bunny off the cereal commercial.

Two weeks later, I was at chilling, watching "Set It Off," when I decided to call Oz, and see what he was doing. To my surprise, he picked up the phone after the first ring, asking when he could see me, and I told him if he wasn't busy later on that night that we could hook up. I could hear a person's voice in the background telling him something about finding the location to "Nigga's he had been looking for where-a bout's." He quickly ended the conversation, telling me that he would call me later on, and I knew in my heart the person was talking about Ize, and Cazh.

"What you gone do, Teaz?" I thought as I paced back and forth.

I hadn't talked to either of them since before we all got locked up, three years ago. I tried writing Barbie a couple of times before but never got a response so I stopped trying to write her long ago. I knew what she had to be going through living the prison life, so I figured I would just let her be. There are certain people, and things you have to leave in your past in order to move forward, and I guess Barbie was one of them. I knew I had to somehow get word to Ize about this whole Oz, situation. I couldn't just let something happen to him knowing that I could have at least tried to warn him. It was so crazy that after all these years I would still felt the need to talk to Ize. This was one chapter of my life that should have been closed by now, but for some odd reason, I still felt bonded to, Ize. What were the odds of me running into Oz, and finding out what I did about Ize? I probably wouldn't even be thinking about Ize right now if that hadn't of happened. Of course, he crossed my mind periodically, but I was good now that I had Mega. I felt like I was right back to square one. Wrapped up in Ize's drama after I finally escaped it all because of the love I had for him. I decided to write him a letter using our secret language code that we had made up as kids. As kids, we would communicate like this often, especially when we wanted to write dirty letters to each other so I wouldn't get caught by my Mama. Zarbreah hated it, too, because she never could decode any of our secret codes. I typed his name into the prisoners search website to find out his prison information and once I found out everything I needed to know, I started my letter. The first letter I wrote, I balled up, because I didn't really know what to say to Ize. I wasn't really sure I was ready to open up the can of worms I knew would crawl out. The second letter, finally expressed all I needed to say. I even added my new number, and then thought maybe that wasn't such a good idea after the envelope was sealed. I had moved on with my life, and I didn't really need to hear his voice after all these years. It was crazy that after all the hurt and betrayal, I was still loyal to Izir.

The next morning, I woke up feeling "grrr-reat,' like Tony the tiger exclaimed. I was playing my jam "Until The End Of Time," by Tupac making breakfast, when Mega came into the kitchen. I could tell something was wrong with him off rip.

"Good morning," I beamed, walking up to give him a kiss as he opened the refrigerator.

He didn't even bother to respond as he poured his glass. He just shot me a look I couldn't quite distinguish, and walked out the kitchen.

"Is he ignoring, me?" I asked myself, while singing along to Pac.

I finished cooking breakfast then took him his plate in the living room where he was sitting.

"What's wrong, baby?"

"Did you sleep okay?" I asked concerned, handing him his plate.

"I'm good, Teaz," he responded dryly.

"Are you, okay?" he asked me, and I was confused.

I was good up until a few seconds ago. I didn't understand why he was acting funny towards me when we were all lovey-dovey right before we went to bed last night. I took a seat next to him on the coach then leaned in to give him another kiss and out of nowhere, he was telling me to "Come on with all the mushy shit".

"Ok, Mr. Attitude," I said standing up to head back to the kitchen to fix my plate.

I wondered what got his panties in a bunch, but I wasn't about to press the issue. I fixed our plates as "Jazzybelle," by Outkast played, and I was really starting to get annoyed by all the ignoring me games he was trying to play.

"Damn!"

"I can't even offer this Nigga some jelly for his toast without him saying: I don't care," I mimicked his last remark.

I heard him turn on the television after that. He even had the nerve to turn it up loud as if he was trying to say: "Fuck Me".

Well, that did it. I was about to get down to the bottom line of this little attitude problem he was having.

"What's up, Mega?" I asked, deliberately standing in front of the television.

"Hello, can you hear me now?" I asked, mocking the people on the Verizon commercials.

I took a seat beside him then cut the television off.

"What I don't understand is why you're mad at me right now," I stated, clueless.

"Don't I treat you like a queen, La'Teazya? Mega inquired, and before I could answer, he cut me off.

"I do everything you ask of me, and beyond without a hesitation just like I always said I would, right?" he asked, but his eyes were pleading with me.

"So please tell me why I find a balled up letter to your ex on the table in my guess room?" he asked, and I was speechless.

I thought I had thrown the first letter away, but apparently, I forgot, too. I guess it is a good thing that he didn't get to see the one that was in my overnight bag. I was so embarrassed being caught up in some bullshit, but I wasn't about to let this whole letter situation fuck up a good thing.

"I'm saying, Mega, you're sitting here mad over a balled up piece of paper!" I snapped.

"Think about it, Boo," I said moving in closer to him.

"I haven't talked to Ize in years," I added, because that was the truth.

"I was just going to write him, and see how he was doing," I lied, and then cuddled up to Mega.

"As you can see," I nodded towards the paper he had on the table, and then kissed his cheek.

"I decided against it."

"I would never intentionally try to hurt you, Mega," I promised him, while looking him deep in the eyes.

In all honesty, I meant every word I had said about not wanting to hurt Mega. He was a good man despite his upbringing, and I knew he loved me dearly. I didn't ever want to lose that love all, because I was trapped in a web of chaos from my past. Something had to give, and I damn sure wasn't giving up Mega anytime too soon. This little white lie isn't going to hurt anyone, I thought. This was going to be the first and only day Mega would ever have to question my loyalty, because I wanted him in my life forever. We actually had a breakthrough in our relationship during our talk we had that evening. We found out that we have a lot in common as far as our viewpoints were on love, loyalty and life. We also decided that were just going to take things slow, because we are all just "Ordinary People," like John Legend, sang. We both were content with just seeing where the future leads us, but it was clear Mega was in love with me. I also realized that maybe I was more in love with Mega, than I could have ever imagined. I was just too stubborn to admit it. He told me he understood how I felt, and that I could tell him in due time. That night, we made love for the first time to "Steal Away" by Mary J. Blige, and I wished we could just leave Michigan right then, and there. We had, had sex plenty of time before that night, but I swear it was something very different about it this time. Once we were done, I noticed that I had eight missed calls from, Oz. I wasn't really up to any conversations with him after the last one we had, so I erased my log then fell asleep. Oz even went as far as to pop up at the club a couple nights just to try to get my attention. I could tell the way I kept spinning him whenever he was around, was really starting to piss him off, but I could care less. I didn't really give a fuck about his attitude, because he was my enemy as far as I was concerned. Some nights, if I were bored enough, I would dance for him, and then leave without saying a word before the song was over. Others night, I would just blow him off completely, acting as if he didn't even exist. At club, I lived by the motto: "The Money Make Me Work," but Oz was about to learn the hard way that Teaz didn't play.

I was walking to my car one night after we closed, and a black on black BMW with tinted windows pulled up on the side of my car. I was nervous at first, thinking I was about to be robbed, or car jacked but to my surprise it was Oz.

"Get in the car," he said once he rolled down the passenger window.

I hesitated to get in at first, because his demeanor was more aggressive than before.

"Come on, Teaz," Oz demanded, and I thought he had figured out I was Ize's ex-girlfriend.

"It's like that?" He added, looking at me as if I was crazy. I, just let out a deep breath, walked up to the car, got in the passenger seat, and he pulled off.

"Heaven or Hell," by Meek Millz was playing as he punched the BMW up the street, puffing on a blunt.

"I guess a Nigga just gotta kidnap your ass to get your attention, huh, Lil' Mama," he said, trying to pass me the blunt.

"I'm good," I answered, turning down the bunt while trying my best to stay focused.

I didn't want the weed to start clouding my judgment.

"Take the blunt, girl," he coaxed, passing me the weed again.

I snatched it this time, hit it once, and then passed it back.

"You ain't scared, are you?" he asked as the song changed to "Round Here," by Paul Wall.

"Should I be?" I asked calmly, but I was nervous as fuck on the inside.

"Never," he stated, hitting the blunt, and passing it back to me.

"I just wanted some of your time, Lil' Mama," he continued, and I rolled my eyes.

"Even if that meant I had to take it," he explained, now sipping his cup.

"I planned on just talking to you in the parking lot for a few, but I have an errand to run, then I'll drop you back off to your car," he assured me, and I felt a slight relief.

"Hello," by T. I. began to play once we approached the Lodge freeway, and he turned up the volume. I didn't say much as we drove, because I was too busy paying attention to where he was taking me. Once we reached our destination, he called someone of his cellphone. A couple minutes later, a short, cocky built, dark-skinned dude, came out of the building. They didn't say a word to each other when he approached the car. He just handed Oz an envelope, gave him some dap, and was out. On our drive back to my car, I couldn't help but wonder what was inside the envelope. I put on my thinking cap as we drove, and I remembered Oz telling me earlier that he wanted to spend some time with me.

"Perfect timing." I thought to myself as I began to put my plan into action. Mega would be out of town for a couple days, so this was the perfect opportunity to spend time with Oz to be nosey.

"So what are your plans for the rest of the night?" I asked as my song, "Don't Love Me" by Lil' Wayne and Trey Songz began to play.

"It's whatever you want to do, Lil' Mama," he responded, licking his lips, and rubbing his hands across my thigh.

"Whatever I want to do, huh?" I repeated, but I knew what he really wanted.

It was a price to pay for everything in life, and I knew tonight mine would be my pussy. Nothing comes cheap, and I was willing to pay that price to find out what his next moves were. You know what they say: "Curiosity kills the cat," and this little kitty was willing to make some sacrifices to get what I wanted. I swear, the more I put the plan in motion in my head, the more attractive Oz started to look.

"I'm tryna use a rubber, tonight." I joked, and then laughed thinking this would be easier than I thought.

"Whatever you want to do, I'm with it," he repeated as "I Luv This," by August Alsina began to play.

The next thing I knew, we were at a room in the Casino, and I was fucking Oz's brains out. You heard Pinky XXX's song, right? This "Pussy That Good," and right now, all I could think about was sometimes you gotta do, what you gotta do; to get what you want. As soon as Oz went to sleep, I crept over to the table where he left the envelope and opened it. Just liked I expected earlier, it was information about the jails Ize, Cazh, and Barbie were in.

"Oh My God," I whispered, while making sure to keep an eye on Oz the entire time.

"I can't believe he wants Barbie dead, too," I thought, shaking my head.

I almost cried reading over all the information I had just found until I saw the information about myself. I instantly removed the papers with my information on it trying, not to be too loud, and that's when the picture fell out. My heart sank looking at the picture of us four attending the yacht party that Cazh had. I quickly, put it with the other papers, and closed the envelope when I saw Oz move.

"Wassup, Lil' Mama," he asked, sitting up on the bed, and I slowly slid the papers into my bag.

"Nothing major, just trying to find this bag of weed." I lied, rambling through my purse.

"Look in my pocket and just roll up the weed that I have," he instructed, and I did to try to calm my nerves.

After we smoked, we fucked again, got dressed, and then Oz gave me $700.00 dollars, to go shopping. I was feeling emotional once he dropped me back off to my car. I pulled out the picture of us at the party, and tears rolled down my face as "Nite & Day," by Lloyd played. I felt so bad for fucking, Oz, now. I hated that I had just betrayed Mega, for the second time, but that was nothing compared to how I felt just knowing that it was a ticket on Ize and Barbie's heads. I didn't really care about what happened to Cazh, though. It was his fault that we were in this mess in the first place. I couldn't take it anymore, nor did anybody else deserve to die because of our mistakes in the past. I couldn't just sit back, and let them get hurt knowing what happen the last time I failed to open my mouth. I had already lost Zarbreah to this dirty game, and I damn sure wasn't willing to lose anyone else. I decided it was time to go pay Ize, and Barbie a visit. I cried all the way home, while listening to my jam "Good Times" by Styles P as my mind drifted off to when we first moved here. I even thought about the night of the party, and how smooth Ize played it when he was introduced to the same La'Teazya he grew up with. I, remember being so shocked when I found out the fine brother who was watching me all night was my childhood sweetheart. Nothing happens by chance in life, and there is a lesson in every obstacle. Everything you learn to overcome, down to the people you cross paths with during your life was predestine. The key was to try to walk away with your sanity still intact at the end. I knew many people who didn't always walk away with the sane mind they once had. We were not going out like that if I could help it. The first thing I had to do was create a new identity. I didn't want to just stroll into each prison as myself, so I got Mega to get me a fake birth certificate, and social security number. He had been living under an alias himself for a few months now, all because he decided to stop reporting to his probation officer. After, I got my new identification card in the mail, I called the federal prison Ize was in to get his mailing information. There was a two-month waiting list to see him, and I had to have a police clearance. After calling Barbie's prison, and going through the process to be added onto her guest list, I decided to go visit her the following week. I, purposely got the same last name as hers on the new identification card, so it was easy to convince the officers that we were siblings. Since no one had heard as much as a word from anyone on her side of the family in years, they didn't ask a lot of questions when I sold them the story about one of our parents being ill. Everyone always said we looked like we could be sisters during our college years so I knew this was one plan that I could easily pull off. It was a cold and rainy day when I decided to go visit my old friend, Barbra. I had to drive six hours away in a thunderstorm and the roads were flooded so it was detours everywhere. The moment I pulled into the parking lot,

"Someday" by Scarface came on, and a chill came over me. I grabbed my umbrella then headed up to the prison. All kinds of thoughts raced through my head as I sat there waiting for Barbie. It was so much I wanted to talk to her about in so little time. I could tell that she was surprised to see me when she walked into the room. Once she took a seat at the table I was at, I couldn't help myself from crying, and telling her all I'd been through. After I calmed down, I listened to her tell me about the past three years of her life that I had missed. She wasn't the same Barbra anymore that lived for the glamorous lifestyle and drug dealers. She had changed, and in a way, I envied that she found the one thing I still had not. I guess when surviving is the only thing you have left, giving up is never an option.

"No matter what the situation is you face, unless it's the bitter end; You have to always try to make a way out of no way." I rationalized.

"The real reason I'm here to visit, Barbie," I paused.

"Is because I ran into the brother of the guy Cazh had killed," I explained to her through more tears.

"I don't know what I'm going to do to stop his plans," I paused, again clutching my hands to my chest.

It was so sad to be sitting with my friend after all these years just because someone wanted her to die.

"I felt I should give you a heads up," I continued while whipping away tears.

Barbie's face was blank, and I could tell what I had just revealed to her was a lot to take in.

It wasn't every day you find out a person wants you dead for a murder you didn't even commit. It was already bad enough that she was going to be in prison for a long time.

"Alright, La'Teazya," she responded dryly.

"It was good seeing you again," she smiled, while standing up.

"I'll take care of things on my end," she stated, and then walked up to the guard and left.

The drive home was long, and quiet. After, I listened to "Prayer For The Dying," by Seal, I decided against listening to the radio. I just wanted to be alone with my thoughts. Lately, I had been focusing all my attention on Ize, and Oz's bullshit that I had totally forgotten to focus on my own man. It had been a week since I last seen Mega, and I missed him so much right, now. Every time he tried to have a real conversation with me after I had gotten the Id, I would somehow manage to cut it short. I hated myself for putting everything before my new relationship, and I swore this was the last time it would ever happen.

Once I got home, I popped in my Musiq Soulchild cd, and "Love," came on. I called Mega, and he answered on the first ring as usual.

"Yo, Babe," he yelled into the phone, and I just laughed.

"Hey, Baby," I giggled.

Mega always put a genuine smile on my face. It was the little things that Omega did out of love that kept me happy. He was my "go to" person to cheer me up whenever I was feeling down. I loved Mega's natural fun-loving personality, and positive energy. He was like a daily dose of medicine that I needed to take regularly in order to remain a sane individual. Oh, how I desperately needed inner peace, and I was trying my best to get to that point in life. I knew I still had some mental growing to do because the past had taken a toll on me. After talking for a few more minutes, I let him know that I would be waiting for him at my place if he wanted to stop by later. I even told him that, "I loved him," for the very first time, and felt good about my decision to love again. I was so tired of holding back on love just because it always showed me its ass.

"If God could continue to love us after all we have done, and then who was I to not give love another chance." I concluded, before I hung up the phone, and got in the shower.

"Rose Colored Glasses," by Kelly Rowland was playing while I picked up around my place before Mega came over. I felt Kelly lyrics because I was so glad I didn't have to wear those glasses anymore. Love had completely taken over my soul, and I just wanted to use this opportunity to show Omega how much he really meant to me. I walked into the kitchen, and turned down the boiling pot of crab legs that I was making us for dinner. Omega was definitely "The Truth," I thought, while humming to India Irie. I was happy to have someone like him in my life. By the time Missez started to play, I was ready to sing Mega a "Love Song" all right. I picked up my cell phone, and called Mega but he did not answer. I even called his other phone but it went straight to voicemail.

"I wondered why he's not answering," I thought, and then went to make me something to eat.

I put in my old school cd and zoned out to some of my favorite songs waiting on Mega to call me back.

"Destiny," by Myron started to play, and I noticed two hours had passed since I last talked Mega.

I checked my phone, and saw that he didn't return any of my calls. I decided to call him back but this time both phones went to the voicemail.

"Maybe, he's still out handling business and both of his phones died," I concluded as I turned off the music to turn on the television.

As soon as I hit the power button, Fox2 news came on, and I damn near fainted when I heard the breaking news report before I could change the channel.

"A young man's body was found gunned down in front of an abandoned building," The news reporter announced.

They flashed to Mega's car, and I almost died.

"Please, God, let this be a dream," I screamed, falling to my knees.

I, literally felt my heart hit the floor, so I began to pray.

"Lord, please forgive, Mega for all his sins." I prayed.

"Have mercy on the fools who took his life away, and watch over his son he left behind," I cried even harder.

I was finally starting to fall in love with Mega, and he was gone. Love didn't play fair. I thought as I dropped to my knees, and broke down in tears as I continued to talk to the lord.

"Lord, I also ask you to give me strength," I continued to pray.

As much as I hated to admit it, they had just taken away the love of my life. I didn't know who else to call on so I screamed: "Help me please, Jesus," right before I said "Amen".

I thought back to the last conversation I had with Mega that day. He was so happy when he answered the phone and just his happiness brought a smile to my face. Then I thought about a couple weeks prior to his death. He had wakened me out my sleep at 5:00 am, in the morning scared to death from a nightmare he had. He was trying to tell me what had happen to him during the dream, but I cut him off before he could even tell me.

"Whenever you have those kinds of nightmares, Mega, you have to pray," I advised him.

I even told him to start "Rebuking, Satan in Jesus name," whenever he felt like something was wrong. I had learned that from Mrs. Franklyn when I would have nightmares as a teen about my Mama. I always dreamed my Mama was still alive, and that I was still living with her, T'Aira, and Bozo in that townhouse in the projects. It took a long time for me to convince myself that my Mama wasn't always the boogeyman. I hated my Mama's guts. I still couldn't bring myself to forgive her for all she had done to me, even after all these years. Mama hated me, and in a lot of ways I hated her, too. Mrs. Franklyn always read the bible to me, and took me to have regular talks with the pastor, because of this problem I had. I guess she didn't want the hatred I felt for my Mama to lead me straight to Satan's doorsteps. I remember Mega telling me that, "he never wanted to die violently in the streets," yet the irony of his death made me cry just thinking that good people really do die young.

"Who in their right mind would want to kill, Mega," I wondered, as I was lying in my bed listening to the radio.

"Who Can I Run Too," by Xscape had just come on, and all I could think about was Mega. My heart couldn't believe that he was dead. The news reporter said that it was a robbery, but the amount of bullets they put into my baby tells me, differently. This was personal, somebody wanted him dead, and I needed to know why. I cried even harder as Xscape sang thinking that there wasn't anyone in the world that I'd rather be running to right, now. Xscape was absolutely, right! It wasn't a soul on this planet that could fill this empty space I was filling in my heart. I felt miserable inside, and I desperately needed somebody to call "911". I knew my wounded little heart was bleeding out from all the pain it always felt. I cried myself to sleep that night. I didn't understand how I could have two people I loved just taken from me so suddenly. I was starting to feel like I was damaged goods because everybody I crossed paths with ended up dead or in jail.

The next morning, I woke up at the break of dawn and hit the streets.

"If you woke up without a goal, go back to sleep." I thought, as I cruised around my neighborhood thinking about Mega, and my life. I felt like a total failure thinking back to Mega's favorite morning quote. I really didn't have a purpose for being up this early except trying to free my mind from all the bullshit I had been through lately.

I even put in my "My Life" cd by Mary J. Blige, and I began to cry when "Only Woman," came on. Mega was the only man that ever really loved me, and now he was gone. I was back to square one all over again, and I hated love. At that very moment while I was sitting in my car feeling miserable for myself, that I realized I was the only woman Mega ever needed to make it out the hood. He always used to tell me that no one ever compared to me and that we could leave this all behind once I got off papers. I just wanted to "Steal A Way," like Mary J. said in her song, but the chance was now gone. All I had left of Omega were memories, and no matter what star I wished on, he wasn't coming back. I pulled up by the water trying to ease my mind but the songs were making it hard for me to find peace.

"Ain't Nobody," by Monica came on, and all I could think about is how the lyrics fit my current situation.

"Ain't nobody ever loved me like you do,"

"Ain't nobody who compares," Monica sang as I cried.

"That's why I love you, baby," I repeated along with Monica.

I then closed my eyes, pictured Mega's face, and then whispered, "I Will Always Love You," to the wind.

The next day, I went shopping with Rozi to clear my mind. I wasn't really up to hearing any rap music, or R&B, so I put in my alternative cd. I loved the fact that Rozi always tried to keep a smile on my face when she knew I was feeling down. I was truly lucky to have a good friend in my life like her after all I had been going through, lately.

"Lighting Crashes," by Live began to play, and Mizz came to mind. It was ironic that all the emotions I was feeling inside for Mega's passing kept taking me back to the love I had for Mizz that I tried to bury. Other than Mega, she was the only real love I ever had in my adult life.

"How many more people do you have to lose to know when you are really being loved, Teaz?" I pondered.

I damn near had a nervous breakdown just thinking about having to bury another friend of mine. I didn't know how I was going to get through this whole funeral ordeal. I knew if the shoe was on the other foot, Mega would've been there for me; but some things were better left said than done. I was glad that I had found an outfit in the first store that we went in. I was tired from lack of sleep, because I was depressed. I couldn't even eat the days leading up to Mega's funeral. I was "Lost," like Gorilla Zoe rapped, and the road to my recovery seemed so far away.

The day before Mega's, funeral my phone rang. I wasn't really up for any conversations so I decided not to even answer. Once I checked my messages, I saw that it was Oz who had been calling, me. I could tell that he had an attitude, because I wasn't fucking with him, or returning his calls.

"What the hell did I get myself into?" I frowned, reading his text.

"Hope you're having a great day, beautiful," he wrote, and I was pissed that he was wishing me well on the day of my dead boyfriend's funeral.

"I would have at least got to see my baby for the last time, if I wasn't with your ass," I sobbed, putting the phone down as if it was Oz's fault that Mega was dead. I needed somebody, anybody, to blame for the way I was feeling inside. The emptiness was slowly taking control of my sanity, and I knew I was going to black out at any given moment. It was even worse that it was a possibility that had we not met that one night at Buffalo Wild Wings, I would be dead, too. I cried, just thinking that my fate could have easily been the same as Mega's. Somehow, I had managed to escape death, and I was wishing that I could have done the same for him. I was dying just thinking about the fact that I would "never" see Mega again.

"If I wouldn't have been six hours away trying to warn Barbra, maybe Mega would be alive,"

"I sat thinking about every possible way I could've saved his life, but there wasn't one." I convinced myself.

A part of me knew that if I had been with him instead of visiting Barbie, he would not have wanted to go outside that day. Just the thought of him still being alive if I had just been there sent me into a rage. This was all Oz's fault, for real. Why did he have to want to kill everybody? Why did I have to run into his snake ass? Most importantly why does being loyal to a fault suck, sometimes.

"Oz had to go," I thought, and then popped in my new Doughboyz Cashout cd.

I had played this game to long with him, and it was time to rid myself of this evil.

"Setup Bitch," started to play, and all I could think of was "You gone get yours, OZ"!

I laughed thinking Mizz was absolutely, right.

"Revenge was a dish best served lethal," and I was going to make sure he got what he deserved.

The next week, I was at Mega's funeral with my right hand chick Rozi. It was so unbelievable seeing my love in a casket knowing this would be the last time I would ever see his face again on earth. I was also shocked to see Haji there sitting with Mega's brothers, and son. This was the craziest situation I had ever been in. Before today, I could turn every corner, and I never saw Haji after the night we had met. At the repast, I learned that Haji was Mega's god-brother, and that he was out of town at the time of Mega's death. That explained whom Mega was always going to see in Ohio. Haji was taking Mega's death hard, and I could tell that he was hurting deeply because of it.

"How did you know Omega?" Haji asked me while I was making my plate of food.

"I was dating him," I admitted to Haji and a light bulb went off in my head.

"I can't believe he's gone," I told Haji, because it was all so surreal to me.

"Me, either," He sighed.

"When I find out who did this," he continued.

"I'm going to personally make sure I put them in the dirt, too," he stated, and I was happy to hear those words come out his mouth.

"Well, you know I got my eyes and ears open," I assured him, pulling Haji into my master plan.

"Being that I'm in the strip game," I paused.

"You'd be amazed how much these dudes talk like bitches once you got 'em open," I bragged, putting my plan into action.

"Take my number down, and call me if you hear anything," he insisted, and I agreed.

"I just sealed your fate, Oz," I laughed inside feeling like an evil villain.

I also promised myself that I was going to find out exactly what happen to Mega if it was the last thing I did. I'm sure the streets will be talking soon about the truth behind his murder. So all I had to do was be patient, and in due time everything would come to the light.

The next couple of weeks went by in slow motion literally. Life just wasn't the same anymore now that Mega was gone. I was so used to seeing his car everywhere that it was starting to take a toll on me knowing that Omega would never be around again. Oz was blowing up my phone as usual, and I was really getting sick of it. I secretly wished I hadn't even fucked him now that he was becoming a bug-a-boo. He clearly had to be pussy whipped after that one night the way he constantly called my phone. I always said, "There was a price to pay for everything in life".

"Oz just didn't know what he was paying for," I laughed.

He was just like all my other victims I had been with sexually. They all seem to be hypnotized off my juices during lovemaking, and my name imprinted on his brain like a tattoo, afterward. I call it the "CUMBACK," because I loved the power I had over men once I gave them a taste of this vagina.

I was at the club one night drinking my life away, when I called Haji, and told him to meet me for drinks. Once he got there, I took him to a section in the back of the club so we could talk privately.

"Emotional," by Detroit artist Hardwork Jig began to play, as I told Haji the fake story about Oz killing Mega over a chick they were both fucking. I even started crying to make the story more believable. Haji was pissed as I sold him the lies that were going to lead to Oz's downfall. The fake tears was exactly what I needed to get Haji on board. I had a masterplan in my head, and I wasn't going to stop until it manifested into reality. I also could have won an Oscar award for Actress of the year. "

What a performance," my inner thoughts screamed as Haji, and I chatted.

"I'mma take care of that Nigga," Haji promised, and I just rose my glass to make a toast.

"Paybacks a Bitch," I announced, and then drank the entire glass.

Weeks had gone by since I last spoke with Haji, so I decided to go pay Barbie another visit to let her know she would be okay. I wanted to ease her mind about the whole situation she was in, because something never did sit quite well with me after our last visit.

"I'mma handle things on my end," kept playing over, and over in my head.

I knew Barbra didn't have anyone looking out for her on the outside. Everyone she knew had turned their backs on her, and, the only other man that ever loved her other than her father was in prison with a price tag on his head. Barbie told me that she had found God while she was in prison, but I knew faith alone wouldn't stop Oz's plan.

"Dead?" I screamed.

"What the fuck do you all mean Barbra's, dead?" I yelled at the officers.

"Barbra committed suicide a couple days after your last visit," the officer explained.

"We notified your parents," the rookie went on to say, and I was dead inside.

I cried as I sat in my car in the parking lot. Everybody, I loved was dying, and I knew in my heart Barbra's death was my entire fault. I felt like Ize after he accidently had Zarbreah killed.

"If I hadn't told her about Oz, she'd still be alive!" I cried, while beating my hands into the steering wheel.

"Jesus take the wheel." I shouted, and then pulled off.

The next week, I was at home watching movies on Netflix. I changed the channel to see the news. It was cloudy outside, and I wanted to catch the weather report before I went out for the day. Once the commercials I was watching went off, the news came back on and I was speechless when I heard the breaking news.

"Two local drug dealers found dead in an alley," the reporter reported, and I was happy as hell when I saw Oz's face. The other man they found murdered was the person he went to pick up the envelope from the day he made me ride with him.

"Snitches get put into ditches," I laughed.

"That's what you get, bitch ass Niggas!" I smirked, and then turned off the news.

I had totally forgotten about watching the weather as I popped in my DMX greatest hits cd and went straight to my jam, "Bring Your Whole Crew".

"I just love when a Nigga bring his whole crew,"

"It's just a bigger piece of cake for me to chew a hole through," I laughed, as I rapped along with DMX.

The next thing I knew; my cell phone was ringing. I almost didn't answer when I saw that it was a "Restricted," caller.

"Hello!"

"You have a collect call from an inmate in a federal prison," the automated teller announced.

"To except this call press, one."

"To decline, press the star key," the woman instructed, and I immediately pressed the number one button.

"Ize!" I yelled into the phone.

"Sup, Teaz,"

"It's been a long time since I've heard your voice, baby," he replied, and I melted inside.

"I got your letter, and I saw the news recently,"

"I guess that's Checkmate huh, Teaz?" he asked, and I just let out a deep breath.

"Listen to me, Teaz, because my time is limited," he continued, and I did not say a word.

"You hear everything where I am, and I truly appreciate you trying to warn me."

"You have two minutes remaining," the operator interrupted.

"I have a confession to make now that I'm a changed man," He stated, and I just prepared myself for whatever he was about to tell me.

"One minute, remaining," the woman announced, and I almost told her to shut the hell up.

"I'm listening, Ize," I replied after she stopped talking.

"I've been meaning to get this off my chest for some time now, but I figured this was the best time to do it being that you handled that one situation for me," he confessed, and I wanted him to get on with the story.

"I illed kaysky our yaysky other maysky," he admitted, and I could not believe what he had just said.

"Did Ize just admit that he killed my Mama?"

"I'll talk to you about it more whenever we're face to face," he explained, and then the phone hung up.

I was appalled as I sat there deep in thought. I didn't even hear the cd

change until "Dear Mama," by Tupac started playing. I went into the

kitchen and poured myself a drink as I listened to the words Tupac was

saying. Ize had just told me that he was the one who killed my mother all

those years ago in our secret language we made up as kids.

My mama wasn't the mother Tupac was talking about in his song, but it

was ironic that the song was on at this very moment. Mama was a cruel

and evil Bitch the whole time I stayed with her, so I couldn't really feel

sad even after knowing Ize was the cause of her death. He did always

promise to protect me once I was his girlfriend, so maybe he was just

looking out for my best interest back then. I remembered Ize witnessing

my Mama mistreat me for no apparent reason a lot of times while we were

growing up, and I was happy he removed my life's demon.

"If Ize hadn't taken my Mama's life that night, I never would've gotten

the chance to have a real life," I reasoned.

The Franklyn's did more for me than my Mama ever would have done,

and I couldn't see life without them. I was sad thinking back on my

experience I had at the girls' home, and me moving back to Michigan to

discover that they had moved away. As destiny would have it, that move

with Barbie was the reason I ended up back with Ize. I guess now I

understood that love was something deeper than we all knew. Love had kept me loyal to Ize after all these years, even when I knew I should have left him. In a way, I guess that same love is what had me have Haji murder, Oz.

"Maybe, Ize was my soul mate," I thought, and then finished my drink. Love was one of the craziest feelings to explain, because it made people make bad decision sometimes. I understood Mizz completely, now.

"A life for a life," I concluded as "You Can't See Me," by Pac began to play.

Sometimes in this dirty game, it is all about who wants their life more. I, for one, wasn't about to let anything get in the way of my survival. This very moment reminded me of my favorite author, Raven Soars Quote.

"Sometimes, You Have To Apply Pressure..."
That's the only way you can see who strong enough to really survive each storm with you."

I guess we are even, Ize.

Cruel Intentions

Dear Dairy,

November 10, 2014

"One of the greatest feelings a person can have in this world is knowing that Jesus loves you unconditionally!"

This lady told me as she handed me a pamphlet. I just shoved it inside of my purse and kept walking. I had a big show to do tonight. I was throwing my 25th birthday party at Dirty Secrets, and I knew it was going to be epic. It was truly amazing what a year could do for you if you truly applied yourself towards being successful. I had accomplished every goal I had set for myself, and I was making major progress in completing probation. I was truly proud of myself for coming home, getting my Associates degree, and keeping my promise to the Franklyn's. I had also recently moved into my new apartment, so I was spoiling myself rotten with all the extra money I was making outside of school. I stormed into the mall as fast as I could. I was already late picking up my outfits from my favorite little boutique. I had my girl, R'e, the owner of the store made me three special outfits for the evening. I really didn't have time to hear the rest of the ladies ranting, so I just said "Thanks", and kept it moving. My entire birthday décor was Tiffany blue. My cake was a Tiffany's box with a diamond on top. I purposely picked that color because it was the closest thing to my birthstone, and I loved Tiffany & Co. I strutted through the mall in my Michael Kors outfit with the matching, handbag, and diamond studded sunglasses. I was annoyed as hell by the time I got to the entrance of ExquizIt CreAtions.

"You should let me get to know you better, Ma," The dude that followed me into the store hinted as I continued to walk towards the counter.

I just wanted to get my outfits and bounce. I had a ton of things to do before the party, and meeting dread head wasn't on the agenda. I didn't need any more distractions in my life at the moment; so whatever he was selling, I wasn't even trying to buy. I wasn't the type for small talk, and little did he know I was about to cut the conversation real short. I walked up to the woman sitting behind the counter and told her my name. I watched her punch the information into the computer, and then disappear to the back of the store.

"Look,"

"Moe," he interrupted in his Jamaican accent.

"Look, Moe," I repeated, while checking out his overall appearance head to toe.

"It's nice to meet you, but I'm not really looking for any new friends." I bluntly state.

The woman had just returned with my outfit before he could respond, and I was glad she did. I just wanted to get my things and leave.

"I respect that, Sweetheart," I heard Moe reply, but I was too busy listening to the price of my outfit.

The next thing I knew Moe handed the girl $300.00, and started walking towards the exit. Once I paid the remaining balance of $275.00, got my bags, and receipt, I headed out of the store. I looked around for Moe for a minute but he was nowhere in sight.

"Oh Well," I shrugged!

"I guess its Happy Birthday to me,"

"Compliments of Moe the dread head," I laughed.

I hit a couple more stores in the mall, and then I jumped in my ride to head home so I could get myself together for the evening.

"Girl, your ass is just the fattest,"

"If I can I wanna grab it,"

"I'm the man, and you can have this,"

"What I'm sayin' is you a Bad Bitch, a Bad Bitch," Trey Songz sang as I started my car.

"Da Baddest," by Big Kuntry King had just come on before I parked, and I was feeling it as I pulled out of the parking lot. I was about to put on a hell of a show later on that evening for my birthday, and I was happy to just be alive at the age of Twenty-five. Barbie and Zar crossed my mind as I drove blasting our favorite song "The Resistance," by Drake. I wondered what we would all be doing right now if they were both still alive. I thought back to the last time we were all together and us toasting to us being the "Three Musketeers," forever. I felt like Jada as I drove to my house at the end of "Set It Off". Just the thought of them brought tears to my eyes. Here I was about to have the best time of my life tonight, and I was sad that my two best friends couldn't be here to share it with me. I smiled just thinking that Zar would be a mother, and Barbie would be partying her ass off right now had she not been in prison, and took her own life. That whole experience is one I knew we would all recover from differently. I didn't regret it but, I wouldn't wish prison on anyone. I had to learn at an early age that only the strong survive in this game called "Life". Being that my life started out rough when I lived with my Mama. I didn't really have a choice but to learn to protect myself. I knew that I was given this second chance at life to do better, so I wanted to do right with the rest of my days on Earth. It is amazing how lifeworks. I always told myself: "never touch the ground once your wings are spread", but I guess everyone has to climb fools hill at some point. The hard part is getting back down once you get so far up it. I knew I was standing on top like Jill just waiting to go tumbling down one day. I have also come to believe that there is some truth to the saying: "three strikes and you're out". I was literally on my third strike with God, and I knew I needed to do something about my actions before it took me under. I couldn't help but reminisces over my past my whole drive. Even though, I knew I had made a lot of mistakes before today, I wouldn't trade a moment of my past life. Just thinking about everyone, I knew, and the fact that Barbie loved the lifestyle that her, and Cazh had built together made me smile just remembering how the two lovebirds started dating. They were really the true definition of "Until death do us apart" without marriage. I admired the genuine love they had for one another despite how things had turned out between them. I can honestly say they had a love for each other I could only dream of having. I could literally wish upon every star for the love, and bond they shared but I knew that kind of love wasn't meant for Ize, and I. I shook my head finally realizing the truth about our tainted love, and then thought about Mizz and Mega, as I drove. They were both the loves of my lives now gone over stupidity. I hated that they were, deprived of their young lives, all because of someone's personal greed, and envy. Secretly, I wished I would find that same love one day, with less drama. So far, Mega was the best man I ever fell in love with. It was a shame that he was also a product of his environment. The street life cut our love short. I felt like Monica as "Street Symphony," began to play. Had I known Mega would end up murdered the very way he always said he did not want to leave this Earth, I probably would have tried my best to convince him to leave this city with me.

"I love you so much," I whined aloud as the song played.

I also thought about Ize again, and the fact that he still had not wrote me back after our first conversation. Ize was good for keeping me on edge when he knew I needed him most. I hated the way he treated me sometimes, but I expected nothing less from him being that he said we would talk more about it face to face. I felt like Pac as I drove reminiscing over my past while staring at the world through my rearview. I desperately wondered "If Heaven Had a Ghetto," yet I knew I would never know the answer as long as I lived on earth. If there was a possibility that Heaven did have one I knew Mizz, Mega, Zar, and Barbie were having a party for me right now. I laughed just thinking about them all hanging out together in heaven on account that they all were a part of my life. I smiled, and cried just thinking about all the fun moments I got to share with each one of them while they were alive. I was sure they would be four out of the five people I would meet in heaven. I thought back on a book I had read by Mitch Albom, and I knew Stazy would probably be one of the first people I would met in Heaven. She was the one who introduced me to

God. I was so happy that Ramir got me that book now that I had read it. I knew that in my grief of missing them all there would come a time of comfort. I was riding down my block while the snow fell as I thought about my current relationship with Ramir. Things between us were not the same as they were before our weekend at the cabin, but Ramir didn't even seem to notice. I played my role just as if I had done many times before while dating, Ize. Secretly, I wished we were back to the old carefree us. Well me at least, because I was the one with all the secrets. The harsh truth was that my infidelities had lead me to make a foolish decision. I had vowed to find out exactly how much Ramir knew about the whole Haji situation. I knew Ramir wasn't a cheater, and that it was a possibility he knew nothing about us, but I had major trust issues. I had really fucked up, and it kept me from falling in love with the person who probably really loved me. The most I had gotten out of Ramir since I'd been doing my own private investigation was how much he hoped one day I'd become his wife. I knew Ramir loved me deep down inside, but I had my guard up until I got down to the bottom of things. Tonight, I just wanted to put everything in my past behind me and enjoy this birthday. Nothing could ruin my evening I had planned, and I was glad that it had been three months since I last seen Haji. It was always good to be one up on a person who thought they were your opponent, so I always had to be on my "A" game when it came to these two. At least until I could figure out which one of the two was my real enemy and mastermind behind the whole plot. As far as I was concerned, I knew I had the upper hand on them both.

"May the best man win," I mused pulling into my driveway.

"Or in my case, Woman," I laughed some more cutting off my car.

I found myself getting dressed that evening as one of my favorite movies, "Fresh" played.

"Classic," I marveled at the television while I put on my panties.

The movie fit my current situation that I was dealing with just knowing these two fools. The main character in the movie devices, and executes a brilliant plan to eliminate all his enemies using the chess game techniques to kill of his opponents. I felt his pain, because if it came down to it, I would be on the same page. Once, I got dressed I went to see what Rozi was wearing. I knew she was going to look ravishing being that Rozi was such a Diva, and trendsetter. Her native background was a major part of her natural beauty. She always went above, and beyond when it came to her appearance, purposely ornamenting her natural attributes. In many ways, she reminded me of less fortunate version of my friend, Barbie. The only difference is Rozi was independent, were Barbie depended solely upon Cazh's success. Rozi had a hard life coming up as a child like I did, yet she slayed life as if the struggle had to make it through her not the other way around. She promised herself that she would always live the lavish life once she made it out the projects. At the age of fourteen, Rozi knew she had to depend on herself once her mother overdosed off Heroin. She was left in legal care of her father until he disappeared for good one day. Her parents were well-known Crackheads, all her life that spent more time chasing their drug addiction then raising their children. Rozi, and her two younger brothers would often get teased because their clothes stayed dirty, and her hair was always nappy. Rozi did the best she could for them when they were little but, eventually child protective services were called on her father, and the kids were split up. It wasn't long before she was adopted but, her foster parents only cared about one thing, "Money". Once she started developing, the mother got jealous of Rozilan, which often lead to beatings and her being put out. She decided to run away, and try to make it on her own in the streets after being waken up out her sleep at 5:00 in the morning and accused of sleeping with the woman's new boyfriend. She lived on the streets for a couple months until a friend of hers that she went to school with Mother saw her sleeping on a park bench during her morning jog. The friend just so happened to be the boy, that Rozi liked. Ivan had recently lost his younger sister due to a hit and run accident. His mother took one look at Rozi, and instantly fell in love with her. For years, Rozi slept with her foster brother after losing her virginity to him one night while they watched movies. She always suspected that the mother knew about their secret love for one another. It never affected their household until she got pregnant. She didn't want to have an abortion, but she also didn't want his mother to find out about their love child. The woman had already taken Rozi in and treated her like her own. Rozi decided to just keep the whole baby situation a secret until she could figure out what she was going to do. One day after school, she took a bunch of pills, which caused her to have a miscarriage. Once the boy found out he told Rozi he would never forgive her, and he even stop talking to her. The fact that he never even knew Rozi was pregnant, or was given the opportunity to decide with her the fate of their unborn child made him resent Rozi. He started to see other people right after that and it broke Rozi's heart to see the boy she loved with other girls. It crushed her heart even more that he started introducing Rozi as his sister to his new friends. Once she graduated from High School, she went to college out of state to get a break from it all. She eventually moved back home to Detroit to be close to his mother once he was killed. She started dancing after that to make some fast money while she worked on earning her degree in college. Once she achieved her financial goal, she had set for herself, along with her Bachelor's, degree in Business. She stopped dancing for good. She used the money she had to open up a little salon with a friend, but that didn't go as planned. Once she brought herself a house, and got a license to be a bartender, she knew she was going to be more than a dancer. One night while she was on a date with one of her Sugar Daddies, he mentioned that he would be opening up his own club in a couple months. He also asked her to be the Manager, over the bartenders and the main attraction for the club. She agreed, and that's how she started working at "Dirty Secrets". She's even the person who named the club. She was Duty's "dirty little secret," aside of his married life. Rozi didn't mind being Mr. Furtunato's side chick as long as she got what she wanted, and never had to depend on another soul a day in her life. She was a real "Maneater," like Nelly's song, and the price always had to be right to even speak to Rozi. She was the host of my party I was having tonight, and I knew I was going to love every minute of it. We had been through hell and back in our childhood to get where we were today so we deserved a moment in pure bliss. I was truly blessed to just be here. I thanked God for another year, and then I opened the door to her room. I could tell she was feeling herself as I entered the room. Her jam, "Walk Thru" by Rich Homie Quan was blasting while she sat at her vanity table. Once "Lifestyle" by Young Thug came on, I knew it was on tonight, and I couldn't wait to get to the club.

"You ready, Boo?" she yelled over the music when I walked in.

"You looking real cute, Teaz," she stated, and I did a little twirl around so she could get a good look at my entire outfit.

"R'e is the coldest seamstress in Detroit," she acknowledged after admiring my attire.

"Thanks, Boo." I replied, and even I had to admit that I was looking exquisite in my crocheted one piece. Rozi, on the other hand was "killin' em" like Fab said in her form fitted dress.

"Wait until later," I told her, because she hadn't seen anything yet.

I had R'e make me a couple more outfits for the party, and I knew everyone I wore, I was guaranteed to slay it.

"I'll be ready in a few," she claimed, but I knew Rozi.

"I just have to do my makeup then we're out," she assured me grabbing her makeup kit.

"I'm thinking the Benz tonight," she giggled, applying her mascara.

"It's time to pull my baby back out," she continued and we both laughed.

I walked back to my room to get my bag and purse.

"Ooh, Na Na,"

"Look what you done started," Trey Songz sang when I walked into my room. I did a little two-step while I sang along. I gathered up my belongings, cut off the radio and walked out the door. By the time I got to the living room, Rozi was ready to go. It was 11:00 pm once we got to the club. Everything was set up just like I wanted, and I was ecstatic because for once in my life everything was going "JUST RIGHT"! My phone rang while I was turning up in the dressing room with my girls. I was setting out all my outfits and explaining to the girls what I wanted them to do for the last show of the night.

"Hey, Ramir," I say answering the phone in mid-conversation.

"I see you're busy" he replied.

"I just wanted to let you know I'll be on my way in a few," he informed me, and I told him I'd see him once he got here.

An hour later, the DJ was playing all my favorite songs, and I couldn't wait until it was my time to perform. I was in a zone as I watched my girl, Stormii dance to "If I Ever Fall In Love" by Shai. I headed back to the dressing room and smoked a blunt until I heard Rozi on the microphone. Pinky XXX "Pussy That Good" began to play and I knew I was up. I did my thing on stage as crowds threw money at me. Once "Make That Money" By Rich Homie Quan came on, I had dudes surrounding the stage making it rain bills. Local artist Icewear Vezzo song came on and ended my last show before I took my break with "I Won". I felt him, because I was definitely on top of the game. Once I got back in the dressing room, I counted my money that Sazhay had collected for me. $5000.00 I counted, and the night was still young. I smiled as Gorilla Zoe played.

"I was living one hell of a life, alright," and tonight it was all paying off. Rozi came to tell me that Ramir had finally made it, and I quickly changed into my clothes. I had an hour to play with until we sang the happy birthday song, and I did my last performance. I decided to take some time to collect all my gifts and mingle with some of the people who I invited. I walked out of the dressing room into the crowded club, and I was shocked when I saw Moe seated three booths away from Ramir. My first stop was at Lucky Lex's table. She didn't waste any time pilling off a couple hundred dollar bills, and giving them too me.

"Thank you, Lucky Lex!" I smiled, giving her a hug.

"Anything for you, baby girl," she replied, and then poured me a glass of D'usse.

 I finished my glass, thanked her again, and then made my way through the crowded club towards Ramir's table. The minute Moe spotted me; he stopped me dead in tracks.

"What a coincidence, Lil' mama," he flirted, grabbing my hand.

"Let Me Hit That," by August Alsina began to play, and I could see the lust in Moe's eyes, as he looked me up and down.

"You like?" I teased, as he pulled me in close to him.

"I'm diggin' you for real, Ma," he replied whispering in my ear.

Moe smelt so damn good that I almost forgot about Ramir sitting two booths away from him. I played it off releasing his grip while assuring him that I would be back to talk later. In a way, I was wishing Ramir wasn't here, because I wanted get to know Moe a little better. I could see Ramir staring at us as Moe hugged me again while grabbing my ass, so I politely ended the conversation telling Moe we would talk later, and made my way over to Ramir's table before he got jealous.

"Who was that?" Ramir, asked me once I got to his table.

"Just someone who wanted to tell me, Happy Birthday." I teased, giving him a hug, and kiss.

"Don't be kissing all on me with the cooties," Ramir joked, wiping off his cheek.

"Ramir was so jealous at times," I thought, and then kissed him again.

"If he only knew what I was really thinking," I laughed inside while looking over at Moe's table.

"So, how's the party been going so far?" he asked me, then told the waiter to bring me a bottle of my favorite champagne, Luc Belaire Rare Rose Fantome.

"Great so far," I announced, cheerful as "Circle" by Lil' Ronny played. The night was going great, and I planned to keep it that way.

A couple drinks later, I informed, Ramir that I had to get dressed for my last show. I had a special show planned for everyone attending my party that evening. I always wanted to redo Grace Jones's version of the stripper she played in the movie "Vamp", so I had R'e make me an outfit like the one she wore in the movie. I even wore a red wig, and ordered a zebra print chair to do my performance. I left the audience in awe after "Katrina's Club" from the original soundtrack went off. I even got naked and removed the wired bra, and panties once "Come To Me" by Brad Fiedel came on. Afterwards, we sang Happy Birthday, and a couple of girls and I performed to "Freek-a-Leek" by Petey Pablo. We gave random selected people free lap dances while they unwrapped our bows. I purposely chose Moe over Ramir, and I could tell Ramir was pissed.

"Tuesday" by Drake ended my show of the night, and I was "PAID". After Rozi wrapped up the show, we all headed to the dressing room and all the girls thanked me. They had made more money in one night just by doing my party then they would usually make a week. I laughed as I counted my money while "Freak Like Me" by Adina Howard played because this was the norm for me. This wasn't shit to me, because I bring home a bag full of money every night. I paid Sashay $1500.00 that night and told her to give Duty what she wanted. I was feeling so good nothing could take me off the cloud I was sitting on. I was on my own damn planet, and I was starting to feel like I was in a new world. I got dressed, and headed out of the dressing room to find Ramir. He wasn't anywhere in sight as I made my way towards the exit while glancing around the club for him. I did run into Moe right before I reached the exit, and we exchanged phone numbers. Once I got outside, I found Ramir talking to Haji.

"What a way to end the night." I thought when Ramir called me over to the car.

I was annoyed as the hell the whole walk over towards Haji's car, but I kept a smile on my face. I hadn't seen Haji in months, and I damn sure didn't want to end my night seeing his face. I was in shock once I got to the car, and he handed Ramir a gift for me.

"My brother told me you were having a party, and I couldn't get her, sooner," He smiled, but I knew better.

"So a gift!"

"A little peace offering for missing your little extravaganza," he chuckled looking around at all the people leaving the building.

"Looks like you had a good turnout" he added, and I just took the box Ramir was holding and said "Thanks".

I was really starting to wonder what the fuck was up with Haji. What was the real reason behind all these games he kept playing? I hated that he was using Ramir as a puppet in his sick and twisted little game. I couldn't stand Haji, as I sat there listening to him talk to Ramir. I sneered at the sound of his voice but was broken out of my thoughts by the sound of Haji saying bye.

"I'm about to get out of here, and let you two love birds enjoy the rest of your night," He told Ramir as they slapped high- fives, and he pulled off.

I was never so happy to see Haji leave. I was really starting to hate his guts the more I saw him.

"My brother's really a cool guy once you get to know him" Ramir explained, but I knew better.

Haji was a mystery I desperately needed to solve, and Ramir didn't know half the truth about his evil brother. I could tell he really admired and loved Haji in so many ways by the way he spoke of him highly as we walked towards my car. Ramir's father would have been so happy at the man Ramir was, because he turned out to be exactly how he would have wanted him to be. Haji on the other hand was the total opposite. He reminded me of the step-sister off my favorite movie "Cruel Intentions". I hated that Ramir was in the middle of all of this just because he was associated with me.

"Bae?"

"Are you there?" Ramir asked me as I realized I had zoned out on the whole Haji was a good person speech.

I was so lost in my own thoughts and feelings about it all I decided against seeing Ramir tonight.

"I'm good, Bae,"

"I think I just need some rest," I lied.

"I might have truly over done it tonight," I continued to say while playing the restless role all the way to my vehicle.

We just walked hand in hand to my car, chit chatting as he carried my bag of gifts. Ramir was such a perfect gentleman, and I hated the fact that I ever messed with Haji behind his back. Once we got to my car door, I gave Ramir a kiss and promised to call him as soon as I got in. After he put my bag in the car and gave me another kiss I put my key in the ignition, and drove off. I sang along to "Keys Under Palm Trees" by Nicki Minaj as I drove on the freeway to my house.

"I'm in Jamaica with them keys under palm trees"

"Them leprechaun see's what my palms reads"

"And if my heart seized."

"Please call my Aunties,"

"I hear them girls telling,"

"I hear them boys yelling,"

"Get Down." I yelled with Nicki Minaj as I drove thinking about Haji's slick ass.

I really was starting to wonder when he would ever realize his tricks were no fucking good.

I pulled into my driveway as "Heels On," by Lady Saw began to play. I was starting to wish I had told Ramir just to follow me home. I was horny as hell all of a sudden, and I could use some good birthday sex now that I was all alone. I decided to just give him a call once I got out of the shower to tell him to come over. I gathered all my belongings and headed inside the house. Once I was settled in I popped in one of my mix cd, and headed towards the bathroom as "Skin" by Rihanna started to play. I couldn't wait to see Ramir, and feel him inside of me. I started fingering myself just thinking about him fucking me later on. By the time "Own It" by Drake ended, I was feeling ecstatic. I couldn't wait to take the ride I knew I'd be taking once Ramir got here. I have to admit. He is the first man to definitely know how to handle my body. He did things to me that you only read about in the Kama Sutra books, and I was addicted to him like a drug. The boy couldn't keep his hands off of me, and when I wasn't around he'd leave me text messages saying: I need my "MEDICINE". It was sinful just thinking about all the things we done since we started having sex. Even

worse, that I loved every minute of it. It was good to know I was the only

person Ramir was with even though I had slipped up and fucked his

brother. I couldn't help myself from comparing the way he fucked me to

the time I had sex with Haji. They both had skills in the bedroom, and I

probably would've fucked Haji again had he not turned out to be Ramir's,

brother. I quickly shook off the thought of ever fucking with Haji's

retarded ass ever again. The only way he was ever going to have me was

in a dream or when hell freezes over. I laughed as my old school jam

"Freak Hoes" by TRU began to play, because I was a mess for even

thinking about Haji's ass. I guess it was the soul ties, I read about recently

that you get once you sleep with a person. A part of me always knew after

you have sex with a person a part of them is always attached to you. I

stood in the mirror admiring my beauty, but I also knew it was the reason

behind some of my main problems. I attracted all the wrong people for the

same reasons. I just wanted to be happy for once, and I knew it wasn't

going to be with Ramir as long as Haji was in the picture. I wrapped my

towel around my body then headed out of the bathroom. I walked down

the steps towards my living room, and grabbed my purse off the couch. I

was looking for my phone, so I could call Ramir and tell him to come

over. I glanced down at my towel, and smirked. I was feeling like a real

nasty girl tonight. I was so horny, I planned on being naked the entire time

Ramir was here. I walked into the kitchen as "She Will" by Lil Wayne began to play, and I just twerked along to the song as I got out a bottle of wine. Wayne was right I was about to pop this thang all over Ramir once he got here. I grabbed a glass and sat it on the counter by the bottle. I was pouring myself a drink when I was just about to hit the "call" button on my phone. I was startled when the doorbell rang, but happy all at the same time.

"Damn Ramir is the shit." I boasted to myself thinking we were having some kind of mental telepathy moment.

I sat the phone down on the counter without thinking twice about it being anyone else at the door.

"Haji!" was all I could say as I stood in the door with my towel on.

The whole moment was so surreal to me. Everything about this very second reminded me of the time I opened the door for the police in my robe, and was arrested.

"Smiley face, smiley face." I thought but I wasn't feeling happy on the inside.

"What the fuck do you want, Haji?" I blurted out without even thinking.

I was annoyed as hell seeing Haji at my doorstep at 3:00 am in the morning instead of my man.

"The Devil is a lie!" my mind screamed, but my reaction was a loud sigh.

"Haji really is the Devil's best friend," my mind yelled to my guilty conscious.

"I know what you're thinking, Teaz," Haji managed to say when he noticed I had an attitude.

"But, I really just want to talk to you," he explained, and a part of me wanted to say just leave.

"I swear, Teaz." Haji continued to say while raising his hands in the air.

I knew he was lying. People always swear on God, deceased people they know, family members, or their own kids when they want you to believe the bullshit lies their trying to sell you. I hated that I had danced with the Devil in the past, now I was paying for my stupidity. I invited him in instead, even though it was against my better judgement. I regretted the minute he walked through the door as if he had out witted me. Honestly, I didn't need Ramir riding past seeing his brother on my porch at this time of night while I was in my towel. Once, I saw Haji take a seat, I quickly went into the kitchen, and grabbed my phone and drink. I took a seat at my bar that was facing the couch were Haji was seated, and drank my whole glass of wine because I was so pissed. I didn't have time for Haji's shenanigans, and it seems like he was willing to do anything to get under my skin.

"So what's the deal, Haji?" I asked with irritation all in my voice.

"Calm down, Teaz," he suggested while asking me could I pour him a drink.

"Are you kidding me?" I inquired, frowning at him.

"Damn you rude." Haji replied as "Nobody" by Keith Sweat began to play.

I was secretly wishing that Ramir were here right, now. Instead, I had to deal with his psychotic brother who liked to play childish ass games with me for no reason.

"Fine, you want a drink, Haji?" I snapped, grabbing him a glass from behind the bar.

I huffed, and puffed as I made it, too. I was so sick of Haji's bullshit. He was seriously getting on my last nerves, and it was time he knew. I handed him his drink, and then made me another one.

"You good, Teaz?" he asked, and I couldn't help but speak my mind.

"I was until you showed up, and ruined the rest of my birthday," I answered sincerely.

Haji was not only killing my vibe, but he was blowing the high I had before he got here.

"Smoke this, and calm your nerves," he stated, passing me a blunt he had lit.

"Seriously…" I frowned.

"What type of games do you think you're playing, Haji," I snapped, snatching the blunt from him.

"Games?" he mocked me with a laugh.

"Who said I was playing games?" he questioned, and I just rolled my eyes.

"Come on now, Haji,"

"You and I both know you're up to something," I stated letting my speculations be known before I lost it.

We were too old for this cat, and mouse chase game he kept playing. Haji didn't even respond. He laughed, and it pissed me off even further that he thought I was a joke.

"Is that what you've been thinking?" he finally asked, drinking his glass.

He then had the nerve to ask me for another drink when I handed him back his blunt.

"You looking really good in that towel, too, Teaz," he announced as I walked over to the bar.

"Is he just dumb, retarded, or just plain stupid?" I asked myself, and then shot him an evil look.

"I bet if I were Ramir you would've taken that as a compliment," he jested, and I ignored him.

"That's just it, Haji," I stated, handing him his drink.

"You'll never be, Ramir," I sassed as the song changed to "I'll Be Your Other Man" by Trick Daddy.

"I see," he smirked, sipping his drink.

"I'm just the other man," he smiled, and I choked on my drink.

"Other man my ass, Haji" I coughed, sitting my glass down.

"So why are you here, Haji?" I asked him one last time before he had to leave.

Haji had overstayed his welcome, and I didn't care what he wanted.

"First off, did you even open the gift I got you?" he asked.

I had totally forgotten about the gift he had gotten me. To be perfectly honest, I only took it because Ramir gave it to me, and I didn't want to seem rude. Truth be told; I could really care less what this fool had gotten me.

"No." I answered, and before I could explain, he asked me to open it.

I walked over to the dining room table where I had sat all my gifts, and snatched up the box Haji gave, Ramir.

I began to open the wrapper, and inside was Tiffany & Co.'s box. I opened it, and inside was the bracelet I had been asking Ramir to get me since after Valentine's Day.

"I can't accept this," I stuttered, placing the bracelet back in the box.

"You can and you will," Haji coaxed as he stood up and removed the bracelet from the box.

He walked over to where I was and placed the bracelet on my wrist.

"Perfect fit," he beamed from ear to ear.

I have to admit; it was a perfect fit. This would have been the perfect gift and evening had it been the other brother standing in front of me now. I imagined Ramir here with me instead of Haji, but was quickly broken out of my fantasy when I felt Haji's hands on my thighs.

"What are you doing, Haji? "I yelled while trying to move his hand off my body.

He pushed my hand away from his, and then placed a finger to my lips. I watched the towel I was wearing fall to the couch as Haji devoured my breast with his mouth. I wanted to say: "stop," but my mouth didn't say a word. I tried to push him away, but I couldn't move. I just let him have his way with me as the horny feeling I was having earlier took control of my body. I wrapped my legs around his waist pulling him in closer to me as he unbuckled his pants. He started kissing me all over as he put his penis inside of me. I was so into the moment that I never even paid attention to the fact that this was the second time that we had, had sex without using a condom. I moaned as Haji sank his teeth in the back of my neck as if he were a vampire while he fucked me from the back. I just threw my ass back at him as "Pound Her Out" by Doughboys Cashout played. I knew it wouldn't be long before he was pulling my hair while growling to let me know he had ejaculate. I threw my ass at him even harder trying to make him come faster. A sick part of me, loved it when he growled during sex, but my guilty conscious was starting to get the best of me. Haji was actually a better fuck than Ramir, and I knew it was all because of the liquor.

"I'm about to cum!"

Was all I heard as he grabbed a handful of my hair, and finished. Reality quickly started to set in when he released his grip, and stood up. I shook my head realizing that I wasn't on any type of birth control. I was dead wrong for what I had just done being that Ramir, and I always used condoms after the first time we had sex. We both agreed that we weren't ready for children. I knew I had lost my damn mind after letting his crazy brother fuck me twice without any damn protection. I couldn't believe I had just slept with the enemy again, and I damn sure didn't want to end up with Haji for a "Baby Daddy". I knew I was lucky before today to have not gotten pregnant, so I had to start making better decisions.

"I Mean It" by G-Easy started to play, and Haji began to sing along.

"If I said I fucked your bitch,"

"Just know I mean it." He sang with the song, and I shot him an evil look.

"I'm fucking your girlfriend, and there's nothing you can do about it," he rapped while lighting another blunt, and walking to the bathroom.

"Oh hell no!" I thought.

"I know this cocky son-of-a-bitch isn't trying to hoe me in my own damn house?"

I was fuming on the inside but I tried my best to hold in my attitude. I was so mad at myself for the situation I was in, but I knew it was my fault. I kept letting Haji play me like a fool, and I finally realized, just that.

"I'll be damned if I let the Devil disrespect me in my face any further!" I ranted aloud as I walked out of the bathroom.

I pushed open the door as "Don't Trust No Nigga," by Khia began to play.

"I think you should be leaving once you're done washing up," I advised him.

I was fed up with, Haji. He had me wrapped up in some kind of spell, and I wasn't about to keep acting like we were cool. I hated him for the control he had over me, and my body.

"We still haven't talked yet," Haji replied, nonchalantly as if I was joking.

I frowned, turning to walk back into the living room. It was obvious that I was talking to death ears, so I was going to have to show Haji better than I could tell him. I grabbed his keys, and removed the bracelet from my wrist. I shoved it back into the box, wrapped the towel around myself, and headed to my front door. Once I heard him open the bathroom door, I opened the front door. He had a look of disbelief once he reached the living room, but, my attitude was on "**I DON'T GIVE A FUCK**" mode.

"Like, I was saying, Haji," I smirked.

"It's time for you to be leaving," I announced while dangling his keys out the door with my free hand.

Haji slowly walked over to where I was standing, gave me a look that could have killed me, and then removed the keys from my hand while stepping onto the porch.

"We will talk the next time I see, you," he promised me before I shoved the box into his chest.

"I'm sure you have someone else you can give this too," I added right before I shut the door in his face.

I felt so bad once Haji left that all I could do was pray.

"Lord, I know I don't always pray to you the way that I should, but I ask you to protect me. Please watch over me, and guide me in the right directions. I know I have been foolish, but I ask that you to forgive me, and please, please, please, do not let me be tempted by this fool Haji… Amen."

I knew I needed Jesus to fight the demon I was battling. I wasn't spiritually strong enough to fight off the evil that was inside of Haji because I kept falling into Haji traps. I reached into my purse, and removed the pamphlet this woman had given me earlier.

"The Daily Bread," I read aloud as I opened to the present day.

This was actually my first time ever reading one of these even though I had seen them plenty of times before. The lesson of the day was on soul searching, and I knew I desperately needed to invest some time into that.

The next morning, I was pissed off when I opened my front door, and saw the box I gave Haji was in my mailbox.

"Haji was such an asshole," I grunted as I hopped in my car, tossed the box in the back seat, and turned on the ignition.

"Save Me," by Nicki Minaj started to play and all I could think about was what I had read in the Daily Bread last night and this morning. All I needed right now was God to save me from my own self. I had been on a destructive path lately and it seemed like no matter how hard I tried to avoid drama it seemed to follow me. I felt Nicki, because I could slowly feel myself giving up. I knew in my heart that it was time to find myself and change the person I was. Good grades and a bunch of degrees could not make up for the other secret life I was living outside of school. I knew I needed some kind of help whether it was God or counseling. Seemed, as if I had been through hell and back, lately. I was just happy that I could admit I had a serious problem. Denial, had lead me to make an ass out of myself, and I couldn't afford to do that ever, again. I pulled up at the salon to get my hair curled, and all eyes were glued to me once I walked in.

"Hey, Teaz, boo!" Niecy announced as I took my seat.

"I heard the party was bangin' last night," she added, and everyone was waiting for me to respond.

'Yea, I really enjoyed myself, and the party was overall a good turnout," I replied, flipping through a magazine.

"I told you to fall thru, Boo," I reminded her even though I already knew she wasn't gone show up.

"Girl, you know I would've been there if I didn't already have plans with my one Boo," Niecy explained while waving me over to take my seat in the chair.

"What I don't know is why you ain't been told me that your little boy toy of yours had such a fine ass brother?" She asked, and I was lost for words.

I never mentioned Ramir to her before, so I was shocked just hearing those words come out her mouth.

"Yea, this handsome brother was in here a few months back getting a haircut from Rio, and in walks you boo thang."

"Never even knew you had a boyfriend," Niecy said, giving me a crazy looked then continued.

"I'mma let that slide since I haven't seen you lately." She joked.

I was all in once he mentioned to his brother that he was taking his new girlfriend that he was falling in love with named, La'Teazya to their cabin later on that evening."

"He went on to say that he wanted it to be a romantic weekend outing so that he can get you to open up, and really trust him." Niecy smiled, and so did I.

My smile was replaced with a frown when she told me what happened next.

"His brother," Niecy paused.

"He's a hot mess because he bragged about some freak he'd hooked up with the night before, and even said he fucked on her front porch."

I almost choked sitting there listening to Niecy repeat their conversation, Haji's real thoughts about how he feels about me, and I was fuming on the inside. I felt a slight relief when my hair was done, and I left the shop. Niecy was my girl because she was cold when it came to the hair game. I also knew she loved to gossip. Nothing got past her ears without it leaving her mouth. She reminded me of my best friend Zar in so many ways when it came to people's business. They loved to keep their lives' private, but they knew any, and everything about everybody else's. I didn't mind her knowing that I had a Boo or the fact that he had a brother. I knew she was just letting me know she had found out that bit of information, because she was scoping out Haji. I also knew she knew she didn't have a chance with him being that she was really born a man. I was glad to find out a small piece of the truth I had been looking forever since I found out that Haji and Ramir were brothers.

"Haji was one twisted as son-of-a-bitch," I thought as "No Juice" by Boosie began to play.

He knew all along that I was going to be at the cabin with Ramir the night he showed up there unexpectedly. Like Niecy said: "It's only one La'Teazya that she knew of, so it wasn't too hard to put two and two together".

"I got you, Haji," I smirked, applying my lip-gloss, and turning up the music.

"I see that I'm gone really have to just show you," I snapped, closing my visor.

"Two can play this game."

"And, I just so happened to be a cold-hearted dirty, Bitch!"

Twisted
November 21, 2014

Ever since, Ize dropped the news on me about him killing my Mama our first conversation, I started writing him frequently. He didn't write me back which was the typical Ize thing to do, but I was sure he knew that I needed clarity. A part of me had to know why he killed Mama. I knew he told me that we would talk more once we were face to face, but something inside of me couldn't rest until I knew exactly what happened.

"Twisted," by Keith Sweat was playing as I danced on old school Sunday. I hated the way Ize always left me hanging on strings! Loose ends sang it best, but I felt more like Teena Marie as I danced. I was "Out On A Limb," and I was slowly giving in to Ize all over again. It had been a year since Mega was murdered, and I was finally off probation. I hadn't been in any more serious relationships since Mega, but I was playing the field here and there. My new passion was traveling with my best friend Rozi, and living my life to the fullest. Everything, Mega, had embedded in me during our short period of us knowing each other was starting to pay off. My bank account was growing by the weeks, and everything I did in life after his death was definitely beneficial to my future.

"You have to cherish people while they're still here," Mrs. Franklyn always told me. I now understood what she meant about the "borrowed time," we were all living on. I was turning into the female version of Mega, because everything I did was for the benefit of my better future. I now see why he admired me so much. Our life stories weren't the same, but we both had managed to overcome our struggles. Good or bad, I knew it was only one-way to stay ahead. My only goal was to stay alive, so I could make it out the hood. Therefore, I chose to live, and not just exist. I was on my way to the library when I bumped into an old friend of mine name, Lyriic.

"Life had a crazy way of connecting people," I thought as "Everybody Wants To Be A Star," by Beanie Sigel poured out of my stereo system when I put my key in the ignition. It was funny how the perfect songs played at the right moments, as if God were trying to tell you something through music

To be perfectly honest, good people were hard to come by in this lifetime. It's rare to find loyalty as a quality in the people you meet now-a-days. Everybody seems to be looking out for self, so friends aren't very common. You're lucky if you are blessed to have any real friends in your corner. Which is why I always use to ask myself "What is a girls' best friend"? Once I came up with all the obvious answers, I started to ask myself what would I do when life wasn't always as easy as the simple question like what is a best friend. I had to learn early on in life that I was my own best friend. I didn't pity myself either for feeling this way, because I didn't expect anything less than what Jesus got out of life here on earth. If the only perfect man that was ever born to this Earth was persecuted by his friends then who was I to expect some perfect life I accepted my life for what it was during my time I spent in prison. I wasn't a sinner, but I damn sure wasn't a saint, like Jesus. I was a realist, and I knew everything in life that happened to me whether good, or bad was because of the decisions I had made. My downfall was always putting more trust in others, than I did myself. I never backed down from any situation I faced. Instead, I learned from every obstacle, so I would never have to live a life of regrets. I looked all my fears in the eyes, facing even the harshest realities, and overcame them all. I admit that I didn't always use the best logic in each situation. Sometimes, I would let my emotions get the best of me due to me being a Pisces. No matter how things turned out, I always played my hand the best way I saw fit. It was a constant battle learning to be the master of my own destiny. I wasn't a person who gave up just because something was hard to me. Victory was always mine, even if that meant walking away with scars. The way I see it; "Sometimes your best cards are the ones you haven't played". I was just using what I grew to know, and that is to survive by any means necessary. It's a dirty world that we live in, and sometimes: "In order to play the game; you gotta learn the rules"! I also learned that sometimes breaking the rules came along with paving the right path for yourself. It was hard becoming the master, even when I knew I was the key factor in my life. This time around, I vowed that once I was up, I would never come back down. I was too smart to not use all the wisdom I had obtained to achieve some obtainable goals. The first thing I had to do was get off probation. Now, that I am back in school I can finish up my major in Business Management, and get the hell out of Michigan for good. I had evolved as a person, and I knew in my heart change was gone come. I guess there really is some truth to the books I read in prison by Betrice Berry called "When Love Calls You Better Answer, and Redemption Song". I reminisced on reading her message at the end of the book. I was inspired to have read something so endearing to my soul.

"There are always signs around trying to warn you and lead you down a different path if you just pay attention."

I was starting to become a firm believer of that now. I had to learn the hard way that "There are no shortcuts to any place worth going".

"Beach Chair," by Jay Z came on, and I could definitely hear my Angels singing to me that day. I was finally living, and I knew they were smiling down on me from the Heaven's above. Somehow, I knew Mega would be one of my guardian angels now that he was in Heaven. Stazy always said, "There were people in Heaven who are always with us to protect us daily," and I believed that now. I had survived so much in my life that I knew it was someone other than me looking out for my crazy ass. I was grateful to have them all up there looking out for me even when I couldn't. It was a beautiful summer day in the city. The car show was going on Downtown, and I decided to hit the streets with my girls in honor of my Boo. I knew if Mega were still alive he'd be cruising through the "Dream Cruise," in one of his fancy rides, so I was "out here, killing shit," like Barbie always said.

"Lil Nigga Snupe," was blasting by Meek Millz as I got stares and waves from all directions. I would just do my normal "Salute" to a couple crowds admiring all the vehicles driving by, and let my girls handle the rest. It wasn't every day you saw an Aqua colored Lucky Lexus full of bad bitches. I was blessed, and you heard T.I., "I didn't fuck with mediocre".

"Every day A Star Is Born,"

"Clap for 'em, Clap for 'em, Clap for 'em, Ayeeeee."

We all sang as the song changed to Jay Z. It was a good ass day, and I was feeling myself as we cruised through the streets. We set it off that night in the club too! Rozi and I were both pulling in hella tips by all the different groups of people and chicks in the club. It was a good night for the bar, and the strippers because we all were paid.

A local club promoter was in the club promoting one of his parties, and some local artist even performed. My girl Candy Kane was also having a birthday party so we we're rolling in dough. I had the whole club in a zone as I danced to "Clubbin'" by Marques Houston. Once "Tell'em What They Wanna Hear" by Rashad Morgan, a local Detroit artist, came on the dollars were flying, and I was feeling like U.S.D.A song. I loved the way these tricks kept throwing their money at me. I had these people in a trance, and I knew later on, I was gone go home, and "Throw This Money" all over my bed while rolling in it like Scrooge McDuck. Candy Kain performed her big "Birthday Special Surprise" performance that ended in us both naked, licking cake icing off each other bodies. Everything seemed to be going great in my life lately, and I was finally on the winning end of things. It wasn't shit that could take me off my winning streak now that I was up. The following week, I was chilling by the bar kicking it with my girl, Passion when Haji showed up. I hadn't seen him since I invited him for drinks that one evening, and sold him the story about Oz killing Mega. It is ironic, that tonight he is in the club patiently waiting to have drinks with me at the same table he was at the first night we had met.

"Hey, Haji," I smiled as I took a seat at his table.

He didn't say a word. He just opened the bottle of D'usse he had on ice and poured us both a drink.

"Long time, no see," I added, trying to spark up a conversation.

He just nodded, and sipped his drink.

"I see you've been good, La'Teazya," he finally responded.

Then I sipped my drink.

"You're looking good," he said more sarcastically than sincere.

"I can see that life has definitely been treating you good these days," He continued then swallowed the rest of his glass, and pored himself another.

"I can't complain," I said, taking another sip of my drink.

It was something different about Haji's demeanor so I made a mental note to only make small talk to get down to the bottom of his showing up unexpectedly.

"It's a bit hot in here, wouldn't you agree?" he asked, and I just played along.

I wasn't hot at all, and I already knew he was playing out the whole first date again. Once I agreed that I was hot, Haji suggested that we step outside to get some fresh air. We walked out the club, and he asked me to accompany him to his car to catch up a bit. I didn't really want to, because my first mind was telling me something wasn't right about seeing Haji after all this time.

"You aren't scared are you?" he inquired, and I could not admit that I was.

"So, what's good Haji?" I asked once we got in the car.

"Just checking on an old friend," he replied with a smile.

"I'm sure Mega wouldn't mind me checking up on his most loyal companion he had before he left this earth," he added, making sure to put emphasis on loyal.

Even the way he was talking to me was making me feel uncomfortable.

"I'm sure Mega would be proud of the person I have become," I stated.

"He always loved me for just being me, and I admired him for that," I explained making sure to put emphasis on my last statement.

"I'm sure he did," he mumbled.

"So how have you been?" I asked, trying to change the subject.

"I've been good, just staying under the radar, and off the scene. I need to always remain as low key as possible." He smirked.

"That's why my nickname is Ace, because I've always been a loner, and I like to make all moves myself." He told me, and I just listened.

I didn't know much about Haji, so I had to feel out the situation so I could know exactly what I was up against.

"I'm kind of like a ghost you know, nobody really knows me, but I'm tied into everything."

"I'd hate for my name to get in the wrong people mouths," he added, and I just rolled my eyes.

"It's only two people that know about that one situation, and I'd like to know that it'll always be that way," he finished, and I could have snapped.

"Did he really expect me to acknowledge the fact that I had people killed?"

For all I knew, he could have been wearing a wire, and I wasn't going out like that. I had to play it smooth. The truth had just come out about Haji, and his true colors were starting to shine through.

"I really don't understand what you're asking me right now?" I stated looking at Haji confused.

"What's understood should never have to be explained," I stated unlocking my door.

"You have a nice night, and be safe out here," I replied, while unlocking my door, and opening it.

I understood completely where Haji was coming from, but I didn't think that was information for anyone else's other than me, his, and Gods ears.

"It was hot, alright," I laughed.

I laughed some more thinking Haji was a hot ass mess for thinking I'd be talking to people about what I'd done after all this time.

"Was he serious?" I asked myself.

I know he didn't actually think; I'd tell someone that I had people murdered in the past. I never even told Mega about Mizz, or me killing Ladibug. I did not understand why Haji would think Oz was even worth speaking on now that he was out of the picture. I couldn't put anything past anyone after, tonight. Trust doesn't come easy, and I knew that I had to watch my back, especially when it came to Haji, now. I wasn't sure what he was up to, but I knew he was trouble the minute he walked in. I did have him kill Oz, so I couldn't really blame him for being suspicious. I knew he was also thinking I was capable of anything, and I was thinking the exact same thing about him.

"Trick No Good," I thought back to our very first encounter.

I laughed thinking about him trying to get me to shove the dope up my pussy. Then I thought about my Mama walking up to me, grabbing me around the arms, looking me deep in my eyes. In a drunken state of mind, she would slur, "Don't trust these Niggas".

"They're all snakes, Eve," she continued, and then made me promise to; "Never let their tricks be any good".

She always loved to call me Eve, every chance she got. Mama really acted as if it were my fault that all women was cursed by, God. I hated when my Mama went into her drunken rants because I would just stand there thinking she had seriously lost it as she chanted over, and over that she was "shaking the Devil out me".

The next evening, I was at home getting ready to go out with a dude that I had met a month ago at the club. I was listening to "The Last of The Mohicans" soundtrack, and my song "I Will Find You," by Clannad came on. I couldn't hold back the tears after thinking about all the people I had lost in the past few years. I even thought about my childhood best friend, Stazy.

"I will find you all again," I promised myself, as the song played while tears rolled from my eyes as the lady repeated the words, "No matter where you go".

A couple hours later, I was out having the time of my life with a young dude that had been pressuring me for a date. I finally decided to give him a chance once he showed up at the club practically begging me to go on a date with him. I was lucky that I agreed, too. So far, I was impressed with Ramir. Our first date was short, and sweet. A simple movie, dinner, and then he took me straight home. We ended up talking on the phone all night once he got home, and I felt like a schoolchild with a crush.

"He was the perfect gentlemen, despite his age." I thought, but I knew better.

Guy's always seemed to play it cool until they got what they wanted, and then they change once another opportunity presents itself. Only time would tell who Ramir really was, and trust me, people always show you exactly who they are. So beware! It is up to you to take heed, or not once their true selves showed up. Our second date really impressed the hell out of me; I have to admit. As a surprise, he took me to a new bookstore called "Sinful Publications," and I got two good books there. The first book I purchased was called "The Five People You Meet In Heaven," by Mitch Albom. It was one of Ramir's favorites and a must have because he always talked about it to me. The second book I brought was by one of my favorite authors Vickie Stringer called, "Let That Be The Reason". Ever since I read the whole "Dirty Red" series by her, I was addicted. The only author I liked better than Vickie was Raven Soars. Raven, is an author the whole world can relate, too. She is truly an inspiration to youg girls' as myself, and a lot of her work helped me get through my day-to-day struggles in life. I was very appreciative of Ramir for doing things with me that I knew others men wouldn't have even thought of doing with me on a date. The fact that we had met in a strip club while I gave him dances, never seemed to bother him in our life outside of the club. It felt good to be treated like the woman that I was for once, and not just a stripper. I hated when people tried to play me like a whore. We ended the night partying with his mother for her 50th birthday. This was kind of a weird way to end a second date being that I wasn't his girlfriend, or planned on being it. I felt honored nonetheless by the end of the night to have even met his mother. He told me that meeting her was a rare privilege that many girls before me didn't get. In a way, I felt kind of special. I had danced the night away with his most precious possession in life, and just knowing that he trusted me enough to meet his mom on a second date said a lot about his character. He also told me: "We all lived a double life somehow". Mine just happen to be taking off my clothes for money". We eventually starting going out more after that. Ramir took me to museums, plays, boxing, and we even took some art classes. We had regular walks in the park on Sundays and regular picnics whenever we had some extra free time. I loved spending quality time with Ramir, because he made me feel a sense of freedom. I loved his positive energy, and the peace that was starting to take over me. There was never a dull moment being with him, and I was grateful to have him in my life. A couple of great dates later, and a lot of getting to know one another over the past month. I find myself in a bar enjoying the juiciest steak I had ever eaten.

"I must admit, La'Teazya," Ramir announced, as I watched the band performing.

"Before you came along I wasn't going on many dates."

"Most of the girls I went out with only wanted one or two things, mostly both,"

"Dick and Money," he laughed.

"Trust me thou; that shit gets boring," Ramir continued.

"Sometimes, I really just want a woman I can talk to with some common sense, good sense of humor, and a decent conversation," he explained.

I just sat there listening to him go on, and on about his dislikes and likes in a woman. I felt him, because many of these chicks now days were still waiting on "Captain Save-A-Hoe". I shook my head, and laughed at their feeble minds. Nobody wanted real love anymore so they settled for anything, and fell for everything. People's morals stopped matching their values a long time ago, and women started thinking their best assets were their asses. Nobody wanted to work for anything anymore, especially if a Nigga was willing to give it to you. The easy way out is, the best route to go for most people. Any thing that makes you a quick couple of dollars considered a blessing. To most people growing up in the hood, an honest living was stealing other people's goods, selling everything from their souls to prescription drugs, and living off the government. Mama was right, having "kids" were some people's sick blessing to do absolutely nothing with their lives. Everybody, and his or her daddy was a drug dealer, or rapper, but nobody was saving for down the line. Everybody, I knew was always living for the moment. I was looking forward to a great longevity once I finished college. I never wanted my reputation to exceed my legacy, and falling in love was one of the furthest things on my mind right, now.

"So what about you, La'Teazya," I heard Ramir ask, breaking me out of my thoughts.

"Do you know what real love is?" he asked me, and I almost choked on my wine.

"Oh, Lord," I thought to myself.

This was turning out to be a good night until Ramir started talking about love, and asking me about it.

"Well," I mumbled as I thought about my next line.

"I do believe real love still exist in this world." I recalled, thinking back to the Franklyn's relationship.

The Franklyn' had been together since junior high school. Once they got married during college, they would soon have to overcome the fact that Mrs. Franklyn would never have children of her own. Mr. Franklyn never left Mary, nor did he cheat on her after finding out she had to have both of her ovaries removed due to complications of ovarian hyperactive stimulation syndrome. It amazed me that, love to them meant more than having children. Their bond was built solely upon love, loyalty, communication, and understanding each other's needs. I am sure the thought of marrying someone who couldn't give my foster-father a child was a hard decision to make as a man, but the bond they shared was worth more in the end. I, guess when you meet your soulmate, nothing can compare, or break you two when you stand as one unit. I was always hoping that I would find the same love in Ize, being that we were childhood sweethearts

"As far as love and I go," I answered, breaking myself out of my thoughts.

"We've had our tainted relationship in the past."

"And, I'm not sure if I'm ready to play that game, again." I giggled.

"You have heard George Michael classic song "Careless Whisper," right?"
I asked him.

Then told him; "I never wanted to dance that dance again".

I had to laugh again after saying that, because I was as serious as a heart attack when it came to not falling in love again. Love was not for me as far as I was concerned, and I was letting it be known, early. At this point, I really only had time to love "Me, Myself, and I," like Beyoncé said in her song. Apart of me was actually starting to accept that bittersweet reality of my future. I, guess what I had said was enough to satisfy his interest as far as the whole love thing went, because he left the subject alone completely. Once we got in his car "Down Ass Chick," by Bow Wow came on, and all I could think about was Mega. I knew if he were still alive, we would have been out of town, somewhere. We were always planning to move to Arizona, and start a new life once I got off probation. Now, here I was carrying on pointless converstaion with a temporary thrill I picked up to past time. I was feeling like J. Cole said about the girl in his "Losing My Balance," song as we drove. It always seemed like somehow, some way, whenever I wanted to take some time out for self, someone would manage to weasel his or her way back into my life.

"I'm sorry, Ramir," I thought to myself.

I am on some Annie Lennox, mixed with TLC shit, right now. There are "No More I Love You's," left in my heart, and I damn sure don't chase "Waterfalls".

Maybe, it is a good thing Ramir really wasn't looking for love right now, either. Then things between us will never have to get complicated. If he needed a chick to just chill with occasionally, and I am available; I guess we could hook, because I enjoyed his company. It was cool having someone around that I could just kick it with, and even have a good time with on a friendly level. I needed a good male friend around, but I knew Ramir being so damn handsome would be a distraction. I couldn't help but watch him out of my peripheral as we drove admiring his smooth chocolate skin. He was the perfect shade of mahogany with a hint of coco, and his wavy hair looked like the ocean ripples with every movement, because he also had a good grade of hair. His long eyelashes complimented his spellbinding, yet alluring eyes that would make any girl fall in love at first sight. Ramir was every woman's dream man came to life, and I knew then he was too good to be true. I secretly knew that was the real reason why I didn't want to get too involved with, him

"Turn On The Lights," by Future began to play once we reached my house. I thanked Ramir for a lovely evening, grabbed my carry out bag, gave him a big hug, said goodnight, and then walked up to my house.

"I sure wished that Ramir was coming with me," my mind thought as I reached the door, and gave him a little wave once I was I safely.

That night while I was lying in bed, I started to feel lonely as I listened to "Scream" by Timbaland. By the time "Scent Of Attraction," by Patra came on I knew I was long overdue in the sex department as I played with my pussy until I fell asleep. The next night, I went to work, and as usual, the club packed with poeple. It was a beautiful August night, and I was having a "Back To School," party. All the girls working the floor had on schoolgirl uniforms, but I was wearing a girl's scout uniform. I was selling the hell out of these goodies, and these fools couldn't keep their hands out my cookie jar as I danced to "Shake That Ass For A Rich Nigga," by Doughboyz Cashout.

"Slow Motion," by Juvenile was playing as I danced for a usual customer of mine name Alexis. Lucky Lex was a stud who ran a couple spots in Southwest Detroit. Lex's facial features and coloring proved that she was of the Latina race with ancestry probably going back to Central, or South America given her very noticeable indigenous traits. She was a very beautiful woman on the outside, but her nonchalant attitude towards life earned her a reputation after her brother was murdered, and she retaliated on his killers. She was one of my favorite clients, because she always paid me well.

"What are your plans for tonight, sweet cheeks," Lucky Lex asked, while I was giving her a lap dance.

"Nothing major." I lied.

"I was actually thinking about turning it in early, tonight,"

"Why what's up?" I replied, because Lucky Lex was my lance dance for the night.

"Well I was thinking about grabbing a bite to eat at my favorite little Mexican restaurant, and wanted your company,"

"If you not to busy," she said in her sweet Spanish accent.

I agreed, and then headed to the dressing room to change into my clothes. I followed her to the restaurant in deep Mexican town. After dinner, and a few drinks I ended up at Lucky Lex's house. She had paid me $600.00 dollars, just to go home with her. The entire night all she wanted to do was cuddle. The next morning, she thanked me before I left. She also confessed that she had missed having a female around due to a recent break up, and just me spending the night with her helped her get over her ex. I also got home, and discovered that Ramir had been texting all morning to invite me to breakfast at his house. By the time, I was dressed, and made it to his house it was lunchtime. I was pissed at first, because I had to ring the doorbell five times before he finally answered it in his towel.

"Damn, Ramir reminded me of Trey Songs," as I stood the admiring his physique.

I was starting to feel like 112 in the "Anywhere" video, because the boy was turning me on as he stood there with water glistening all over his body.

"I had left the door open for you, "he said, letting me in.

"I figured you'd do like any other crazy chick after the first couple rings, and check the door knob," he laughed.

"But, I guess you not like most chicks," he stated, while heading back to the shower.

I just laughed, thinking that had this been Ize, or Mega's house I probably would have.

"I'll just be a couple more minutes," he announced, and then told me to make myself at home.

I decided to check out the kitchen. I was curious to know what was on the menu since he invited me to breakfast. To my surprise, it wasn't a single food item in sight.

"I guess we're going out for breakfast," I laughed, and then turned right around to Ramir standing directly behind me.

"Did I frighten you," he asked me before I could say a word.

I just shook my head "No", but I was scared as hell on the inside. I never even heard Ramir come back into the kitchen I was so lost in my own thoughts. The kiss he laid on me next, took away any feeling of fear I was feeling inside. Ramir was going to work on my mouth with his, and I was starting to imagine how his tongue would feel between my thighs. I swear he had to be reading my mind, because he picked me up, threw me on top of the counter, and dove in between my legs face first. He was eating my pussy so good all I could do was call for God, himself. I had been trying so hard not to fall for Ramir, and here I was giving in to temptation. He was always full of surprises I thought as he did magic with his tongue. Every, Friday, Ramir sends me flowers to the club, he calls me every morning just to tell me I was the first thing on his mind once he woke up and the sun was shining. He even compares me to the stars, because every time that we are out together at night the stars are out, too. It was something about these past months with Ramir, and this moment that made me realize that maybe I had been too hard on the boy.

"What more did I need him to do to prove that he really wanted me," I asked myself through moans.

He had already proven that he was an amazing person, and right now, he had me soaring over the clouds. I couldn't believe I made him wait eight months to even get this close to the pussy. I couldn't resist anymore. I let Ramir have his way with me right there on the top of the kitchen counter, and table. Afterwards, he carried me to the shower, and I loved feeling all 6'5 ft of his frame against mine as the water covered our bodies. His skin was the smoothest, dark chocolate, I've ever seen. I admired his physique as he fucked me in ways I didn't even know I could do, and I was feeling like MiMi on her sex tape, because he had me wide open. After we got dressed we went to Bucharest, and enjoyed lunch then he drove me back to my car so that he could meet with his older brother. I didn't know much about him other than they had the same father, and he wasn't in town a lot. Ramir was the only child on his mother's side of the family. Ramir and his brother weren't close growing up. The two boys never knew each other until their father was murdered. No longer than a few months after that, they ended up meeting by chance at a grocery store when their mothers bumped into one another. At first, Ramir's mother was bitter about the encounter being that she was married to their dad. The other woman was a fling from time to time who ended up getting pregnant first with Ramir's only brother. They agreed to let the boys see each other on weekends, but his brother eventually moved out of town, and he didn't see him again until they ended up at the same college. I thanked Ramir for the lovely morning, and then told him to bring his brother to the barbeque Rozi, and I was having later on if he wasn't busy. When he did show up, he was alone claiming that his brother couldn't make it. We ended up having a ball that night. I was having so much fun, I almost stripped for our guest. Ramir stayed over that night, and we had so much sex that I knew Rozi was going to be pissed the next morning. Ramir had put it down all night with his young ass, and for the first time I thought, I had met my match sexually. I loved the way he growled once he came. I swear I had taken him to heights not even he knew he could achieve by making him fuck me thirteen times in a row. I guess that is why he was asking me to commit this morning. He didn't want anybody else getting a piece of these goodies, anymore. I laughed, thinking about how he kept whispering that in my ear the entire time we were doing it the last time we fucked. I always knew I was a beast in bed, but I honestly thought I had just met my match. My motto on sex is simple. Take me to your boudoir, and a lovesick, stuck on me, sex nympho is bound to leave out behind me. Moments later, your bodies yearning for an instant replay of my session of straight fucking. Just like magic. Ramir was knocking on forbidden doors with all this relationship talk, but I went ahead, and told him I would be his girl. Technically, he was the only person I had been seeing lately, so being faithful wasn't a problem for me. I just really hope that it all works out for us. I would really hate to be wasting my time all over again.

That night, I was at the club doing my last show of the night to "2 On" by Tinashe, and right before I finished Haji walked in.

Just like the first time we'd met, my Lucky Lexus was in the shop. I was getting some new custom painted rims, and pink tiger stripes on the hood, and both doors. It was time to spice things up in my life, and my car was always the first on my list. My love life seemed like it was taking off, and I was happy that I had given Ramir a chance.

"Sup, Teaz," Haji greeted taking a seat by the bar as I talked to Rozi.

"Hi Haji," I replied then asked Rozi to bring me a drink.

"Who's the handsome guy, Teaz," Rozi inquired, and I introduced her to Haji.

"Good Job," I thought to myself.

If this Nigga ever tries anything crazy, at least Rozi will be able to pick him out of a lineup. I also made a mental note to put her up on game later on that night once we were at home. I knew I was going to have to leave out a few major details being that he killed Oz for me. I just needed to tell her enough to make her keep her eyes open, and alert whenever he is around. After she gave us our drinks, he asked if we could talk privately. I accompanied him to a booth not too far from the bar. I wanted to be in plain view just in case this fool tried anything. I wasn't too sure about

Haji's intentions after the last visit we had, and I damn sure wasn't about to let my guard down.

"Freak No More" by Migos started to play, and I just sang along.

"So what's up with you, Teaz?"

"I know I came at you wrong the last time I saw you, and I don't ever want you to feel uncomfortable around me." He stated.

I was honestly glad he had addressed that issue. Haji was really starting to creep me out with all the pop up visits he kept doing.

"I know it seems like every time we run into each other it's something up with me" he continued shaking his head, while letting out a deep breath.

"I swear though, Teaz, all I need is a friend right now," he confessed, and I didn't know what to say.

I just listened to Haji tell me about what he was doing since I last saw him. By the time, he finished talking I felt like I had known him for years. My thoughts about him possibly being a potential enemy had flown right out the window as we sat talking about life. He offered to give me a ride home, I agreed, and then told Rozi I would see her at the house. The ride to my place had me thinking about our first date. I wanted to put it down on Haji's fine ass once I got home, but never got the chance too, because of how the night ended. As fate would have it, he would end up being the

God-brother of my deceased ex-boyfriend, and the man I had murder my other ex's enemy.

"Life was twisted," I thought as "My Story" by local artist Eastside Peezy began to play.

I felt him, because even if I told you my life, I would not know where to begin. I learned that you can't change your past, but a better future is determined by your present. Sometimes progress should always be your current situation. You have to evolve now, and let growth ensure a promising destiny. Samuel L. Jackson said it best on one of my favorite movie, "The Samaritan".

"Nothing changes unless you make it change."

"I'm just trying to soar above dry land, while remembering to never leave, abandon, or neglect my dreams".

We pulled up at my house, and I was just about to get out the car when Haji asked me to chill for a few. We kicked it for a little while longer as he rolled a blunt listening to "Astronaut Chick" by Future.

"That's all I need in my life," he declared, passing me the blunt to light it.

I couldn't refrain from asking him, "What"?

"My Ace," he stated.

"My better half, or just somebody who loves me for me" he continued, and I was all in.

"Life would be so complete," he smiled then hit the blunt.

My mind did a flashback of me asking him was he married, or single the first night we had met to flirt with him. I couldn't see why any girl in their right mind wasn't trying to push up on Haji. He was handsome as hell, and the feeling of temptation was definitely hard to resist. I hit the blunt, and quickly passed it back to him. I had to keep reminding myself that I had just gotten committed to Ramir. If this had been a week ago, I probably would have been all over Haji's fine ass by now. I fantasized about us being together as my buzz kicked it. The weed we were smoking was so strong it felt like it was doing magic to my pussy. The more I sat there having lustful thoughts about fucking Haji while smoking, the wetter my pussy got. My phone rang, and I knew in my heart it was, Ramir. He always called me around this time to make sure I made it home safely. At first, I wasn't going to answer, but I knew trust was the key to every successful relationship. I picked up the phone assuring him that I was okay, and then I told him I would call him before I went to sleep.

"One of your little fans," Haji joked, and I just shook my head.

"Slow Your Roll," by Young Buck came on, and I was starting to get tired. I told Haji, I had a good night talking with him, and then gathered my things to go in. He offered to walk me to my door once I stepped out the car. Once we reached the porch, he asked for a hug then pulled me in close to his body before I could say yes.

"It was good talking with you, Teaz," he smirked, and I wanted to frown.

"We should do this more often," he told me and before I could say, "I agree" he kissed me.

I was so shocked, as I stood there with Haji's lips pressed to mine.

"Where the fuck did that come from Haji?" I snapped pushing him away.

He just kissed me again, and this time I gave in. The next thing I remember was waking up the next morning with a banging ass headache, and praying that my neighbors didn't hear, or see me and Haji getting it on right there on the porch. I must admit, that fucking Haji on the porch might have been one of the best nights of my life. It is just something about that, "we're not supposed to be fucking" that thrills my spirit. Haji went to work on my pussy all over the porch, and I loved every minute of it! I had never experienced a night as wild as last night, and just the thought of being caught turned me on as he fucked the shit out of me from the back against the railing. It was a good thing I didn't let Haji spend the night, because Ramir showed up at my house the next morning.

"Love 'Em Like My Doe," by The Streetlordz was blasting outside my bedroom window, and caused me to wake up out my sleep. I answered the door half naked, and I could tell Ramir had an attitude.

"What happen to you calling me back last night," Ramir asked, and I instantly thought about Haji.

"I fell asleep," I lied.

"I had a long night at the club, Boo," I whined.

"I apologize," I added, walking up to him giving him a kiss.

"I bet you did," he responded, releasing my grip.

"So what we doing today, Daddy," I asked, trying to brighten up the mood.

I wasn't about to feed into the bullshit.

"I have to go meet my bro before he goes back out of town."

"When I come back, I plan on taking you out," he explained.

"I'm so geeked up," I giggled, going over to where he was sitting.

I wasn't really in the mood for having sex after last night but I knew he didn't show up this early in the morning for nothing. I quickly popped him off as "Quickie" by U.S.D.A. played, and then sent him about his way when we were through. I needed some time to relax, and get myself together for later on.

I was feeling myself as "Boss Ass Chick" by Nicki Minaj played. I had to laugh while she rapped her verse. Last night I had done the unthinkable and fucked Mega's best friend. I felt bad; because that was the third thing, I ever did to betray Mega. If he hadn't of got killed, and the situation would've played itself out any other way I probably wouldn't have fucked Haji. I couldn't take it back now that it was done so I'd just have to learn to make better decisions. I had also just cheated on my new boyfriend, and I wasn't even sure if I was in love with him yet.

"What type of shit do I be on?" I wondered.

Then I thought about how if I hadn't of ran back into Haji that Oz would still be alive. I still couldn't believe Barbra had taken her life. Everything thing happens for a reason I guess, and her death was one thing I will never truly understand. I had to tell somebody about all the drama I had going on so I went to talk to Rozi. I filled her in on all my dirty little secrets, and I even told her that I would be hooking up with Ramir later on that night. I joked about how he popped up that morning with an attitude, and how I was going to fuck the shit out of him later on to make up for last night. I also told her I'd text her later that evening to let her know how it all works out, and for her to let me know if Haji pops up looking for me while I'm gone. She told me to have a ball as usual, and I sure as hell planned on it.

It was 9:30 pm, when Ramir came back to pick me up. He claimed he had something "Real Special" planned for me, and I couldn't wait to see what it was. Ramir was always so romantic and spontaneous who knew what he had up his sleeves. He did text me an hour before he pulled up to remind me to pack an over-night bag.

"If you could have anything in this world Teaz, what would it be?" he asked as we drove.

I thought very hard before I answered, because all I could think about was, peace.

"Peace," I answered, and he just nodded his head.

"Would you ever have a threesome?" he inquired, and I laughed.

Men seemed to ask me this question often, being that I was a stripper. I wasn't really into sharing my men. The closest I ever got to a threesome was licking icing off, of Candy Kain while a bunch of men watched. Ever since Mizz, I had been strictly dickly, and I didn't see myself going back down that road again. The only way I ever saw myself having a threesome is if I could have two men of my choice fuck me at the same time. Just the thought of it made me think about Ramir, and Haji fucking me at the same damn time.

"That would be some crazy shit," I thought, and then told Ramir, "Never".

I did say that I didn't mind arranging them if someone wanted one but then dude wouldn't be my man, he'd be my client.

"Money talked," I teased, and then asked him a couple questions of my own.

He popped in a cd after that, and "Somebody Gotta Die" by Biggie, "24 Hours To Live" by Mase, and "I'm Supposed To Die Tonight" by 50 Cent, were they first three songs to play. A chill went through my entire body as we drove past nothing but trees.

"Crazy song choice," I thought as I listened to the cd.

I just looked out the window as we drove into the night. I started to feel a little better once "The Watcher," by Dr. Dre came on but for some reason I felt paranoid. I pulled out my blunt I had put out earlier, and lit it to calm my nerves. Three hours later, we were at a little cabin by the lake. It made me think about the time Ize invited me to the cabin in Lexington. To my surprise, the cabin wasn't as nice on the inside as the one Ize invited me, too. Ramir must have been reading my mind as I looked around the place. Once we were unpacked, Ramir explained that the cabin had once belonged to his father, and was given to him by his mother on his eighteenth birthday. They would go there a lot as a family when he was a child, but once his father was murdered; his mother neglected the cabin until he asked for it before he went to college. He also neglected the cabin for years to avoid the memories they all shared, but decided to use the cabin as a hideout, or a place to have sex with random girls during his first years of college. I was the first person he had ever brought to the cabin that he cared about since then. He also told me that he hoped we would be in love by our next visit. I was all over him after that. I have always believed in the quote "Actions speak louder than words", and Ramir's actions were always showing me he cared. I wasn't about to wait until it was too late to fall in love like I did with Mega so I decided right then and there to just go with the flow. After we had sex I took a shower, and all kinds of thoughts flashed in my head. At times, I just wished I could turn back the hands of time.

"What is twisted cannot be straightened; what is lacking cannot be counted," my mind told itself.

"It was all a part of the many meaninglessness pursuits of humans under the sun, simply because nothing is new. We all have different journeys to face in life, yet our stories are all similar. Life is like one big "Urban

Legend," that continues with each new generation. History constantly repeating itself.

"I don't ever want my journey to be meaningless, just a chasing after the wind." I thought back to me hearing that somewhere.

"It's truly a struggle to remain humble through chaos," I reasoned, while lathering up my rag with soap.

"It's even harder to keep your head when all those around you are losing their heads, and blaming you" I reminisced on Mr. Franklyn telling me that after a fight I had.

"It seems like my whole life, I have been up against the wind," like Lori Perry's song, I explained to him.

"You can't always feed into other people's negativity, Teaz,"

"It takes two people to argue, and walking away doesn't make you a punk," he advised.

"Wise people choose their battles," He continued, while looking me in the eyes.

"Not every fight is meant to be yours," he added, and I knew he was right.

It took me until now to really understand what he meant by that. I now understood my Mama's favorite little saying about not letting men trick me any further like the snake tricked Eve.

"Trick No Good," she would always say.

"We're all damned, because of the sin Eve committed," she would slur.

"Innocence is a blessing amongst the cursed, and I've never been that fortunate," she would yell.

"Ain't shit getting past these eyes, because I always knew more than I ever let be known." she would finish with a laugh.

It was always some crazy logic behind Mama's drunken rages. What she would never understand is that my innocence was gone the minute she allowed Bono to let the drunken man into my bedroom. If she was ever trying to protect my innocence, she sure didn't try hard enough. My Mama was the first person in this world I couldn't trust, because of her problem with drugs, and alcohol. I never did understand how the person who brought me into this world could hate me the most. I was sure that family was the one thing you could always depend on without a shadow of doubt. Besides, blood is always thicker than water, right? If there were one thing I could honestly say I have learned out of everything I had been through, it would have to be to choose your friends wisely. Enemies came in all forms, and you can never truly know who is out to get you. Sometimes you have to sit back, and correct the demons within yourself before you can correct the demons in other. People only do what you allow them to do, and believe me when I say they always show you their true colors. The key to survival is never giving your opponents the bullets to shoot you down. Sometimes you have to face your worst fears to become the true master of self. The revelation of knowing self-worth is priceless, and the wisdom you get is worth it.

I could hear Ramir talking to someone once I stepped out the bathroom. He ended the conversation once I entered the bedroom where he was.

"Is everything okay?" I asked him.

He looked somewhat frustrated after hanging up with whomever he was talking too. I just took a seat at the end of the bed, and put on my lotion. I wasn't going to let anything negative get in the way of our evening.

"Yea, everything's cool," he replied nervously, and I just continued to get dressed into my nightgown.

"I'll meet you in the living room," he told me, and then left out the room.

Once I got dressed, I texted Rozi and told her everything was going good with us. When she didn't text me back right away, I figured she was having a good night of her own. I cut my phone off for the rest of the evening so no one would disturb my time alone with Ramir. I walked into the living room, and Ramir was watching some old homemade movies. I took a seat next to him, and got cozy under the throw blanket. I saw a little boy who I knew was Ramir having a birthday party. I heard a man's voice in the background, and I knew it was his Dad.

"Say hi to the camera, Ramir," His dad instructed, and Ramir said "Hi".

"How old are you turning today?" His dad asked, and Ramir replied "Three," while holding up three of his fingers.

"My big boy," His dad responded, and then zoomed into Ramir.

"I am a big boy," Ramir announced, showing off his muscles.

"Now who is that lovely lady?" the man asked, and Ramir smiled.

"That's my, Mommy silly," Ramir giggled, running up to her.

The camera focused in on her as she gave a little wave, and twirled Ramir around.

"I married the most beautiful woman is this world," He stated, and then it went off.

I was almost in tears seeing how his parents genuinely loved one another. I wanted that kind of love someday and I thought it would be so cute if that turned out to be our ending. I always dreamt of a knight in shining armor coming along to rescue me from the evil villain called, "life". It was a strong possibility that Ramir could have had been sent here to do just that. He took his time to win my heart, by showing me a different lifestyle. He wasn't as flashy as I thought he would be when we first met, and he actually came from a decent background. Ramir worked hard for everything he had, and he carried himself with dignity. He knew his self-worth unlike the other men I had met before him. He wasn't the average street nigga just trying to become a hood legend. He still lived by the traditional family rules, and morals. We shared some of the same values when it came to raising kids, and what a husband needs in a wife. We both had just hit rock bottom in the love department so we were taking things day to day. He worked as a chef in upscale restaurant, and was on his way to receiving a Bachelor's degree in Culinary Arts. Ramir wasn't perfect, but he was the perfect gentleman when it came to my well-being, as well as protective. If anything, he was a man I could build a life with in the future. We both didn't have any kids, and with both of us being on the right track I could see us one day becoming a power couple. The next thing I knew another clip came on. It was Ramirs father, and for a split second, he looked like Haji. The sex we had must have put a spell on me, or something I thought, because Haji kept popping up in my head. His dad was saying how he loved his family, but he knew he had messed up by having another child with another woman. I guess that was the story of everyone's household who had a single mother. Papa was nothing more than a rolling stone was, and wherever he chose to lay his hat was home. It ended with Ramir's father promising him to raise both boys, equally. He also promised that his actions wouldn't affect their home, and told Ramir that he hoped one day he would understand, and forgive him. He wanted Ramir to promise that he would never do women the way he did. I watched Ramir look at his father, taking in his every word. The next clip that popped on was a party. It had to be something Ramir recorded during his first college year.

"Sup, everybody," a younger Ramir spoke.

"Tonight, it's about to go down!" he continued.

"Me, and my big bro are about to have the party of a lifetime."

"I'm talking epic moment people," he yelled, and I burst out laughing.

"You heard Whodini, the freaks are about to come out tonight,"

"Trust me," he laughed, pulling out a box of condoms.

"My ace boon coon and I are well prepared," he laughed, and I laughed even harder thinking he always thought he was a ladies' man.

"He was quite the little charmer," I smiled, thinking about how he persuaded me to go out with him.

He would literally come to the club every night looking for me until I agreed to let him take me out on a date. I was starting to feel like I was lucky for once. Ramir was everything I expected him not to be, and I was glad to have a good man, finally. After Mega, I had really given up on love, but I guess you can't let love knock you down like Keri Hilson sang. I was so busy smiling at Ramir that I never saw his brother when he flashed the camera on him. I heard him say a quick couple of remarks and by the time I looked up again the camera was back on Ramir. It was something about his brother's voice that reminded me of someone I knew. Ramir cut the television off after that.

"What's wrong?" I asked.

He didn't say a word, so I concluded that he must've been feeling kind of emotional after watching all those different flicks of his family. I figured seeing his dad after all those years triggered some feelings he had hidden deep down inside. I could tell he didn't want them to surface in front of me but I knew what he was going through. I knew men tried to hide their feelings often, but I wanted him to know it was okay to cry in front of me. We all needed to cleanse our soul every now and then, and crying was always what did that for me. I reached in to hug him once he took his seat, and he just stood up and walked over towards the cabinet.

"Don't pity me, Teaz," he stated, staring at some trophies.

"My fathers' been dead for a long time now," he continued, removing a picture for the cabinet.

"I became the man he wanted me too, and I've done exactly what he asked of me, and more."

"I can honestly say, I made him, proud," he stated placing the picture back where it was.

I had to agree, because despite how we met, Ramir has treated me with nothing by the utmost respect.

"I just wish I could find a woman as loyal to me as my mother was to my dad, and then I'd be complete." He continued turning to face me.

I thought about when I was little, and Ize had told me those same exact words about his parents. I also thought about Haji telling me this the other night while we kicked it. This was the third time I had heard this in my life, and I knew it was a sign.

"Are you a loyal person, La'Teazya?"

"Can you honestly say, I trust you with my life?"

"Most importantly, can I always trust you to be honest with me?" he asked me.

For a minute, there was complete silence.

"I guess what I'm asking you is, do you really love me?" he pleaded with me, and I could have fainted.

'Where was all this coming from?" I wondered.

I never gave Ramir a reason to doubt me, but I knew he wanted answers. I just wish the timing were different. I planned to enjoy this night and here he is ruining it with all these love questions.

"Of course, I love you," I replied.

"You can trust me with anything," I assured him.

"Umm Hmm," was all he managed to mutter sarcastically.

After all, they were short and simple without any real explanation behind them. I was trying to get over the whole "21 Questions," game. I didn't know why Ramir was always hitting me with these damn questions at the most obtund times.

"I know I asked you this before, but I'm going to ask you again," he stated, and I just shook my head.

"Are you ready to commit to me?" he asked, and all I could do was look off into space.

I wasn't really sure if I was ready to commit, but since I already agreed to it the first time he asked me, that's what I was sticking too. I did slip up and fuck Haji the night before so I knew I was far from being faithful. A part of me wanted to feel Haji inside of me one more time before I turned into a one man, woman. My mind was telling me to slow my roll, and my heart was telling me it could be true. I just played my role in this game when it came to the men I dated. I was in it while it was good, but once the thrill is gone… you know what they say.

"Yes," I replied.

"Have you been faithful to me since we started messing around?" he inquired, and I laughed.

"Come on now, Ramir," I whined, walking up to him.

I put my arms around his neck, and looked him deep in the eyes.

"You been so good to me since we've met," I smiled.

"Why would I ever want to let go of all this," I teased, snuggling up to him.

"I already have everything I need right here," I continued, pulling him in closer for a kiss.

"So you haven't fucked anyone?" he repeated, and I quickly said "NO".

"The one thing I hate most in this world is a liar," he stated, and I felt nervous inside.

"I'd hate to find out the truth in the streets when you could've just told me yourself," he advised, and for a second I wanted to rid myself of my sins.

I wanted to take back the lie I had just told. I knew it wasn't anything I could do now, but stick to my story now that I had told it.

"I swear, Bae," I promised, while pushing him up against the wall.

"You'll never hear anything about me other than what I've already told you" I assured him then gave him a kiss.

Just before I unbuckled his pants, the doorbell rang.

"Who could be coming to visit at 1:30 in the morning?" I thought then watched Ramir disappear to open the door as I took a seat on the couch.

"Who was that Bae?" I inquired when I heard footsteps.

I almost fell out on the floor, and died when I looked up to see Haji standing there instead of Ramir.

"OH MY GOD!" I mumbled as Ramir entered the room.

"What the fuck is really going on?" My mind wondered but my mouth said nothing.

"What's wrong, La'Teazya?" Ramir asked, and I was speechless.

I just wanted to blink my eyes, and hope that what I was seeing wasn't really happening.

"N- N- Nothing," I stuttered over my answer looking from Ramir to Haji.

"Oh, it just looks like you saw a ghost," Ramir replied with a smirk, and I instantly knew something was up.

"How did he find out about Haji, and I?" I pondered.

"Could he have been sitting outside my house that entire time the other night?" I quizzed my own brain trying to find all the right answers.

Nothing I came up with was a logical explanation to why Haji was here right now, and why Ramir had not said a word to me if he did know about me, and Haji fucking. I didn't know what to expect being that they were acting as if they knew each other for years. To make matters worse, I didn't hear them say a word to each other once Ramir opened the door.

"Maybe, Haji was the one Ramir was on the phone with the whole time I was in the shower," my mind yelled.

"Is this a set up?" I feared, thinking the unimaginable was about to happen.

I kept thinking about the songs Ramir was playing on the way here, and the line of questions he was asking me all night. It was all starting to make sense to me now. This had to be some sick twisted joke, and I was secretly hoping the little Devil from the show "Cheaters" would appear. I knew in my heart he wasn't coming out though. It was about to go down, and whatever happened tonight would be between us three, and God. Everything about this very moment felt wrong! All I could do was hear the lyrics from the song "Heaven" by Bebe, and Cece Winans that I listened to earlier while I was in the shower before Ramir picked me up. Something inside of me told me I would be going there very soon, and I was hoping it would be everything they sang about if that was my only option. I sat there in a daze as they chitchatted, laughing, joking with one another, and I couldn't find anything funny about this situation I was in.

"Are you sure you're okay?" Ramir asked me again, as Haji walked over to a chair, and took a seat.

"Yea, I'm sure," I lied, and then tried to force a smile.

I was shaking on the inside, and I was hoping to God that it wasn't showing on the outside.

"Bro," Ramir finally acknowledged, and the piece I needed to put the puzzle together had just come out.

"Let me introduce you to my girl, La'Teazya," Ramir announced.

Haji just shot me a look that said it all.

"Your girl?" Haji replied, and I just wanted to disappear.

"She's a real piece of eye candy, Mir," Haji added, sarcastically.

Ramir just looked at me with a smile.

"You know how I do it, big Bro,"

"If she ain't fly then she ain't me," he teased.

I was getting more, and more disgusted by the minute just sitting there listening to their bullshit.

"So, La'Teazya," Haji said.

"Mind if I call you Teaz for short?" he inquired, and I wanted to slap the grin he had off his face.

"Sure," I answered, trying to only make small talk.

"So you're the new girl I've heard so much about that's been holding my brothers interest lately?" he smirked, and I was frightened by the sinister look he gave me.

"You must be really special to have won the heart of this man right, here," he added, and then walked up to Ramir and put his arm around him.

"I guess, I am," I teased with a smile then looked at Ramir.

He was smiling from ear to ear with that same happy-go-lucky attitude he always had. I watched Haji frown looking at how happy Ramir was to have me as his girl.

"Must be nice," Haji mumbled, removing his arm from around Ramir's neck.

"Pay my brother no mind," Ramir stated, taking a seat next to me on the couch.

He had to literally, turn me to face him, because my attention was still on Haji. It was something about the whole situation that didn't feel right no matter how Ramir tried to justify it.

"So where were we," Ramir inquired, but my focus was on Haji.

This was by far the craziest shit I had ever experienced in my life.

"Who would've known that they were brothers?" I concluded, and then started to feel panicky.

The thought that I had earlier about the threesome with both of them wasn't looking so good now that I knew they were brothers. I was secretly wishing I didn't know either one of them now that the dark was finally coming to light. The reality of this situation could be deadly, and I was sure I would end up burnt. Who knew I was playing with fire? I had just lit the match in a room filled with gasoline. I had been sleeping with the enemy, and it felt like my ending would be a burning bed. I thought about my song by Eminem "Love The Way You Lie", and what Ramir said earlier about finding out about me lying from someone else's lips other than mine. I thought about Haji exposing our little secret to his brother, and the possibility that he already knew and this was my last day on earth. Then I thought Haji was taking too long to come out the bathroom for me, and I was wondering what he was up too. I kept wishing this night was a dream I could wake up from, but I knew that would never happen. I remember my number one rule, and that would be the key to get me out of this mess. Your opponents only have so much advantage against you once they think they know your weakness. Now it was time to be unbreakable even with the odds against me.

"Could they have been playing me all this time?" I theorized.

I could hear Ramir asking me something about love, and I almost snapped.

"Not this love shit again!"

"Excuse me?" I responded, confused.

We already had this whole love conversation before today. I didn't see why he was bringing this up again when I just answered the question for him less than five minutes before Haji walked in. I sighed, because I didn't really want to be having this conversation with Ramir while psycho Haji was around.

"Don't you think this is something we should discuss in private?" I asked.

They were not about to just sit there, and play mind games with me the entire night. It was time to reverse the conversation, and flip the script on these fools.

"I just wanted to know if you could see yourself possibly falling in love with me one day." He stated.

"I never got to ask you this, because we were interrupted by my brother," he continued, and I ignored the question all together.

Haji came out the bathroom, and I wanted to excuse myself. I needed to gather my composure. I could slowly feel myself losing it on the inside, but for some odd reason I couldn't move.

"I'm curious to know the answer to that myself," Haji chimed in, walking towards the kitchen.

"Damn," I whispered.

I wondered just how long he was ear hustling before he actually decided to leave the bathroom. Haji was really starting to annoy me. Not only did I want him to leave, I was starting to wish I never met him at all. He was the worst type of enemy of them all. Anybody who could smile in your face and stab you in the back right afterwards had to be pure evil. He was my modern day Judas, and his kiss was death.

"I'm sure if you're half as incredible of a woman that my brother always makes you out to be you'll be getting engaged, soon," he taunted, and I rolled my eyes.

"I am my brother's keeper, you know," Haji added, and I just watched Ramir.

"I would love to be the best man at your wedding," he finished, walking out of the kitchen with a bottle in his hand.

These fools were starting to remind me of the two brothers from the movie "Funny Games". I just happened to be the target of their twisted game, because of the bad decisions I had made.

"Do you drink, La'Teazya?" he asked, placing three glasses on the table.

I just sat there in disbelief, and I didn't even bother to respond. All I wanted to know was how long were they actually going to keep up with this bullshit? I couldn't put up with the crap anymore. They were "Killing Me Softly" with words liked the Fugee's sang, and all I could do was play along as the lyrics were being written. I watched him pour us all a glass of wine. Then he took a seat in the love seat that was next to me.

"It's cool, Teaz!"

"You don't have to answer that right now,"

"You can just tell me your answer another time," Ramir explained.

I watched Haji finish his drink then smiled at me.

"I wasn't interrupting you all was I?" Haji finally asked, and I almost answered for Ramir.

"You good, Bro," Ramir replied, but I wished Haji would leave.

I hated the fact that Haji ended up being our uninvited guest, but it wasn't anything I could do about it. I sat there patiently waiting for him to leave thinking that this could possibly be my last night. I couldn't wait to tell Rozi about this mess when I got home. Then the thought crossed my mind that I might not get home.

"Why did I cut off my phone?"

I thought about me turning it off before I came downstairs with Ramir. I had to get to it somehow.

"So what brings you by Bro?" Ramir asked, and I wanted to know the same thing.

"I was actually driving past here on my way to the freeway, and decided to stop once I saw lights on," Haji paused, and asked for a bottle of water.

"I haven't been out here since we were in college, and for some reason Dad's been on my mind a lot lately," He explained, and I started to excuse myself right, then.

I had a flashback of the last conversation I had with Haji. He did mention his Dad to me briefly, but I didn't know he was talking about the same man, Ramir had briefly mentioned. It wasn't like I saw Haji on a day to day basis, but I remember him telling me that he always felt abandoned as a child by his dad, because he loved his brother's Mom more than his own. I did notice that their father looked a lot like Haji when we were watching the old movies of them. The fact that I didn't get to see Haji when the camera flashed on him had me clueless to what his brother looked like until now.

"I know," Ramir agreed.

"I was just telling Teaz that she is the first person I've brought out here since those days," He said with a smile.

"Like I said earlier, baby Bro," Haji replied staring at me.

"Lucky girl," he smirked, and I rolled my eyes.

"Well I won't hold you two love birds up any longer," he announced, drinking his glass, and standing up.

"It's getting pretty late, and I gotta hit this road," he added, walking to the door.

"I'll catch you when I'm back in town," He told Ramir, but he was looking dead at me.

Ramir stood up to walk him to the door, and I let out a sigh of relief.

"You have a great night, La'Teazya," Haji yelled from the door.

I didn't say a word I just headed for the bathroom.

"What the fuck just happened?" I asked myself starring at my reflection in the mirror.

"Can I really trust this nigga, Ramir after knowing that he's brothers with the guy I fucked?"

I was in too deep to turn back now, so I had to play it smart until the end. The first thing I had to do was distance myself from both of these fools after this little weekend escape is over. I also had to find out just how much Ramir knew. I knew that when you assumed things you tend to make an ass out of yourself, so I always went on facts, and the facts was the very thing I needed right now.

"Three can play this game," I smirked, listening to Richie Homie Quan from the bathroom.

"I guess I'll have to show them both I'm not to be played with," I thought splashing water on my face.

"They don't know what I've been through. They don't know the half." I laughed.

"They only know what I tell them," I sang, while opening the door.

So, The Games Begin
Dear Diary,
December 11, 2014

"Ain't no sunshine when she's gone". Bill Withers sang as I pulled into the parking lot of my doctor's office. Lately, I had been feeling a little under the weather, so I made an appointment to have a checkup. I was in total disbelief when the doctor announced that I was pregnant. I felt like the girl Jane from my new favorite show, "Jane The Virgin" except I knew my pregnancy was a result of my own foolishness. A few weeks later, I wanted to faint as the doctor did my ultrasound. Being pregnant was the last thing I needed to hear with everything else that was going on in my life. I was so mad after seeing the baby that was growing inside of me that

I stormed out the doctor's office afterwards. I banged my head repeatedly on the steering wheel once I got into my car. I began to cry while "Walk On By," by Isaac Hayes played as I stared at my ultrasound picture. I was never going back to the dark side now that I was in search for the light in my life. I knew everything that I was going through was the, Devil. It was starting to feel as if he was playing a sick game with my life, I thought as I cried. I knew that I was going to have to make one of the toughest decisions a woman ever had to make about their first unborn child. I didn't approve of abortions, but I knew I couldn't keep this baby for two reasons. First off, I didn't know which brother I was pregnant by, being that I had slept with both brothers, unprotected, recently. The second problem was that I had slept with Haji unprotected twice, and he was the last one I had slept with before I started to get sick. A part of me knew this baby I was carrying was Haji's because Ramir and I always played it safe in the bedroom until about a week ago, so there was no way in hell I could have this baby. It was crazy how my mind tried to justify, and make sense of the entire situation. I didn't have any other choice in the matter. I had to have an abortion and this was nothing more than the consequences of my foolish decisions. As a result, I would have to get rid of my first child. This would be the last little secret added to all the other skeletons in my closet. I promised myself that day to clean it out soon. I was tired of walking around with all this negative weight on my shoulders weighing me down. It was really time to let it all go and start over while I still had a chance. "Thought U Was The One," by Bow Wow came on as I drove to my hair appointment. I sang along thinking about everything I was doing behind Ramir's back, and how I knew it would break his heart if he knew. I felt so bad thinking that for once I was the one destroying my relationship. I knew that, I could not turn back the hands of time but secretly, I wished I could. I pulled up in front of Niecy's shop, Unique Stylez, and parked. I shoved the picture of the ultrasound into the glove compartment. I was still in shock as I walked into the salon trying to put on my happy face. I was surprised when I walked through the door, and saw Haji there getting a haircut by Rio.

"This day couldn't get any better," I thought sarcastically as Nicey greeted me.

"You ok, Boo?" Nicey inquired breaking me out of my thoughts.

"You look like you're irritated as hell," she announced as I took a seat.

"Irritated was an understatement," was all I could think as I sat there feeling, annoyed.

I hated being in the same room with Haji. This day had just gone from bad, to worse, and I couldn't wait until he left. I laughed on the inside as "Use Me," by Bill Withers played while I sat reading a magazine. I felt used up by life, and I was pissed that Haji was a possible sperm donor. I also hated that he kept staring at me from across the room as if he knew I was hiding something. I hated that Haji was a major part in me having to make such a life changing decision. I knew this abortion was going to haunt me the rest of my life. Up until now, I had had no regrets about anything I had done in the past but killing your child was truly a heart breaking decision. After Rio finished cutting Haji's hair, he paid him, gave me a little smile and then walked out the door. I felt a slight relief being that the last time we saw each other; he promised that we would talk. Frankly, if you want me be honest, I didn't have anything else to say to Haji. I just wished he would stay out of my life, but I knew that was too much like right. He was becoming a burden and it was time I got rid of my headache. I had to come up with a plan, and quick.

"It's not enough room in this world for the both of us, Haji." I concluded, flipping through another magazine.

Somebody had to go, because I was tired of playing these childish games. An hour later, Niecy had done the hell out of my wrap; I beamed to myself as I walked to my car. I loved the way the wind blew through my curls and the fact that they fell right back into place. I felt like a model in a photo shoot as I admired myself in my car window. I was flawless and the day was starting to look a little brighter just seeing how beautiful I was standing there.

It was two weeks before my favorite holiday, which was Halloween. Ramir had texted me while I was in the salon getting my hair done offering to take me to a haunted house. I quickly texted Rozi to see if she wanted to go with us, and of course she was down. I turned on my car and the cd instantly changed. "Woman's Worth" by Maxwell came on blasting right before I could pull out of my parking spot. I reached to turn down the volume and then noticed someone was tapping on my passenger window. When I looked up to see who it was, I was pissed off that it was Haji.

"What now?" I mumbled as he reached for the knob.

"So you gone let me in or what, Teaz?" Haji asked, and I almost thought against it.

I was hesitant about hitting the unlock button at first, but I let him in anyway. I didn't need Niecy adding this unexpected encounter of ours to her gossip list. I also knew I had to play it smooth just in case Ramir ever came back to get his hair cut by Rio. The way my luck was going Rio would be the barber he goes, too, also.

"I told you we were going to talk the next time we saw each other," he stated, and I didn't respond.

I really just wanted to end the whole conversation with Haji before it even started. Whatever he had to talk to me about at this point was pointless. I could really care less about talking to Haji because he was starting to ruin my life.

"I really don't like the way you've been trying to avoid me, Teaz!"

"You don't answer my phone calls or text," he added, frowning up his face.

"I know that you're with my brother, and maybe I should respect that."

"But I want you, too," he smirked, and I knew he was lying.

"Just like the song: I know your worth," he smiled while turning to look at me.

"If you give me a real chance, I'm sure I could be a better man than, Ramir," he stated, and I just flipped him the middle finger.

Haji's ego really had him thinking he was some type of Demi-God out here in these streets. I truly believed that he thought he was invincible or maybe even suffering from a serious case of bipolar disorder. It was clear he was narcissistic the way he always tried to make everything about him, but he was even crazier for the way he always flipped the script. Ramir and Haji were different as night and day. It was also ironic that I had met them both at Dirty Secret years apart. Everyone knows that first impressions were everything, and my first date with Haji ended on a bad note. Ramir had to beg me to go out with him, and yet, he turned out to be the sweet and sincere one. He has also been nothing but a good man since our first date. On the other hand, Haji was cold and callous. He reminded me of Damien Omen. Only the Devil, himself could have created someone as evil as Haji. I thought back to my mom telling me once I was the spawn of the Devil himself. She was wrong on so many levels, because I wasn't as cold hearted as I always portrayed myself to be. I knew I had done some bad things in my past, but I didn't deserve this, and I needed to know why it was happening to me.

"Why are you doing this to me, Haji?"

"Do you think I owe you something for that one thing you did?" I yelled confused.

"I mean technically, I already let you fuck me twice for free, so I'm just wondering what it is you want from me,"

"I've never spoken to anyone about that hit you did, and yet, you're bragging about freaks you fuck on their front porch." I inquired.

"I also know you showed up at the cabin where Ramir and I were on purpose," I screamed, hitting my hands against the steering wheel.

"You're not fooling anyone, but yourself with all the foolishness you've been on lately, because even a blind man can see that you've been stalking me. You can say what you want Haji, but it's no coincidence that you keep popping up in my life at the strangest times." I added, frowning at him.

I was a ticking time bomb ready to explode and it was time this lunatic knew it. Had I known then what I know now, I never would have talked to Haji past seeing him at Omega's, repast. I had told myself that I would be respectful the first day we met just in case we ever ran back into each other later on down the line. As I sat there, asking him questions while watching the blank facial expression he held, I knew I was talking to dead ears. This very moment in the car with Haji made me realize the main reason I couldn't have this baby I was carrying. I had prayed so many times to rid myself of the whole Haji situation, but he was becoming a nuisance. I guess it is some truth to the saying: "If you walk with demons they will eventually consume your soul". I was really starting to wish I never even opened up, Pandora's Box. I knew I had to break free of this demon somehow before it destroyed me. I promised myself right, then, and there that once I was free from this cycle of destruction I would never look back. All I heard was the song change to "Wrong Idea," by Snoop as Haji began mumbling something. I watched his knee bump the glove compartment, and all my papers fell out onto the floor. I had been meaning to get the latch fixed weeks ago, but I kept putting it off due to all the bullshit I always had going on. Haji instantly started to pick the papers up while rambling on. I wanted to scream "NO," as I watched him fix the envelopes containing my registration and insurance. He was still rambling on about only God knows what, but I had completely tuned him out. I watched him place the envelope inside the glove compartment, and then pick up the ultrasound picture. I could tell he was reading it over, but I didn't say a word.

"Wow!" he smirked, placing it back in the glove compartment.

"So you're pregnant, huh, Teaz?" he inquired, and I just slammed the glove compartment closed.

I felt so embarrassed about my secret being, discovered by Haji before I could even get to hide it. I honestly felt like I didn't owe Haji any explanations about anything I was doing. I didn't even address his question. Instead, I demanded that he got out of my car. He looked at me with a smirk on his face then opened my door without saying a word. Once he got out and closed my door, I took off out of the parking lot in tears like a mad woman. I saw a car a turn out the parking lot behind me as "Traffic," by Usher played. I knew it was Haji's sick twisted ass, and I hated that I had ever met him. I pushed the pedal to the metal watching the car in my rearview mirror as Usher sang. I sped up switching lanes trying to dodge Haji as I made my way towards the freeway. I was pissed off when we both ended up stopped at a red light. The moment the light turned green, I took off like a bat out of hell towards the entrance of the freeway. I knew Haji wanted to know was it a possibility that this could be his baby I was carrying. At this point, it really didn't matter whose baby I was carrying, because my mind was made up. I did everything I could to loose Haji as I drove on the freeway, but he was right on my tail the entire time. After fifteen minutes of being, chased down I-96 by a nutcase, I finally reached my exit as "I Love You" by Lenny Williams played. I knew Haji was enjoying every minute of making my life a living hell by any means necessary. I, on the other hand, wished it all were just a dream.

"Why do I have to be pregnant now?" I asked myself aloud.

I thought back to the last time I had sex with Haji, and I shook my head in disgust. I prayed so hard to God that I didn't get pregnant, but look at me now. I guess I deserved this, being that I kept playing with fire. I can't even blame God for not helping me this time around. Sometimes it takes you to bump your head really, hard to know you have been walking towards a brick wall all along. I still didn't understand for the life of me why it had to happen while I was dealing with this crazy nut out of all the men I ever slept with. I felt disgusted as I drove down my block just looking back on how I was fucking over a decent man. Ramir was always the compromising one when it came to our relationship, and I hated that I had betrayed him. Haji was really the last person I wanted to be pregnant by on this Earth. The very fact that I was even pregnant by him right now irked my very soul. How could I have been so careless? I was starting to feel like the lyrics to George Michael's song "Careless Whisper", because I never wanted to dance this dance again. I pulled in my driveway and snatched the keys out the ignition. I walked as fast as I could to the porch, and I was never so grateful that these guilty feet still had rhythm. I could hear Haji shouting my name as I fumbled with my keys to open the door. I felt like I was being chased by Michael Meyers once I finally managed to open the door.

"Wait, Teaz!" Haji shouted, but I keep walking.

"I really need to know if that's my baby?" he yelled, right before I shut the door in his face.

This petty bastard just stood outside my door banging and shouting, while desperately trying to cause a damn scene. I just ignored him and prayed he would leave before the neighbors called the cops. I finally heard his car pull off ten minutes later, and I never felt so relieved. I knew this was just the beginning of my problems, and eventually, I would have to deal with him. My phone rang a couple times, but I didn't even bother to answer as "IDFWU," by Big Sean played letting me know it was none other than Haji. For the rest of the afternoon, I ignored all my calls. I really wasn't in the mood to talk to anybody. I ran myself a nice hot bubble bath, and I even added some Calgon to help take me away. I laughed, because I felt like one of the women on the commercial as I stepped into the tub as "Cuffin' Season," by Fabolous played. I laughed as I sang along while soaking in the bubbles.

"These hoes keep calling I ain't picking up,"

"Told these hoes I'll be back around June,"

"Better yet I change my number for the whole winter,"

"Damn it's so cold in the fucking winter," I laughed.

 After my bath, I took a quick nap before I had to meet with Ramir and a couple of our friends later on that evening. I couldn't believe how my day had started, but I was sure I was going to have a good night. I felt so bad for my first unborn child. The fact that I had to get an abortion was tearing me up in the inside, but, I knew it was no way in hell that I could keep this baby. I was even sadder once I woke up from my nap, because I had dreamed about my baby the entire time I was sleeping. Even in my dream, I had mixed emotions. I had, had the baby, and at first, I was happy to be a mother. I saw myself bringing my handsome baby boy home from the hospital with Ramir, and us smiling as we entered the nursery. I sat in my rocking chair as I began to remove his blankets, humming "My Little

Sunshine," while Ramir sang along. I was ecstatic, filled with love and never so happy to be with the two men I loved the most in this world. I had never felt this kind of joy in my entire lifetime as I uncovered my babies face only to see Haji's. I screamed, and when I turned to look at Ramir, I woke up. I was in the same mood I had been in before I even went to sleep. Rozi knocked on my bedroom door, and I almost didn't answer, but I secretly wished I could've just canceled going to the Haunted House to sulk in bed with my misery. I decided right then that I wasn't about to let this whole baby situation ruin my favorite month of the year. Once I told her to come in, she informed me that she had made my favorite food while I was sleeping, and wanted me to meet her in the kitchen. I was getting hungry anyway so I agreed. I knew I needed to put something on my stomach before we left, so I slipped on my gown and left out behind her.

"So what's been up with you lately, boo?" Rozi asked as she fixed my plate of food.

"I know with me being gone all the time for Duty on these business meetings, I've been missing out on a lot lately," She stated, handing me my plate.

"Girl, I don't even know where to begin," I mumbled.

"Well, you know you're like a little sister to me, and as long as you're here with me, nothing will ever happen to you," she explained, and her words were so sincere that it reminded me of Mrs. Franklyn when she promised me the same thing.

"I'm cool, boo," I reassured her, but I really wasn't sure of anything.

"I know you, Teaz," she replied, concerned.

"I'm here to talk whenever you're ready, though," she added, fixing herself a plate and taking a seat at the table with me.

"I have something I've been meaning to talk to you about," she stated shoving food in her mouth, and I became worried.

"Maybe she already knows," my mind told itself right before she reassured me that the news she had might just cheer me up.

"I think I'd rather hear the news you have to tell me before I tell you my crazy stories," I informed her, shaking my head.

Rozi looked at me with a concerned look on her face, and kept eating.

"You're never going believe the mess I got myself into, so I'd rather hear anything to take my mind off this bullshit," I added while shaking my head some more.

It was such a relief to confess to someone else that my life was secretly falling apart. I hoped Rozi had some of that good old fashion hard truth for me after I told her about everything. She always did try her best to give me some solid advice whenever I felt things were falling apart for me.

"Well, you know that Duty has been looking to expand his business by opening a couple more clubs. I also always wanted to own my own nightclub in Vegas after I got my Master's Degree in Business," she added, beaming from ear to ear.

I just listened to Rozi talk while I continued to eat my plate of food.

"Duty has his heart set on opening a club in either Atlanta or California, which I also think would be a great location for a night club. These past few months, we have been meeting with some investors who gave us some great deals on a couple of buildings in all three areas. "We've decided to buy all of them," she beamed.

"This is where you come in, Teaz," she smiled while taking a sip of her glass of water.

"Since you've always been about your money since Duty hired you and a great investment to Dirty Secrets," she paused, giving me a big smile and wink.

"We would love to make you the manger over one of the new clubs of your choice!" she clapped as she announced the good news.

"I figured this would be a great start for you once you receive your Bachelor's degree," she explained.

"This could also be a fresh start for you, and help you get over whatever you've been going through lately," she smiled.

I always wanted to live in California, and I was being, presented with the chance of a lifetime.

"The building in California has so much potential, Teaz," she informed me.

I knew she already knew where I would choose to go. I was just honored she even thought about me to have this position. I really hoped I still had enough time to correct all the wrong things I had done in my life.

"I believe in you, La'Teazya."

"I also know that despite everything you've been going through, you are truly destined for greatness," she smiled at me sincerely.

I just sat back, and took in every word. She was offering me another chance to be the woman; I always knew I was destined to be. I knew this was the moment I had been praying for finally coming true.

"You haven't seen the best of me," I thought as Rozi continued to talk.

This wasn't like the move I had made when I was Nineteen years old, with my friend Barbra that turned out to be a bad move. This was my future. My longevity was always a major priority in my life, and for the first time in a long time, it looked promising. I didn't see myself stripping for the rest of my life, and I was so proud of the fact that I already had a couple thousand in the bank. I was never so thankful that Omega had told me to do that, because it was definitely paying off now.

"A woman should always have something saved in case of an emergency or rainy day." Omega always told me.

I smiled thinking this move to California was one of my dreams come true, and I wasn't willing to let anything get in the way of me making it a reality. It was so funny how life could take you through hell and back just to bring you closer to heaven. Rozi was absolutely, right. Despite my current situation, I was blessed, and it was time I embraced it. I knew that I had to start making some wiser decisions about the things I did in life from this point on. I also needed to stop taking my life for granted, and the good people in my life. I was finally starting to appreciate everything I had. I knew brighter days were going to be ahead of me. I told Rozi that I would think about the whole situation and get back to her with an answer for Duty in a timely manner. I had a couple things to clean up in my life before I could even think about moving to California. I was also very grateful to have such a good friend in Rozi. I always knew she cared for me like a sister, but her loyalty to me always spoke louder than any words. She was the true definition of the word friend, and I appreciated that no matter what I told her about my personal life it never left her lips. It's like she cherished our friendship and really knew what it took to be a true friend. These were all rare qualities to find in people now days. Talking to Rozi that day about my life and everything I had be going through allowed me to get some of the anger that was starting to build up inside of me off my chest. I desperately needed the talk we had, and I couldn't think of anyone better to be having this conversation with. I was shocked that Rozi didn't try to talk me out of the abortion when I told her about the whole baby situation. I figured telling Rozi was the least of my troubles now that Satan's little helper Haji already knew. After listening to the whole story, Rozi told me to do what I felt was going to be best for my life ahead of me. She also advised me to get a P.P.O. against Haji's crazy ass. I wasn't one for involving the police with my issues, so I knew I'd have to handle this situation on my own. The first step was to try to avoid him as much as possible. We talked some more as I finished my plate of food. I decided to do the dishes since Rozi cooked. It was the least I could do after all she had done for me. Once Rozi was done eating, she wiped down the table, grabbed a bottled water out the refrigerator and was just about to head to her room to get dressed when she turned to me, and said:

"The road to success is not straight. There is a curb called failure, a loop called confusion, speed bumps called friends, red lights called enemies, and caution lights called family," she laughed.

"You will get flats called jobs, but if you have a spare called determination, an engine called perseverance, insurance called faith, and a driver called Jesus. You will make it to a road called success!" she finished before walking out the kitchen.

"I read that on a plaque on a wall my first year of college, and I knew then that I was meant to survive by any means necessary."

"Believe me, Teaz," she added.

"You're not the first person to make some terrible mistakes in life, have an abortion and fall from grace to finally stand up on your feet,"

"Just keep moving forward and don't you ever give up on yourself," she smiled.

"Sometimes in order to truly stand you have to literally kiss the ground once you've fallen to know you never want to go back down again." She smiled, and I just smiled, and walked up to her and gave her a hug.

"I'm gone always be here for you, Teaz," she repeated.

"You just have to start making some better choices from this day forth,"

"Once you start believing in La'Teazya, again," she smiled, looking me in the eyes.

"The knowledge in which you have obtained will help you become much wiser and trust me," she beamed.

"No one will overlook you when you've reached your full potential." Rozi smiled, and then reached in to hug me again.

"Now enough of the mushy stuff!" she laughed, wiping away my tears. We both need to get ready for this fun evening your boo has planned!" she cheered while dancing away.

She was right! Life wasn't always perfect, but it damn sure wasn't all bad, either. It was time for me to put on my big girl panties, and put an end to all the non-sense. I was done fighting fire with fire. For the first time, I was going to do the opposite of what I would usually do. I always blamed me growing up in the hood for thinking "an eye for an eye" was the solution to all my problems. Now that I was getting older, I began to see the bad in all our stupid codes of the streets. Today, I decided I was going to give all my problems to God, and hope that in the end, I would turn out a better person.

"Jesus, take the wheel," I sighed, and then headed to my bedroom to get dressed.

I only hoped that this time around time gave me enough time to make things right. I needed closure, and the only way I felt I would get it was to make right of my wrongs, right. I was getting dressed as I sang along to Little Big Town.

"Yeah, I'm gonna lift this house, spin it all around,"

"Toss it in the air, and put it in the ground,"

"Make sure you're never found!" I screamed to the top of lungs, wishing I could really do that to Haji.

I cut off the radio just in time to catch the ten o'clock news. I was trying to see what the weather would be like for the rest of the evening since it was raining earlier. I wanted to faint when I heard the reporter announce that the police had arrested two men in connection with a murder that took place a year and a half ago. I knew they were talking about Omega. I also knew that it was a possibility that Haji had just heard the news I did. The news should have made me feel happy, but I felt guilty, inside. All I could do was pray that my crazy stalker hadn't been anywhere near the television. I really wanted this day to be over with, now. I was hurting, but I had to try my best to keep cool. I put on a damn smile and got ready to go out with my boyfriend who knew nothing about my twisted past life. I loved the fact that we never talked about our past relationships, which I seemed to use to my advantage. We always said the past didn't really matter to us. It was ironic that today, my past was catching up to me in more ways than, one. I seriously felt like I was on the verge of a breakdown.

"What the fuck!" I yelled to the air, as I got dressed.

"I just need a break from it all, God and I promise to be better this time around,"

"If you give me one more chance to prove myself, God," I prayed, and then cut off my television.

"I swear this time I'll come out on top the right way, and I also promise to become a better woman," I finished before saying, Amen.

At that point, I could honestly care less about the weather. I just wanted to get this night over with so I could crawl back in bed with my misery. I was so pissed at myself for letting things get this out of hand. For the first time in my life, I looked in the mirror and saw the monster I was becoming.

"What's done in the dark always comes to the light," I thought as I cried, thinking about all the skeletons that were falling out my closet today.

My phone rang, and I answered it without even looking to see who the caller was.

"I know you saw the news, Teaz," Haji yelled, and I didn't say a word.

"All I want to know is if these two guys that got arrested today have any connection to Oz?" he screamed into the phone.

"Or is it really true that Oz was the brother of the guy your ex-boyfriend Ize had killed?" he laughed, but I knew it was more sinister, than jokingly.

"You and I both know the streets talk, Teaz,"

"So before you even open your mouth to try to lie to me again, I need you to know that I already know the truth," he added, and I was in shock.

"I'm guessing your silence means I'm right about why you had me murder, Oz," he laughed some more.

"You really are a selfish bitch, Teaz!" he yelled.

I just removed the phone from my ear, and stared at it while he yelled out more insults. I was just about to hang up on Haji, but I didn't. It was time I let him know how I really felt no matter how wrong I was. I put the phone back to my ear as he changed the subject.

"I want to know if that's my baby you're carrying?" he inquired, and I snapped.

"Listen up, Haji."

"I've had it up to the ceiling with all of your bullshit!" I yelled.

"You have some fucking nerves calling me, and demanding that I tell you anything after all the shit you've been putting me through, lately. Furthermore, I don't give a damn how you feel right now, because you don't really care about me, anyways. You love making my life a living hell, and a part of me always knew you were nothing but trouble. It all began the day I walked into your life with the dope up the pussy crap you tried to pull, and yet I still tried to be cool with you, despite my intuitions," I added smacking my lips.

"You're so fucking dumb though, Haji," I laughed, before I went into my next sentence.

"You deserve every bite of the shit I dished out to you!" I laughed.

I was truly annoyed having to have this conversation with him after I just tried to put all this out of my mind.

"My intentions for knowing you after Omega's funeral were about as good as the tissue I use to wipe my ass with and then toss in a toilet," I snickered just thinking about how he was a piece of shit.

"I know you're probably too slow to get what I just said so let me dumb it down for you," I smirked before he could say anything.

"You're nothing more than a miserable piece of shit, and so are your motives for being in my life," I laughed to keep from crying.

I couldn't show him how I really felt inside, because he already thought he had the upper hand on me.

"Trick No Good Boo!" I added, shaking my head.

"You mad or Nah?" I inquired, but I didn't care about the answer.

"Oh, and to answer your question," I paused.

"Whatever I do with this baby is purely my decision and trust me, it's nothing you can do to change my mind," I added.

"Maybe it is your baby, maybe it's not," I laughed some more.

I didn't even give him a chance to speak because I was so mad.

"Now if you don't mind,"

"I have a date with a real man," I teased.

"Goodbye," I announced before I just hung up in his face.

"That son-of- a bitch really has issues," I said to myself shaking my head.

I was really starting to hate Haji more and more with each breath I took. He was the second person I ever met next to my Mama who could get under my skin. It was exactly 11:00 pm, once we headed to the haunted house. I felt weird the whole drive there. I figured the butterfly feeling in my stomach was the baby, so I sipped some water to try, and soothe it.

"Take a shot with me, Boo." Ramir offered, while handing me a bottle of Remy Martin 1738, but I declined.

"Damn, you can't even turn up with your main, man," he joked, and I just laughed.

"Why did Ramir have to be connected to my worst nightmare," I thought to myself.

"I tried to get Haji to come with us," he stated as we drove, and I choked on my water.

"Are you okay, Boo?" he asked, and I just nodded my head yes.

"Haji's been acting real funny, lately," Ramir said, sipping his drink.

"We kind of got into it earlier today before I asked him to come out with us," he continued, and I was all ears.

"Haji called me to tell me that he had messed around and got some chick pregnant."

"He also said he regretted it, because he hated the cold-hearted bitch," he laughed, but I didn't see anything funny being that it was me he was talking about.

"He even went as far as to tell me some scandalous shit the bitch had him do for her that furthermore made him not trust her."

"Really?" my inner voice screamed as I listened to Ramir while we drove.

"Then he hits me with some shit about how our Dad never really loved him," he laughed.

"He was really trying to convince me that our Dad showed favoritism between us two, Teaz."

"He was really starting to sound like he was jealous of the fact that my mom was married to him instead of his mother," he stated.

"When I went to address what he had just told me about our father, who I knew loved us both,"

"Haji, basically chewed my head off about how he had to take care of his sick mother until she died," he stated, shaking his head.

"I just ended the conversation with him after that."

"I couldn't just listen to him try to belittle the man that raised us," Ramir frowned while shaking his head.

Ramir took a sip of his drink after that, and I wanted to do the same thing.

"I didn't talk back to him until about an hour ago, and I could tell he was still mad so it really didn't bother me that he couldn't make it," he said shrugging his shoulders.

"The boy has some real issues," he added, looking into space, and I could tell Ramir was offended.

"I always knew he felt like Dad loved me more." He sighed.

"I was just hoping I was wrong for all these years," he also confessed.

I knew at that very moment that Ramir honestly knew nothing about Haji's, betrayal. Haji was nothing more than a low-life backstabber was. How did I end up meeting such a narcissistic psychopath was beyond, me.

Once we got to the haunted house, and paid our admission fees, I felt a little better walking towards the entrance with Ramir's hand in mine. I knew I had to stop Haji before he seriously tried to hurt Ramir, and I. I was both sad and happy at the same time, but I wasn't about to let Haji get the best of me. I couldn't wait to get through these four floors of terror. I was ready to have fun with the people I loved most. Rozi recorded us all with her video camera right before we went in, and I was just happy to have good friends in my life. I was nervous as hell on the inside as I hung on to Ramir's arm when we entered the building. Everything was going great until we reached the third floor, and the floor dropped splitting our group up. I found myself walking alone down a smoky hallway. I was feeling around for the exit when someone came up behind me.

"I know you're there," I announced, still trying to find my way to the next room.

"Teaz," the voice said, and I was scared to death just knowing it belonged to, Haji.

"How the hell did I end up in the same room with this nutcase?" I pondered while I walked towards the flickering light that was moving towards me.

"Wait!" Haji yelled, trying to grab my arm but I pushed his hands away.

"Don't touch me!" I yelled.

"Why can't you just leave me alone, crazy ass bastard!" I screamed as we both entered the next room.

The next thing, I knew the walls were closing in on us. I moved quickly through the dark maze trying to get out of Haji's sight, but he was right on my heels. I hated that I was alone in a haunted house with his fool Haji. I felt even worst knowing that I had a real life lunatic right behind me.

"Will you just listen to me?" he yelled, while grabbing me once we reached the swamp area.

"You gone tell me the fucking truth about everything whether you want to, or not!" Haji demanded tightening his grip on my arm.

"What the fuck you gone do if I don't Haji?" I snapped snatching away from him.

"You can think I'm playing if you want, Teaz!" he stated tightening his grip.

"We both know what I'm capable of!" he threatened, and I turned to walk away.

He just made the last threat he was ever going to make towards my life. I was done with Haji's non-sense. He wasn't the only one who had capable of killing somebody.

"Please don't make me have to hurt you, Teaz." I heard him say as I made my way through the next couple of rooms, and I just laughed.

"We gone see about that," the sinister voice in my head laughed.

I was never so happy to see the exit sign. I ran, and jumped in Ramir's arms once I saw him waiting outside for me. I was never so happy to see him in my life. I hated myself for fucking over him with his brother, but I was going to make it right. The first thing tomorrow, I was going to make arrangements to go visit an old friend. I was sure once I tell him everything that has been going on with me lately and give him a couple dollars, and my problem will gone, forever. I was glad that Ize squashed the beef with Pzyco over Zar's death before he went to prison. Now it was time for him to do an old friend a favor, being that I am the one that talked Ize into making amends with him. I knew I had said I was done with the whole "Eye for an Eye," lifestyle, but Haji had to go. This was the only way I knew I could get rid of my problem before it got rid of me. I popped Jay Z's cd in as we drove back to my place. He hit it right on the nose with his lyrics, too. I had ninety-nine problems, and Haji's bitch ass was no longer about to be one. Haji reminded me of an old saying my Mama always use to say when she talked about my Daddy.

"Even if you remove the venom from a snake; is it still not a snake?" Mama who always say. Today, her words stood out more than ever, and I knew then, that I couldn't let Haji get away with his psychotic behavior or he would seriously try to hurt me one day. Once we got home, I fucked the shit out of Ramir. I made him have sex with me so many times that night, I couldn't even move the next morning. I was happy when I woke up to him bringing me breakfast in bed. He was always such a sweetheart, and I couldn't wait until I could give him all my love. I opened my journal, and began to write all about my like, and everything I had been through to get to this point. Writing and music were always life therapy to me. After I finished pouring my heart out to my journal, I popped in my favorite movie, "The Breakfast Club" and cuddled with my Boo all day. The movie ended just as Ramir fell asleep.

"Don't you forget about me is right." I smiled, kissing his forehead.

I then grabbed my phone, and slid out of the covers. It was time to put my plan in motion.

"And so the games begin," I thought.

Wrong Turn
Dear Diary,
December 21, 2014

It was two weeks before Halloween when I finally decided to go pay Pzyco a visit. I popped in my alternative cd and "I Alone" by Live came on. I drove through the streets of Chicago in my rental looking for the street that Pzyco stayed on. He had been hiding out here with his baby mama that no one other than Ize, and I knew about since we all got in trouble. I pulled up at the house, and found his little girl Hydi outside playing. For Pzyco to have been a big untamed gorilla looking ass Nigga, he sure did make a beautiful baby with Katina. Katina, also known as Kat, was a white girl from around the way that Pzyco helped clean up her act. Kat was a prostitute who used meth, and heroin. One day while he was serving a customer he found Kat in an alley beaten, and clinging on to the little life she had. He made her promise to get her act right if he helped her, and she did.

"Hi Hydi," I smiled, walking up towards the house.

"Where are your Mommy and Daddy?" I asked when she ran up to give me a hug.

It had been years since I last saw Hydi, and just seeing her made me think about my own child I was carrying. After hugging Hydi, and telling her I missed her, she ran up to the door and opened it for me. I watched her storm through the living room into the kitchen to tell her mom I was there. I laughed as I took a seat on the couch thinking about how good life is for a child with both loving parents at home. Pzyco was a cold-hearted killer, but he took good care of his family.

"Teaz," Katina beamed once she reached the living room.

"What a pleasant surprise," she announced giving me a hug.

"You look good, girl. How have you been?" Katina asked, taking a seat next to me on the couch.

"I've been maintaining," I told her as Hydi handed me a book.

"Green Eggs, and Ham" by Dr. Suess I announced reading off the title, as I picked Hydi up, and sat her next to me.

"Can you read this, big girl?" I asked Hydi. She just smiled, opened the book, and started reading to me.

"Pzyco will be down in a few," Katina announced then walked away to go tell him I was there. After Hydi finished the story, Pzyco came into the living room. I kissed Hydi, and then asked him if we could talk in private. We went into his office, and I told him about the whole situation I was in dealing with Haji. I told Pzyco how Haji and I met, and how we reconnected years later after my ex Omega's death. I also explained to him that I had Haji murder Oz to stop him from killing Ize. This he already knew because Ize had reached out to him from prison to put a hit on Oz himself, and found out Oz was already dead. I even confessed that I had been recently dating Haji's younger brother. I was in a twisted love triangle, but all I could think about doing was cutting the squares up out my circle. Once I told Pzyco all the information he needed to know, and paid him $5000.00, I left, promising to come get Hydi for a weekend after everything dies down. I was ecstatic as I hopped in my car just knowing that my burden would be gone for good in a couple of weeks or so. I sang along to "Bow Down (No Man)" by Hogni as I drove back towards the freeway.

"Checkmate," I said aloud thinking I was one-step closer to being free from the mess I had gotten into. My only focus was getting rid of this baby, and the business I would be running in California next year. I was so excited about the second chance I was being given at life as "Butterfly" by Crazytown poured out of my system. Nothing in this life comes easy, and

I was just thankful to turn out a champion with all the chances I was always taking.

Four hours later, I had reached my exit back to Detroit, and was all smiles once I got to my block.

"I came out of the darkness with a bullet in my hand," I sang along with Redlight Kings before I cut off my car. In two weeks, I would have rid myself of all ties to Haji. Once I got in, I watched a documentary on Marilyn Monroe. In so many ways, I was just like her. I loved her style and the way she carried herself. I always wondered how such a sex symbol could commit suicide but then again I felt her. Sometimes being the object of people's sexual desires and fantasies only can get tiring when you want to be much more. She was absolutely, right with her quote: "I am good, but not an Angel. I do sin, but I am not the Devil. I am just a small girl in a big world trying to find love". I cried when the documentary explained how her life took her in many different directions just to lead to her death. All I could do is pray that my life got better before it got any worse. It was 12:30 in the afternoon, when I strolled into Dirty Secrets. I almost decide against going in, because I had been throwing up all day. I was sitting in the dressing room kicking it with a couple girls when Duty came in. I knew Duty had hired someone new, because it's the only time he comes out his office.

"Sup Duty," I greeted him as he took a seat.

"What brings you to my neck of the woods?" I asked before the new girl walked in the door.

"You know I like to show off my new ladies their first day here, Teaz," he chuckled as I applied my lip-gloss.

I was just about to go do my first show of the night, so I really just wanted to get this little meeting was over. The next thing, I knew the door opens, and in walks, my long lost Sister T'Aira! I hadn't seen her since we were both put in the girl's home after our Mama was killed.

"I'd like everyone to meet T'Aira" Duty announced but I was too shocked to even speak.

I heard my song start, and the DJ announce that I was coming to the stage, but I couldn't move. All I could do was stand there and stare at T'Aira, who looked exactly like my Mama while acting as if I was listening to Duty.

"If you need anything you can ask Teaz," Duty informed her while walking up to me to put his hand on my shoulder.

I just smiled, and continued to stare at T'Aira.

"It was nice to meet you," I finally said, walking past them both towards the door.

"I'm sure we'll get to know each other later" I smirked heading out the dressing room into the crowded club as "Freak At Night" by Sixmile Malik and Raven Soars played.

I couldn't believe I had just run back into my sister after all these years. It was truly amazing how my life always seemed to take the craziest turns. I couldn't help but watch T'Aira and Duty's every move while I worked the pole. A part of me wanted to know what they were talking about as I watched them wrap up their meeting. Once T'Aira finished talking to Duty, she walked over to a table, and to my surprise, she was sitting with "Dread Head Moe," who I met on my birthday. I hadn't seen him since then but I made a mental note to find out about them. I wanted to know just how involved she was with him. I watched T'Aira whisper something in his ear, then he finished his drink, and they left. The next day, I was at the cider mill with Rozi enjoying the beautiful fall weather. We kicked it for a few about life, the next moves we were about to make, and I was never so happy to finally be getting away from Detroit for good. We were like two big kids once we got to the pumpkin patch. After picking out pumpkins to crave later on that night, and walking through a corn maze, we decided to go on a haunted hayride. We were excited as we drove to the movies afterwards. For the first time in a long time I was genuinely happy just being able to be me. I felt like no matter what I had been through before today I was sure to make it to the top despite everything I came across in my path. Nelson Mandela was right when he wrote, "There is no easy walk to freedom anywhere, and many of us will have to pass through the valley of death again and again before we reach the mountain top of our desires".

The following week I found myself in the library studying for a group assignment with my new friend, River. In so many ways she reminded me of myself when I was her age. River was so full of life at the age of twenty-one. I just smiled listening to her read off some resources she had found over the weekend. I loved that despite her upbringing she was trying to pave her own way. It was hard trying to make it out here in these streets alone without the proper guidance. I was truly happy to see her making wiser decisions at that age then I ever did. If she stayed on this path, I knew in my heart one day she would be destined for greatness. My only concern was that she had recently started dating a hot head that reminded me so much of a mixture of Cazh, and Ize. Destin had some big shoes to fill being that he'd taken over his father's organization once he was murdered, and I knew how much pressure that could be on a person to keep his father's legacy alive. It is funny how everybody wants to be a star and shine brighter than the person before them, and yet they all forget one simple thing: It is nothing new under the sun and not everybody can survive on these streets. Albert Einstein said it best: "Before God we are all equally wise and equally foolish". Yet, it is one thing we all seem to forget. I hated that I had been living so long trying desperately to gain the approval of others when all I ever needed was my own approval.

"So how's everything been going with you?" I asked as we wrapped up our little meeting.

"Are you enjoying the new move with Destin?" I added, while gathering up my books.

"We've been ok," River smiled putting her papers in her folder.

"It's really the norm with us. If you know what I mean," she laughed.

I knew exactly what she meant without her going into details. I didn't know much about Destin except what I'd heard on the streets. It was weird how life kept connecting me with people of my past because Destin's father just so happened to be the man my Mama use to cop her drugs from, and, later killed by Legend. I knew that if he was anything like the man I knew his father was it was only so long before his true colors came shining through.

"You be safe out here, River," I told her, as I gathered up my bags and books to head towards the checkout desk.

"See you in class next week for presentation," she replied, walking out the door as I waved goodbye.

River was such a sweet young girl, and I only hoped she knew what she was getting herself into by living with a man before marriage. Destin was her everything literally, and without him I don't know what River would do. It was a good thing she was trying to finish out her degree just in case they ever did break up so she would have that to fall back on. In addition, she had a God-mother who loved her dearly, so I prayed she would be ok. I hated to see young girls so lost in love that they forget who they are and end up working at the club just to make ends meet. I hoped that she never has to learn the hard way that "God blesses the child who has their own." We all know you cannot get to comfortable when depending on someone else, because people switch up every day. One of the best things the Franklyn's ever taught me was how to be independent, which I had developed as a little girl. That alone, and the fact that Mr. Franklyn always told me: "There is no price too high to pay to own one's self," is partially the reason why I was able to survive the way I do in this world. I was sitting in the abortion clinic nervous as hell on the inside as I waited for the woman to call my name. At one point, I had to hold my legs closed to keep them from shaking. The abortion had my emotions all over the place. No one could take away the feeling of guilt I had in my heart after letting them basically rip my first born child out of me. I was disgusted at myself as I laid on the cold table with my thoughts haunting me. I never really gave my child a chance just knowing that the father of my child was Haji. I felt so bad once the medicine they gave began to kick in, because I knew it was no turning back. I was sad that I had to go through this whole process alone, but I wasn't going to let that stop me from doing what I knew was right.

"God forgive, me," I thought as the doctor told me to relax, and take a deep breath. That experience was far worse than any pap smear I ever had. I just closed my eyes, and prayed to God that he would forgive me. I knew I was committing the ultimate sin, but all I could do was cry. A few days later, I was getting ready for the Halloween party we were throwing at the club. It had been three weeks since T'Aira started working there and I still hadn't spoken to her since Duty introduced us. Our childhood had left us both bitter inside after our Mama's death. As a result, we didn't have much of a connection once we were sent to the Girl's home, so I didn't see a point in one now. I honestly didn't have time to focus on any other drama in my life now that I had a clean slate. I had just gotten my abortion so I wasn't really up to having any feelings for my long lost sister other than the ones I already felt towards her. I never really cared for T'Aira growing up, and I damn sure wasn't about to start caring for her today just because we worked at the same place. I was getting dressed into my" Red Riding Hood" costume that I had made by my girl, Tiger when T'Aira walked into the dressing room. I noticed she had some bruises on her face, and was crying, but I tried my best to ignore her as I continued to get dressed. I really didn't care to know about her problems when I already had enough of my own, but I had a gut feeling today would be the day we had our first conversation. It was a thin line between love, and hate; and this here is where I wanted to draw the line. I strapped up my last pump, grabbed my wrist bag and was just about to head out the door when she called my name.

"Damn," my inner voice screamed.

"I know this is awkward, Teaz, but I really need someone to talk to," she stated, wiping her eyes.

"What's up, Rain?" I asked, calling her by her stage name.

"Come on now, Teaz."

"You can't just go on forever without talking to me when we both know that we are sisters," she said looking in the mirror at the bruises on her face.

"Ok, what's up, T'Aira?" I replied, taking a seat.

"I need some good advice," she sniffed, while applying makeup.

"I'm listening," I stated dryly, folding my arms.

"The guy I've been with ever since I ran away from my foster home is really starting to become an abusive asshole. He beats me for anything and everything and now it's starting to become harder to hide it," she confessed, taking a line of the powder she pulled out her clutch purse.

"Sad to say, I think I liked the verbal abuse much better than this physical shit he's been on lately," she laughed, taking another line.

"In so many ways I feel like Mama and my Daddy. I dance, drink, do drugs occasionally, and live a fast lifestyle to escape all the bullshit I am going through. I also hate that Moe takes all my money."

"Wait, Moe?" I interrupted her before she could finish.

"Yea, Moe, why?" she asked confused.

"Do you know him or something?" she inquired, turning around to face me.

"We met awhile back in the mall but it's nothing serious," I assured her, and I was never so happy that I had never tried to pursue Moe.

"I really don't know what to do," she continued, taking another hit of the cocaine she had.

"I've tried to leave him on numerous occasions, but he finds me wherever I go. I feel like I'm dating Ike Turner, or even the Feds the way he just knows my every move, but I know that's far from the truth, because he's to fucking grimy to work with the police," she added, laughing.

"I know I can't blame anyone but myself for the mess I'm in, but I just wanted to tell somebody what I was going through just in case this fool ever tried to hurt me. You're my blood, whether you like it or not, and I don't have anyone else that I trust to share this information with" she said through more tears.

I just sat there taking in the whole story as I watched her make sure all her bruises were covered. Death was all our lives seemed to offer us, and yet I felt like I was having some sort of resurrection now that T'Aiara was back around. Was I ready to have a connection with my long lost sister that betrayed me so much in the past? That was the question I desperately needed to answer but one I wasn't ready to really focus on just yet.

"You don't have to say anything, Teaz. I really just needed someone to hear me out before it was too late," she continued, standing up to face me as the DJ announced my name again.

"I'm going to leave that bastard alone for good if it's the last thing I do," she said, breaking the awkward silence that had crept in the room.

"I just need to get my money up" she added slipping on her cat costume.

"Let That Be The Reason," I quoted as I stood up to walk towards the door.

It was always a part of me; that stood up for those who needed my help. This time I could only hope she got out of that situation, and fast. This wasn't my battle, and I wasn't about to let my emotions cloud my better judgment. It was unfortunate that T'Aira was in this predicament and needed my help after all the bad things she did to me in the past. Even worse than that, I wasn't going to let some sob story get me off my square. She never once had my back when we lived at home with Mama, or when we were at the girl's home, so why should I help her now. I wished her the best, and then walked out the door. She was right about one thing, listening was all I could do. I was driving home blasting my jam, "A Tribe Called Red" by Angel Haze when I noticed the car behind me was following me. I instantly thought it was Haji as I pulled up to the red light, and the car pulled next to me. I was shocked when the driver rolled down the passenger window, and it was Moe.

"You gotta be able to smile through all the bullshit," I thought about Tupac when I noticed he was trying to get my attention.

"Well, well, stranger. You just never gone call a brother?" he asked, and I laughed.

He was damn right. Calling him was never an option from day one, and I damn sure didn't want anything to do with him now that I knew how he really was.

"Yea, I'm already in a relationship," I stated, flashing my ring I brought myself to wear to turn down creeps like him.

"To bad, Lil' Mama," he replied as the light changed.

I just drove off and rolled up my window without a word.

"It's too bad that you're such a fucking loser," I smirked, and then thought back to my talk with T'Aira.

I didn't respect a man that put his hands on a woman, and Moe was nothing more than a weak link in my book. I also knew: "Love could be unfair, but there's a fool out there for everybody".

T'Aira happened to be Moe's fool for years, and as a result, she is getting the bitter, end of the stick. A price you have to pay when you date creeps like Moe.

"Work," by Iggy Azalea came on as I drove down my block. I felt her, because I was definitely working on getting my life in order. That night, I stayed in watching movies with Ramir. I felt like Elizabeth Taylor as I entered the kitchen to grab a bottle of wine. Sometimes you have to just, "pour yourself a drink, put on some lipstick and pull yourself together". I was going to do that, and so much more once I got everything in order again. The following week, I did my presentation with River, and we received triple A's on the entire project. I was so excited that everything was going better in my life that I decided to celebrate. I invited River and her boyfriend to join me, and she agreed. I also invited Rozi, and her new boo Sage. I was blasting, "Celebration," by Lil' Wayne as I drove to my hair appointment. I couldn't wait until next fall when I'd be running my own business in the state of my dreams. Once I got to the salon, I called and made reservations for the Whitney downtown on Woodward. I love the architecture of the building, and I couldn't wait to have fun with my friends that evening. A couple hours later, I was chilling, looking at different clubs in California in a magazine to get an idea of how I wanted to do my club when the phone rang. To my surprise, it was T'Aira. She was crying hysterically, so I asked her where she was. I had a couple hours before dinner, so I hopped in my ride to meet her at a hotel she told me she had been staying at lately. Once I got there, she explained that she left Moe for good, but he had been looking all around town trying to find her. She also expressed to me that she felt he would try to kill her once he did find her this time. As much as I didn't want to be involved, a part of me felt that I had to help her.

"I could give you some money to move out of town," I suggested, even telling her she didn't have to pay me back, but she refused.

"So what do you want from me T'Aira?" I asked puzzled.

I never knew a person who could turn down some free money, so I knew she was serious or either high off all the drugs she always took to comprehend my offer.

"I don't want your money, Teaz," she stated, crying.

"I need you to help me get rid of my problem for good," she replied, and I just listened.

"I know he likes you," she continued.

"I stole your number out his phone the other night after he told me he saw you. We could set him up," She suggested, and I shook my head "NO".

"Look, T'Aira" I snapped.

I wasn't about to let her talk me into getting wrapped up in her bullshit when I already have enough problems of my own. T'Aira whined a little bit more, but my mind was made up.

"I'm willing to help you but this was way over my head. I have enough problems of my own," I explained, grabbing my purse.

"Please help me, Teaz," she begged, walking closer to where I was.

"I'll do anything you want me to if you help me get rid of Moe," she added, grabbing my arms.

"Anything, I swear," she repeated through tears.

"I don't want to die, Teaz," she added, walking over to the dresser.

"I wouldn't have asked you Teaz if I really didn't need your help" she proceeded to say while doing some coke she pulled from a plate she had in a drawer.

The look in her eyes were pleading with me the whole time she begged, but I tried my best not to cave in. She really needed my help for the first time in life, and I hated that I was the only person she had. Karma was a bitch and it was ironic the person who always told me she would never need me for shit was sitting in my face in desperate need of a handout.

"Okay, T'Aira, I'll help you," I agreed, and then told her to pack her things.

"You owe me though," I informed her, as she ran up to give me a hug.

"Thank you, Teaz!" she replied, as I loosened her grip.

"The first thing you gone do is stop using this bullshit," I stated, walking over to the dresser where the plate of coke was.

"This is the reason why your judgment's is so clouded," I added, throwing the plate in the trash.

"This shit won't correct your demons nor will it get you out the mess you've made so what's the purpose?" I ask, shaking my head in disgust.

"Now finish getting your things together, and meet me in the car." I snapped.

"I got somewhere to be in an hour, and I'm not about to let this ruin my evening." I told her before walking out the door.

She was really, hopeless out here in this world, but I was sure being around me would help her grow some tough skin. I always did have to protect T'Aira from kids in our neighborhood growing up about her big mouth she couldn't back up. No matter how bad I wanted to let the kid's beat her up to teach her a lesson, I knew my Mama would kick my ass if I did. All I could think about was that I hoped T'Aira did not bite the hand that was about to feed her this time around as I walked towards my car. She was always a little back stabber growing up, and I hope she knew that, that type of behavior would have her missing right along with Moe. If she ever betrayed me, again after this only the Lord knew what I would do to her. It was bad enough I had to clean up my own spilled milk, and now I had a completely different plate of food to eat that I didn't even order. I was going to have to give Pzyco another phone call, soon. I needed him to hit Moe, too. I dialed his phone as I waited for T'Aira to come out but it went straight to the voicemail, so I left a message.

"Hey Pzyco, this Teaz,"

"Hit my line up ASAP. I have another puppy for you to look at." I giggled.

"Oh yea, you better hurry, too,"

"They're going like hotcakes," I giggled some more, and then hung up.

Thirty minutes later, I was dressed and ready to have a night of fun. We took pictures before we entered the restaurant, and I was enjoying every minute of life. After we all ordered, I excused myself to the ladies' room. Ramir was looking so good that I sent him a text asking him to meet me in the bathroom, and he did. I needed a quick fix before dinner to hold me off until later on that night. The next morning, I was pissed when Haji showed up at his house. I could hear him fussing to Ramir about something but I stayed in the bedroom. I didn't have time for his bullshit today, so I let Ramir deal with Haji by himself. Once Haji left, I asked Ramir what was wrong, and he told me that Haji was pissed about the chick he had told him about having an abortion. He also said he was going to get her back for doing it behind his back.

"How the hell did he know I even had the abortion?" I thought as Ramir rambled on.

I heard him say he tried to talk some sense into Haji, but he wasn't hearing it. Haji, was dead set on hurting the girl.

"Oh yea," the evil voice inside of my head screamed.

"We'll just see about that," I thought as I continued to listen to Ramir.

He dropped me off at my house, and I was pissed off. I had to put an end to Haji, and I needed it to be a lot sooner than I expected. A light bulb went off in my head as I called T'Aira's name. I could set him, too. We already had planned to set up, Moe, so why not add Haji to the hit list. T'Aira did say she would do anything for me if I helped her out of her situation. All I would have to do is get them in the same place at the same time and he was sure to take the bait.

"Wassup, Teaz," T'Aira asked once she came into the living room.

"I think I just figured out a way for you to pay me back," I said changing the television to "Usual Suspects".

I knew Haji liked to get his haircut every other Friday, so I arranged for them two be in the same place at the same time so she could get his number. I called Niecy, and made an appointment for T'Aira the following Friday. I also called Pzyco again to let him know the puppies would be ready a lot sooner than I thought. I told T'Aira what I needed her to do for me, and I even had Duty ban Moe from the club. I made up a lie about Moe being a pervert who likes to follow the girl's home, and he fell for it. Duty was good for keeping up with the well-being of each girl at his club so I knew that would piss him off once I told him the lie about Moe. The next day, I helped T'Aira get a P.P.O. against Moe, and even helped her look for some apartments to move into once he was gone. I was lying in bed listening to "Rules," by Mario when the bell rang. Rozi had been gone out of town on another business adventure for Duty, so I got up to answer it. Once I got downstairs to open the door, something inside of me told me to look through the peephole first. I was shocked when I saw Haji standing there. I instantly checked all the locks once he started ringing the bell, again. After about five more minutes of him knocking and ringing the bell, he left. Later on that night, when I was at work, Haji walked in. T'Aira was just about to go out to the stage, when I told her Haji was there.

"I need you to get his number tonight," I told her, and she said okay.

I laughed as my jam, "We Do What We Wanna," by Kay Yay and Gorilla Zoe played. I hit the stage to do my last show as I watched T'Aira work her magic on Haji to "Tell'em What They Wanna Hear," By Ray Ray. I chuckled inside thinking back on how I set up Ladibug after she killed Mizz.

"Silly Rabbit," I laughed.

"You just sealed your fate," I smiled when I saw him giving T'Aira his number.

"I loved it when a plan came together," I thought as I walked off the stage.

That Friday afternoon, Ramir took me to the Detroit Institute of Arts museum. The museum was highlighting a display on Motown's history, and I was excited to see all the good that came out of my city. It seemed like the news always tried to make Detroit out to be the murder capital. Every city had their scandals but that wasn't all Detroit had to offer. Some of the greatest artist in history came from here and if it wasn't for Detroit, I believe people would still be riding horses everywhere. I loved the Motor City for what it was worth, but I knew my time here was up. We decided to take pictures at the photo booth they had, and I couldn't help but smile looking at all the cute pictures we had taken together. We looked so good together, I thought as we stood in line for popcorn. It was a shame that it was only on camera I thought back to my favorite Drake song. The photo captured a love that I knew wasn't really there. I loved Ramir dearly but the whole thing with Haji made it hard for me to love, Ramir the way I should. All I could think about on our drive to my house was the fact that T'Aira was at the shop meeting up with Haji right now. Soon, him, and Moe would be history, and we would both be free of our demons. I sang along as "Come Close," by Common played as we drove. It was unfortunate that I was in this situation, but that never stopped me from pretending to love Ramir the way I knew he loved me. That night after Ramir went to sleep; I stayed up writing in my journal and reading quotes by some of my favorite artists. I stumbled across this quote by Edgar Allan Poe that made me question my own integrity. All I ever wanted was real love, and here I was playing on someone else's emotions.

"We loved with a love that was more than love," the words of Edgar kept playing repeatedly like a broken record in my head, and all I could do was cry.

A couple days had passed since I last saw Haji. He had been out of town a lot lately, so I had to reschedule the hit I had put out on him. I was lying in bed with Ramir when I got a "restricted" call. I almost decided not to answer being that it could have been Haji on the other line but something inside of me told me to pick up. I really wasn't in the mood to deal with anything else at the moment. My plate was very full wit T'Aira living in fear of Moe, and Haji stalking me every chance he got. The operator informed me that I had call from a federal prison, and I was surprised to hear from the caller on the other line.

"What's up, baby girl?"

"It's been a long time since our last conversation," Ize spoke, and I just shook my head.

I was at a loss for words, so I took the time to take the call in the other room while Ramir slept. Ize was the last person I was expecting to hear from!

"I'll be home in a couple of months," he informed me, and I was shocked.

I wasn't sure if I was ready to see Ize after all I had been through.

"I also talked to Pzyco recently,"

"He'll be down there to look at them puppies in few days, so be on the lookout." He stated, and I shook my head okay instead of answering him.

"You have one-minute remaining," the operator announced.

Ize just told me to take care after that, and that he would be home to see me soon. I couldn't even sleep after that, so I left Ramir in the bed as I listened to music.

"Rocket Love," by Stevie Wonder came on, and I felt the lyrics in so many ways as I sat drinking my daiquiri. Every time I felt like I was close to heaven, something always seemed to knock me back down to this cold, cold world. I walked into my room to get my journal and tears began to fall down my eyes as I watched Ramir sleep. He looked so peaceful, and I knew in my heart that part of his life wasn't coming from me. I walked back into the living room just as the song changed to "Reasons," by Earth, Wind, and Fire. I loved this particular song but I couldn't think of any good reason for the love I was in and it made me feel like the lyrics from "Colorblind," by Counting Crows. I didn't know a damn thing about love and it was all a result of me not having any real love growing up. Mr. Franklyn was the only man that ever really loved me, and even that wasn't enough for me. I thought about my biological father for a second as I let the tears roll wildly down my cheeks. I bet he loved his other children, and yet he turned his back on me. I hated him, and my Mama. I couldn't understand why he didn't try to at least get to know me despite my Mama's actions in the past. I cried some more just thinking about all the blood I had on my hands. I couldn't believe my life outside of school was turning out to be the hell I always tried to run from. I was grateful that the Franklyn's had tried their best with me by giving me everything I asked for as long as I did a good job in school. I wish they had set the same rule for my real life. Lord knows I needed more guidance in my everyday life than I ever needed in a classroom. The Franklyn's tried to do everything they could to fix my broken past, and all I did was let them down. The only thing I really had to show from there upbringing was the fact that I was a straight "A", student who just happened to be on the Dean's list in college and a Lexus I didn't deserve, because of that. I definitely wasn't the evolved woman I always portrayed myself to be at our usual Sunday dinners, and it was killing me on the inside. Secretly, I knew that they knew I wasn't fully on the right path just yet but they never looked down on me for that. They always let me work out my own problems and even promised to be there when the roads got to rough.

A couple of days later, I was on my way to meet Moe at a Jamaican club for our date, because I got the "Go" from Pzyco.

"Chosen One," by Future poured out my stereo as I drove to the club and all I could do was laugh thinking about the irony of the song lyrics. Tonight was going to be Moe's last on Earth, and he damn sure was the chosen one. I laughed some more knowing that I was the one who would bring his megalomaniac, bipolar, yet abusive ass one-step closer to the reaper.

"A life for a life" I heard Mizz say to me as a sinister smile appeared on my face.

"In order to be irreplaceable one must always be different," I thought as I checked over my make up before getting out the car. I knew I was different from everyone else in my life, because who else would have helped their sister whom they hated for so many years, especially when they weren't even close. I also felt Mizz now. I was going to help T'Aira out of this situation, and in return, she was going to help me out of mine. I smiled some more as I walked up to the club just thinking that it took all these years for T'Aira and I to finally see eye to eye on anything. The club was crowded when I finally made my entrance, and I loved the choice of music. "Nice and Naughty," by Chevelle Franklyn played as I danced with some fine ass young dude with dreads down his back. "Calabria," by Enur had me in a zone as I continued to dance by the bar waiting for my drink. I rolled my ass all kinds of ways to the beat in my short dress once I saw my mark of the night hit the door.

"Game on," I said taking a sip of my drink as I texted Pzyco our code.

I watched Moe make his way over to the bar through the crowded club as the song changed to "Why Not Take All Of Me," by Casserine. We sat by the bar chatting for a while then made our way towards the dance floor. I was grinding all over Moe to "Scent Of Attraction," by Patra, and Aaron Hall, when I saw the clock strike 12:00, exactly on my phone. I rolled my ass on him even more then knowing that his time would soon be up. For a moment, I felt like I was back at the strip club the way all the dudes were watching me dance with Moe. The next thing I knew. I saw Pzyco enter the club. I was grinding on Moe so hard that he was starting to get an erection.

"What are you going do about that?" I asked him as the song changed.

"What are you going to do about it?" he replied, and I started massaging his penis right there on the dance floor.

"We should leave," he insisted, and I agreed.

"Let me just run to the bathroom really quick," he stated, and I just kissed his cheek.

"That was the kiss of death, you fool," I laughed, and then told him "See you later".

He just laughed, gave me a little wink and then headed towards the bathroom as I made my way back towards the bar. Before I could even reach the bar, the sexy brother from earlier grabbed my arm to ask for another dance, and then people starting screaming. Once people started running towards the exit, I knew it was over for Moe's trifling ass. I heard a person say something about shots fired in the bathroom, and I smiled.

"One down, one to go," I said to myself as the cop cars pulled up.

"Game Over," I smirked, walking to my car where Pzyco already was.

Once I got home that night, I jumped in the shower to wash off the smell of Moe's scent. "Wrecking Ball," by Miley Cyrus came on blasting, and I laughed. This was easier than taking candy from a baby, I thought back to the last moments of Moe's life. The next morning, I was up watching the news while banging my jam, "Black Barbie," by Little Jackie when the reporter came on reporting the news about last night's events.

"A local drug dealer gunned down in the bathroom of a night club," was all I heard before I cut off the television and cut up my jam. I didn't need to hear the details when I already knew the truth. I pulled out my journal, and started to write in it. I desperately needed to get some things off my chest, and my journal was the only person I was willing to confess too. Writing always seemed to make me feel free, so I poured my soul out on paper as "Roses," by Mos Def played. I really hoped things got better for me once Haji was removed from my life. I knew that the privilege of a lifetime was being who you were, but I hadn't been able to be much of myself for a very long time. I also regretted the fact that I would have to break up with Ramir soon. I knew I would have to wait until Haji's unexpected death. I sat there in my thoughts and feelings until it hit me that Ize would also be coming home soon. My life was nothing more than drama on top of drama, and I just wished it would all go away. I hated that Ize still had to tell me the real reason why he killed my Mama, and I really didn't know if I was prepared to take anymore bullshit. Everything seemed to be hitting me like a ton of bricks, but I knew with every dark cloud comes a positive aspect, and silver, lining. I saw past this day, and I was looking forward to working in California. I was ecstatic just knowing the Franklyn's would be proud of the woman I had finally become, and I smiled. A few minutes later, T'Aira walked in the door from the mall, and informed me that she would be hooking up with Haji later on at a hotel.

"Oh really," I thought.

"The ghost finally came out of hiding," I laughed, thinking he was never going to make it to that hotel. I told her the plan, and called Pzyco to let him know the Boogieman was in town and then told him to meet me at the club later that night. It was around 10:30 pm, when I went into work that night. I did my show to "Some Bomb Ass Pussy," by the Dogg Pound, and then headed to the dressing room to make sure T'Aira was ready for later on. She told me she had everything covered and then we both left out the dressing room to do my next show. T'Aira shook her ass all over me to "Move" by Migos, and for the first time, I felt some type of love for her. I sang along to "Brain" by Banks as I watched Misty dance while T'Aira got ready to meet up with Haji. I got dressed after that. It was exactly 1:45 am, when we both left the club. I hopped in my car and called Ramir to let him know I was on my way there. I wanted to be there with him the next morning once he got the news about Haji's death.

"Crazy Bitch," by Buckcherry came on blasting when I started the ignition, so I sang along. I damn sure felt like a crazy bitch as I drove on the freeway to Ramir's house. I loved every moment of knowing tonight would be Haji's last night, and yet I felt bad just knowing that Haji was a big part of Ramir's life. I felt so bad about all the hurt I was about to cause Ramir that I sat in his driveway smoking a blunt to try to ease my pain before I even went in the house. "Dreams," by Fleetwood Mac came on, and I felt like shit. I hated knowing that Ramir would be the one hurt by all of this, but I knew it was no turning back the hands of time. My secrets from last summer were haunting me, and I had to get rid of them by any means necessary.

"Leave Me Alone," by Michael Jackson started to play, and I turned up the radio. If Haji had just left me alone I could have been happy with Ramir, and he would be able to keep his life. Instead, he just had to push my hand with all the stalking and threats he kept insisting on making towards my life as if I was some punk ass Bitch. I hated Haji, and I felt bad for Ramir.

"Oh well," I thought opening up the door to my car.

"A girl's got to do, what a girl has to do," I said aloud as I walked to Ramir's door.

I couldn't even take my coat off fast enough as Ramir pressed my body against the front door while biting on my bottom lip. After I managed to slip my coat off, I watched it fall to the floor as Ramir carried me over to the dining room table. He fucked me all over that table and then carried me to the living room couch were we continued to make love until we both fell asleep in front of the fireplace. The next morning, I woke up, and made breakfast. I was so happy, because I had the time of my life last night, and I knew my problem was, solved. I was just waiting for the confirmation. I ate then headed out to class. I had a ten o'clock Theatre class that morning and a hair appointment right after that. I knew if my little plan had worked, Niecy would know all about it. Class ended at 12:00pm, and I made it to the shop thirty minutes later for my 1:30 hair appointment. I could tell something was wrong when I walked in the salon by the look on Niecy's face.

"Girl have you heard the news?" Niecy whispered when I took my seat.

"Word on the street was that somebody had been killing all the top drug dealers in the city these past couple days," She alleged, and I tuned in.

"Tell me something I don't know," I thought as my little pawn filled me in on the latest gossip.

"I heard Moe Diddy got killed a week ago at a Jamaican club because he owed up some big money to a guy named Ace," She stated, smacking her lips while shaking her head.

"Ace happens to be your new boo's brother, Teaz," she continued, shaking her head some more.

"Some folks call him Haji, but everybody 'round here calls him Ace," Niecy added, and I just put my hand to my chest, and did the best role of looking shocked as I could.

"Oh my God," I replied as Niecy continued to talk.

"What are you saying, Niecy?" I asked, as if I was clueless as to what she was trying to say.

"They found Ace last night dead in his car in front of a hotel. The police think both murders are connected: because the girl that was with him claimed that him, and Moe had been enemies."

I laughed inside as she told me what else she had heard through the grapevine, and then my phone rang.

"Hold up, Niecy," I said answering the phone for Ramir.

He was crying, so I knew he had just found out the news about Haji's death.

"I'm at the hairdresser, Bae,"

"I'll be right over afterwards," I assured him then hung up.

I felt bad for Ramir, but I knew I had to kill Haji before he killed me. I stayed with Ramir that entire evening. I tried my best to comfort him despite the fact that I didn't care about Haji being dead. It hurt me deep down inside to see Ramir hurting. I smiled on the inside as I watched "How To Get Away With Murder," thinking about how I had just done that. The next day. I went home and wrote about it all in my journal. Two days later, was T'Aira's twenty-third birthday. I took her too this hot new club over in Canada, and she loved it. We had a ball that night, and I was glad to see T'Aira genuinely happy. I was starting to a have a change of heart towards her now that she was around me all the time. I was starting to think with the proper guidance, and love we could have the relationship I always wanted out of my sister. I knew that loving T'Aira wasn't going to happen overnight but I was willing to let bygones be bygones, and try start all over again. She was my sister so maybe it was time to bury that grudge I had been holding on to for so long. The following week was Haji's funeral, and Ramir practically begged me to go with him, but I didn't. I made up a story about me feeling under the weather the day before, and I could tell he was hurt. I wasn't going to see Haji's dead body when I knew I was the reason he was really in a casket. I was many things, but I really wasn't the cold-hearted, Bitch that Haji tried to make me out to be, despite how things ended between us. As I waited for Ramir, I decided to take a bubble bath. I was sitting in the tub listening to "Black Horse and Cherry Tree" when my phone rang. I was going to call the person back once I got out the tub but my first mind told me to answer.

"Hello," I answered as Ize told me to open my door.

I jumped out the tub, dried off a little bit and then slipped on my robe still wet. I couldn't believe Ize was at my front door. I walked down the steps as "Dark Horse," by Katy Perry played. I had so many questions in my head as I walked towards the door. It was so surreal hearing Ize say:

"Open my door," after all these years. I took a deep breath before I opened the door. Just seeing Ize standing in front of me in one piece with that perfect Colgate smile made me jump in his arms. I was so happy to see him free again, and I was even more excited about the fact that we would finally be able to have that talk I had been waiting a year to have. I had been dreaming about this day ever since the day he told me he killed my Mama.

"Come in baby," I smiled, taking his hand to lead him towards the couch.

"You looking really good, Teaz," he stated, staring at my ass jiggle through my robe as I walked.

"Thanks Boo," I replied, shaking my ass for him a little bit before we took our seats.

My bottom didn't get a chance to hit the cushions good before I starting drilling Ize with all kinds of questions. I had to give him the third degree, because I wasn't about to put up with the same shit I did before he left. I needed to know where his head was at, and I needed him to understand I wasn't that naïve little push over who was blinded by love anymore.

"So where are you going to be staying now that you're out?" That was the first thing I needed to know.

"How have you been my love?" I asked, looking Ize deep in the eyes. Even with a scruffy looking bread and braids, Ize was fine.

"I can't wait until you cut this off," I joked rubbing his beard.

"Me either," he laughed pulling me in closer to him.

"Come over here, girl," Ize replied, kissing me on the cheek.

"I've been waiting years to have a moment like this with you," he smiled, and I almost melted.

"It's good to be home with my main girl again," he added, seductively kissing me on the lips.

I couldn't help but kiss him back. It had been so long since I felt his touch and right, now it felt so right. I was enjoying every moment of the chemistry that was slowly starting to cause friction between my thighs. We always had that fiery connection that causes instant passion. Maybe that is why I kept yearning for more. Ize was definitely the definition of the "Bad Boy," that always made me lose my cool. Before I knew it, we were getting it on right there on my living room floor. I had to give him some after he damn near sucked my pussy dry. I knew he needed me after doing all those years in prison and as crazy as it seemed, I needed him too. I had been with a couple men, but none of them compared to Ize. He knew how to turn me on by just looking at me. I let him fuck me all kinds of ways after we first did it. I even lied to Ramir so I could spend the rest of the day with Ize. After we made love a couple more times, we took a shower, and then I took him to the barbershop. It felt good being able to do things for Ize now that he was home, and I was on my feet. I wanted to show him that I was still loyal and always going to be there for him no matter what we had been through in our past. I truly believed that everyone deserved a second chance to prove themselves if they truly cared about you in the first place. It's a wrap on whatever we once had after that. You only get one time to cross me, and I'll cut you off. If I allow you back in my life, and you make a fool out of me. You deserve everything I dish out to you down the line. I had to learn that when you start looking at people's hearts instead of their faces life becomes much clearer. I was going to see where Ize's heart really was this time around. I promised myself that I would not let the sex, or the physical attraction cloud my better judgment. I couldn't just go off his looks, money or words anymore. I had to trust his actions. People's actions always told you exactly how they felt about you no matter what their mouth said. We went to the mall and then out to dinner once we left the barbershop. After dinner, I dropped Ize off at his loft he had Pzyco get for him while he was away. He asked me to come up to talk before I left, and I did. I knew this was the moment I had been patiently waiting for. Once we took our seats, he poured me a glass of wine.

"I'd like to propose a toast. I know I haven't always treated you like the Queen that you are, but I promise from this day forward to treat you like nothing less than the Queen you've always been to me".

I just smiled. I knew he was serious. I loved this side of Ize because he reminded me of the old Izir that I fell in love with when I was twelve years old.

"I love you," I replied, and then we sipped our drinks.

I sat my glass down after that then took Ize's hand in mine.

"Tell me why you killed my mother, Ize," I inquired and, he grabbed my hand tighter.

"It was really an accident." He told me, but I had to know what happened.

"I was coming to get you the night I killed your mother. I was going to sneak around to your window and wake you up so you could come talk some sense into me. I had gotten into it with a group of boys from my school that was picking on Pzyco."

I laughed, thinking I couldn't imagine anyone picking on Pzyco now but the look Ize gave me told me it wasn't a laughing matter.

"We were supposed to set the boys up after school the following week, but my plans got changed. The plan was for Pzyco to steal his dad's gun, and together we were going to lead the boys to the park. Once we got there, we going to pistol whip the boys, and beat them up. Before I reached your house, we met in the field behind our townhouse to discuss our plans. I guess your mom was buying her drugs from Old Man Dillard, and overheard us talking. When I was done talking to Pzyco, I headed over to your house but to my surprise your mom was there waiting for me. She threatened to tell my mom and the police on me. She even told me I couldn't see you anymore when I tried to explain to her what I was going through. She also knew we liked each other, and said she was going to kill you if she ever caught you hanging around me again. I was furious on my walk back to my house. I paced the floor trying to figure out what to do so that your mom wouldn't tell mine. After twenty minutes of pouting, I decided to go try to talk her out of it. I saw your mom in her room getting high, and for a second I thought about just leaving thinking that she will probably forget all about this once she got her daily fix. Instead, I climbed through the living room window and snuck around to her room. Once I got to her room, I confronted her. I begged her not to tell on me, but she just cursed me out, and threatened to kill you for letting me in. I tried to reason with her, but she jumped out of her chair, and was just about to head over to your room when I grabbed the bat she kept behind the door. I hit her in the head, and she fell to the floor as blood began oozed out the side of her face. When I went to check he pulse, I couldn't feel anything and I panicked. I ran in the front, climbed back out the window, and grabbed the gas can by the side of the house. I climbed back into the house, poured the gasoline all over her body, lit the lighter and threw it. The next thing I knew, the police and fire fighters were outside, and ya'll were being removed from the house. I never meant for you to get sent away, Teaz." Ize said through tears.

"I know I've messed your life up in more ways than one, but I promise that I'm going to make it all up to you if you just forgive me, and continue to be by my side," He added sincerely.

All I could do was cry. I didn't know what to say after hearing Ize's confession. I loved Ize dearly, but I was already in a relationship. I was glad to know the truth about my Mama after all these years. The fact that she wanted to kill me for loving Ize justified his actions. I was glad Ize killed that demon of mine called my Mama. My Mama was never there for me anyway, so I'm glad death chose her instead of me that night.

"I forgive you, Ize," I replied, through tears as I gave him a hug.

"I have something I need to tell you," I added as my phone began to ring.

"One second," I said, holding up a finger as I answered.

"Hello,"

"Hello is this La'Teazya Scorns?" a woman asked me.

"Yes, this is her," I told the woman as I cleared my throat.

"This is Officer Kelly with the Detroit Police Department," she replied, and I was shocked.

"Umm, yes," I stuttered, because I had no idea why the police would be calling me.

"I'm sorry to be calling you this late, Ms. Scorns, but we just found a body of a young lady in her apartment and the note attached to it told us to contact her sister," the woman said, and I almost lost it. First, I find out the truth about how my Mama died, and now I have to go identify my sister's body.

"Ok, officer," I stuttered some more as a tear rolled down my cheek.

"I'll be there as soon as possible," I replied, then hung up.

"T'Aira's dead."

"I'll explain later," I told Ize in shock.

I felt like him the day he had to go identify Zar's body knowing he was the reason behind it.

"What's understood never has to be explained," he stated giving me a hug.

This night wasn't turning out the way I had expected. I felt like I was having an outer body experience as we walked to the car. I told Ize to drive me, because I wasn't sure if I could steer straight with everything going on in my head. "Autumn Leaves," by Chris Brown played as we drove to the morgue, and all I could think about was my life growing up with T'Aira as a child. I had spent most of my time with her lately. I wanted to play a positive role model in her life since she started going to rehab. T'Aira was really trying to become a better person now that her demon was gone. It was a shame that her guilt made her take her own life. I only hoped that death could offer her the peace she never received in life. I felt so bad looking at my sister's lifeless body. She actually looked like an angel just lying there.

"I'm sorry I wasn't a better sister too you growing up," I whispered through tears as they placed the sheet back over her body.

We were both just products of our environment. We shared the same blood, but we were nothing more than different results of being black trying to make it in the hood. It took years for me to look at my sister, and feel some kind of love for her. That fact alone made me hate my Mama even more knowing that it was all her fault that me, and my sister's bond wasn't as close as it should've been. Since T'Aira didn't have any insurance I cremated her. I scattered her ashes in the Detroit River right by this spot in Canada that we went to for her last Birthday. We even set off balloons in her, and Zar's honor during the party I was having for Ize on the Princess Boat.

"I was so in love with Ize," I thought as we danced together at his party.

He was really living up to the promises that he made me, and I felt special to be the only girl in Izes' life for once. Ramir, on the other hand, wasn't as happy as I was once he found out Ize was home. I tried my best to convince him that everything would be the same between him one night during dinner.

"I hear you Teaz." Ramir stated as I sipped my glass of water waiting for my appetizers to arrive.

"Do you love him? He asked, and I couldn't lie.

"Yes I love him, Ramir, but I'm also in love with you," I replied, but he just shook his head.

"Whatever, Teaz," he stated pouting.

"Just be with Ize," Ramir added, as the waiter walked back up.

We didn't talk about being together anymore after that, and we eventually ended up going our separate ways. I hated to hurt Ramir after everything else I had already done behind his back, but I needed to be happy. I knew that would never happen being with Ramir. It was a good feeling to have my King back by my side. Ize was the only man I ever really loved next to Mega anyway. I was going to follow my heart, and hope love lead me in the right direction this time around.

A couple weeks later, at work I did a private show for Ize as we chilled in the new V.I.P. section they just put in. "Often" by The Weeknd was playing as he began to ease his penis inside of me. I was happy that everything had been going good between us now that we were officially a couple again, and even more happy that Ize was finally starting to get back on his feet. I felt like the lyrics to "You Know You Like It," by DJ Snake & Aluna George as I rode Ize. I knew in my heart I was on my way to better things after next year. It was also very ironic that no matter how hard we both tried to deny it: we both knew the truth. We shared a rare connection that even I couldn't explain at times, and I loved it. I just hoped the love we had didn't drive us both insane in the end. I was never so happy to be able to put all the shit before today, behind me.

"Last summer was cruel one," I thought as we finished our little quickie.

"I love you Ize," I whispered as I adjusted my clothes.

"I love you more, Bae," Ize replied, but little did I know my relationship move I had just made was about to take a wrong turn.

Un-Fuckin' Believable
Dear Diary,
December 29, 2014

"We're about to get fucked up, tonight!" I shouted along with Shawty Redd as "Groupie Love" began to play. It was the day of club, Dirty Secret's Christmas party, and I was feeling myself. Everything was finally going right in my life, and I was ecstatic about the New Year ahead. "2015," was going to be my fresh start at life. It had taken seven long years of blood, sweat and tears for me to accomplish my dreams, and I was proud. I was finally happily in love with the man I always wanted, and I was very excited to be graduating at the end of spring. My parents were so proud of me, and all I had overcome. Despite, all the things I had been through I managed to achieve beyond my own expectations, so life couldn't have been any better for me. I wasn't valedictorian of my graduating class like I would have liked to have been, but I was happy for the girl that was. I didn't have a bad bone in my body, and I was finally starting to humble myself. The bar was crowded with people from all over, and I damn near bought the bar out for my entourage. I had been celebrating all week, because I had a lot to be grateful for outside of school with me starting my own business next year. I was grateful for Rozi and Duty, because they offered me the chance of a lifetime. I was literally on cloud nine, and it wasn't a damn thing that could bring me down. Once my jam "Masterpiece" by Noni off "Beyond The Lights," came on I had the entire V.I.P. section turned up. Sparkling bottles were on every table in my section, and I was in heaven. In my own little way, I felt like a masterpiece. I was dressed to perfection as usual in my all gold Saint Laurent dress. Complete with matching gold accessories, and the matching gold Giuseppe heels. I was feeling like a queen so I wore a Nefertiti necklace with the matching earrings. I looked like I could have been one of the modern day version, Egyptians. All my hard work was finally starting to pay off, and I was truly, blessed. For the first time, I was shining bright like the star I was born to be so I was letting my little light shine. Mrs. Franklyn always told me to, "Never let the sun go down," and I wasn't planning too. Who would have known that all I had to do was believe in myself, and the impossible could happen?

 "There's no blueprint on how to beat me," I laughed inside sipping my drink as I thought back to Floyd Mayweather's interview I watched, earlier. We all know that you can't spell believe without the lie in the middle, and to be honest some of the lies I told is the main reason why I'm sitting so pretty right now.

"I love you so much!" Ize whispered in my ear as I danced to "Twerk Dat Ass" by Juicy J.

"I love you more, baby!" I replied, giving Ize a kiss on the forehead.

The party lasted until five that morning, but I decided to leave early to spend some quality time with my man. Ize had just bought this new house in Gaylord, Michigan, and I absolutely loved the place. I really loved the bathroom attached to the master bedroom, because it reminded me of the one from the movie "Scarface". I was happy to see my baby back on his feet like the man I always knew he had become.

"I still don't understand why you won't just move in." Ize said taking a seat on the couch.

"You're always over here anyways, telling me how to decorate this place," he added while motioning for me to come sit next to him.

I just laughed. I had been thinking about it a lot lately. It really seemed like things had been good between us. A part of me, wanted to take Ize up on his offer, but I never wanted to play "house". I didn't believe in moving in with a man without marriage, especially when I could reap the benefits at the end if our relationship failed. "Meant To Be," by TLC came on, and I made Ize dance with me.

"We should get married Ize," I smiled, pulling him in for a kiss and he stopped dancing.

"What?" I asked walking away to get a drink from the bar.

"I really don't see what the big deal is with you, and marriage Ize!" I snapped confused.

I knew Tazha had did Ize bad in the past, right before their wedding, but I wasn't that bitch.

"You want me to move in, and play house but you can't marry me." I pouted pouring myself a glass of D'usse.

I hated that Ize always had these commitment issues when it came to us when I have been loyal for years.

"You do know that I'm in love with you, right?" I inquired sipping my drink as the song changed to "Pose To Be" by Omarion.

"Yes I do, Teaz." He mumbled walking over to the bar.

"Then what's the problem, Izir? Why won't you marry me?" I asked him again, slamming my glass down on the table.

"We've been through everything together so I don't understand why you're not jumping at the opportunity." I yelled.

"We're soul mates don't you see that?" I whined sipping some more of my drink. I loved Ize, but I wasn't completely satisfied with us just dating after all wed been through together.

"I'm the Bonnie to your Clyde, the Juliet to your Romeo," I stated, getting up to walk over to Ize's seat.

"We're like art."

"Just the right combination of everything to create a perfect picture," I stated, wrapping my arms around his neck while showering him with kisses.

"I agree with everything you just said," he replied, but I could tell he wanted to change the subject.

His smile was slowly starting to fade at the thought of marriage, but I needed answers.

"I'm just not ready for marriage right now, Teaz. I'm just really starting to get my life back on track from that minor lost I took, and to be honest you're not ready either. So come on with all this marriage shit, Bae." Ize continued giving me a hug.

"You still have so much to accomplish, Teaz. I would never want to be the reason why you didn't fulfil your dreams. What happened to us just living for right now?" he asked pushing me away to face him.

"I don't really think you're ready to give up your other life outside of school, either," Ize added referring to me dancing at Duty's club, and I was hurt.

"I know you won't leave that club to be my wife." Ize said, walking over to the radio to turn it off.

"That's your bread and butter, baby!" he giggled, but I didn't see anything funny.

"You know I'd leave the strip game alone if you really wanted me, to, Ize." I replied, but I wasn't really sure of my answer.

Ize was right. Dirty Secret's had been my way to make cash until I graduated, and move to California. Speaking of, I still hadn't gotten around to telling Ize about my next career move. I wanted to see how things between us would work out before I broke the news to him about my job in Cali. I see now that waiting to tell him was a good decision. I had to be absolutely; sure, that Ize was the one before I just included him in my plans. I didn't want to just run off in the sunset with Ize on blind faith knowing that somewhere along the lines we'd come to an end. I needed something solid this time around, and I was willing to risk it all if it meant there was going to be someone else down the line. Things with us were good for the moment, but I always kept my third eye open. People always act a certain way until they get everything they want out of you. Ize was a total asshole in the past, and I was only hoping that he was telling the truth. In my heart, I really felt that he had changed, but I had to be sure.

Ize phone began to ring, and I noticed that he ignored the caller by sending them straight to voicemail. The caller called back five more times after that, and I knew off rip it was one of his little sidekicks. I wasn't jealous that girls called Ize, because he told me that the girls from his past didn't compare to what we had built together. I admit I was curious at times, but, I knew a major advantage of age is learning to accept people without passing judgment." I always wondered if the other women in his life were secretly the real reason Ize wouldn't fully commit. I didn't bother to press the issue after that night. I slept on the whole marriage concept, and asked God to lead me in the right direction. I also promised myself that I was going to make Ize chose before I left.

I was driving to my home girl, River's office to go over a part in her play that I helped her write. River had been working on her new label, and lately she had been spending a lot of time in the studio with her new artist whenever she wasn't in Drama class. Destin had recently brought an abandon building that had another small building attached to it. The smaller building was River's main office for "Trending Sounds Inc.", and the larger building was going to be a nightclub. He was really trying to make their dreams come true, and I knew my girl was on her way to being the producer she always dreamed of becoming. I was happy things were going good for the young couple. I had to give River her props. They were doing what I only could have dreamed of doing with Ize at that age. I kept thinking about Destin's father Old Man, Dillard. He was the biggest drug dealer in Michigan when I was coming up, but ended up being murdered by, Legend. How ironic. A lot of people seem to think that the world is small, but the truth is nothing happens by chance, and we are all connected. Life is predestined for us, so everyone you meet whether good or bad was supposed to be there. That's why we have moments we call, déjà vu. We just simply imprint in our footsteps that were already created for us before we were born. It's also ironic that the person who killed Destin's' father would die by the hands of my boyfriend, Ize. We all know that when you live by the sword, you die by that same sword. Life doesn't offer a lot of rules, and yet we all have to play the game. As twisted, and cruel as life could be at times; it always seems like you're lucky if you are one of the ones that survives. Not everyone is meant to make it out sane or alive, but that's the circle of life.

"No Juice" by Lil' Boosie was blasting when I walked in the building. I love how River had the place decorated. The main hallway looked like you were traveling inside the ocean until you reached the studio.

"Sup, Teaz." River greeted when I walked in the door.

"I love what you all have done with the place so far." I smiled, and so did she.

Looking at all the potential of her building, made me start to think about my own club I was going to be running in California. I couldn't wait to move there, and decorate. It was time I put my creative side to good use. Once I took my seat, she pulled out a folder, and passed it to me.

"I just need you to read over everything, and let me know if you want to add anything or change something. I also need you to make sure everything is the way you want it before I send in my final draft." River instructed.

I was happy to be able to help her out with this project. I always wanted to write my own movie, or book one day once I retired. That's part of the reason why I love the author, Raven Soars. I smiled just thinking about the interview I watched about her life earlier. The woman who was giving the interview spoke highly of the creative, heartfelt autobiography about her life with a twist added to it. I remember reading that book when I was in prison, and thinking she was such an inspiration to young girls like me. Raven's only goal in life as a child, was to spread genuine love to all the lives she ever touched, and to try her best to walk a righteous path in the eyes of God even when life wasn't as good to her. As she grew older, she began to realize that she was most misunderstood, and mistreated by those she loved and trusted the most. I truly admired that no matter what she had faced in life, she was able to overcome every obstacle she faced since birth, and then made her dreams reality. This is one of the main reason she became my favorite author during my prison years. Raven taught me that in order to change and move forward you have to forgive your past as well as yourself. This is the first step of changing your life with "acceptance and forgiveness". Once you conquer those two you are free to move forward towards "repair and restoration". One day, I knew I was going to do great things once I finally forgave myself. I had just begun to read the script when River starting talking to me.

"So, I hear you and Ize are back together?" River stated while I read over my words.

"Warning…"

"This is a test. The next thing I say is a very important piece of information for your mind to analyze. You think you got it all figured out, don't you? I can just about guarantee that you're not even close to the truth." I laughed, just thinking about my own life.

"I did it. I murdered that bastard right there in his own bathroom in cold blood. I was hypnotized by his tricks that were starting to be no good, and I wanted in on his wicked little game. His cruel intentions sent me into a fury, and I wanted to be free from everything. It's not my fault the Devil made a wrong turn. I'm just the Angel that put him out his misery." I read, and then answered River's question.

"Yea, we're back together," I replied while continuing to reading some more.

"I don't care what people think about me as of this point in my life, because I'm free of my burden. Folks love to swear they so perfect, but the truth is nobody really is. We are all out here searching for something we know nothing about, and settling for less. Then have the nerve to get mad at the choices you make when you realize you have been a fool. I know everybody's been secretly waiting to say, I told you so, but they need to remember one thing; I reached every goal I ever set for myself before I pulled the trigger." I laughed thinking this girl; Shari was one crazy ass bitch that reminded me a lot of myself.

"Now whose up, Bitches?" I read right before I heard River say, "Oh,", and then noticed she had a slight frown on her face. I just kept reading. I was all into Shari's character that River had created. It was something about her main character that felt like, Déjà vu.

"Well, I saw Ize the other night, while I was out, Teaz." I heard River say, but the storyline was so interesting I couldn't pull my eyes from the paper.

"I'm sorry, what did you say River?" I asked giving her my full attention.

"I was saying that I saw Ize the other night with a girl," River repeated.

"I was out looking for local artist on amateur night at this new club when they walked in," she continued.

I had to stop reading, because I was speechless. It was as if I knew what her next line was going to be before she even opened her mouth.

"Well, Boo,"

"You know I'm not one for gossip. If you know what I mean?" she added, and I closed the folder.

"The thing that bothered me the most is I knew Ize saw me, but that didn't stop him from being all over the girl he was with." River stated giving me a crazy look.

"The second thing that really bothered me was the fact that the girl kept telling everyone they were married." She added, and I frowned.

"Married?" I snapped.

"That bitch is lying." I yelled, slamming the folder on the desk in front of me.

"Calm down, Teaz! I'm just the messenger" River replied, raising her hands in the air.

"It's all good." I laughed, and then gathered my composure that I was starting to loose.

I grabbed up my purse, snatched out the car keys, and told River to keep the script the way it was. Shari was about to be my new inspiration as far as I was concerned.

"We're going to see about that." The crazy voice in my head repeated over, and over until I reached my car. The minute, I got into the driver seat, I dialed Ize's phone, and got the voicemail. I was so pissed I could not even start the car. I dialed his number back just to get the same thing. I found myself calling back a couple more times after that, and then I pulled out the parking lot in tears.

"Lying King" by Jhene Aiko played as I drove like a mad woman to my house in the rain. Three hours later, Ize showed up at my house drunk, and upset about losing $10,000 dollars at the casino. The next morning, I confronted him about his so-called wife and the allegation about them two being seen hugging in the club. Of course, Ize denied it all. I knew damn well River would not just sit up, and make up a lie like that. She had no reason to hurt me, so I knew I had to do my own investigation. The next couple of days were rocky between us. Ize was back to pulling his old tricks. I was starting to wish I had left his ass in the past with the rest of my problems. In so many ways, I believed River now about ole girl being his wife, because he sure as hell was not with me anymore.

One morning, around 5:00 am, he showed up at my doorstep demanding I pack some bags. At first, I thought he had gotten into so more trouble until he explained that he just wanted to go on a weekend getaway, and talk. We drove to Chicago, and the whole time he gave me every excuse in the book for him being away for so long. He also claimed that he had been investing money in a new business he was starting in Vegas. That I believed. After a long weekend of good food, entertainment, and sex, things were back to normal with us. Ize even left a set of keys to his house over to my place the last time he was there, and every time I offered to return them, he was conveniently too busy to get them. I figured this was his own special way of letting me know we were exclusive no matter what people had to say.

"Cross the line, speak about mine."

"I'mma wave this tech,"

"I'm a geek about mine." I sang as I drove to work

It had been two weeks since all that wife non-sense, and I was about to take my first trip to California with Rozi to see my building. I had planned to break the news to Ize later on that evening during dinner. I called Ize about 6:00, which was right before I decided to go into work. I had not really been dancing lately, but one of the girls was sick, and Duty practically begged me to come in. I was thinking about leaving this whole dancing life behind me once I became the manager of my own club. I had bigger goals to accomplish in life and it was time to start pursuing them all. I was so happy to get this chance at a better life that I felt like Sean "Puffy" Combs. "I had learned to enjoy the ups for what they are, because those are the moments that go by the quickest". I was almost about to hang up when Ize answered.

"Hey, Baby," Ize said.

"You gone wear that one thing I brought you in Chicago for me later?" Ize then told me to hold on before I could answer.

"I gotta call you back a little later, Love," He promised after clicking over.

"Make sure you wear the red one." Ize instructed before hanging up.

I was looking forward to seeing Ize later. I had something very special planned for him being that this was the day I was going to let him in on my secret. When we were in Chicago Ize showed me this watch he had seen in a magazine that was worth a couple thousand. I knew he was going to lose his mind when he saw that I made his wish come true. With me rushing to go to work, and planning the perfect evening I forgot to pick up the wine I'd had ordered for the evening. I decided to call Ize back to ask if he could pick it up before coming over. The phone went straight to the voicemail and after calling back three times to get the same thing, I decided pick the bottle up myself. Once I got to the club I called one more time, but this time I left a message.

"Whenever you get this message call me back." I sighed, before I hung up.

I was starting to have a bad feeling in my gut, but I ignored it. A part of me was hurting on the inside as I gathered up my outfits, but I quickly forgot about my attitude once I felt this sharp pain in my stomach. The minute I stood up, I rushed to the bathroom to throw up.

"What the fuck?" I thought walking out the bathroom to the dressing room.

Lately, I had been feeling weird a lot, but I summed it all up to stress or bad nerves. I had been going through an awful lot with life. My tainted relationship with Ize was beginning to get the best of me. I knew I was driving myself insane.

"I was seriously going to have to let all the bullshit go." I thought as I sat listening to "Hello, MFers," by Raven Soars & DJ.

"Hello Mutha fuckers,"

"It's a no bullshit zone!" I sang along with them, as Sazhay kicked it with me about her relationship issues. The whole time we talked all I could do was think about Ize, and his latest bullshit. I was so happy that I grabbed his key off the nightstand, because I was going to return them if he did not answer once I got off work. The whole date, I had planned for us that night was about to be history if Ize did not pick up the phone. I was really hoping Ize called me back before I had to go through such drastic measures, but it was no telling with Ize. After talking to Sazhay for another thirty minutes, she left, and I was alone with my thoughts. It was clear that we could not be together no matter how hard I tried. One person could not keep a relationship together. If we really wanted things to work, Ize would have to start doing his part. I was not about to let Ize ruin my fresh start for me, and I damn sure was not about to go back to the old days. As far as I was concerned, we were over. I was fed up with, Ize.

"Everything has been figured out, except how to live." I thought back to my favorite quote by Jean-Paul Sartre. I almost cried. I was so disappointed in myself for allowing my heart to fall in love with Ize all over again after all these years. I did a couple shows before I decided to try to call Ize back. It had been exactly five hours, since the last time Ize, and I had spoken. I was fuming when I noticed Ize had not even attempted to call me back.

"How could I have been so fucking foolish?" I asked myself as my mind flashed back to Ramir. I knew things had ended on rocky terms between us, but I knew he was the better man. A part of me still wished Ramir were mine. It was sad that Haji blew my chance at real love all because he found out I was dating his brother. I knew Ramir was at a good place in life, despite the fact that he lost his only brother. I hated that I had broken his heart by leaving him after all that had happen. I could not bear to see Ramir hurting all the time over a brother that I knew did not give a flying fuck about him. I kept playing the last time I had ran into Ramir at the mall over in my head. I was walking into Footlocker with Ize, while Ramir was leaving out. He just smiled, and gave me a little wink while I tried my best not to acknowledge him. Secretly, I wished Ramir were the one I was calling right now. I was hurt just sitting there thinking about Ramir, and all the bullshit that lead to us not being together, so I went to the bar. I needed a drink to escape the pain I was starting to feel. Ize was never going to love me the way I wanted him to, and it was time I learned to face the music even when I did not like the tune. After a couple shots, I was mad at myself as I sat with my empty shot glasses. I always found myself putting Ize on this pedestal that he did not belong on. I really needed to check my own insecurities. There was absolutely, no way reason why I should be feeling like this right now. I was constantly stroking his ego by letting him come back after all his random infidelities, and it was time I let go. I wanted to cry as I watched Mona dance to "Outside Your Door" by Meshell Ndegeocello. The lyrics touched my heart in so many ways that I ran into the dressing room, and busted into tears. I was pissed as I sat staring at my screensaver. I had taken this picture of us the weekend we were in Chicago at a fair, and I hated looking at the false love we shared. I was in such a rage that I never even heard Sazhay walk into the dressing room.

"I hate you, Ize!" I mumbled aloud, before I almost threw my phone against the wall.

"Wu-sa," I heard Sazhay say before I threw my phone.

"I hate Ize for you." She laughed, and I just wiped away my tears.

I was not about to let Ize ruin my night when I had so much to look forward to. In another week, I will be in California with, Rozi preparing for my future. I finally felt blessed, I thought thanking God.

"It always seems impossible until it's done." Sazhay told me, and then offered to pray with me. I loved that I still had some good people in my life. Sazhay may have worked here at night, but that was only a way to make some extra cash. We all knew how she felt when it came to God. She pulled out her little bible she carried on a daily, and read me a passage from James.

"My dear brothers, take note of this: Everyone should be quick to listen, slow to speak and slow to become angry," Sazhay read.

I could feel my spirit being lifted right then.

"Thank you, Mama," I told her once she finished praying for me.

"I really needed that." I continued fixing up my lip-gloss, and massacre.

"The prayer of a righteous man is powerful and effective," she added as we headed out the dressing room.

I was on a mission, and money was the main thing on my mind. I did my last show then headed back to the dressing room to get dressed. I was pissed once I checked my phone to see that Ize still had not called me back yet. I even tried to give him the benefit of the doubt, but I knew something was up. I got dressed as quickly as I could, paid Sazhay, and bounced. I had to know what was going on, and I was really starting to believe it was some truth to River's story. My gut was telling me that Ize had been lying to me about everything. I jumped in my car, and instantly started to cry some more.

"One of these days, these shoes are going to walk all over you," I screamed at the air. I really hated the way Ize had me feeling.

"Why do I have to be the one in love with, Ize?" I asked myself aloud, as I sat disgusted pondering over our relationship. No matter how I sat there trying to analyze the whole "Us" thing, I knew in my heart that I loved Ize more then he would ever love me. Love is so crazy to me! When it's just us two he really makes me feel like he could be the one. Now, the one thing Ize always said to me from the beginning to be clear now:

"The one, who loved less, was the one who always controlled the relationship."

I was pissed as I sat with my thoughts that kept going from zero to a hundred really, quick. He was right, and I hated it deep down inside. I was the one sitting in my car with all the crazy thoughts while Ize was out somewhere in La La Land, literally. I stuck my key in the ignition and drove off with a purpose. I was "Dangerously In Love," with Ize! I put in the song at the thought of it and bumped Beyoncé on repeat as I drove all the way to his house.

"No the fuck he doesn't have the nerve to be home!" I yelled to myself more a loud than in as I pulled in front of his house.

"I can't believe this shit," I chanted over, and over like a mad woman to myself then I noticed a silver Mustang parked in my usual spot right next to Izes' Challenger.

"Oh Hell No," I screamed as rage began to fuel my now flaming mind... "Who the fuck car is that?"

"And, has the nerves to be in my spot?" was all I could muster up before I cut off my car, and parked.

"This nigga, Ize must've lost his damn mind," I screamed out loud to the wind as I snatched opened the glove compartment, and removed the set of keys Ize had left a t my house the other night. I stepped out the car, and slammed my door so hard I had to check and make sure I didn't break my own window. I marched up to the gate like a drill sergeant ready to command his troops and entered the security code, then crept around to the back of the house. Opening the back door to the kitchen, I could hear music playing.

"Damn, Ize, you couldn't even make it to the bedroom," I mumbled, then started instantly get madder than I originally was walking into the house.

I stood there in a state of shock with all kinds of wild thoughts in my head as "Secret Garden," by Quincy Jones played. I could hear the woman Ize was with moaning and begging him to fuck her. I shook my head in disgust as I continued to tip toe closer to where the sound of the voices was coming from. The whole thing was so surreal to me. Of course, I knew Ize had been with other women before today, but he always told me they didn't compare to what we had built together. I was mad as fuck on the inside as I walked down the dark hallway. It's just something about catching a guy you have feelings for in the act that makes you question yourself. What happened to the loyalty Ize swore he had, and is always stressing me about? Where is the bond, I thought we once shared? Right now, I swear if this is the link I gotta be chained to forever, you can best believe I'm about to break it. This shit right here just shows me that no matter how much a guy lays under you, tells you sweet nothings, and you provide, there is always going to be somebody who can fuck him other than you! I stood at the entrance of his entertainment room listening until my heart couldn't take the pain it was starting to feel, and then I walked in.

"You piece of shit!" I shouted as I entered the room throwing his keys at him.

Ize couldn't believe what he was hearing as the keys came crashing into the back of his head right before he could manage to pull his face from between the bitch legs.

"Teaz?" Ize responded in shock as he began to slightly, rise to his feet.

"What the hell are you doing here?" Ize managed to ask me with a bit of attitude in his voice.

I just cut him off with my "**WATCHING YOU EAT THIS BITCH PUSSY**," reply, like I hadn't just snuck up in this mans' house while he was clearly making another one of his homemade dirty movies he loved to watch so much.

"Teaz are you, crazy?" Was all I heard before I charged him like some raging bull. We tussled for a few minutes while Ize tried to gain control of the situation. I was so mad the only thing I heard were the screams from the "other lady" to be released from the pole he had built into the ceiling months ago. I was furious listening to this bitch. All I could think about at the time was the fact that this hoe was cuffed to the pole I asked him to install so that I could give him private shows. I was enraged by the sight of it all, so I wasn't backing down. He finally grabbed me up in a bear hug and then carried me kicking and screaming all kinds of profanity to the couch and slammed me into it. As soon as my bottom hit the couch, he smacked the shit out of me, causing me to calm down.

"Teaz, how dare you sneak up in my shit and attack me because you see me with another Bitch!" Ize finally spoke.

All I could do was concentrate on was the stinging feeling I was having in my face.

"Are you fucking crazy or something?" He asked with a sinister laugh as he looked at his arm where scratches were now starting to form.

"You know what, Teaz, don't even answer that." Ize snapped.

"It's obvious that you are crazy the way you up in here trying to kill a brother like we're married and you came home to find me, cheating." He yelled.

"What the fuck is up with this shit, my baby?" He inquired but I was at my wits end with Ize, and all his cheating.

"I guess you just straight disrespecting me now, huh, Teaz?" He grunted, raising his hand to slap me again, and I screamed.

"Wait Ize please, baby," I begged, knowing that I probably wouldn't be able to stop the obvious.

"I'm so sorry for acting like this," I whined, putting on a little waterworks to make it look believable.

"I was calling you to return your keys, baby," I thought quickly.

I can't tell you where I was going with my story, but I hoped to God it worked. I paused, and took a deep breath before I went into my next line.

"I was trying to surprise you by coming in, and giving you some head, and this good pussy while you were sleep,"

"But,"…

I stumbled over my words as I lied, watching his penis go from soft to erect as my words began to sink in.

"Baby," I sighed, now dropping to my knees and taking his manhood deep into my mouth.

" I got kind of jealous when I saw you with her," I confessed.

I then started licking all over his shaft that was now at full attention begging for more.

"You know I would never act like this on a normal basis," I added, while letting spit roll out of my mouth as I sucked vigorously at his penis playing on the vulnerability of the moment.

"You mad at me, Daddy?" I cooed.

It's just something about good oral sex that makes men weak even in their strongest moments.

"I can make this up to you," I promised pulling his penis out of my mouth, and walking over to where ole girl was still hand cuffed.

I gave her a look that said, "I was doing this more for him, then you." Before, either of them could say a word, I went down on that hoe. I sucked that bitch's pussy until she begged for us both to fuck her. I couldn't believe I'd just ate out some hoe I didn't know from a back alley, but when it comes to my man there was absolutely no limits to what I'd do. Once, I felt like Ize was satisfied with my behavior. I, told Ize to come fuck us both, and little did I know this was just the icing on the cake. In my mind, this was the beginning of a war; because I will be damn if another bitch was gone ever have, what I felt was rightfully mine. I had been down with Izir since we were twelve years old. I had lost him one time to life, and I meant it when I vowed that I would never lose him again.

Once I returned to my house the next morning after the crazy incident I had at Ize's house, all kinds of thoughts ran through my mind.

"A life is like a garden; perfect moments can be had, but not preserved, except in memory." I thought, as I opened my front door. I knew I, had not been planting the right seeds in mine, so I was sure to grow some weeds next year. There was so much that I wish I could just erase from my past, but I knew the only way to really correct my mistakes was to create better Karma in the near future. The only real question I needed answered as of this moment, was if Ize was really worth all the trouble I had been going through these past few years? I knew last night was just the icing on the cake for me, as far as our relationship went. I was fed up, and there was no way in hell I was going to compete with any bitch just to have a title. I could not believe that I had let the situation get that far out of my control. I knew deep down inside that I should have been left Ize alone. I also hated that I opened back up the door God had closed, just to get it slammed back in my face. This was definitely the straw that broke the camel's back, and I was officially over it all. I guess there is some truth to that saying: "We attract what we expect, and mirror what we reflect". The harsh reality was that with Ize, I did not expect much. All I ever wanted was for him to love me, the same way that I loved him. I do not know how I ever expected that to happen when I never set any real boundaries. Ize was everybody's property, and I was tired of his community dick. All I could think about doing when I stepped in the front door was washing away all the sins I had just committed. How was I ever going to move forward if I kept allowing myself to take steps back? I honestly did not understand why I kept letting Ize hurt me when it was clear that he did not love me. I was nothing more than another one of his side bitches just like the rest of his little freaks. Ize did not love anybody, but his damn self and it irritated my soul knowing I had wasted my time trying to make him love me. Love was just a word he used to his advantage to get what he wanted from people who he knew actually cared about him.

"Ghosttown," by Madonna came on the radio as I ran my bath water. I wished love was that easy, but I knew better, though. Ize always told me he loved me, but his actions showed me differently. It was really starting to seem like Ize was using all my weakness against me to get what he wanted, and still keep me. He knew I had not been with women since my prison days, and yet I hated just knowing that he enjoyed every minute of the unexpected threesome we had last night. I felt like a piece of trash as I walked back down stairs. As much as I thought I was playing on the vulnerability of the moment last night; it was ironic realizing Ize had did the same thing to me. I was heated as I snatched open my door to get the mail. I did not even bother to look at any of the envelopes. Instead, I threw the stack of mail on the living room table, and then headed back upstairs to take my bath. I cried the entire time I was in the tub, and then I promised myself these would be the last tears I shed over Ize this lifetime without him being dead. All I could do was stare at the plaque on the bathroom wall as I soaked in the tub. I cried just thinking about the years that I spent being such a fool for Ize as I read the words: "Some revolutionary events, which we call wild cards, will inevitably occur".

John L. Peterson was right, because this was the last thing I expected to happen in our relationship. Ize had hurt me so bad this time around that I was starting to feel worthless. I knew that Nat Turner once said, "No man, woman, or child was meant to be a slave of another. Let it come rough or smooth surely you must bear it." I was tired. I had bared all I could endure when it came to this tainted, "situation ship". Once I was dressed, I headed down stairs to watch the episodes of "Once Upon A Time," that I had missed. I sat down on the couch, and began to snuggle up with my pillow. I wished my life could have that happily ever after ending, but I knew that was only in the fairytales. I decided to have a glass of wine to calm my nerves as I watched my show so I headed into the kitchen. Once I returned to the couch, I took my seat, and reached for the remote controller that was sitting next to the stack of mail I had brought in earlier. I noticed a manila envelope, and wondered what it could be. I immediately snatched it out of the pile, and then noticed it did not have a return address. I figured it was the final draft of River's script, because I saw my name printed on the back in big red letters, but I was dead wrong. Still, I was excited as I ripped open the envelope that revealed the truth.

"What the fuck?" I snapped, while looking down at the picture of Ize and the bitch I had just did the unspeakable too. I was pissed as the contents of the envelope fell onto my lap. "I Can Tell" by 504 Boyz played in the background, but sex was the furthest thing on my mind. My heart almost hit the floor as I pulled out the next piece of paper in the envelope. All I could do was cry as I stood there holding a copy of Ize's marriage certificate, and a wedding picture at some wedding chapel in Vegas. Etta James was right; "I would have rather went blind,' then to be standing here looking at this shit. On the back of the picture in big red letters it read, "He's mine now, Bitch. You may have had him once, but I'll have him for life." I was fuming as I sat staring at her, "Laughing my petty ass off" signature.

"Lord, I'm going to kill Ize," I screamed into the air.

I was so mad at Ize. I knew even God's forgiveness wasn't going to stop

me from making my next move. I also knew that if I followed my first

mind this time; it would damn my soul, forever. I was furious, and I

wanted some temporary comfort for the pain that was forming in my

heart. My mind did a flashback to me walking in on Ize last night with ole

girl as I searched frantically for my car keys. The whole night played

itself back to me as I looked for my keys. I saw Ize, and I fighting, me

lying about why I was really, there, and us all having a threesome. I was

so busy focusing on pleasing, Ize that I never noticed the ring on the

woman's finger until now.

"How could Ize hurt me this bad?" I asked myself as I cried

uncontrollably.

"I've always been true to Ize, and this is how he repays me for my

loyalty". I screamed, throwing my phone.

I watched it scatter all over my living room floor into pieces. The phone

was nothing more than a reflection of my broken heart. Ize had crushed

my soul, and I did not know how I was going to fix it.

"This shit is un-fucking, believable," I yelled, and then stood up out of the

corner that I managed to crawl in like some child on time-out.

The little piece of sanity that I had before I stood up; left my body the moment I looked at the picture of Ize, and the woman, again. Furious, I snatched it up with the rest of the papers that were in the envelope, grabbed my car keys, and was about to head out the door then the house phone rang.

"I wonder who the fuck this could be?" I snatched the phone of the charger, and answered with an attitude.

"Hello," I yelled.

"Hi, is La'Teazya Scorns-Frankyln in?" The woman on the other end asked.

 I was ready to go to war as I paced my floor back and forth with the phone in my hand. I had a one-track mind, so I was not really in the mood for talking to anyone. I was mad as I listened to the woman on the other end of the phone, that I started gaging. I felt like I was having a panic attack as I tried my best to concentrate on her words without snapping.

"Yes, this is her," I answered back trying my best to calm down.

"This is Natalie, from Midwest Medical Center. We need to schedule an appointment with you to do some blood work as soon as possible. We were supposed to freeze some of your blood during your last visit, but didn't get a chance, too," she paused.

"But, I can see here that you had to leave early, and never rescheduled," she continued, and I just said, okay before I hung up in her face.

I had a one-track mind, and the only blood work I wanted to hear about was the one the news would be reporting after I saw Ize, and that bitch of his again. I ran upstairs, opened my nightstand, and pulled out my Tiffany & Co. decorated .9 millimeter Swiss & Wesson then headed out the house with a terrible vengeance. I hated Ize, and I damn sure didn't care about the consequences I would have to face down the line.

"Hatred is acquired through good deeds as well as bad ones." My mind repeated to itself as I unlocked my car door. I had so much hate built up inside of me right now, I could not even think of anything good about Ize. I wanted my revenge, and I knew it was going to be a dish best served cold. I wanted Ize to look me in my eyes, and feel the pain I felt just before I pulled the trigger.

"How could you, Ize?" I asked the wind as I drove in, and out of lanes crying to his house.

So many memories of us played over, and over in my head as I drove. I thought about us as kids, and the first time Ize ever told me he loved me. I was dying on the inside, and I felt betrayed that Ize was the cause of it all. How did we even get to this point, and where is the love? Those were two questions I desperately need answered, or not. I had been down this road before, and I knew if the first time Ize did not change when he promised he would, he was not going too.

"People will forget what you said, people will forget what you did, but people will never forget how you made them feel," the Dj said before he announced the title of the next song.

"Shout out, to Maya Angelou," he continued as I approached my exit. I wanted to cry as Janet Jackson's "This Time," played as I drove down Ize's block. I shed one tear, and then let the lyrics take total control of my feelings. Janet was absolutely, right.

"This time Ize had gone to fucking far".

I pulled up in front of a vacant house that was for sale and parked. I sang along with Janet, as I felt the crazy woman inside of me screaming to be set, free. After the song was over, I got out of the car and sighed as I walked calmly towards Ize's house. I knew the back patio was unlocked on Sundays, because he liked to take afternoon swims. I knew I would not have a problem getting into the house after returning the keys. I entered the security code into the gate, and then crept around to the back door. I was never so happy that the cameras were out of order. The show "How To Get Away With Murder," was definitely paying off, now. I had done this so many times before today that I was starting to become a pro at killing people, and getting away with it.

"Maybe I should become a professional hit woman," the sinister voice in my head joked, but I was not in the mood.

All I could think about was the lyrics to Janet's song as I walked into the house, and removed my gun out my bag. I screwed the silencer on the barrel, and then tiptoed around to Ize's bedroom where I heard voices. I was disgusted listening to them talk about how much they loved each other, and what their future plans for their life. I could not believe the nonsense I was hearing, and I hated every minute of it. This fool Ize had just committed the ultimate betrayal against me. I was the one who asked Ize to marry "me," and rejected just so some bitch he barely knew could take my place.

"Now ain't that a bitch?"

"I'll show you both, better than I could tell you," I thought.

"You love that Bitch more than you love me huh, Izir?" The rage in my mind screamed.

 I could not wait to shoot his ass.

"You coldhearted, son-of-a-bitch," I whispered tightening my grip on my gun.

"We gone see about them future plans, Nigga." I frowned.

Then Ize's bitch had the nerves to add more insult to injury.

"I wonder what your little Bitch gone do once she finds out we're married," The bitch had the nerves to say.

 That was it. If Ize did not come to my defense soon, I swear I was going in guns blazing like back in the Wild, Wild West, days.

"Fuck La'Teazya, Amere!" Ize stated laughing.

I wanted to run in the room, but I couldn't move. I felt glued to the spot that I was standing in, and my heart was crumbling into pieces, and then fell out my chest with every hateful word Ize spoke against me.

"You're the only one always worrying about what Teaz might do." He laughed some more.

You scared, baby? "He asked the woman, and she put on a show that had me fuming on the inside.

"You know I got Teaz in check," He added and then told her, too, "Trust him".

This whole situation had me feeling as if I was in an episode off the series, "Power".

Ghost kept cheating on Tasha with his old fling from the past, but Tasha was the one who had his back when his past caught up with him.

Now, here I was finding out I was the Angela in the relationship. I hated listening to their conversation about me. Ize must have really thought he was, Ghost, because he kept playing with fire thinking he wouldn't be burnt.

"I got this, Bae." Was all I heard before, I blanked out, and entered the room.

When I finally snapped back to reality, I was sitting next to Ize's dead body asking him why. I was shocked as I sat rocking uncontrollably next to the man I thought I loved. Flashbacks of every moment of our life played to me in my head as I quickly tried to gather my composure. Ize was dead, and I was the person who murdered him. I couldn't believe it. I felt disoriented as I checked around the room. Once, I retrieved all the surveillance videos from his video camera, I left out the bedroom making sure I did not leave any more evidence behind me. I was in total shock as I walked back to my car.

I knew I looked suspicious, too. I was shaking, crying, and chanting my entire walk.

"Why?" I, asked, myself again before I put the key in the ignition, and drove off.

I was, startled, by the sound of Raheem DeVaughn's song, "You" once I turned the key, so I cut the music off. I did not have time to hear any love songs when I was feeling so unloved and hurt. I had just killed my first love, and it hurt like hell on the inside. The drive to my house seemed like it took forever with all the thoughts in my head. I felt so guilty for killing Ize once I pulled in my driveway as I cried. He always had a way of making me feel bad about my decisions, even when I knew I was right. Once I got in the house I took a shower to try to wash away my sins I had just committed, and then burnt my clothes. Later on that evening, I watched the news report the double homicide of Izir, and his wife while I cried myself to sleep. The next morning, I woke up feeling nauseous, and watched reruns of the Oprah show. I was still devastated behind what I did yesterday, but there was no turning back.

"The biggest adventure you can take is to live the life of your dreams,"

Oprah said, and I was never so happy to have a second chance at this game called, life. We all know you do not get to play it twice, but somehow I had managed to come out on top. California was something to look forward, too. The tipping point in my life was about to become my turning point. In six more months, I would be far away from the state of Michigan, and I was never so grateful. I was closer to my dreams than the eye could see, yet my heart was shattered from my tainted past. I knew it was God's mercy that I was still living, and breathing. I had only been on this earth for twenty-five years of life and I already felt like an old woman. The craziest part to me was all the obstacles that I had to face, and overcome in this short period of time. Sometimes, the harsh reality of life makes us stronger individuals, even if you have to fight all your life just to come out a champion. I, also guess dreams really do come true, because everything I went through was preparing me for today. I had lost everything from my past, and I was finally able to see the truth. I had been so distracted with trying to find love, and feel loved by a man that didn't love me, so I often walked around like I was blindfolded just to cope. It was definitely time to start believing in La'Teazya before my time ran out. My thoughts were all over the place as I tried to watch television, so I read the bible instead.

"Therefore I will not keep silent; I will speak out in the anguish of my spirit, I will complain in the bitterness of my soul," I read once I opened the bible coincidentally to Job. I immediately knew what I had to do to fix

my life. I knew I needed a change, and for the first time in my life, I was

going to take some real steps in a positive direction. I could not go on

living life like this. I had to start setting better goals for myself. The very

first step to recovery was to forgive myself, and let go.

   It was exactly two weeks later, and I was on my way to my doctor's

appointment. I was so excited about it being closer to the day I was going

to move, that I sang loudly as drove listening to "Time" by Culture Club.

"Time won't give me time

And, time makes lovers feel

Like they've got something real

But, you and me we know

We've got nothing but time

And, time won't give me time

Won't give me time." I sang, as I pulled up in the parking lot of the

doctor's off.

 Before I could step out of the car I had an epiphany, and the last meeting

with Rozi, and Duty popped into my head. We had just finalized the deal

on the club that I would be running in California, and I could not wait to

open up my club, "Evolve".

I walked into the building feeling ecstatic about my choice to leave

Detroit, and it's awful past behind me. I had not been this happy in a long time, and I was enjoying every minute of my new stress free life. As, I stood in the empty club admiring the architecture gunshots rang out. I, ducked thinking the sound of the gun seemed close, and realized that I was hit in the chest. I quickly shook of the thought, and went into the office. It was going to take more than a creepy thought to scare me, so I prayed. I knew the Devil liked to try you when he feels you're getting closer to God, or a blessing.

After twenty minutes of waiting in the lobby, my name was finally, called. I had a long day ahead of me so, I was really hoping the blood work they needed me to come in and give went by fast.

"So how are you today, La'Teazya?" the nurse asked as she drew my blood.

We held a conversation for a few more minutes, and then she left and so did I. The next couple of weeks I prepared myself for the big New Year's Eve party Rozi was throwing at the club.

Rozi wanted to announce the opening of Duties' three new locations that would be opening this year. I was at home getting dressed when my phone rang.

"Hello!" I answered all bubbly.

"Hello, is La'Teazya Scorns-Frankyln home?" The man on the other end asked.

"Yes, this is she," I replied, while putting on my jeans that seemed to have gotten a little tighter since I had last worn them.

"Hi, La'Teazya this is Doctor, Herman from Midwest."

"I just got the results of your blood work back, and I wanted to call you

personally to let you know you have to come in for further testing," He

stated, and I was confused.

"Can you tell me, why?" I asked frightened.

I knew I had done some stupid shit in the past, but God please do not let

me have AIDS.

"Well one of your test results came back positive," I heard him say before

I cut him off.

"Positive,"

"Positive for, what?" I asked as he said, pregnant.

"Pregnant?" I replied in shock.

"This has to be a mistake," I shouted into the phone.

I just hung up. I damn near lost it. A baby was the last thing I had in my

plans now that my life was turning around.

"Oh my God," I screamed taking a seat on the edge of my bed.

"What have I done?" I cried realizing that I would be having Ize's baby.

"Fuck it, like fuck it though!"

I had vowed not to ever have another abortion after my first one, and I

was keeping my word. I guess you can run from the past, but eventually it

all catches up to you.

"Fuck you, Karma." I yelled.

I was finally going to have to re-evaluate my life's plans now that I had a baby on the way. My mind raced, and I even thought about writing a book.

"There's no greater agony than bearing an untold story inside of you." I thought. Maya Angelou was right about that, because I knew my life story would probably end up on a New York Times best-sellers list. I just needed some extra time to actually sit down and write my story. Once I got dressed, I headed to my car. I was excited about River's album release party, for a couple of the artist signed to her label. I was trying to put the whole baby situation behind me. I needed a night of fun, and tonight I planned to have just that.

"Don't Fear The Reaper," by Blue Oyster Cult was blasting as I drove. I was all into the song when my phone began to ring. I reached over to turn down the volume, and grab my phone when I noticed the caller was "restricted".

"Who could this be?" I asked myself aloud before answering.

"Hello?" I asked, and the person did not respond.

"Hello," I repeated, just before I hung up.

I heard, "Hey, Teaz." It was Ramir, and I was shocked.

I had not heard from Ramir since we broke up, and it was ironic that he would just call me out the blue.

"I see you've been keeping yourself up," he stated, and I instantly started to look around.

I quickly shook off the nervous feeling I was starting to have once I noticed I was the only car on the entire block.

"No, I'm not in your area, but I promise I'll be to see you real soon," he added with a laugh, as if he could see me.

"Oh really," I stated putting on my sexy voice.

"Trust me, Teaz,"

"I wouldn't miss seeing you for the world," he continued, and I laughed thinking he was flirting.

"Teaz," He snapped, breaking me out of my fantasy.

"Before you start thinking our little reunion is going to be all lovey dovey, and shit," I heard him say before the smile I had on my face turned into a frown.

"I know what the fuck you did last summer, Teaz." Ramir calmy said into the phone right before he hung up in my face.

I was scared as hell as I starred at my phone in shock. I began to pray as I walked franticly back to my car. Once I pulled back up to my house, it took me at least thirty minutes to gather my composure enough to call River. I was so terrified that Ramir was following me that I gave her some lame excuse about me not feeling well, and then I ran into my house and locked myself inside.

"This shit is un-fucking believable," I yelled as I got undressed.

Falling to my knees, I prayed one more time.

"God, as I lay down to sleep,"

"Protect my soul, and give me strength. My weakened heart has grown so weary. I need you now, please hear me clearly. In you, I put all faith and trust. High hopes for peace from up above. Please help me spread your love that is always, true. Restore my spirit, and make me new. In Jesus name I pray, Amen".

I got up off the floor, looked at my stomach, and shook my head.

Just when I, thought my life was getting better…

Shit got real.

Made in the USA
Columbia, SC
20 February 2020